The Visiting Girl

A novel by

Madge Walls

This book is a work of fiction. Names, characters, places, and incidents are either the product of the author's imagination or are used fictitiously. Any resemblance to actual events or locales or persons, living or dead, is entirely coincidental. Although every effort has been made to ensure the accuracy and completeness of information contained in this book, the author apologizes for any errors, inaccuracies, omissions, or inconsistencies herein. Any slights of people, places, or organizations are unintentional.

Cover design by Heather Walls

Other Novels
by
Madge Walls

Paying the Price
Buyers Are Liars

To gaël Doyle Oroyan and Kenn Grimes

Cheerleaders of my writing career

The Visiting Girl

CHAPTER 1

Caroline Crawford smiled inwardly as her daughter Nancy turned away from the tulips she was trimming on the dining room sideboard.

"But Mother, you can't!"

"Of course I can, my dear. Your father's been gone for three years. You are married and soon to be a mother; your brother is off with his horses in Tennessee. Who or what's to stop me?" Caroline pulled a loose tortoise shell hairpin from her graying top-knotted hair, secured it back into place, and gave her daughter a look wreathed in innocence.

"But by yourself, all the way to Oregon? I've never heard of such a thing!"

"Don't be silly, Nancy. It's 1923. Mr. Pullman's passenger cars are like small hotels on wheels. Remember when I took the train to Washington, DC, to march for women's suffrage?"

Nancy put down her shears and slipped the tulips into a crystal vase already filled with water. Turning to face her mother again, she crossed her arms over the tucked bodice of her white shirtwaist.

"Mother, that's not the same. You were with a group of friends on a day trip. Long-distance trains are dirty and uncomfortable. There are all kinds of dangers along the way. Broken tracks, avalanches in the mountains, wild Indians, train robbers. Not to mention uncouth salesmen who prey on women traveling alone. How many times have you told me to beware of traveling salesmen?"

Suppressing a grin, Caroline pulled herself a little taller, but still not eye to eye with her willowy daughter. She had indeed preached the dangers of traveling salesmen, for some reason now forgotten. She must have heard it from her own mother and simply passed it on.

"Darling girl, I'm forty-three years old and perfectly capable of taking care of myself. Haven't I done a splendid job these past three years? I've been no burden to you and your brother. And you know very well that train-chasing Indians and robbers on horseback are things of the past. Besides, I'm well beyond my prime. No man would give me a second glance, traveling or otherwise. I'll be perfectly safe."

Nancy untied her apron, folded it, and laid it on the sideboard.

"Mother, come here and sit down." She led Caroline by the hand into the solarium. Their white wicker chairs, cushioned in blue and green plaid, creaked pleasantly as the women made themselves comfortable. Through the wide bay window, morning had unfolded across the sprawling lawn in pristine summer beauty.

Hands relaxed in her lap, Caroline waited for her daughter to launch into a lecture. Since her father's death, Nancy had taken on the role of her mother's protector, much to Caroline's amusement. The timing of Lily's letter could not have been better. Being apart for a while would finally ease Nancy back into her proper daughterly role, or so her mother hoped. For now, Nancy would have her say; then Caroline would do exactly as she pleased.

"Now then, Mother, you haven't seen this woman—Lily—in twenty years! It's sure to be a wild goose chase."

"This woman, as you call her, was my best friend at Bryn Mawr College. We were roommates for two years until I left to marry your father. She often spent weekends and holidays with us, and lots more time after she graduated. I've never had a closer friend, before or since."

2

Nancy glanced at the ceiling. "I know, Mother. You've told the story often enough. You always get upset when you talk about it, even after all these years. Why does it still bother you? And why do you think you owe Lily anything? She's the one who disappeared from your house without explanation and left you with a pile of unpaid bills."

"Her bills were modest, only to the shoemaker and the dry goods store. I was happy to pay them. I've worried about her all these years but never heard a word until this letter arrived late last week. Here, take a look."

Caroline slid her hand into the pocket of her dress and pulled out an envelope, creased from frequent handling over the past few days. She offered it to Nancy, who hesitated for an instant, as if wary of the letter's power of persuasion. Once in hand, however, Nancy slid out the single sheet of paper, covered in an elegant script.

"Go ahead," said Caroline. "I'm sure I have it memorized by now, but read it aloud anyway." She closed her eyes, invoking a picture of her friend at a writing desk, setting her thoughts down in her unique, left-handed style. She'd have recognized it anywhere.

Dearest Caroline,

I write in great trepidation, trusting that you still live at the address in Philadelphia where I found such a haven in my youthful travails, yet fearing you will drop this letter into the fire without reading it. On the happy chance it finds itself open in your hands, let me begin.

I am ill, Caroline, quite ill. As I sit here, listening to the robins make merry on the lawn below my window, watching the afternoon leaf shadows dance on the wall beside my bed, I hope for a swift end when things become unbearable, as I'm told they will.

I find myself asking what I might have done differently in this life and what regrets I have. I suppose I must count my life successful, as I can only dredge up one true regret that cannot be undone.

And that my dear friend, if I may still call you friend after so many years of negligent silence, is having left you so precipitously with no explanation. I assumed you would think the worst of me, and I couldn't face it. Perhaps my youthful struggles had worn me down. In any case, cowardice won out, contrary to the person I believed myself to be. I was offered an escape and an exotic adventure, so I walked out of your home to a new life in the West.

Here I am, then, daring to hope that you too might be tempted by an adventure. Will you come to me in Portland, Oregon, Caroline? I'm told travel on the Pullman cars is luxurious these days. Would you even consider it? I would so love to see you, to hear about your life, your children and grandchildren, and finally, if you are still interested, to explain myself.

I know this is asking a great deal, but pride falls away when one's life nears its end. Please forgive my optimistic smile as I picture you walking through my bedroom door and lifting the gloom that surrounds me. Do say you'll come, dear Caroline. I sleep little these days so we can talk all night if we want, just as we did at Bryn Mawr. What memories!

Sending love and hoping it is welcome,
Lily Paxton Giannotti

Nancy's hand holding the letter dropped onto her lap.

"Giannotti? What kind of name is that?" Before Caroline could answer, she blurted, "Why, that's the name of our florist. Mother, surely your best friend didn't marry an Italian florist?"

Caroline smiled. "It seems she did. I stopped by the flower shop yesterday to inquire."

Nancy handed the letter back to her mother. "To inquire? You mean you asked the *florist* if any of his relations had married your friend Lily?" She emphasized the word *florist* as if he were a frog squatting on the windowsill.

"Yes, the solution to the mystery of Lily's disappearance was just down the street, if I'd only known to ask."

"Well, what did you find out?" asked Nancy, tapping a foot impatiently.

Caroline sighed. She and her daughter were polar opposites in almost every way, but beneath Nancy's straightlaced and often judgmental surface, she was a staunch friend to all who knew her, a dedicated wife, and her mother's favorite companion.

"Old Mr. and Mrs. Giannotti have long since passed on, but their younger son Antonio now owns the shop, along with his wife Elisabetta."

"I know that, Mother. We all know the Giannottis. What would we do without their flowers for our dinners and parties? But what about Lily?"

"It seems she married the older son, Marco, and they ran off to Oregon all those years ago. Marco eventually communicated with his parents, but unfortunately it never occurred to them to share the news. Undoubtedly they were angry, disappointed, or perhaps embarrassed. At any rate, it seems Marco owns a successful flower business in Oregon. The brothers weren't very good at staying in touch, so Antonio and Elisabetta were surprised to hear that Lily is ill. When I mentioned I might visit her, they asked me to give Lily and Marco their love and send word as to her condition. Now I almost feel obligated."

"Surely more than a misplaced sense of obligation is driving this idea?" Nancy asked.

Caroline leaned forward with her hands clasped on her knees. "Oh, Nancy, I want so much to visit Lily. Without your father, life seems so dreary and insignificant. So dull! Ever since receiving the letter, I've been buoyed by a kind of vitality I haven't felt since my marching days. I'm restless, energized, seeing the world in bright colors again! I truly want to go, darling. I do hope you'll give me your blessing."

Nancy chuckled. "Mother, you were always headstrong in your own quiet way. It's usually the parent who says that about a child, but not in our case. I often admire you for it. Other times I want to box your ears. What on earth am I going to do with you?"

Sensing she'd won, Caroline rose and strode the few steps to the bay window, absorbing her victory. A pair of dogwood trees in white bloom at the far corners of the yard seemed to echo her joy. Between them stood a gazebo where wisteria hung in lavender cascades all the way around the roof. What kinds of trees and flowers do they have in Oregon, she wondered. Spinning back to face Nancy, she clenched her fists at her sides in an effort to still her exhilaration.

"I take it, then, you've no further objections." A statement, not a question. Nancy's opinion mattered. Caroline did not want to leave with her daughter's disapproval clouding her journey.

Nancy shook her head and flicked her hand toward the window. "Go."

"Excellent! I've checked the schedule. A train leaves the city every morning for Chicago, where I'll transfer to a train headed to the Pacific Northwest. The Pacific Northwest! Doesn't that sound exciting? I'll leave on Thursday. That gives me three days to pack and close my house. I can't wait! Oh thank you, darling, for being so understanding."

She rushed over to give Nancy a hug, which Nancy returned with gusto, good sport that she was. Pulling away, Nancy's eyes twinkled. "As you seem to have had it all planned before you walked in the door this morning, Mother, I don't see I have any choice."

"No, you don't," teased Caroline, relieved that she'd be leaving no hard feelings behind. She'd already dashed off a note to let Lily know she was coming, trusting it would arrive before she did.

CHAPTER 2

Thursday morning at eight o'clock Caroline and Nancy stood in line at Philadelphia's Broad Street Station to purchase Caroline's ticket to Oregon. A Red Cap porter stood guard over her traveling trunk, a woven wood food hamper, a valise packed with immediate necessities for the journey and a round hatbox containing a broad-brimmed straw summer hat. For the journey her brown felt hat with grosgrain trim would do.

The past three days had passed in a frenzy of activity: choosing what clothing to take for a stay of indefinite length and unknown weather and making sure everything was clean and pressed and carefully packed in her trunk, cushioned with tissue paper to discourage wrinkles. She squeezed in a drive to the countryside to select a gift for Lily that might bring her comfort.

She kept on her gardener and Tildy, her live-in housekeeper and cook. Tildy had been with the Crawfords for nearly fifteen years. She deserved a rest and would keep an eye on the house. Caroline had no idea if this would be a short cheering-up visit, or if her friend would want her company for the duration.

Caroline and Nancy jostled their way through the noisy crowd to the platform and found her car. As the two women hugged goodbye, Nancy couldn't help offering some last-minute advice.

"Now, Mother, do be careful. Don't talk to strangers, and send us a wire as soon as you get there."

"Oh, for heaven's sake, Nancy. Of course I'll talk to strangers. That's what one does on a long train journey. You can't sit across from someone for five days and never say a word. I'll be fine. Don't waste your time worrying about me. Take care of your husband, and I promise to be home in plenty of time to greet my first grandchild. Just think what stories I'll have to tell you when I return!"

She gave Nancy a final peck on the cheek and turned to climb the steps into her car. A blue-uniformed Negro porter stood by with military bearing, ready to take her elbow if needed.

The back-to-back sections of facing seats were comfortably upholstered in plush Pullman green, later to be made up into sleeping berths by the car's porter. She located her section, set her valise and food hamper on the aisle side of the seat that faced forward, and sat down beside them next to the window. She had paid an extravagant nine dollars extra for the forward-facing seat, which gave her the lower bunk at night. Her section mate, whomever it might be, would have the upper bunk, something Caroline was happy she wouldn't have to deal with.

She didn't have long to wait to meet her traveling companion. A slender, modishly dressed young woman traipsed down the aisle carrying a birdcage and a tasseled gray traveling rug. She wore a red and white polka-dot frock, with a white organdy collar and a wide navy sash at the hips. She dumped the rug on the aisle end of the seat and set the bird cage atop it, a bit too roughly to suit the poor canary. It fluttered back and forth, clutching the wicker bars on one side of the cage, then the other, before finally settling on its wooden perch. The young woman meanwhile plunked herself down next to the window across from Caroline, grimaced as if sitting down were painful, then quickly dispelled any hint of discomfort with a winning smile. Despite her unruly golden curls, or perhaps because of them, she was, in the argot of the day, "a blue-eyed stunner."

"Well, here we are," the young woman said. "Are you traveling all the way to the West Coast?"

"Almost. To Portland. And you as well?" answered Caroline.

"Seattle. I got on in New York City, but despaired of my section mate, such a grumpy old bat. She took one look at me, and declared, 'I have never traveled with a flapper in all my life'. She didn't say another word all the way to Philly. So when we got here I asked the porter to move me somewhere more congenial. And here I am! I'm going home to my wretched brother. I just hope I can stand it for the next six months. Then I'll be free." She hugged herself in delight.

Before the girl could explain, if in fact she intended to, the train whistle blew and a blast of steam shot out from the sides of the locomotive, temporarily obscuring Caroline's view of the bystanders. The car jerked a couple of times, then slowly rolled forward. As the steam cleared, Caroline glimpsed Nancy waving energetically from the platform, doing her best to look cheerful as she receded from view. Perched on the edge of her seat, Caroline blew her daughter a kiss.

She was on her way.

Caroline watched, enthralled, as the train passed by blocks of tall office buildings, shops, then quaint residential neighborhoods. Parks, vacant lots, and ramshackle tenements sped by. Fascinated by the unfolding vista, so different from her own sedate section of Philadelphia, Caroline started when the young woman spoke again.

"I'm Donalee Wagner. Since we'll be together for the next few days, we might as well get to know each other." Removing her red cloche hat and tossing it on the seat beside the birdcage, the young woman held out her hand.

Caroline smiled and reached across the space between them.

"Pleased to meet you. I'm Caroline Crawford." Of all the possibilities—a pipe-smoking man or a mother with an unruly child—this young woman might prove a pleasant companion, provided she didn't chatter from morning 'til night.

"You're wondering, no doubt what I'm doing on this train all by myself," said Donalee. "Frankly, I'm rather surprised I pulled it off. I'm on my way home to get a divorce, you see." She leaned back, crossed her arms and legs, and waited for Caroline's reaction.

Caroline tried to contain her astonishment. She had never spoken to a divorced woman, nor one who intended to be. "A divorce? Why, you look as if you're barely out of school."

Donalee picked up her hat and cycled it through her fingers. "I'm nineteen, old enough. I did a terrible thing. My mother warned me I would regret it, but the more she objected, the more determined I became."

She leaned toward the aisle, peeking past the birdcage as if to make sure no one could overhear them. Turning back to Caroline, she whispered, "I ran away with a soldier. He was so handsome and romantic! When Mother and I were in a shop one day, he caught my eye and winked. At first I was insulted. Then I heard him tell the proprietress he was buying a gift for his mother. What a thoughtful young man, I said to myself. Boy, was I wrong!"

Donalee tossed her hat aside again, sat up straight, and eased off her shoes. Pretty little things, Caroline thought—navy blue to match her sash, with chunky heels and a narrow band across each arch. Her polka dot dress, though fetching, had a scandalously high hemline, entirely inappropriate for train travel. Caroline smoothed the long skirt of her own brown traveling suit, certain she looked as dull as she felt in comparison.

"I attended a convent boarding school," Donalee continued. "We had no contact with boys other than our brothers. Imagine dancing with girls at our senior prom! I felt like my canary, poor little Peck, caged up with no hope of freedom. How was I ever going to meet a man to marry?"

She rushed on, not waiting for a response. "After graduation, I saw nothing ahead but stuffy afternoons calling on my mother's friends and their unmarried daughters, and boring dinner parties with people I didn't care about. And endless matchmaking by my mother and her friends. If I played my cards right, I thought, this fellow could be my ticket out of here. So I winked back at him!" She demonstrated, dimples and all.

No wonder the young man was captivated, thought Caroline. And raised in a convent school—small wonder the girl yearned for freedom. Caroline remembered her own first intoxicating taste of freedom as a freshman at Bryn Mawr. Bewitched by Lily's high spirits, she had joined her in one bit of nonsense after another. Caroline smiled at the recollection and wondered if Lily recalled their hijinks as vividly.

Donalee brought her back to reality. "When my mother wandered off to another part of the store, I scribbled my address on the back of a calling card and gave it to him. I think he was just as shocked as I at my boldness, but he appeared the next afternoon at our front door with a single pink rose. My father was at work, my mother out visiting. So I grabbed my coat and walked out with him. What delicious fun!" She cocked her head to one side, daring Caroline to comment on her boldness.

Caroline frowned, ill at ease with so much sharing of personal information. Nevertheless, they had a long trip ahead of them and she was intrigued. Suddenly Donalee gasped and gripped the window-side armrest. She closed her eyes, then seemed to recover and continued her breathless tale.

"Charles was in town for four more days before returning to his Army base in Oklahoma City. We met for a walk every afternoon. He was charming and amusing. On the last day he asked me to marry him. I was so shocked, I didn't know what to say. I mean, it wasn't as if he was going off to war or anything. The Great War was over. Besides, how could I up and marry somebody I'd known for less than a week?" Her cornflower eyes widened as if the notion still surprised her. She blinked and carried on.

"But, oh my, he was persuasive. He told me to pack a bag with clothing to last a week, and when things calmed down we'd write my parents to send the rest of my belongings."

Caroline was reluctantly impressed. "My goodness, how daring of you. Didn't your parents try to stop you?" She thought again of Lily, who had done something of the same sort.

Donalee shrugged. "I snuck out in the evening while they were at a party, with my suitcase and my birth certificate—I found it in my father's office files—to prove I was old enough to marry. By the time

11

they got my letter, we'd found a justice of the peace and said our vows. To be honest, I knew neither of them would care. I have an older brother, you see, who looks and acts like a Greek god. He's the only one they care about. Gaudy, I always called him."

"Gaudy? That's an odd name."

Donalee hooked a stray golden curl behind her ear. "His name is Gordon, but I couldn't pronounce it as a child. So I called him Gaudy. Later, when I learned about Greek gods in school, the name sounded like God-y, so it stuck. He's insufferable, if you want to know the truth, but he's the one charged with keeping tabs on me when I get home. He's just out college, about to start work as an accountant. I'll bet he's licking his chops over yet another opportunity to lord it over me."

"And your parents?"

"They left for Europe a few days ago. They were extremely annoyed about this whole divorce thing popping up right before their trip, but happy, no doubt, to leave it all to Gaudy. Such a disgrace upon the family, and all that. Not to mention that the Catholic Church isn't sympathetic toward divorcées. Doesn't that sound wicked—divorcée?" She shivered.

"That doesn't bother you? You might be excommunicated. My Catholic friends say it's one of the worst things that can happen."

"Not in the least," Donalee replied. "Anyway, I'd only be excommunicated if I remarry, which, believe me, I have no intention of doing."

"But how long have you been married?" Caroline asked, not sure she believed all this.

"Just over a year. Within a few months I knew I'd made a terrible mistake. Charles left all his charm in the chambers of the justice of the peace. All he wanted was—you know what men want from women—any time, whenever he felt like it, whether I felt like it or not. Let me tell you, romance went right out the window with his incessant demands. I mean, I'm all for a good time, but I had no idea this was what married life was all about. Why don't our mothers warn us?"

Caroline shook her head. It hadn't been that way with John.

"If I told him I had a headache, he moaned about until I gave in. If I pretended I was asleep, he pestered me until it was easier to get it over with so I could go back to sleep. A few times when he'd had too much to drink and I told him I wasn't in the mood, he popped me a shiner. Then one night he twisted my arm until I thought it would pop out of its socket. Whew, painful! That was it. The next morning after he left for a two-week training exercise, I packed my bag and took off. Seems I'm getting pretty good at running away!" Donalee grinned at her own cleverness, but beneath the surface Caroline sensed a brittleness, her outward show of bravado masking deeper wounds.

"But what has this to do with your brother?"

"My father hired a lawyer for me before they left on their trip. I'll give him credit for that. The lawyer said I have to establish residency again in Washington state before I can get the divorce. He also said that I have to stay squeaky clean, have nothing to do with men, not even casually. I can't give my husband any ammunition that would allow him to blame everything on me and cause the judge to deny the divorce. So my brother has been assigned to keep me pure for as long as it takes. Can you think of anything more ridiculous? I must stay in the house, mind my Ps and Qs, and go out only when chaperoned by Gaudy or a trusted woman friend. What a bore." She crossed her arms over her chest again and pouted.

Caroline could see that such cloistering would weigh heavily on this animated young sprite, who had endured enough of it while in school. She silently wished Gaudy luck.

"But you were in Oklahoma City. Didn't you say you boarded the train in New York?" Caroline asked, still trying to fit all the pieces together.

"Yes. I wanted to get as far away from Charles as possible. I had enough money to buy a one-way ticket home to Seattle, or to the East Coast. I feared my parents would say 'We told you so' and boot me out onto the sidewalk if I turned up at home. So I went to my aunt and uncle in New York, Long Island actually. Arrived on their doorstep unannounced. At first they were bricks about it. After a couple of weeks, though, they sat me down and told me I couldn't stay forever. I had to face the music. So I swallowed my pride and wired my parents that I wanted to come home. I swear the telegraph wire sizzled with their angry reply, but they sent me a ticket— amazingly they sprung for sleeper class—took off on their trip, and here I am." She tapped an index finger on her temple and grinned. "There's always a solution if I put my pretty little head to it."

Caroline scowled, thinking this pretty little head had a devious aspect. But sometimes that was what a woman needed in order to survive in a man's world. Murmuring a few noncommittal words, she turned to the window, feeling overwhelmed by her seatmate's emotional outpouring. Donalee, apparently out of steam, rested her head against the seat back and closed her eyes. Caroline welcomed the peace and quiet.

Shortly before noon their porter, Terrence according to his nametag, strode down the aisle, announcing luncheon service in the dining car.

Donalee jumped up, patted her hair, and stated her intention to partake. Caroline waved her off. She didn't have the strength for more of the young woman's gregariousness, nor to chat with strangers, should she have to share a table. She pulled her picnic basket over.

Lifting the lid, she found a cold chicken breast, a crock of potato salad, a couple of apples, half a loaf of freshly baked bread, several cheeses wrapped in cloth, and a packet of Tildy's triple citrus cookies—two thin butter wafer rounds filled with orange marmalade, topped with a lemon sugar glaze and sprinkled with powdered sugar and grated lime zest. God bless Tildy! For her first meal on board, Caroline dined in solitary splendor while the world rolled by.

By mid-afternoon, the scenery had turned to small towns, flat farmland framed by rolling hills, and cottonwood trees clustered on occasional stream banks—a jumble of Americana unfolding before her as they hurtled ever farther west. The vastness of the country was stunning, yet the journey had barely begun. Donalee must have found someone else to amuse her, as she had not yet reappeared. For that, Caroline was grateful. Even Peck had settled down in his cage, thanks to Terrence kindly refilling his water cup.

The *click, clack, click* of the wheels and gentle sway of the car finally caught up with her. Caroline leaned against the window and rested her eyes, just for a moment, or so she intended. The charged excitement had worn off, replaced by a deep contentment. In less than a week her dreary life had turned a cartwheel, rushing her into the vast unknown and a reunion with her dear friend Lily.

Her drowsy mind recalled an earlier time when she had felt a similar contentment: the morning after her wedding when she awoke snuggled under a down comforter in a Vermont country inn beside her young husband. Enough time had passed since John's death that those memories were no longer tinged with grief. Reliving them now brought her comfort.

The weeks leading up to Caroline and John's wedding had been insanely busy. But underlying it all was the gnawing mystery of what to expect on their wedding night. She knew by way of whispers that stopped the moment she entered a room, and allusions in romantic novels that she and her schoolmates smuggled into their Bryn Mawr dormitory, that married couples did more than lie side by side when they climbed into bed together. Something mysterious took place that resulted in children. But what?

Their big chance to find out came when one of the girls returned to the dormitory late one night, disheveled and agitated. Caroline, Lily, and several others pounced on her, demanding to know if she and her boyfriend had "done it." Their questions infuriated the girl, who had hitherto been more than willing to share the details of her romantic exploits. She was by far the fastest in their set and loved bragging about it as much as they, who would never have dared, loved hearing about it.

"Leave me alone," she cried as she stumbled down the hall to her room. "I don't want to talk about it." Three months later she dropped out of school, never to be seen again. After much pestering, her younger sister, a grade behind, confided that she'd "gotten into trouble" and was now married and living in New Jersey, where she could no longer bring shame upon the family in Virginia. While remaining unenlightened as to the details, the girls concluded that "doing it" was not all it was cracked up to be.

Caroline was among the first of her classmates to marry, leaving school after two years, so she'd had no friends her age with whom to discuss these things. Even if there had been, she doubted that she would have dared venture into such forbidden territory. It was the great unknown, the terrifying cliff toward which a well-bred young woman raced during her engagement, knowing nothing about what lay beyond, but somehow expected to survive the experience and emerge in good cheer. As for her mother, Caroline had tried several times to pin her down but was always rebuffed, the last time severely.

"We don't talk about those things, Caroline. Ever. Just be sure your private parts are clean and powdered. That's all you need to know." Her mother actually shuddered as she said it. Caroline concluded that it must be awful indeed.

One afternoon, as she and John took a leisurely stroll through her parents' garden, she suggested that perhaps they shouldn't plan on having children.

"Not have children?" he asked, stopping on the gravel path and turning to face her. "What an odd thing to say. You've always said you wanted children, Caroline. Me, too. Whatever has happened to change your mind?"

She felt herself sinking into quicksand, the subject nobody would discuss.

"I…I don't know exactly. I…guess I'm…afraid."

"Afraid? Afraid of children?" He huffed at such a preposterous idea.

"Well, no. Not exactly." Feeling her face grow hot, she turned away from him to hide her embarrassment. She desperately wished she had never started this conversation, but how could she enjoy her wedding day with the great unknown looming at the end of it? Oh, why couldn't she just have left things alone and take whatever came, she thought. Every married woman apparently survived it. Surely she would too.

John smiled in sudden understanding, that gentle, boyish smile she had come to love. He guided her into the shade of a nearby tree, where they would be sheltered from anyone looking toward the garden from the house. He took her into his arms and spoke softly, holding her close with his mouth near her ear to save her the indignity of looking at him while he addressed her fears.

"Darling Caroline, I'm sure all young women like yourself feel some trepidation on their wedding night. Please don't be afraid. I'll be as gentle as I possibly can. You are my treasure, Caroline, my golden treasure. I value you above everything and everyone on this earth. I will never hurt you, I promise. Can you trust me, my precious one?"

She slowly pulled away and dared to look up at him. A sense of calm settled over her at the sight of his concerned expression.

"Yes, John. I do trust you. If you say I have nothing to worry about, then I shall set it aside and enjoy our wedding day. Thank you." She had not felt as reassured as she sounded. More than anything she wanted to put an end to the uncomfortable discourse. But now that he was aware of her feelings, she trusted that he would honor his word.

He pulled her close again and kissed her, softly at first, as he had done several times before. Then his arms tightened and the kiss went deeper. Her eyes flew open in surprise. As she started to pull away, he slid one hand down her back, past her waist to her bottom. He pressed her closer as his kiss moved from her lips to her neck. Her body ignited with the most delicious flames. Enthralled yet frightened, she struggled, but he kept her close and nuzzled her ear.

"Relax, sweetheart, and enjoy the feelings. Let them flow. This is just the smallest preview of how wonderful everything will be when we are finally man and wife."

Having looked forward to the fulfillment of this promise, Caroline found their exploration of the marital mysteries puzzling and rather disappointing. John was quick about it, treated her gently, and thereafter only bothered her once or twice a week. Her happiest memories in those early years were of cuddling with him afterward, when he was satisfied and they both were drifting off to sleep.

When she opened her eyes again Caroline realized, by the deepening dusk of the landscape and the crick in her neck, she had dozed away the afternoon. There was still no sign of Donalee, but who was this woman staring at her through the darkening car window? She blinked several times, thinking for a moment it was her late mother. But Mother wearing Caroline's brown suit with the cameo brooch from John pinned to the collar?

Of course not! She was staring at a reflection of herself—her disheveled graying hair twisted into a loose topknot, her deep-set blue eyes. But when had she become so middle-aged, and yes, looking more and more like her mother in her later years? She quickly pulled out her hairpins, ran her fingers through the waves, regathered them atop her head, and pushed the pins back in. That was the best she could do.

As she stood to make her way to the lavatory, Terrence came through the car again, announcing the first seating for dinner. This time she looked forward to a change of venue and a hot meal.

To reach the diner, Caroline walked through three Pullman sleepers and a lounge car, each linked to the next by a small, noisy vestibule. In the cars she passed families getting ready for dinner, single travelers reading or chatting with one another, and porters, one to a car, efficiently tending to the needs and comfort of their passengers. In the lounge car a few gentlemen and several couples enjoyed pre-dinner drinks from their private flasks. Prohibition had become the law of the land, but folks who wanted to imbibe found their way around it.

The sounds of clinking glasses and silverware, interlaced with conversation, greeted her as she pulled open the final vestibule door. The dining car was softly lit by wall sconces, with a row of square tables along each side, all topped with freshly pressed linen, china, and polished silver and glassware. The walls and domed ceilings were richly panelled in dark-grained mahogany, intricately carved with gilded detailing.

The Negro maître d' welcomed her with a pleasant, "Good evening, Madam," and showed her to a table occupied by a middle-aged couple and their adolescent son. He politely inquired if they might share their table with her, a single woman traveling alone.

The Winsteds were on their way home from London to Chicago, she learned. Mr. Winsted, vice-president of sales for Marshall Field's department store, had traveled abroad with his family to see for himself the latest in British merchandising techniques. Caroline was fascinated by his description of Selfridge & Co., a department store whose theatrical use of sidewalk display windows had taken London by storm.

"Marshall Field's lost a genius when Harry Selfridge left us to open his emporium in London," Howard Winsted stated. With a long-suffering look, his wife patted the top of his hand, as if reminding him this was not the place to air his grievance. Mrs. Winsted diverted the conversation with a light-hearted description of the tombs and memorials of kings, queens, famous statesmen and other notables they had seen in Westminster Abbey. As Caroline rose to leave at the end of the meal, she thanked her new acquaintances for an entertaining evening and wondered with a chuckle what Nancy would have thought of these dangerous strangers on the train.

Making her way back to her car, Caroline spotted Donalee in the lounge car, sitting with a flashy-looking young fellow, one of those fabled traveling salesmen, no doubt. They were smoking and sharing his hip flask, entirely too engrossed in each other to notice her as she strolled past them. Having listened to Donalee's tale of woe regarding her husband, Caroline was surprised to see her cozying up to this young man. Perhaps the liquor had loosened her inhibitions. She shook her head and moved on.

As she progressed through the sleeper cars, Caroline passed porters preparing berths while their passengers dined. They moved swiftly with economy of motion, creating lower berths by folding down seat backs and pulling upper berths from the ceiling. Sheets and blankets were swiftly tucked in, pillows fluffed, upper and lower privacy curtains attached, and ladders affixed to upper berths. As she passed, each attendant flattened himself against the berth he was working on to let her by.

Finally entering her own car, Caroline found it transformed, with most of the berths made up, including her own. Donalee's upper berth had been lowered and made up, too, with the canary cage set high upon it. How Donalee was going to sleep with that bird, she had no idea, but perhaps the young woman could offer Terrence a tip to take care of it until morning.

With no place to sit, Caroline decided to prepare for bed and read propped up on her pillow until she felt sleepy. She made a trip to the cramped but clean lavatory at the end of the car, then returned, eased onto her berth, and pulled the curtain shut. Trying not to jar open the heavy green fabric that separated her from her fellow passengers, she kicked off her shoes, rolled down her stockings, shrugged out of her dress, and quickly pulled her flannelette nightgown over her head.

Donalee's lowered berth eliminated much of the headroom, forcing her to accomplish all of this while kneeling on her mattress. Only then, under the tent of her nightgown, did she struggle out of her underthings. Goodness, she thought, I'm glad I only have to do this for four nights. It's enough to tempt me to sleep in my clothes, however uncomfortable that might be.

Seated cross-legged, she folded her garments as well as she could and stowed them in the mesh bag that Terrence had hung hammock-fashion against the window. She rolled over onto her stomach and slid her shoes under her berth. There was still no sign of Donalee, but Caroline assumed she would be along soon enough. She hoped the young woman would climb up the ladder to her berth and tuck in without any fuss.

For the next hour or so, Caroline luxuriated in her small private space, reading her book by the light of a lamp above her head and feeling quite pleased with herself for having managed so well the awkward business of undressing. Beyond the curtain she was aware of all sorts of noises, muffled and otherwise, as her fellow passengers arranged themselves and their belongings for the night.

Occasionally someone called out for assistance, and Terrence hustled to attend. Soon things quieted down as passengers turned off their lights, one by one. Before long Caroline turned off her light and fell asleep.

She awoke to a series of rustles, murmurs, and giggles from above, not sure at first where she was or what she was hearing. Then her surroundings came into dim focus. What could Donalee be up to, she wondered. She had no idea of the time, but by the total darkness outside the window and the snoring that rumbled through the car, she assumed it was well into the wee hours.

She was just dozing off again when another round of rustling and giggling jolted her awake. This time a deep voice from elsewhere in the car hollered, "Quiet down! Respectable folks are trying to sleep."

This caused an outburst of hilarity in the berth above, male and female. Why, Donalee must have a man up there with her, Caroline realized. What kind of a loose young woman was she? Was she drunk? In all her years she had never witnessed such wanton behavior. And by someone who had earlier expressed her dislike of intimate relations, not to mention whose pending divorce, a scandal in itself, required unblemished moral conduct.

The discreet clearing of a throat came from the other side of the curtain. Terrence, Caroline realized, who was responsible for maintaining civilized behavior on his watch. This would give him a racy tale to tell his fellow porters, and probably not the first one.

Within moments anyone who was still asleep was awakened by a crash and a series of squawks from Peck. Caroline sat up and threw her curtain open, heedless of her state of *deshabille*. Peck's cage had tipped off the upper berth and landed on its side on the floor, birdseed scattered everywhere. Before Caroline could rescue the poor bird, Donalee squealed from above.

21

"Stop! Stop! You're hurting me!" A great tussle ensued, then Donalee cried, "Get out of here, get out! You're hurting me! Go!"

A pair of naked male legs slid off the edge of Donalee's berth and landed on the floor in a crouch, trousers accordioned at the ankles above shoes and sagging sox. The eyes of the attached fellow blazed open, staring straight at Caroline, just inches away. Neither Caroline nor the young man could have said who was the more startled.

"She's a little tease!" the man blurted. "She drank my booze and led me on. Good riddance to all of you, I say." He pulled up his pants, grasped the unbuttoned fly with both hands, and ran out the far end of the car, shirttails flying.

Disembodied heads poked out from behind curtains; curious eyes stared their way. Terrence stepped forward, speaking to Donalee discretely through her curtain. "Do you need any assistance, Miss?"

"No, thank you. I'm all right. He…he mistook my berth for his own." Her shaky voice belied her declaration of wellbeing and the truthfulness of her statement.

"Happens all the time, Miss." Terrence nodded and turned to the curious passengers. "Nothing to worry about, folks. Just a case of mistaken berths. You can all go back to sleep now. Everything is fine, just fine." His voice was soothing and mellow, with a distinct northern accent. The other porters she'd heard speaking all seemed to hail from the Deep South.

He picked up poor old Peck's cage, which somehow had survived its fall undamaged. Peck clung to the side bars, waiting to see which way would ultimately be up. "I'll take care of the bird for you, Miss," Terrence said, again through the curtain. "You go back to sleep now."

Terrence returned to his post at the rear of the car, from which he could continue to observe everything that went on, with Peck's cage on the floor beside him. When or where did he find time to sleep, Caroline wondered.

She settled in once more, tucked under her sheet and blanket, feeling as if she should offer Donalee some kind of comfort, but not knowing exactly what to say or do. The girl was obviously upset and in some kind of pain. Had the callow fellow forced his attentions on her and hurt her in the process?

From what she had seen of Donalee's flirtatious, tipsy behavior in the lounge car, there was no doubt he'd felt his advances would be welcome. But to actually present himself at her berth and climb in, well, that was beyond any kind of propriety. Then again, what was all that giggling about? It appeared as if Donalee had welcomed him—until the going got rough. It hadn't been a matter of spurning his affections, Caroline surmised, but more about his coarse treatment of her.

What on earth did one say or do in such a situation? Caroline's desire to be helpful, if indeed help was needed, conflicted with her extreme embarrassment on Donalee's behalf. Not just at the moment, but how in the world was she going to behave normally for the next few days in this flighty young woman's company?

Perhaps the best thing was to let it go and concentrate on their arrival in Chicago in the morning, where they had to change to another train line. With luck the girl would awaken feeling better, and they'd find themselves in entirely different cars.

Although Donalee tried to muffle it, her continued crying kept Caroline awake. It didn't sound like the crying of loneliness or heartache, as she might have expected, but rather cries of fear and pain that got progressively more difficult to ignore.

Unable to stand it any longer, Caroline threw her curtain open, stood up on her bare feet, pushed the upper curtain aside, and peered in at Donalee. The young woman, dressed in nothing but a slip, crouched on the mattress, chin to knees, rocking back and forth, moaning in pain.

"Donalee? What's going on? Are you injured? How can I help you?" Caroline now realized this was more than a casual incident of clumsy attentions.

Donalee moaned again, then arched her back. "Oh, God, I've done it now. What a fool I was. It hurts! I...I think I need a doctor."

As Donalee continued to moan, Caroline spotted a dark stain on the sheet beneath her. She pulled up the edge of Donalee's slip and stepped aside to allow more light in. Fresh blood had pooled on the sheet—a great deal of blood.

"What's happened?" cried Caroline. "What did that man do to you?"

"It's not his fault," Donalee gasped. "Please, fetch a doctor. Please!" She began to whimper again, huddled with her head in her hands.

Caroline backed away to call for Terrence, who had already materialized beside her, frowning in concern.

"Is there a doctor on board?" Caroline asked. "I'm afraid she's ill. She's bleeding badly." Caroline suspected she was having a miscarriage, but didn't want to be so indelicate as to say so.

Terrence turned and addressed the passengers in a loud voice. "Is there a doctor in the car? We have a young lady in distress."

Half way down the aisle a middle aged man backed out from behind his curtain, snapping his suspenders over his undershirt. "I'm a doctor. Let me take a look at her."

Caroline and Terrence stepped aside. The doctor leaned in, murmured a few things to Donalee, then backed out and whipped the curtain closed.

"Who did this to her?" he asked, eying first Caroline and then Terrence.

"I'm sure I have no idea," replied Caroline, not wanting to mention the nocturnal visitor. Terrence remained silent. A lady's reputation was at stake, a lady who was on her way home to obtain a divorce. Foolish girl! Terrence remained inscrutable, no doubt fearing that his skin color could cause him to be blamed for everything.

"Get me some towels," the doctor ordered Terrence. He turned to Caroline.

"Your daughter is in serious trouble, Madam. She'll need to be removed from the train in the morning when we reach Chicago and taken to a hospital."

"But…she's not my daughter! We are sharing this section, but I just met her today—well, yesterday. She's traveling home to Seattle. Surely she can continue the journey and be taken care of there?"

"No, Madam. She needs medical attention immediately. There is nothing I can do for her on the train. She needs expert and discreet intervention, right away."

"Discreet? What do you mean?"

The doctor eyed Caroline for a moment, his bushy gray eyebrows bunched together in a scowl. "As she's not your daughter, I hesitate to say. But take my word for it—her parents will not be pleased."

Terrence arrived with an armful of clean white towels. The doctor turned back to Donalee, opening the curtain enough to maximize the light from the dimmed ceiling fixture, while sheltering the young woman from the gaze of curious passengers. As Terrence handed the towels to the doctor one by one, Donalee continued to moan and occasionally cry out. Caroline yearned to hold her hand and comfort her, but the doctor effectively blocked her access.

Finally he backed away, let the curtain fall shut, and wiped his hands on the last clean towel. "That should stop the flow for the time being, but she needs to be seen to the minute we arrive in Chicago. George, wire ahead to have an ambulance meet us there. Her life is in danger. And you, Madam, I exhort you to do your Christian duty, not that she deserves it, and stand by her, at least until she is delivered into medical hands. I've done all I can, and more than I wished." With that he tossed the red-stained towel at the startled Terrence and strode back to his bunk.

What a sanctimonious bastard, thought Caroline. Calling Terrence "George," even though his name tag was in plain sight. And how dare he judge Donalee like that? She's a married woman, and miscarriages, she knew only too well, were commonplace. It was entirely likely that Donalee hadn't even realized she was pregnant. No wonder she was frightened.

Caroline turned to Terrence. "It's just about dawn. I'm going to change into my day clothes. If you would reconfigure my seat, please,

I'll look after her until we arrive in Chicago. And I apologize for him calling you George."

"Don't be concerned about that, Ma'am. Passengers often call us George, after Mr. Pullman. We're one and the same to them. I'll stand by until you return, in case the young lady needs anything more."

When Caroline returned from the lavatory, dressed for the day, Terrence departed to dispose of the soiled towels and arrange for the telegram to be sent at the next station. She looked in on Donalee and found her dozing. The pain must have eased up, she thought with relief. She sat down to wait.

Terrence returned and bent over to ask how Donalee was doing.

Caroline replied softly, not wishing to disturb anyone who had managed to fall back asleep. "Her pain seems to have eased. I think it's best to leave her sleeping."

He nodded. "No point in waking her. Sleep is sometimes the best medicine."

"You must see your share of medical emergencies on the train." She spoke less out of curiosity than a desire to share her distress.

"We do indeed. Me more than most. I've actually just finished medical school, Ma'am. I'm often called upon when there's no doctor in the car."

"You? A doctor?" She blurted it out, and immediately regretted her rudeness.

His handsome smile spoke of regret and disillusionment. "Almost. I worked my way through medical school on the cars. In the fall I'll begin my internship at Harlem Hospital in New York City. After that I'll be fully qualified. No one will ever call me George again."

Caroline regarded his sincere countenance. "That is admirable, I must say. I'm sure you will be a wonderful practitioner. Your patients will be lucky to have you. I wish you all the success in the world."

He smiled again, this time with confidence and good will. "Thank you, Ma'am. It's meeting folks like you that makes my work here tolerable."

CHAPTER 3

With the sky outside the train window softening into dawn, the passengers began to stir, dress, and head to the dining car for breakfast. After they departed, Terrence began changing their berths back into seats. As far as Caroline knew, he hadn't slept a wink. She stood up and shook Donalee gently on the shoulder to awaken her and ask if she felt well enough to eat. As the girl sat up, the sheet slipped off her bare legs. A dark stain of blood had blossomed through the towel the doctor had stuffed between her thighs. Horrified, Caroline backed away and called to the porter.

"Please, Terrence, fetch the doctor again. She's bleeding badly."

He turned to the doctor's section, only to find it vacant.

"The doctor has gone, Ma'am, likely to breakfast. I'll try to find him."

"Please, hurry! It looks very bad."

He rushed off, leaving Caroline alone with Donalee. The girl was dreadfully pale, and the stain, now bright red in the dawning light, was growing alarmingly.

The doctor strode in just as the train began to slow upon approaching the outskirts of Chicago.

"Now what?" he muttered as he peered in at Donalee and took in the situation. He backed away and spun around. "We've got to get her out of here. George, the minute the train stops you run out and find that ambulance. You did wire ahead as I instructed?"

"Yes, sir. They should be waiting for us." His jaw muscle bulged as if biting back a less civil response.

As the doctor turned back to Donalee, Terrence addressed the rest of the passengers. "We have a medical emergency here, ladies and gentlemen. I ask that you remain in your seats while we take care of it. The ambulance attendants will be boarding as soon as we stop. Please stay out of the aisle until they have transported the patient. Thank you so much. We appreciate your cooperation."

The moment the train hissed to a stop at Union Station, close to noon, Terrence threw open the car door, jumped to the ground, and waved above the crowd to the waiting ambulance crew in their white pants and jackets. Carrying a furled canvas stretcher, the two men hastened into the car.

Caroline and the doctor backed out of the way as they unrolled the stretcher and balanced it across the seats below Donalee's berth. Terrence pulled open Donalee's curtain and retreated a respectful step. The ambulance men quickly assessed the situation.

"All right, Miss. We're going to lift you off the berth and onto the stretcher. Can you help us by turning over onto your back and extending your legs?"

Donalee groaned.

"That's it, Miss. On your back. We don't want that soiled sheet, Joe. Just the blanket. That'll keep her warm. That's it. We've got you. Okay, Joe. Hoist!"

In one swift movement they lifted her off the berth and down onto the stretcher.

"Jesus God, Mel. Look at all that blood!"

"Can it, Joe. Come on. Let's get her out of here."

"Wait," Caroline said in a moment of fierce determination. "I'm going with her. We can't just send her off with no one to look after her." She turned to Terrence. "Please have her luggage and mine removed from the train and stored at the station under my name, Crawford. Once this is all sorted out, we'll retrieve it and carry on

28

with our journey." She opened her handbag, pulled out a dollar, and handed it to him. "You've been very kind, Terrence. Thank you so much for all your trouble."

"It was no trouble at all, Ma'am. I trust the young lady will recover quickly."

"I'm sure she will. And best of luck to you as you build your future."

He smiled at her and tipped his cap.

By then the ambulance attendants and their patient were out of the car and onto the platform. Caroline spotted Donalee's red handbag pushed down into the crease at the end of her berth. Not knowing what valuables it might contain, she scooped it up and tucked it into her valise. She rushed after Donalee and the attendants, following them through the milling crowd to the waiting ambulance. Hurriedly they loaded their patient, still on the stretcher, through the ambulance's rear door. Mel scrambled in beside her and held out a hand for Caroline. She lifted her skirt, braced a knee on the bumper of the vehicle, and allowed herself to be pulled inside.

Joe secured the door behind them, rushed to the driver's seat and threw the ambulance into gear. Cranking the siren, he blared them into the oncoming traffic. During the jostling ride Caroline's only concern was for Donalee, who continued to bleed, despite the attendant's best efforts to stanch the flow with towels. She'd turned pale, and was no longer responsive to their frantic entreaties.

"Donalee, speak to me! Speak to me!" She turned to Mel. "She's lost consciousness! And look at all that blood!"

The attendant shook his head. "It doesn't look good, Ma'am. She's losing the baby, there's no doubt about that. She'll need a doctor the moment we get to the hospital."

An orderly met them at the hospital entrance. He took one end of the stretcher, slid it partially out of the ambulance, waited for Mel to jump down and pick up the other end, then led the way inside. Caroline grabbed her valise, hopped down and followed. They transferred Donalee to a cot in a crowded receiving room. The orderly ran off to fetch a doctor; Mel waved farewell and exited with the furled stretcher over his shoulder, leaving Caroline alone with Donalee. Winded, she bent over the young woman, who was now motionless and deathly white.

She grasped the girl's clammy hand. "Donalee, Donalee! The doctor's on his way. Hang on, please. Hang on! Help is almost here."

Surrounded by rushing people—medical professionals and hospitals visitors—and their attendant chatter, Caroline had never felt so alone and helpless. As she looked around, a middle-aged gentleman with curly gray hair and spectacles and wearing a white lab coat, breezed into the cubicle and introduced himself as Dr. Harrison. He bent over Donalee, peeled off the blanket, and drew in a sharp breath.

"Dear God, let's get her down the hall." He looked up, snapped his fingers, and shouted, "Orderly, over here, quickly. Get this woman into a treatment booth."

He turned to Caroline as they rushed after Donalee and the orderly. "You are her mother, I presume?"

"No, I'm Mrs. Crawford. We shared a section on the train. We only met yesterday. She was in such desperate trouble, I couldn't leave her. I thought at least I should stay with her until she's stable and can contact her family in Seattle."

"I see. Well then, if you'll just step aside, Mrs. Crawford, we'll get on with it. Nurse!"

Caroline backed away just in time to keep from being slapped by the curtain as the doctor swished it shut around himself and his patient. She retreated down the hallway to the reception room, where she gave the receptionist the scant facts she knew about Donalee. Then she found a seat and hugged herself to stop from shaking. How absolutely dreadful to miscarry, never mind in such a public and dramatic way. She felt again the pain of her own miscarriage, between Robert and Nancy. It had happened slowly but relentlessly, leaving her heartbroken. Had Donalee known she was pregnant? Surely not, if she had teased that young man into a nocturnal visit to her berth. When the pain and bleeding had begun, had she known what was happening? Considering the circumstances, would she be

30

relieved to lose the baby? Caroline had difficulty believing that any woman would feel that way, no matter what the circumstances.

Not twenty minutes later the doctor reappeared, looking haggard, and accompanied by a uniformed policeman. Confused, Caroline stood to greet them.

"Mrs. Crawford, I'm afraid I have bad news," the doctor began. "Mrs. Wagner has expired. Lost too much blood. By the time she got here, there was nothing we could do. I'm very sorry."

Caroline felt her legs go weak. She fumbled for the chair behind her and steadied herself with the armrest. "Expired? You mean she's...dead?"

"Yes, I'm afraid so," said the doctor.

"And...and the baby?" Donalee couldn't have been very far along, but Caroline felt compelled to ask.

The doctor looked puzzled, but before he could reply, the policeman stepped forward. Tall, mustachioed, and ruddy faced, he projected a no-nonsense air. "Mrs. Crawford, what exactly do you know about all this?"

Her eyes widened in surprise. "Why, I don't know anything. As I told Dr. Harrison, I met her yesterday on the train. I don't know her at all. I can't believe it. She's dead?" That lively young woman, dressed so frivolously in red with white polka dots, flirting with the man in the lounge car, and so looking forward to a new life of freedom—dead?

"Did you know she'd been...in a family way, Ma'am?" asked the policeman.

Caroline met his stern gaze. "I...I surmised. With the loss of blood, I assumed she was having a miscarriage." She looked at Dr. Harrison for confirmation.

"Not quite, Mrs. Crawford," said the doctor. "Mrs. Wagner was the victim of a botched abortion."

The policeman took a step closer to Caroline. "I'm afraid I'll have to take you to the station for questioning, Ma'am."

Caroline gasped. "An abortion? Me? " Her mind whirled as she tried to take that in. "Surely you can't think I had anything to do with it?"

"You were traveling with her, Ma'am," the policeman said. "Taking her home after the operation, perhaps. For all we know, you're in the business of facilitating abortions across state lines."

Caroline let go of the armrest and staggered backwards. The back of one knee hit the seat of her chair, causing both knees to buckle. Dr. Harrison reached out to steady her as she dropped abruptly onto the chair. Dear God, what a disaster, she thought. Donalee not only dead, but by such unspeakable means. And this policeman suspected her involvement? She turned to the doctor.

"Are you sure about this? An abortion?"

"We see them all the time, Ma'am. Sometimes done with an instrument as crude as a shoe hook or a knitting needle. Infections, hemorrhaging, scar tissue that gums up the works if they survive. It's a desperate shame when a woman finds herself expecting and tries to do away with it herself. Or finds a butcher who does it for her. If she lives, she goes home and idiotically gets in a family way all over again. Or she's maimed for life, and will never have another child." He stopped and looked at her as if he were wondering why he was telling her this, believing her a partner in the crime and all.

"But I had nothing to do with it! I told you both—I just met her on the train."

"We'll let the police deal with that," said Dr. Harrison. "Meanwhile, whatever information you can give us will be useful in notifying her family."

"I've already told the registrar everything I know!"

"That's it, then, Ma'am," said the policeman, taking her by the arm. "This way, please."

The next fifteen hours were a nightmare, pure and simple. As Caroline was a stranger in Chicago, she had no one she could call upon for help. Ignored by her jailers, she spent the night locked in a dreary, smelly cell that filled with garrulous streetwalkers as the night wore on. Reeking of cheap perfume and sweat, they all seemed to know each other, and to find their predicament more amusing than distressing. She gathered from their chatter that it was all too common to be rounded up to satisfy the self-righteous politicians, many of whom were their patrons, and released the next morning after paying a small fine, a cost of doing business.

The women eyed her with suspicion, dressed as she was like a lady, but aside from some halfhearted teasing, they left her alone. The best she could do to pass the night was to huddle on a corner of one of the two dirty cots in the room, propped against the damp masonry wall for support while being careful not to lean on any of the other women who had made themselves comfortable, if the term applied, alongside her. The others slept on the floor.

Between episodes of fitful dozing, and a couple of mortifying visits to the reeking bucket that served as a toilet, she had plenty of time to consider her predicament. Being accused of facilitating an abortion, not to mention across state lines, was a serious felony. There was no telling how long they would detain her, or if they would hold her for trial. She'd have to somehow contact her daughter Nancy first thing in the morning, and ask her to get in touch with their family attorney. He would know what to do.

While rehearsing how she would explain this to Nancy in a way that would keep her from bursting into hysterics and rendering herself useless, it occurred to Caroline that if she could prove that Donalee had already been on the train when she herself had boarded, that would show that they weren't traveling together and clear her of suspicion. Not exactly foolproof, but it was all she could come up with.

In the morning she demanded to see the officer in charge. By her manner, her dress, and her speech Caroline was obviously of the upper class; thus her request was accommodated. Her jailers had no idea who she was or who she knew in the city, but they had apparently decided they'd better play it safe.

The duty officer was a stocky fellow with thinning brown hair, seated behind a cluttered wooden desk. He did not pay her the courtesy of rising when she walked in, which she took as a discouraging sign. She resolved to overlook it.

"Officer, I swear I only met Mrs. Wagner on the train after I boarded in Philadelphia. She had come aboard before me, in New York City, she told me. Surely that would demonstrate that we were strangers to each other.

He looked out the smudged, cobwebbed window beside his desk for a moment, as if deciding whether or not to humor her. "I suppose it might. Can you prove it?"

She drew herself up a little taller. "You have my valise in your custody. Within it you will find Mrs. Wagner's handbag and my own. I picked hers up as we left the train for the hospital. I didn't want to leave it for another passenger or a porter to pick up and walk off with." She mentally begged Terrence's forgiveness for suggesting he might do such a thing, but she didn't think he'd mind.

"If you look in both handbags, you will find our tickets. Hers, in the smaller red bag, will show she boarded up the line ahead of me by many miles." She desperately hoped Donalee had not tucked her ticket away in a pocket, or carelessly tossed it out, and that she had told the truth about where she had boarded.

He ran his hand down the back of his head, considering her statement. "How do we know you weren't stealing her bag and planning to walk off with it yourself?"

She took a deep breath and bit off a caustic rejoinder. Her only hope was to cajole this man into believing her and checking their tickets.

"I understand that might seem suspicious, Officer. But put yourself in my place. I made a split second decision to accompany Mrs. Wagner to the hospital when I realized how ill she was, at great inconvenience to myself, I might add, and to the folks waiting for me at the end of the line." She ventured to give him a tentative smile. "Do you have a daughter, Officer?"

He raised his eyebrows, but didn't say "no."

"Then think about it. If your daughter were in trouble in a distant city, far away from home, wouldn't you hope that some kindhearted stranger would look out for her and safeguard her possessions?"

He studied her for a moment, running his tongue along the inside of his cheek. Then he hefted himself out of his chair and disappeared for several minutes. When he returned he had two train tickets in his hand.

"Where did you say she boarded?"

"New York City. And I boarded in Philadelphia."

He nodded and narrowed his eyes. "I rang up the hospital just now. It's the doctor's opinion that the butchery happened several days ago, possibly even a week. Since your tickets were dated yesterday, hers from New York and yours from Philly, neither of you would have been in Chicago when it happened. That puts the crime out of our jurisdiction."

He leaned forward menacingly. "'Course we could ship you back to New York to face charges as an accessory to murder. You could have taken her there to have it done, left her there for a few days to cover your tracks, and met up with her again on the train in Philly to make sure she got home safely to Seattle. Although I can't imagine a cold-blooded arranger of abortions being that considerate."

Caroline gasped. Murder! She hadn't thought of that, but of course, if Donalee had died as a result of the abortion, the abortionist had committed murder. A person who had arranged the abortion would be an accessory. The stakes were much higher than she realized. And how naive she had been to think the tickets proved anything.

Satisfied that she was properly terrified, the officer relaxed his stance, stroked his chin, and continued. "But in all honesty, I believe you, Mrs. Crawford. And the tickets bear you out. Clever of you to have thought of it. In addition, it would be a great deal of trouble to pack you off to New York, where they might not know what to do with you in any case. You are free to go."

"Wh...what?"

35

He cleared his throat loudly. "I said you are free to go. You may pick up your effects at the front desk on your way out. I suggest you continue your westward journey as soon as possible." He held out her ticket.

She stood abruptly, reached for it, turned toward the door, then wheeled about to face him again. "What will happen to Mrs. Wagner's...remains?"

"We'll work with the hospital to contact her family. The hospital will see that the body and her personal possessions, including that red handbag, are sent home once we track her family down." He walked over to Caroline, took her by the arm, and turned her toward the door. "You'd best be gone, Mrs. Crawford, before I change my mind."

She hastened down the steps to the street, fearing her legs would fold beneath her, and hailed the first empty cab that came by. She instructed the driver to take her directly to Union Station. There she redeemed her luggage, leaving Donalee's for the police. Casting aside all thoughts of wasteful spending, she parlayed the unused portion of her ticket into a private roomette for the rest of the journey. She couldn't bear the thought of four more days of small talk with another stranger, not to mention the possibility of another dramatic incident.

"It's done all the time, Ma'am," the agent said as he handed her the upgraded ticket. "A worthwhile price to ward off unwelcome attention, if I may say so, for ladies traveling alone."

Brilliant, she thought as she found her accommodation, set her valise and handbag on the green upholstered seat and closed the door. Hands clenched in her lap, knees rigidly together, she silently urged the train to steam up and roll before a law officer could rush aboard and declare that her dismissal had been a mistake. Her anxiety persisted until the departure whistle blew and the train jerked forward. Exhaling in relief, she slumped back in the seat and closed her eyes while the first blessed miles rolled by.

Try as she might, Caroline could not get Donalee out of her head—the girl's cries of pain, the blood seeping through the towels, and the last sight of her, pale and still, as the doctor swirled the privacy curtain shut and cut off her view. God bless the poor girl. No matter what one thought about abortion—and nothing in Caroline's upbringing had caused her to think about it at all— nobody deserved such an undignified, painful, and lonely end.

How desperate she must have been to have submitted to the illegal procedure and then attempted such a long cross-country trip before she was properly healed, no doubt unbeknownst to her husband. If he had realized she was in a family way, he would surely have moved heaven and earth to find her as soon as he returned from his training exercise.

And to have invited a strange man into her berth, even under normal circumstances, not to mention in her fragile state? The whole scenario beggared belief. Yet it had happened. The shocking memory and distressing feelings it invoked remained with her as the train gathered speed. For one fleeting instant in the Chicago station, she had considered exchanging her westward ticket for a fare back home. But only for an instant. Regardless of the upset, she was determined to have her reunion with Lily.

Only then did she remember Peck. In the tumult with Donalee, she'd completely forgotten him. Poor, dear Peck, an innocent victim of unhappy circumstances. She could only hope that someone in the Chicago railway station, perhaps even Terrence, had taken him home, but she'd never know. The vision of Peck, unfed and unwatered, likely dead and cold at the bottom of his cage, broke Caroline's heart. She burst into tears for the neglected canary. Soon she realized she was really crying for Donalee.

When the emotional storm had passed, Caroline dampened a washcloth at the tiny sink in a corner of her roomette and patted away her tears. Recovered enough now to try to interest herself in the passing countryside, she gazed out the window, her elbow on an arm rest and her chin propped in her hand as the industrial outskirts of Chicago passed in a blur. Inside, the roomette car was designed for privacy, with doors and partitions instead of open seating.

A different uniformed porter had been exactly as courteous and helpful as Terrence. The sway of the train was exactly as soothing, her seat just as comfortable. But everything in Caroline's interior landscape had shifted.

For the first time in her life, she had come up against the reality of an unwanted pregnancy. For herself, she couldn't imagine a pregnancy being unwanted, yet she knew there were circumstances in which it might be: extreme poverty, an unmanageable houseful of children already, an unreliable or renegade husband, the threat of maternal death, and as in Donalee's case, an anchor to a man with whom she'd be unhappy for the rest of her life. If so, should abortion be made available in a medically safe environment? She'd never had such thoughts before, but the vision of Donalee, crouched and bleeding and crying in her upper berth, remained with her as the train rolled on.

Anyone passing her door on the few occasions when she left it open would have seen a pleasantly attractive middle-aged woman, conservatively dressed, sitting alone and happily anticipating her arrival on the West Coast, no doubt visiting family or friends. They would have no idea that she had just been through the most traumatic experience of her forty-three years.

The remaining days on the train passed unremarked. She took her meals in the diner, usually at a table with other travelers whom she enjoyed but was just as happy never to see again. She looked forward to those breaks, welcoming the distraction of the pleasantly inconsequential chatter. Back in her roomette, gazing out the window, she saw for herself the endless prairie, bursting with life in the summer sunshine, always changing yet always the same.

In her quiet isolation, Caroline welcomed the opportunity to let her mind wander, seduced by the gentle sway of the cars. When thoughts of Donalee intruded, she acknowledged the grief that accompanied them, then allowed them to recede while she opened her mind to a flood of memories of Lily.

CHAPTER 4

Caroline had already unpacked her trunk and now paced restlessly while awaiting the arrival of the girl who would be her freshman dormitory roommate at Bryn Mawr College. She desperately hoped she would be paired with someone halfway lighthearted. She couldn't bear the idea of living with a scholastic worrywart or hopeless bookworm. Standing at the window, she bobbed up and down on her toes, keeping watch on the walkway below.

Without so much as a knock, a young woman threw open the door and burst in, followed by a porter with her trunk. They must have entered below when Caroline had momentarily stepped away from the window to rearrange the knick-knacks on her dresser top for the dozenth time.

Taller than Caroline by a good four inches, the girl was slender, with high cheekbones and rich brown hair braided into a bun at her neck. She wore a tailored tan-colored suit with a hip-length jacket over a plain white cotton blouse. Caroline was struck by the contrast to herself, with her almost matronly figure, generous in bust and hips. She wore a suit as well, olive green with black braid at the lapels, collar, cuffs, and hem. Her jacket opened over a pale green blouse a-froth with ruffles and lace cascading down the front. In the mirror over the bookcase, she quickly checked her fair, wavy hair, fixed atop her head in a loose Gibson Girl knot. Her hair and buttercream complexion were her best features. Although the new girl was striking, Caroline knew that she could hold her own in the looks department.

Seeing a hat, scarf, and handbag on one of the beds, the girl directed the porter to stow her trunk at the foot of the other bed. She tipped him a coin and thanked him for his help, then held out her hand to Caroline.

"Hello. I'm Lily Paxton. Looks like we're roommates."

"Lovely to meet you. I'm Caroline Lindholm. I got here early this morning and took the liberty of choosing this bed and dresser. I hope you'll be comfortable with the other?" She waved at the bed and dresser across the room.

Lily nodded. "Absolutely fine."

"Where have you come from?" Caroline asked.

"Upstate New York. Which I hope to avoid as much as possible from now on. And you?"

Caroline pushed aside the possessions on her bed, plunked down on it, and leaned back on her elbows. Her neatly shod feet poked out below the braid-trimmed hem of her skirt.

"Actually, I'm a townie. My father is Professor Lindholm. He teaches first and second year Greek and Latin. We'll both have to suffer through his courses, I'm afraid. But take it from me—his bark is much worse than his bite." Caroline's grin attested to her affection for her father, Greek and Latin notwithstanding. "But where in Upstate New York? Why do you want to avoid going home?"

Lily's face clouded over. "Let's not talk about that right now. Tell me about some of the other professors—which ones have the best reputations and which to avoid. What does your father say about them?"

There was a seriousness about Lily, a quality Caroline, whose friends thought mostly of fun and boys and marriage, sensed would take some getting used to. There was also a hint of mystery about the girl, which promised to be interesting.

Caroline rolled her eyes toward the ceiling. "Oh, I could tell you all kinds of stories. But let's save that for another time. Let's go down the hall and see who else is here. You can unpack later. It'll be so much nicer if we can meet everybody on the floor first off."

Right from the start, Lily was an enigma to Caroline and their dorm mates. She was quiet, dignified, and aloof much of the time, yet pleasant and respectful as a roommate, neat and tidy, with a ripe sense of humor that surfaced unexpectedly. The two girls became fast friends, although Lily continued to maintain a certain level of reserve. They never experienced the kinds of tiffs and arguments that erupted from time to time among the other girls in residence; nor did they become immediate confidants. Lily studied diligently with great concern over her grades; Caroline's approach was much more casual, but she managed to pass her courses with marks that met her father's approval. Lily never mentioned her family and managed to deflect any questions that the other girls asked. Soon they stopped asking.

Despite her studiousness, there were times when Lily burst with uncontainable physical energy, leading the other girls in outrageous pranks. Like the night she rounded up everyone on their floor in their nightgowns at midnight and shepherded them out the door for a ghostly barefooted run across the moonlit campus. They had almost made it back to the dormitory when they were spotted by none other than Dr. M. Carey Thomas, a founder and celebrated second president of Bryn Mawr and vigilant guardian of its reputation. Women might be welcome in select coeducational colleges and universities in 1898, in addition to the few women's colleges, but they still needed to behave like ladies and set a good example.

The next day they were all hauled before the student Self-Government Association. Though it was considered a radical experiment at the time, Dr. Thomas backed up her belief in the association's ability to keep the students in check by refraining from interfering in their deliberations and punishments, whether she considered them just or not. In this case, the errant girls were restricted by their peers from leaving the campus for two weeks and enjoined not to indulge in such foolishness again. All in all, they considered it a fair price to pay for fifteen minutes of joyous midnight exuberance. With each of her pranks, Lily's star rose higher among her fellow students.

As time went on, Caroline noticed that Lily rarely went home for the weekend, nor did she have visitors aside from her younger sister Florence, who spent an awestruck weekend at the college in anticipation of her own enrollment four years down the road.

Once she realized this, Caroline often invited Lily home with her, and their friendship continued to flourish. During a ramble through Caroline's suburban Philadelphia neighborhood in October of their freshman year, when the trees were turning scarlet and gold, she ventured to bring up the subject of Lily's family. Being so fond of her own parents and brother, she couldn't imagine anyone seemingly so unattached.

"I know you have a sister, Lily, but you never mention your parents," Caroline began, prepared to be rebuffed but determined to get to the bottom of it. "You've spoken of an aunt and uncle in upstate New York, but you never mention your home."

Lily took so long to answer that Caroline feared she had crossed an invisible boundary.

"We grew up in Buffalo, New York, but our parents are gone," Lily finally replied, staring straight ahead. "They died within two years of each other, Father first, in a carriage accident, and then Mother. Florence was ten and I was fourteen when Mother died."

Caroline glanced at Lily, expecting to see an expression of sorrow, but her friend's face revealed nothing. "I'm so sorry. It wasn't fair of me to pry."

"It's all right. I'm ready to talk about it, at least with you."

Feeling somewhat reassured, Caroline asked, "So who took care of you after that?"

"Our Uncle Arnold, our father's elder brother, became our guardian and executor of Mother's will. He took us to live with his family in Corning, New York." Lily stopped, lifted her skirt, and viciously kicked a pile of brittle leaves that had accumulated near the base of a tree. Her expression was no longer serene.

"Is Corning your home now? You've never mention going there."

Through gritted teeth Lily replied, "Technically I suppose it's my home, but I don't go back unless I absolutely have to. Summers, school vacations, and monthly summons from my uncle."

"Gosh, is it that awful?"

Lily stopped and looked down at the edge of the gravel roadway. She ran the toe of her shoe along the upheaving root of a hawthorn tree. She was silent for so long that Caroline feared she had stirred up memories that were still too raw and painful.

"I'm sorry. It...it's none of my business. Please, I don't want my nosiness to ruin our friendship."

Frowning, Lily turned to look at Caroline, as if deciding how much information she was willing to share, and how much their friendship meant to her. Without being able to explain it, Caroline understood that if Lily answered the question, it would mean an important turning point in their friendship. It would mean that Lily was beginning to trust her.

Lily turned back to the root in the roadway, kicking it distractedly. "I've never told anybody at school about my family. I don't even like to think about it, but of course one does." She began walking again, faster this time as if trying to outpace the memories. Caroline had to jog a few steps to catch up.

"My father was a pharmacist, a graduate of New York College of Pharmacy. He owned a small drugstore, ran it himself. We had a comfortable life in Buffalo, not wealthy by any means, but I can't remember lacking anything. Father worked hard—long weekdays and half days on Saturday. In the evenings after closing he rolled or pressed his pills, restocked the merchandise and did his ordering and paperwork. He was rarely home except on Sundays. We lazed about in the morning, and on summer afternoons we often took a picnic to the park. In the winter, Sunday afternoons meant a lazy lay-about by the fireplace listening to my parents read from whatever book we were interested in at the time. *Little Women* was our favorite. Father rolled his eyes every time we requested it, but he gamely joined Mother in reading it to us. He was hilarious doing the girls' voices.

Those were wonderful afternoons." Lily slowed down, appearing to relax a bit with the sweet recollection.

"How terrible to lose him at such a young age," said Caroline, unable to conceive of such a tragedy.

"Yes. He was a good man, good to us and good to our mother. Everything changed when he died." Lily gazed toward the autumn hills, drifting along with the memory.

"That must have been dreadful, especially for your mother," Caroline said softly, calling her back to the present.

"Dear, dear Mother. It was so hard for her after he died, especially as she got sicker and sicker. Our only consolation was that Father didn't witness her decline. Tuberculosis is a terrible wasting disease. She hired a young fellow just out of pharmacy school to run the business. His salary took up most of the profits, which left us with very little. She had great hopes that he'd eventually buy it from her—until she discovered he'd been embezzling. In an amazingly short time he'd run the pharmacy into the ground and skedaddled with everything he had skimmed off, leaving us with a pile of debts. To avoid a scandal, Mother decided not to pursue him. Luckily we owned the lot and the building free and clear, so Mother was able to sell them for a good price. But much of it went to pay off the debt. The rest she gave to Uncle Arnold to invest, and we lived off the earnings. I admit he did well by us financially, but it was never enough."

"Is that how you managed to come to Bryn Mawr? Your inheritance from the sale of the property?"

"That, plus the sale of our house after Mother died, and her savings. For as long as I can remember she told us that she was setting money aside every month so we could go to Bryn Mawr. She had followed the opening of the college in 1885 with great interest. In fact she knew several of the college's founders. She believed that, with its exceptionally high standards, Bryn Mawr would be a revolution in women's education. Her biggest regret was that she was born a generation too soon to attend herself. She wanted it desperately for Florence and me, so that we would never have to depend on anyone else, especially men, for our security and well-being. Our father's death greatly reinforced that in her mind. On her deathbed she made me promise that I would carry on with the Bryn Mawr plan for both of us."

Lily reached up and snapped off a dead twig from an elm tree, then tossed the twig aside. "The problems began when Uncle Arnold took over our lives and finances."

"Did he embezzle as well?" Caroline asked as she and Lily lifted their skirts and hopped over a mud puddle.

"Fortunately, no. Mother had scrimped and saved for Bryn Mawr. Added to the money from the sale of the drugstore and the house, it sufficed. Mother had specified in her will—in black and white, duly signed, witnessed, and notarized—that we were to go to Bryn Mawr. It should have been ironclad, but Uncle Arnold told us in no uncertain terms that women needed no education beyond the primary grades; that the only things we needed to know were how to run a household and take care of children. We were at his mercy. Not only that, but he kept meticulous track of every penny he spent on us while we lived with him and Aunt Sophie and all the way through college. I mean every penny. He sat me down every month with a ledger that showed what he had spent the previous month for our food, clothing, schooling—everything right down to a penny for a hair ribbon and a nickel for the Sunday church collection. God forbid he should spend a dime of his own money on his orphaned nieces. I only learned much later that he had invested our funds wisely and the capital was growing nicely. There was no need for him to be such a skinflint with our money."

"How absolutely wretched! Is your uncle not a man of means himself?"

"Certainly, he's a man of great means. He owns a large and successful housewares manufactory in Corning, inherited from his father. You should see their mansion."

"Then why was he such a miser with your inheritance?"

Lily shook her head. "I can only guess. Maybe he just wanted to make things difficult for me, to punish me for pursuing my college dream in spite of his objections. Maybe he just wanted to control me in the one way he could."

"But your mother specified in her will that the money was for Bryn Mawr!"

"Indeed. We had raging battles over it. Aunt Sophie was appalled that I would stand up and fight back against his controlling small-mindedness, but I often suspected she was silently cheering me on. He bullied her as much as he bullied everybody, but there wasn't much she dared do about it. Once again proving Mother's point about a woman's disadvantage in being dependent on men."

For a moment the girls were distracted by a group of noisy boys playing stickball in the empty field across the road. Caroline and Lawrence had played ball with the neighborhood kids in that same field only yesterday, it seemed.

Still curious, Caroline returned to Bryn Mawr. "So how did you manage it? Getting to college, I mean."

Lily cut Caroline a sly sideways glance. "Pure dogged stubbornness. Obnoxious persistence, as Uncle Arnold once termed it. I never gave up. It was what our mother wanted; it was what I wanted for myself; and it was what we both wanted for Florence. Then I executed my stroke of genius."

Caroline raised her eyebrows. "Genius? Whatever do you mean?"

"I hired an attorney to intercede on my behalf." Lily rubbed her hands together as if savoring the memory.

Caroline halted and stared in disbelief. Lily poked her in the shoulder to get her moving again.

"I really did. One evening at the dinner table Uncle Arnold ranted on about a lawsuit in which he was involved, and how much he hated the attorney for the opposing side, Maurice Chapin. I looked him up the next day and made an appointment for a consultation. Once he got over the shock of a fifteen-year-old girl wanting to hire him, Mr. Chapin was delighted to take my case. He even waived his fee, because it gave him another chance to cross swords with my uncle."

"Genius indeed," giggled Caroline. "I'm impressed."

Lily reached up to pluck a few dried oak leaves from a low-hanging branch. She crumbled them up and tossed the bits into the breeze.

"When I met with Mr. Chapin, the first thing he asked was why I was so sure I'd be accepted at Bryn Mawr. I confessed that I wasn't sure at all. I just assumed I would be. He pointed out that the entrance requirements were extremely rigid, patterned after those at Harvard—notoriously difficult even for men—unless they were well connected, of course, or legacies. He advised me to look into it before we tackled Uncle Arnold.

"So I sent away for the college catalog. When I saw the list of subjects that were covered in the entrance exams, I was appalled. Weren't you? All that algebra and geometry, Latin, German, French, history, geography, the classics—and that wasn't the half of it." She turned to face Caroline. "Weren't you shocked?"

Caroline looked at Lily a bit sheepishly. "I didn't have to take the entrance exams, being the daughter of a professor."

"Lucky you! When I realized that my public school education wasn't going to be good enough, I almost gave up. But I couldn't let my mother down, nor Florence, and, even if it killed me, I couldn't let Uncle Arnold win. The idea of him lording it over me, laughing at my folly when my application was denied, was unthinkable."

"Goodness! So what happened?" asked Caroline, stopping briefly to disentangle her skirt from a blackberry bramble encroaching onto the roadway. It wasn't too many years ago that she and Lawrence had gone out with their pails and brought back juicy ripe berries for their mother's pies and preserves.

"By the best of good luck, Mr. Chapin knew a woman in Corning who had been in Bryn Mawr's first graduating class and earned her living by tutoring. Miss Darla Hatton. She'd been a brilliant student but contracted infantile paralysis shortly after graduating. It left her with a paralyzed leg, walking with a crutch. Her widowed mother cared for her, but died within a few years, leaving her the cottage. As she learned to manage alone, she tried to get a teaching job, but was always turned down because of her handicap. So she took up tutoring. She agreed to put me through a rigorous two-year course of study to prepare me for the entrance exams."

Lily leaned against the white trunk of a birch tree and inhaled deeply. The scent of autumn wood fires wisped through the air from the many nearby chimneys.

"At that point, Mr. Chapin contacted Uncle Arnold and told him that I had retained him to help me secure my rights under Mother's will. Uncle marched into the house that evening huffing and puffing, red faced, slamming doors, and hauled me into his study. He sat there like a fat-bellied potentate with his gold watch chain bouncing across his stomach. He bellowed at me, verbally flogged me while I stood at paralyzed attention. He called me every uncomplimentary name you can imagine to describe a woman who puts herself forward. Suddenly I realized this would be our defining battle. I shouted right back at him, flaying him with my long list of grievances that had built up since Mother's death. Oh, it was glorious!"

She pushed off from the tree and spun around, making fighting fists in the air.

"I'd love to have seen that," exclaimed Caroline, enthralled.

Lily stopped and grinned, arms akimbo. "Smack in the middle of this unholy conflagration, Florence came flying in and threw herself at him. She had no idea what was going on, only that her sister was under attack—again. She beat him with her fists, shrieked at him like a crazed hyena. Oh, what a scene! She'd never joined me in battle before, bless her heart. He was stunned, absolutely speechless. When Florence finally ran out of steam, I grabbed her hand, and we marched out of the room. The next day I packed a bag and left for good."

"You left?" Caroline gasped, pulling her shawl tightly around her shoulders. As the sun neared the horizon, the wind had taken on a chill.

"Yes. My only regret was leaving Florence behind. I promised her that if she could put up with living there until it was her turn, I'd get her to Bryn Mawr. Luckily, Florence had always been comfortable at Uncle Arnold and Aunt Sophie's. She was only ten when Mother died and a much more placid child. Aunt Sophie took a shine to my sister as she never did to me, and Florence didn't bring out the worst in Uncle Arnold as I seemed to do. She and our cousin Mavis became quite chummy, so she blended easily into their family. But just in case he decided to turn on Florence, this unexpected show of spirit reassured me. In any case, I couldn't possibly have taken her with me."

Wide-eyed at Lily's bravery, Caroline asked, "So where did you go?"

"When Miss Hatton agreed to tutor me, what she hadn't agreed to was providing me with room and board as well. But when I turned up on her doorstep, suitcase in hand after my big fight with Uncle, she quickly took in the situation and welcomed me graciously. She was such a wonderful teacher. We laughed as much as we studied. God bless her, she even taught me to cook."

"You, cooking?"

Lily affected her haughtiest pose and looked down her nose at Caroline. "I make a mean pot roast. It may come in handy someday. Anyway, Mr. Chapin convinced Uncle that Mother's will was airtight and enforceable. After a great deal of protest, he agreed to release the money for two years of private tutoring, plus room and board at Miss Hatton's, in addition to Bryn Mawr itself. And the same for Florence. It turned out, upon Mr. Chapin's inspection of the accounts—and didn't that just drive Uncle wild—that Uncle had invested our inheritance extremely wisely. Somehow he'd anticipated the financial panic of 1893, and managed to skirt it safely on our behalf. In fact, I once heard him brag that he made a lot of money on it. Between his canny investing and his meticulous accounting, though, he outfoxed himself—he could not deny me my education based on insufficient funds, any more than he could ignore Mother's will. Mr. Chapin was absolutely brilliant in handling the old goat without ever having to go to court!"

Both girls began to giggle. Suddenly Lily picked up her skirts and lit off across the open field, then circled back in the direction of the

Lindholm house, with Caroline dashing after her. They arrived just in time for dinner, flushed, winded, and happy.

CHAPTER 5

Lily and Caroline's friendship continued to deepen during their second year at Bryn Mawr. As often happens, however, the unexpected reared its meddlesome head and tossed things about, at least for Caroline. During the summer between their first and second years, Caroline met John Crawford, a young man who was apprenticing in and would eventually inherit his father's publishing business. They met at a garden party given by one of Caroline's friends on a warm Philadelphia summer afternoon. Both were instantly smitten. Caroline's parents insisted that she finish her second year of college before getting married. Reluctantly, but obediently, she complied.

After the wedding, the two girls stayed in touch by letter—Lily's full of college gossip amid reports on the rigors and triumphs of her studies; Caroline's replete with the details of setting up housekeeping in her new home. In the fall of Lily's senior year, Caroline announced the joyous news of her first pregnancy. Although her studies precluded the frequent visits she'd enjoyed during their first two years, Lily managed to break off now and then for a relaxing weekend at Caroline and John's. Their home was a spacious two-story colonial in a quiet Philadelphia suburb, a few blocks from the city streetcar line.

On a Sunday afternoon in early April, two months prior to Lily's graduation, Caroline responded to a ring of her doorbell to find Lily on the doorstep, wearing a wrinkled travelling suit and carrying her familiar suitcase.

"Oh, what a lovely surprise!" said Caroline. "I'm so happy to see you! Come in, come in. I'm prohibited from leaving the house in my delicate condition. Do they think it would be too taxing for me to walk abroad? What on earth do women do on the farm when the cows need to be milked and field hands fed?"

Lily stepped inside and set her suitcase on the entryway floor. "From what I understand, they just keep on milking and cooking until the baby is born and then get back at it again with nary a blink."

Caroline grinned. "Don't tell anyone, but I suspect the unspoken message is that I must stay sequestered for fear of someone suspecting by the size of my belly that I have had congress with a man!"

The two young women fell into each other's arms, dissolved in mirth. Caroline's married status meant there were no grownups around to keep an eye on them or cast judgment on their behavior. Of course there was always John, but he was a pleasant fellow who, although he enjoyed Lily's visits, usually left the girls to themselves. On this particular afternoon he had closeted himself away in his study, as he often did, editing a manuscript.

"Oh, Caroline, I haven't had anything to laugh about in weeks," said Lily, wiping tears from her cheeks. "What a tonic you are!"

"Leave your suitcase there, and let's fix a sustaining pot of tea."

Once they'd seated themselves in the drawing room, cups and saucers on their laps, Caroline finally took in her friend's distressed condition.

"It's been such a long time, Lily. What brings you here unannounced on a Sunday afternoon?"

"Oh, Caroline. I'm so confused. I don't know what to do. I've just come from my Uncle Arnold's. I'm on my way back to school, but I simply couldn't face it! It's only two months to graduation, and he's forced me to confront the issue of my future. What future, Caroline? I haven't any!"

Caroline listened patiently while Lily spilled her tale of woe.

Four days earlier Lily had received a letter from her Uncle Arnold, demanding that she journey to Corning on the upcoming Saturday to discuss "matters of great import regarding your future." Final exams loomed. She'd fallen behind in several classes, and she needed the weekend to catch up. But such a serious summons from her uncle could not be ignored.

During her almost four years at Bryn Mawr, he had surprised her with his relative non-interference, aside from a letter now and then reminding her of his dire predictions about educated women. In one particularly pointed letter he warned her that his family physician had informed him that she was opening herself to nasty internal disorders and degeneration of the reproductive organs, rendering herself undesirable to men and unable to have children if she persisted in her stubborn pursuit of learning. She crumpled that one up like all the others and threw it in the wastebasket.

However, Uncle Arnold paid Lily's bills to the college on time and, for the most part, without comment. He also sent her a quarterly allowance, miserly in her opinion, but she had learned to make do. Granted, she had built up a debt to the dry goods store for fabric from which she sewed her dresses, but this was certainly better than the larger debt she would have incurred had she hired a dressmaker as most of the girls did. Thank heavens her mother had taught her this skill, which she found a relaxing break between study sessions.

More debt had piled up with the shoemaker, and with the grocer for her frequent and elaborate entertainment of the other girls in her residence hall, an honored tradition at Bryn Mawr. She had no idea how she would free herself of these financial obligations. Perhaps the merchants would be good enough to wait until Florence graduated, at which time she and Florence would receive what remained of their mother's estate. But she knew she'd better not count on much from that quarter. Unless her sister lived like a miser in college, which she herself had not quite managed, the funds would be depleted before the end of Florence's senior year. Her best bet, she decided, was to convince her uncle to release enough funds now to satisfy the three merchants, which would have the added benefit of allowing Florence to establish credit with them without an eye to her own negligent record. If the funds ran out before Florence graduated, perhaps his and Aunt Sophie's fondness for Florence would prompt them to make up the difference. The discussion of "matters of great import regarding your future" was bound to be unpleasant, and she knew he'd throw in her finances as well.

Her future. She'd succeeded in keeping such troublesome thoughts at bay whenever they crept up on her, easily distracting herself with her studies and school activities by day but finding herself grappling with them during the deepest hours of the night. With graduation only two months away, it became harder and harder to ignore them. Uncle Arnold would surely demand to know what her plans were. The terrifying truth was that she had no plans. When she let down her guard and allowed the question to enter, she felt herself hurtling toward the edge of a precipice.

She had survived the years-long war with her uncle. She had exerted self-discipline the likes of which she could not possibly have imagined during her two preparatory years with Miss Hatton, and she had stayed diligently on track during four years of challenging studies in college. Aside from her weekends with Caroline, and occasional visits from Florence, she had kept a rigidly tight rein on herself over the last two years. Her occasional outbursts of pranks and practical jokes provided a welcome release valve, but in her darkest moments she wondered if they were an indication of a serious character flaw. However, that was not what worried her now.

Lily had arrived at the Paxton mansion in the late afternoon, having taken a cab from the Corning train station. Yellow daffodils; white crocus; and pink, red, and orange tulips, the glorious confetti of spring, lined the long driveway beyond the wrought-iron gate. Her Aunt Sophie greeted her in the foyer with polite reserve and suggested she repair to the guestroom upstairs to freshen up and have a bit of a rest before dinner. When Lily asked for Florence, her aunt informed her that her sister was off riding horses with a school friend and would be staying overnight. Lily felt sorry to have missed her, but it was just as well if she and Uncle Arnold were going to engage in fireworks again.

She had just washed her hands and splashed her face at the ceramic bowl on the washstand when Mavis knocked on the door. She hadn't seen her cousin since she'd left for school in the fall. Tall and rangy, with wide shoulders, flat chest, and blotchy complexion, the girl hadn't improved much in the interim. Despite her costly wardrobe, she always looked as if she had just rushed in from a dash through the bushes.

"Hello Lily. Father's just arrived and wants to see you in his study before dinner." So typical of Mavis, Lily thought. No social chatter, just deliver the message in her superior tone and be gone.

Lily dampened a comb and drew it through her hair from her temples to the braided bun at the nape of her neck, plastering the stragglers against her head in a vain attempt to coax them into submission. She ran her hands down the bodice and upper skirt of her gray traveling suit, wishing she'd had time to change but knowing that Uncle Arnold would be waiting impatiently. She drew in a deep breath and mentally girded herself for combat.

Arnold Paxton rose from the chair behind his massive mahogany desk as she entered, one of his many intimidation techniques. The brightly lit west-facing window behind him cast his portly figure in shadow while causing Lily to squint. The familiar smell of old leather and cigar smoke almost made her gag.

He nodded at her. "Lily. It's good to see you. You're looking well."

She didn't believe a word of it. "Thank you, Uncle Arnold. It's nice to see you too." She forced out the requisite pleasantry as she stood with her hands clasped behind her back, feeling a slow trickle of sweat inch down between her shoulder blades. An oil painting of her late grandfather—Arnold, Sr., the legendary founder of Paxton Housewares—stared sternly down at her, suited in the blue wool and gold braid of a Union general atop his prancing black war horse. He had fought at the Battle of Gettysburg, according to family legend, barely escaping death. Lily's father had told his daughter many tales of the general's autocratic and controlling ways. After a final dustup, her father had left home to strike out on his own and worked his way through pharmacy school. As a result, he had been disinherited, leaving everything eventually to Arnold.

Gesturing toward one of a pair of leather chairs facing his desk, Arnold said, "Sit down, sit down, we've things to discuss."

He wasted no time opening the ponderous green ledger which contained the penny-by-penny accounting of his sister-in-law's trust, found the page with the most recent entries, and swiveled the book around to face Lily. He strode out from behind the desk and stood behind her.

"All right, let's take a look." Over her shoulder he peered down at the page for a moment, as if needing to review the figures—not likely, she thought—then leaned over and ran his beefy finger down the column of expenditures.

Posturing, that's all it is, she reminded herself, yet as usual he managed to intimidate her. His masculine control over her life was precisely the state of affairs her mother had railed against. With a slap of his hand on the desk, he retraced his steps and sat back down facing her.

"You've overspent again, Miss. When will you learn to keep your purchases within limits? Extravagance is unbecoming in a young woman who has no way of paying her bills." He laced his fingers across his belly and awaited her reply.

She took a deep breath. "Well, that's just it, Uncle. It's impossible to live on my allowance. I've told you many times I must have clothing and school supplies, and… well, there are so many things a girl needs."

He shook his head. "We've gone over this again and again, Lily. The only saving grace is that you are close to graduation. Soon I will have no further responsibility for you. Frankly, the sooner the better.

Your sister somehow manages to live within her limits. I have no problem with her whatsoever. What do you say to that?"

Lily raised her shoulders at the ridiculous comparison. "She's younger, Uncle, and still lives at home. She doesn't have the expenses I must contend with, at least not yet."

"Clothing and shoes I understand, but your grocer's bill? What in the world is that all about? I pay for your board at the college. Don't they feed you enough?"

'We enjoy entertaining in our rooms. It's done by everyone. I'd be out of step if I didn't do my share."

"*Harrumph*. Utter nonsense."

"The thing is, Uncle, I do have those debts. I need to clear them by graduation."

"Oh, you do? And why should I facilitate that?"

"Because it's the right thing to do. These purchases were necessities, and they must be paid for. We don't want Florence starting out with a reputation for having a sister who's a...a deadbeat." A dreadful word, deadbeat, but she looked him in the eye and said it firmly.

To her satisfaction, Arnold winced. By implication, the term, when applied to his niece, reflected poorly on a wealthy uncle who allowed it. His reputation would be damaged, should it become known among his business associates.

"The right thing to do, eh? 'Twas the wrong thing to rack up these debts in the first place, young lady. Do you think you can keep doing this throughout your life and expect someone to keep bailing you out? All this education has done nothing but make you unsuitable for marriage. No man will want to marry someone who walks around with Latin, Greek, higher mathematics, and what not cluttering up her head. You'll be on your own and responsible for your own finances. You can't carry on in this vein. You'll end up in debtor's prison." His voice rose, louder and more strident.

"Oh, for heaven's sake, Uncle. Debtor's prisons went out with Charles Dickens. Please, grant me this favor. As you say, you'll have no more truck with me in a couple of months."

"Yes, that'll be a milestone indeed—the removal of a millstone from around this family's neck." He grinned, showing his tobacco-stained teeth beneath his moustache, diverted by his sophomoric play on words.

There would be no mention, of course, of her forthcoming achievement in graduating near the top of her class from a prestigious institute of higher learning. Nothing she could say or do would change his mind on the subject of female education. She would remain a blemish on the family's honor, to be compounded by Florence upon her own graduation.

"Speaking of this noteworthy event, and I mean noteworthy in the most negative sense, what exactly do you propose for your future? I see no suitor in sight, unless you're hiding one from me. If so, you'd better bring him out into the open for my inspection."

Aha, now we get to it, thought Lily, the matter of great import. "No, Uncle, there's no suitor. I... I really don't have any plans." Surprisingly, the heavens were not rent open by thunder and lightning; the earth did not quake beneath her feet for having admitted it.

"Well, surely you don't think you're going to come back here to live with us?" Arnold sputtered. "With almost half your mother's money spent on your fancy education and the rest earmarked for your sister, you'll need a better proposal than that."

She paused before answering. She'd elope with a snake oil salesman before coming back to live with her aunt and uncle.

"I had thought of applying for a fellowship to graduate school." She said it with a great deal more enthusiasm than she felt, testing the waters for his reaction and hoping such a threat would make the issue of her merchant bills seem miniscule in comparison.

Arnold exploded out of his chair, sending it toppling back against the window ledge behind him. "What? More bloody education? Not on your tintype, lassie. I refuse to permit anything that would twist your brain into more knots. Absolutely impossible! I won't hear of it."

The idea didn't appeal much to Lily either, but at least it would give her a stay of execution—three or four more years of study before life got real again, with perhaps some of it taken in Europe. Study abroad in Paris or Berlin—either would be pleasant. Bryn Mawr offered a handful of graduate fellowships every year, and she was certain she would qualify for one. But where would that take her? At best, she'd end up being a professor at a women's college, maybe even Bryn Mawr. She admired many of her professors, but the idea of teaching truly did not interest her.

Besides, a woman of her social status didn't become a professor. Her father may have been a pharmacist, a professional man, but her mother came from top drawer Philadelphia society. This was another reason Uncle Arnold disliked her—she was a constant reminder that her late mother's social credentials were considerably higher than those of her husband and his brother Arnold. Mary Louise Atherton Paxton had married for love, and none of this mattered to her or her daughters. But Lily knew it was a thorn in Arnold's side.

Without an advanced degree, she could become a governess, heaven forbid, or take a secretarial course and become an underpaid office drone. What a waste! Then there was medical school. Johns Hopkins University had recently—and reluctantly—begun admitting a few women medical students, thanks to a large grant from an heir to the B & O Railway fortune. Several of her schoolmates were bent on becoming physicians, but that didn't appeal to Lily either. She couldn't see herself dealing with sick and injured people all day and being called out at night to deliver babies. Besides, she'd have to scramble, probably for another year, to take the required upper level science courses she'd avoided by concentrating on literature.

She was tired of studying. That was the simple truth, but red-hot pincers twisting her tongue would never force her to admit it to her uncle. All those years of cramming her head with facts, thoughts, ideas, literature, languages, geometric proofs, and scientific controversies—and for the most part, enjoying the process despite its difficulties—had finally caught up with her. How could she have fought so hard, swum upstream so vigorously, and succeeded beyond her wildest expectations, with high grades and scholastic awards, and now find the future so bleak, so meaningless? The struggle itself had been everything, it seemed. And beyond that—what?

In all her discussions with her mother, they had never ventured beyond the attainment of that Bryn Mawr sheepskin. Mary Paxton, so adamant about the value of education for women, had seen no further than graduation. Of course, none of this would matter if Lily could look forward to an independent income. The most she could hope for, however unlikely, was a smattering left of their mother's legacy after Florence graduated, invested to yield a small income. But she knew, even under Uncle Arnold's brilliant management, that any remainder was likely to be modest in the extreme.

"Well, young lady?" Arnold sputtered, waiting impatiently for her to tell him what she intended to do with her life. Lily had no answer. She rose from her seat and held up a hand.

"Uncle, please. Settle down, or Aunt will get after me for upsetting you. I'll see you at dinner." Before he could object, she hastened from the study, closing the door behind her.

Once upstairs in her bedroom, she threw herself onto her bed and stared at the ceiling. No solutions there, she quickly decided. What was she going to do?

Reluctantly she joined the family for dinner, only to discover that her aunt had invited the Farley family to dine with them. Jackson Farley was a business associate of Arnold's, a member of his Masonic lodge, and a city councilman. His wife Diana, his second wife as it happened, was twenty years younger—pretty but taken to giggling in response to every conversational sally sent her way. She was more the age of his son Colin, who was also at the table. Lily immediately understood. This was her aunt and uncle's clumsy attempt to introduce her to a young man who might rescue her from her overly educated spinster state. She had to admit the fellow was decent looking, taller than she, and no doubt had good prospects in his father's haberdashery business. However, the fact that her aunt and uncle should try to effect an alliance between herself and this unsuspecting young man turned her firmly against him, strictly as a matter of principle.

She managed to keep her conversation civil at the dinner table. She even managed to be pleasant to the ladies as they sipped their sherry in the drawing room after dinner while the gentleman enjoyed their port and cigars in the dining room. But she was shaken by the idea of her aunt and uncle maneuvering to marry her off. Although it would be a solution to her financial problems, she'd marry whom she pleased, when she pleased, and if she pleased, thank you very much.

On Sunday morning the senior Paxtons deposited her at the train station on their way to church. Her refusal to attend was another black mark against her. She'd been raised a Congregationalist and had continued to attend while living with her aunt and uncle, but after moving in with Miss Hatton she no longer considered it necessary. It was one small battle she'd won against her uncle, as he couldn't force her without picking her up bodily and carrying her into the church. Actually, she mused as she waved them goodbye, that might have been entertaining.

Tucked safely in her handbag was an envelope she'd found slipped under her bedroom door that morning. Inside was enough cash to settle her merchant accounts and a little extra, plus a brief note: "Not a word to Uncle. Aunt Sophie."

Instead of purchasing a ticket straight through to Bryn Mawr, she bought one only as far as the Broad Street Station in Philadelphia. She'd lost the whole weekend; one day of skipped classes wouldn't make any difference. She was too distressed to even think about her studies, but God bless Aunt Sophie! At least that immediate problem was solved. She'd been correct all along—Aunt Sophie *was* silently cheering for her. There was unexpected comfort in that.

After patiently hearing her out over several cups of tea, Caroline gave her friend an appraising look.

"Surely you knew this was coming, Lily."

"Intellectually I suppose I did, but it was so easy to push away," Lily replied, somewhat taken aback by Caroline's forthright response. "Life on campus is so…so otherworldly. Now with graduation looming, I suddenly feel like I'm stuffed in a cannon. It's set to fire on graduation day, blasting me off to…to where?"

"Teaching is the most obvious solution. Surely you've considered that?"

Lily bowed her head into her hands. "I can't bear it, Caroline. I'd have to put in three or four more years of concentrated study to obtain a doctorate if I want to teach at the university level. I've had my nose to the grindstone most of my life, and I'm simply worn out. And if I became a teacher with just a bachelor's degree, well, I'll likely end up at a country school out on some godforsaken prairie, which I simply can't imagine. I like children. I believe they should have every opportunity to learn, but I don't see myself standing in a classroom all day, dusted with chalk. Can you understand? Does that make me a bad person?"

"Of course that doesn't make you a bad person, Lily. I don't believe I'd want to be a teacher either. Frankly, I love being Mrs. John Crawford, and I know I'll love it even more once the baby comes."

Lily leaned toward Caroline and took her hand. "May I make a shocking confession?"

Caroline placed her other hand on Lily's, enfolding her friend's hand in hers. "Knowing you as I do, Lily, there's nothing you could say that would shock me. Go ahead and try!"

Lily closed her eyes and breathed deeply. She opened them again and looked directly at her friend. "Despite my bravado on the subject, I want to get married and have a family, just like you."

Caroline laughed, withdrew her hands from Lily's, and clapped. "But that's wonderful! I can't encourage you enough."

"But Caroline, it's heresy! All of my mother's dreams for me! All my years of struggle to get into Bryn Mawr and graduate. Heresy of the worst sort! I'd be caving in to the preordained female fate. What was the point of pursuing my education?"

"Don't you remember me struggling with that very thing, Lily, when I decided to drop out and marry John? My father, the professor—his dreams for me—all down the drain. But the truth is, Lily, education is worthwhile in and of itself. We don't have to 'do anything' with it. We are more valuable to society for being educated, and it opens up an intellectual life that we could never have had otherwise—while we're nursing babies and wiping bottoms. There's nothing wasteful about that. Why, I read and enjoy the most amazing books that John brings home."

Lily looked doubtful, which only spurred Caroline on.

"As for our children, having an educated mother is surely advantageous. We can give them much better guidance for their own futures, and they'll find us more interesting in the bargain, as will our husbands. They may actually see us as people instead of parents and wives. Truly, Lily, you wouldn't be caving in at all. Most women want to get married and have children. It's perfectly normal, our sainted college president notwithstanding."

"Do you really think so?" asked Lily.

"Of course I do! Look at me!" Caroline rubbed her hands on her ballooning belly. "I can't wait to hold the little one in my arms, and then have more after that. Of course I don't want to have too many, but I'll face that dilemma if and when I need to. You see? I'm just as good at putting off big decisions as you are."

"Oh, Caroline, you are a gem. I'm going to think very hard about what you've said. But…"

"But what?"

She raised her hands in a gesture of hopelessness. "Who am I to marry?"

Caroline smothered a grin. "Ah, there is that. We'll have to see what we can do. Have you got anybody in mind?"

"No! That's the problem. I can't just up and tie the knot. I have to find someone to tie the knot *with*!"

Caroline chuckled as Lily fumed.

"It's not funny! My uncle invited the son of one of his friends to dinner last night. It was so humiliating! I can tell you one thing—I won't marry someone just for the sake of getting married. He will have to be someone I truly love. But when will I have the opportunity to meet any eligible men? So many in our circle are already taken."

"Not entirely. As soon as you graduate you'll have to get busy on the social circuit and see who's left. And who appeals."

Lily dropped her hands, intertwined her fingers, and raised her doubled fist to her chin. She looked out the window, to the street along which she and Caroline had taken so many memorable walks.

"Lily? What's wrong? Truly, we just have to get you into circulation."

She looked back at Caroline. "But what if they all think I'm too educated, like my uncle says? A man wants to feel that he is superior to his wife, even though we know that's nonsense."

"Well, we'll just have to find you a man who is even more intelligent and educated than you are; if not, one who finds your intelligence and education intriguing. That can't be too hard. You're a beautiful woman, Lily. With your stunning sense of fashion, heads turn when you walk into a room."

When Lily didn't respond, Caroline prodded further.

"Out with it. What else is troubling you?"

Lily looked up at the ceiling, then out the window again.

"I won't have any money, Caroline. I can maybe wheedle my uncle into sending me a small allowance, but most of what's left of our mother's trust will go to Bryn Mawr for Florence, not to mention the money already spent on her tutoring with Miss Hatton for the entrance exams. At least she didn't have to move in with Miss Hatton, so there's a saving there." She looked back at Caroline, searching for the strength to confront this situation head-on.

"There's no getting around it. I won't have the means to support myself while I search for a suitable husband. I won't even be able to afford an inexpensive boarding house. What a preposterous dilemma. I'm trapped! I may well *have* to go to work, but the minute I become a teacher or a governess I'll be socially doomed. I'll never attract the kind of man I want to marry."

She stood abruptly and began pacing the floor, making fists of her hands and pounding them against her thighs. She turned to face Caroline again.

"How in the world did I get to such an impasse? Bryn Mawr meant everything, *everything*, and now with my diploma assured, it's all turned to ashes." She sat down again with her elbows on her knees, her face in her hands, on the verge of weeping. "What am I going to do?"

Caroline sat up straight and tall. "Lily. Stop it. This is not like you. You are a strong woman. An educated woman, who is not allowed to weep over her fate. Stop it right now." Caroline withdrew a clean folded handkerchief from her skirt pocket. "Here, take this. Dry your eyes at once. Tears will get you nowhere. That's a weak woman's ploy and far beneath you. We'll make a plan. We'll make a plan for your future that will take care of everything."

Lily dabbed at her eyes and blew her nose into the handkerchief. "What kind of plan?"

Now it was Caroline's turn to rise. She took the two steps that separated them and sat on the hassock in front of Lily's chair.

"I know exactly what you'll do. You'll become a visiting girl!"

Lily blinked. "A what?"

"A visiting girl. It's perfect! We'll set you up with invitations to make the rounds of our married friends. You can begin by spending a couple of weeks with me. Then I'll send you on to, oh, let's say Rosalie for a week. And then perhaps to Charlotte, and so on. Between us we have lots of married friends who would be happy to have you. We just need to set it up so that the invitations keep coming until that certain gentleman makes his appearance. Everyone entertains, and eligible young men are always invited to round out the numbers. What do you say?"

Lily sighed and considered. "I suppose it could work. I could be helpful, couldn't I? Writing thank you notes, maybe. Reading to the children. Arranging flowers. Polishing the silver. Adding a single girl's sparkle to their entertainments. Dear God! After everything she sacrificed for my education, my mother would turn in her grave!"

Caroline raised an eyebrow. "There's always teaching. Or... governessing?"

"No! I won't do it. It's a trap. I must find a man who will allow me the freedom to be myself. Is that too much to ask? Mother always said that men have organized the world to suit themselves. We need to take their scheme and turn it on its head. If I can just find the right man, life will be good. But Caroline, is there any man like that out there? A man who will find me attractive and celebrate my intelligence, my learning, my independence?"

Caroline flounced back onto her chair. "We do have a big mountain to climb, but as we've decided it's your best hope, we'd better get on with it. If your uncle will send you that allowance, enough to keep you in dresses, hats, and shoes—oh, and train or tram tickets to get you to your visits—we'll have a chance. You must come here directly after graduation, and we'll organize it. Oh, Lily, you've given me such a wonderful project to work on. I've been so bored these last few weeks of my confinement!"

CHAPTER 6

Lily Giannotti reclined on plump eiderdown pillows in a darkened upstairs bedroom of her home in Portland, Oregon. Her graying hair fell in a single braid over one shoulder and down the front of her padded bed jacket. On a bedside table, along with a glass and a half-full carafe of water, lay a well-worn book of Emily Dickenson's poems and the letter from Philadelphia that had arrived two days earlier. In her hand she clasped the telegram that had followed this morning.

Caroline was coming! She had been delayed overnight in Chicago, according to the telegram, but she was coming! Even now, her dearest and oldest friend was hurtling through the Rocky Mountains, closer and closer, arriving in the morning. Tomorrow! How miraculous that her letter had found Caroline after all these years; even more so that Caroline, by her friendly tone in reply, apparently bore her no ill will.

She wanted to jump out of bed, throw open the curtains, and let the spring sunshine dart through the room. Who had decreed that sick people must be kept quiet and dull, cared for by folks who tiptoed about speaking in hushed voices, the curtains always shut, and only two small lamps to chasten the gloom? If she had the strength, she'd toss off her nightgown, don her gayest frock, and scurry about the house making sure everything was spiffed and polished to welcome Carrie.

As it was, she could only wait in bed, hoping she would sleep enough tonight to be cheerful and alert for her friend in the morning. And that the pain would stay at bay, at least for a while.

Throughout the years she had never thought of Caroline without sadness and guilt, but the more the years flew by, the less capable she had felt of explaining herself in a way that would put things right. She had kept putting it off until she was too embarrassed to follow through.

Toward the end of Lily's time in Philadelphia, Caroline must have known of Lily's increasingly untenable visiting situation—how could she not, when it had become more and more difficult for Caroline to line up the visits—but she could have no idea what had caused the final rupture. It remained a heavy burden on Lily's heart.

As the afternoon wore on with Caroline nearly on her doorstep, Lily's excitement fell more and more prey to doubts. Had she really done the right thing by writing to Caroline? It had not been a spur-of-the-moment act, but rather the result of much thought and consideration. Without realizing it, she began to tear little pieces from the corners of the telegram.

The behavior of their nineteen-year-old son Mark had become increasingly worrisome over the past several years. The cheerful, handsome boy, who adored his parents, excelled in school, had many friends, and showed every promise of being his father's enthusiastic right-hand man and heir to his flower business, was slowly slipping into the shadows beyond their reach. She and Marco had tried everything they could think of to bring him out of it, but the harder they tried, the more elusive and despondent he became. At first he came home to sleep most nights, usually well after she and Marco were in bed; put in minimal hours at the flower shop; but otherwise they saw little of him. When he joined them for an occasional meal, he appeared haggard and was unresponsive to their attempts to engage him in conversation. Lately he had taken to staying away for a week or more at a time. Frustrated beyond measure, Marco had given up trying to keep track of him. He was, after all, an adult.

At first Lily had assumed Mark was saddened over her illness. She had no idea how much his father had told him, but surely he could see she was very ill. Was he too upset to spend time with her, or did he simply not know what to say or how to behave in a sickroom? Either of those things would be understandable, but she sensed that darker demons pursued him. Then again, it was hard to imagine anything darker than his mother's impending demise. Could he just not face it, or was there something else?

The notion that Caroline might hold the key had dawned on her slowly. At first Lily refused to consider it. But it kept nudging her, even to the point of invading her dreams. It was a huge risk. If her notion misfired, not only would it devastate Mark, but it could destroy her family at a time when Mark, Marco, and their daughter Theresa would need each other the most. Caroline, too, would likely be a casualty.

Lily was no stranger to risk-taking. Her precipitous marriage to Marco had been a contradiction of everything society expected of her, and that she expected of herself. In one overnight decision, she had irrevocably changed the course of her life. If Marco had not been the man she had intuited him to be, who knew what disasters might have befallen her. She shuddered to think.

Leaning forward as much as she could, wincing at the pain in her joints, Lily struggled to adjust the pillows behind her. Gasping, she fell back, her eyes frantically searching out the clock on the mantle across the room. In the dim light, she could barely make out the hands, but she thought it said 4:25. Her caregiver, Leticia, would be coming in shortly with her medication, not a moment too soon. Where once the intervals the doctor insisted upon between doses were tolerable, now more and more she found herself moaning for surcease well before the designated time. Just yesterday she had entreated him to increase the amount or decrease the intervals, but he remained adamant that either of those strategies would increase the likelihood of addiction, something to be avoided at all costs, in his opinion. Addiction, indeed, she had scoffed. What did addiction matter at this point? He refused to budge, and Leticia followed his orders.

Settled back with an anxious eye on the door, Lily could dredge up no regrets. Her life with Marco had been richer than she could possibly have imagined—rich in the love of a good man, two beautiful children, and an opportunity to enhance the lives of countless women in the community. How much more satisfying this life had been, she thought, than that of a staid and proper Philadelphia matron for which she had, despite her mother's idealism, been groomed. She had faced many obstacles over the years, she reflected, some successfully and others not. Overall, there had been more successes than failures, and that had to count for something. Yes, she had taken a huge risk in coming out West with Marco, but her life was replete with blessings.

Now she had set in motion another set of potentially cataclysmic events based solely on a hunch. Granted she had given it a great deal of thought—what else was there to do in her debilitated state—and examined it from every possible angle, even sought out new-fangled psychological literature, sparse though it was, with Leticia's help. She wished she could have discussed it with her women friends, but even in the enlightened early 1920s there was still a stigma associated with emotional problems. At least she could spare Mark that.

She was gambling everything she held dear on this one last toss of the dice, acting in desperation and trusting her motherly intuition. Had she not known she was dying, she might have continued to watch things play out, hoping that Mark would somehow find a way to right himself. Every day that went by, however, the latter seemed less and less likely.

If she didn't act, she would take to her grave the one hope, contact with the one person who could fit all the pieces together, albeit unknowingly. No one else, not even Marco, could offer Mark a way back to his once-promising life.

Soft footsteps sounded from the hall, coming toward her door. At last, surcease from pain, and a few hours respite from her tortured thoughts.

CHAPTER 7

Caroline wasn't sure how she would get herself and her luggage to Lily's house, but surely there would be automobiles and drivers for hire at Portland's Union Station. With Lily's address tucked in her handbag and a rush of nervous excitement at finally having arrived, she took her time exiting the train. She let the other passengers sort out their belongings and disperse before she navigated through the cavernous waiting room toward the street. Before she could do more than glance around at the busy outdoor scene, a young man dressed in a green deliveryman's uniform stepped forward, holding a bouquet of peach-colored roses, their stems wrapped in muslin.

"Mrs. Crawford?" he asked, removing his cap with his other hand.

"Yes." She set down her valise and hamper, happy to be relieved of the weight.

"Welcome to Portland, the City of Roses, Ma'am. May I present these blossoms on behalf of Mr. and Mrs. Giannotti? They're the finest roses of the season, freshly picked this morning. The thorns have been clipped off for your comfort." He held out the bouquet with a flourish.

"Why, thank you. How thoughtful." She loved roses, John's most frequent anniversary gift.

"I'm Jimmy, deliveryman for Giannotti Florist West, at your service. Have you got more luggage?"

"Oh, yes. Just one trunk and a hatbox." She opened her handbag, found the claim stub, and handed it to him.

71

"If you'll step outside and wait for me, Ma'am, I'll be right with you."

During the short time he was gone, Caroline willed herself to relax. She took deep breaths of the crisp early summer Portland air and turned slowly around to view the scene. Union Station was impressive, faced with pebbly brown stucco with red brick accents and a red tile roof. Nothing like the grand old stations in Philadelphia, New York, and Chicago, of course, but this was the far west. The central clock tower, a work of art in itself, read just after ten o'clock.

Jimmy soon reappeared, pushing Caroline's trunk ahead of him on a dolly.

"Here we are. Right this way, Ma'am." He wheeled off toward a green and yellow Model T delivery van marked,

GIANNOTTI FLORIST WEST
Est. 1903
DELIVERING HAPPINESS EVERY DAY

"Hold on a moment, Mrs. Crawford. I'll load your things in back with the packed flowers. I've got deliveries to make this morning, but I've cleared a space." Caroline handed him her valise and waited while he stowed it with her trunk in the rear of the van.

As he stepped forward to give her a hand up into the cab, he paused, withdrew a clean white handkerchief from his pocket and wiped off a smudge of mud that had spattered the nearest fender. "Got to keep it shiny," he grinned. For good measure, he stooped to polish several spokes of the underlying wheel.

Caroline smiled. The optimistic slogan on the van and Jimmy's cheery demeanor spoke well for the way in which Marco Giannotti ran his business. She hoped it said as much for him as a husband to Lily.

The cab was roofed, but minus doors in typical Model T fashion. She trusted Jimmy was a cautious driver, and was grateful it wasn't raining. She'd been warned about Portland's wet climate. When they were both settled on the bench seat, the roses on her lap, Jimmy pulled out the choke and started the truck with its new-fangled electric starter.

"So how do you like our fair city so far, Mrs. Crawford?"

"Well, I haven't seen much of it, but everything seems green and bright." She peered around to take in the bustling cityscape. "What a lot of tall buildings you have! I hadn't expected Portland to be such a modern city."

"Oh, yes, we take great pride in being up-to-date. The city fathers have seen to that. You've arrived on a perfect June day. At this time of year the weather can be changeable—rainy one day, sunny the next, more clouds and drizzle after that. We'll have about another month of this, and then around the beginning of July the famous Willamette Valley rain dries up for a solid three months. You can almost set your clock by it. And I guarantee you've never seen anything as gorgeous as western Oregon in the summertime. I trust you'll stay long enough to enjoy it?" He glanced at her inquisitively.

"I hope so too, but we'll have to see how things go." She wished she could ask him about Lily, but this wasn't a subject she felt free to discuss with an employee, no matter how friendly. She'd find out soon enough.

Their drive took them through the commotion of downtown Portland, amid noisy streetcars, automobiles and horse-drawn wagons, all jockeying for the right-of-way. Businessmen, errand and delivery boys, shoppers, and denizens of the nearby Chinatown dodged around one another as they made their ways to their destinations. Within a few blocks, they left the business district, passed through a neighborhood of comfortable-looking wooden and brick homes, then began an uphill ascent. Fifteen minutes later they pulled up in front of an imposing two-storied white house on a large corner lot. A wide covered veranda wrapped around the two sides of the house facing the intersecting streets, projecting a gracious and welcoming aura.

Helping Caroline out of the van, Jimmy gestured to the walkway that led from the street to the house. "Right on up to the front door, if you will, Ma'am. They'll be expecting you. I'll take your luggage around the back."

"Thanks again, Jimmy. I appreciate your help." She handed him a coin, for which he raised his cap, and watched him drive to the far end of the lot and turn into the gravel driveway that led to the rear of the house. As she walked along the flagstone walkway, blue-bordered by low-growing delphiniums, the scent of the sun-warmed, freshly mowed lawn on either side rose up to caress her senses. Halfway to the house, a flower garden extended from either side of the walkway. Multi-colored pansies up front; then daisies of every possible color: white, yellow, gold, orange, red, pink, purple— casually planted with heedless abandon. Here and there a blossom swayed with the visit of a bee. Beyond this riot of summer colors, against the house, stood a row of rose bushes, their candelabra branches laden with red blossoms.

At the bottom of the steps, she stopped to inhale the fragrant perfume of a pair of lavender lilac bushes in full bloom, one on either side of the railing post. I love Oregon already, she silently applauded.

She mounted the stairs, crossed the veranda, and rang the doorbell. It took only a few seconds for approaching footsteps to sound from within. Caroline could barely stand still. She'd been on an emotional roller coaster since receiving Lily's letter, and now she'd finally arrived.

The door was opened by a slender woman in her mid-thirties, attired conservatively in a navy-blue dress with white lace-trimmed collar and cuffs. With a warm smile, the woman extended her hand.

"Mrs. Crawford? Do come in. I'm Leticia Grant, the Giannotti's housekeeper and helper. Mrs. Giannotti has been greatly looking forward to your visit."

"Thank you. So nice to meet you, Miss Grant. I'm very glad to be here."

Caroline stepped in, allowing Leticia to close the door behind her, and surrendered to the homey scent of lemon oil and beeswax furniture polish. The walls were a soft ivory, the floors dark-stained oak scattered with light from stained glass panels on either side of the door. To the right, French doors opened into a comfortable-looking parlor. Immediately across the foyer a staircase with artfully carved newel posts ascended to the second floor. Beside the right hand post stood a round table topped with a magnificent arrangement of pink and white gladiolas, white aster daisies, and yellow dahlias.

Nodding at them, Leticia smiled. "A benefit of my employer being in the flower business. You'll find them throughout the house, fresh almost daily. I see that Jimmy greeted you with roses at the station. If you give them to me, I'll put them in a vase for you." Caroline handed them over and expressed her gratitude.

"Come, it must have been a tiring journey. You'll want to wash up, I'm sure, and perhaps rest a bit. Let me show you to your room. And please, call me Leticia, or Lettie, as the family does." She turned toward the staircase to lead the way.

"And Lily?" Caroline asked as she hastened to follow her, unable to contain herself. "How is she?"

Leticia paused with a hand on the banister and turned back to Caroline. "Mrs. Giannotti was so excited to see you that she didn't sleep much last night. She wanted to greet you the moment you arrived, but I'm afraid she couldn't hold off her mid-morning medication. She'll sleep for the next several hours. Mr. Giannotti will be home for lunch, however, and I'm sure he'll bring you up to date." Her smile this time was tinged with sadness. Caroline sensed that she cared deeply for her employer.

"Lily won't be joining us?" Caroline asked. After all these years, she wanted to rush upstairs and throw her arms around her friend.

Leticia continued up the stairs. "No, I'm afraid not. She takes her meals in her room these days. You'll be able to see her as soon as she's awake, I promise. She'd never forgive me otherwise. Lunch will be served at noon, Mrs. Crawford. When you come down, you'll find the dining room to the left of the stairway." She gestured downward in that direction.

When they reached the second-floor landing, Leticia headed left down the hallway and opened the first door on the right. She stood aside for Caroline to enter. The soft scent of lavender, the stems artfully arranged with narrow-leafed greens in a cut crystal vase on the dresser top, infused the air. She inhaled deeply.

"I see what you mean about living with a florist," Caroline said. "How delightful."

"I never get tired of it," Leticia said. "Now, the bathroom is across the hall. I've put out fresh towels for you. My room is at the end, if you need me for anything. May I assist with your unpacking?"

"Oh, no thanks. I'll be fine," Caroline answered.

"Good, then I'll see you downstairs in a little while. And again, welcome to Portland." With a smile, Leticia stepped out and closed the door behind her.

Too excited to settle down, Caroline opened her trunk and unpacked. With her dresses, skirts and shirtwaists shaken out and hung in the wardrobe, shoes lined up beneath them, and her under-things and nightgowns arranged in the dresser, Caroline paced back and forth across the red and blue Persian carpet, stopping each time she reached the window. What a splendid view of the homes across the street, she thought, each one elegant in its own way, and all framed by the tall pine trees for which the Pacific Northwest was famous.

Wondering what to do with herself until lunch and feeling a bit let down at not being able to see Lily right away, Caroline undressed, slipped on a dressing gown, and sponged off in the bathroom across the hall. Even though she had slept well on the train, at least after the disastrous first night with Donalee, she realized the journey had taken a stripe out of her. The full-sized bed, framed in dark oak with an elaborately carved headboard, looked deliciously inviting.

She picked up a knitted afghan from the back of an easy chair near the window, stretched out on the bed, and settled in. Eyes closed, she relived the rush of the train hurtling through the Rockies. What vistas! Peak after snow-capped peak; death-defying drops from the edge of the train tracks down hundreds of feet to gravel streambeds below; valleys of impossibly stark beauty. And above the dense stands of evergreens, a zone barren of any vegetation at all, only endless swaths of windswept snow and granite. Once again she marveled at the early pioneers crossing those imposing barriers in their covered wagons. Why, according to a map shown to her by one of her dining companions, almost the entire western third of the country was mountains.

And then—the final rush down the Columbia Gorge! Following the paddle strokes of those intrepid explorers, Meriwether Lewis and William Clark. What American schoolchild did not thrill to their adventures in exploring the northwest reaches through and beyond the Louisiana Purchase? They and their companions must have been staggered by this final panorama after all those tedious months of breaking trail and pulling their canoes upstream. The ride through the Gorge had been the highlight of her trip, and, praise God, helped distract her from Donalee's dreadful fate.

But soon to see Lily! She must be very ill indeed to be taking her meals in her room, and to need medicine so powerful that she was unable to greet her long-awaited guest.

Caroline started at a knock on her door.

"Come in," she called, disoriented for a moment before realizing she'd dozed off.

Leticia opened the door, carrying the peach roses in a porcelain vase. "Mr. Giannotti is home and hopes you'll join him for lunch, Mrs. Crawford." She put the vase on the night table beside the bed.

Caroline threw off the afghan, tightened her dressing gown, slid her legs over the side of the bed, and sat up with her hands to her head. "Oh, my heavens, of course. Please give him my apologies. I'll be there in a jiffy."

She dressed quickly, did the best she could with her hair, and hurried downstairs.

CHAPTER 8

Marco Giannotti stood at the round table at the foot of the stairs, sorting through the morning post. He looked up when he heard Caroline's descending footsteps.

"Ah, Mrs. Crawford! How delightful to see you. I'm Lily's husband, Marco. We met many years ago at my parents' flower shop in Philadelphia, but I'm sure you don't remember. How generous of you to come! Lily has been so heartened to know you were on your way. It's done her a world of good."

Beaming with goodwill and gratitude, he held out both hands to her, leaned in, and kissed her on alternating cheeks, European style. She'd never been greeted so dramatically and found herself a bit flustered. He was certainly handsome, in an exotic, foreign sort of way: of medium height, obviously well-muscled beneath his jacket; tanned, with black curly hair shot with silver at the temples, and liquid dark eyes that lingered as he spoke. She indeed remembered him. He had matured magnificently.

He offered Caroline his arm and guided her into the dining room. The table was set for two, with one place at the head and another to its immediate right. A low centerpiece of pink, yellow, and white pompom dahlias set off the Irish linen, English china, and sparkling silverware to perfection.

He held out her chair. "Do sit down, Mrs. Crawford," he said. His English was perfect, with just a hint of an Italian childhood. It only added to his charm.

"Please call me Caroline, or Carrie if you like. As you said, we're not exactly strangers."

"But you never imagined your best friend Lily would marry someone like me." He said it with a disarming grin as he seated himself at the head of the table. "That's how it is in America, isn't it, Caroline? We don't have to stay in our assigned places in society. With ambition, hard work, and luck—never forget luck—a fellow can leave the old life behind and make an entirely new life for himself. Of course it helps to have a wife who is truly a helpmate. I bless Lily every day for that." His voice caught on that last declaration. He cleared his throat but appeared not to be embarrassed by his show of emotion. A man who is truly at home with himself, Caroline thought. She wasn't sure how to respond, but before she could ask about Lily, he adroitly changed the subject.

"We eat somewhat informally, Caroline. I've asked our cook, Mrs. Delfini, to prepare a clam chowder with her homemade Italian bread, both the best you'll find in Portland, followed by ravioli and fresh vegetables. I don't know how familiar you are with Italian cuisine, but when you hire an Italian cook that's mostly what you get. Lily has taught her to make some of her own favorites, Irish stew for example and pot roast, but more often than not it's Mrs. Delfini's old-country favorites, very like my mother's. I hope you won't mind."

"Oh, of course not. I can't say I'm familiar with Italian food, but I look forward to expanding my palate. And hopefully not my waistline."

At that moment a stocky, dark-haired woman, probably in her early thirties, entered the room through a swinging door, carrying a tray holding two steaming bowls and a basket of thickly sliced bread. She wore a white blouse, black skirt, and white apron in what might have been a nod to a uniform. Her dark hair was styled in a modishly short bob; her smile was friendly.

"Ah, here she is with our chowder. Mrs. Delfini, let me introduce our guest, Mrs. Crawford. Caroline, the one secret you must jealously guard in this house is the extent and expertise of Mrs. Delfini's talents in the kitchen. When we have dinner guests, they get a glimpse of it, but we never allow anyone the full picture."

"Oh, Signore, stop it. After being part of this household for so many years now, no one could lure me away. Impossible!" She shook her head in amusement and returned with the empty tray to the kitchen.

Marco passed Caroline the napkin-lined breadbasket. "She's a gem. One of Lily's Back Door Women."

"Back Door Women?" Caroline asked.

"I'll let Lily explain," he said with a wink. "She'll want to tell you all about it."

Curbing her curiosity, Caroline picked up her soup spoon and tasted her chowder. "My, this is excellent! I've never had anything quite like it."

"In Portland we have the finest seafood the Pacific Ocean has to offer. Mrs. Delfini goes to the fish market several times a week and returns with the day's freshest catch. Salmon is a great favorite, as are clams of all sorts."

"Clam chowder is a great favorite on the East Coast, but this is different. What is it that perks up the tomato base?"

"Mrs. Delfini has her own special ways with Italian herbs. She grows them in the back yard."

"And the salmon, shall I look forward to an Italian twist there too?"

Marco nodded enthusiastically.

Caroline put down her spoon. She could keep up the patter no longer.

"And what about Lily, Marco? How is she really? Please tell me. I don't want to wear her out with questions on my first day here."

Eyes downcast, he wiped his lips slowly with his napkin, as if considering how to begin. "Yes, you'd best hear it from me. Lily will make light of it, but her condition is serious. You'll know as soon as you see her." He put down the napkin and looked directly at her. His dark eyes reflected his pain. "Leukemia. Do you know what that is?"

"Leukemia!" Caroline's hand flew to her mouth before she could stop it. She took a moment to collect herself. "I've heard the term…" Yes, she'd heard the term, always linked with such words as "incurable" and "death sentence."

Marco understood her silence. "According to her doctor, it's a cancer of the blood cells. The bone marrow, which produces our blood cells, kind of goes berserk and starts producing an oversupply of white blood cells, the cells that fight disease. Only these white cells are abnormal. He tells me they crowd out the normal white cells and keep them from doing their job. As you might imagine, this causes all kinds of havoc."

"Like what?" Caroline whispered. This sounded worse than anything she could have imagined.

"For one thing, anemia, which means your red blood cells are unable to carry enough oxygen throughout your body, and you get extremely tired. It can also cause bleeding and allow infections to flourish. Swelling of internal organs and pain in the bones and joints are also common. Eventually the pain becomes unbearable and soon everything shuts down. At least that's my sketchy, layman's understanding of the disease."

Caroline grimaced. "Is Lily in a great deal of pain?"

"Yes, although it comes and goes. She takes laudanum for it, an old-fashioned remedy, but effective in her case. It helps more than anything else the doctor has tried. He rails about addiction, but I believe he fears more the increasingly dangerous amount she'll need for it to do the job. An overdose would be fatal. For now, it still gives her a few good hours several times a day and helps her to sleep at night. You'll want to pace your visits accordingly."

"Of course. And…I'm afraid to ask… is there no cure?"

He hesitated. One side of his lower lip trembled. Swallowing, he recovered. "None. Dr. Jaworski has been in correspondence with several physicians back East who have been experimenting with the new radiation therapy. Apparently, if given in the correct dosage, radiation can sometimes shrink a cancer. But the latest development is that the radiation itself is causing tumors in the physicians who are experimenting with it. They try it on themselves to work out the dosage, you see, and suddenly they are their own cancer patients."

"That's horrible!"

"Yes, and it has set the search for a cure back on its heels. No doubt they will someday come up with a better strategy, but it will be too late for Lily."

She placed a hand on her heart. "I am so sorry, Marco. She said she was dying in her letter, but of course I didn't want to believe it. I had hoped that it was just her dramatic way of getting me here."

He shook his head. "Not so, I'm afraid. The doctor is at an impasse. He said just last week that we can only try to keep her as comfortable as possible until…"

"I see," Caroline murmured.

Mrs. Delfini entered from the kitchen again, this time to remove their soup bowls and serve the ravioli and broccoli. Despite being upset at hearing about Lily's condition, or perhaps welcoming a distraction, Caroline closed her eyes and inhaled deeply of garlic and parmesan cheese.

"Oh, my, that does smell delicious. I'm beginning to understand why the Giannottis value you so highly, Mrs. Delfini."

"Thank you, Signora," she replied with a modest nod, offering Caroline the platter.

The ravioli, freshly made that morning and stuffed with minced chicken, mushrooms, cheese, and herbs—lightly seasoned in a creamy tomato sauce—were every bit as tasty as their aromatic promise. Broccoli, unadorned except for a glistening coat of butter, was the perfect complement. While they ate, Marco entertained her with a brief outline of the history of Portland, saving the family details for Lily to share.

"Did you know, according to legend, that Portland got its name by way of a coin toss? Two founders, one from Boston, Massachusetts, the other from Portland, Maine, each wanted to name it after his hometown. They allegedly tossed a coin and Portland won. Of course it's been called a few more descriptive names as well, such as Stumptown, for the many tree stumps left in the streets, and Mudtown—you can guess where that comes from. By 1850 Portland was the largest settlement in the Pacific Northwest. Fortunately things were even more civilized when Lily and I arrived fifty-three years later."

"I'm sure there's a great deal for me to learn while I'm here," said Caroline. "I look forward to all of it."

As they were finishing their tea with butter-rich cookies redolent of cinnamon and orange zest, another Delfini family specialty, Leticia appeared in the dining room entryway.

"Lily is awake, Marco, and most anxious to see Mrs. Crawford."

Marco stood up. "Thank you, Lettie. I'll come up for a minute too before I leave for the shop. Come, Caroline. Let's give Lily something to smile about."

CHAPTER 9

Caroline followed Marco up the stairs. Her heart beat wildly in anticipation, partly from excitement and partly from dread. What would she be facing now that she was here, and how would she react to seeing her friend in such peril? Lily had been a stately young woman, beautiful in an unconventional way—a woman who attracted attention when she walked down the street or entered a room. Her independent air shone forth, an independence that was hard-won yet disarmingly fragile to those who knew her best. How had she matured over the past two decades, and what had this awful disease done to her?

Marco knocked lightly on a partially open door and pushed in without waiting for a response. Caroline followed him, then paused with a hand behind her on the doorknob. Her other hand flew involuntarily to her nose, a reaction to the sour odor of illness, faint but unmistakable. Immediately aware, she lowered her hand before either Marco or Lily noticed.

Despite the ivory-painted walls, the room was gloomy for such a sunny afternoon. Heavy olive green drapes shut out most of the light. The glow of a pair of heavily shaded table lamps on either side of the bed only emphasized the gloom. She could make out nothing more than a shadowy form reclining on the bed, resting against the pillows.

"Hello, *cara mia*," Marco said cheerily as he bent down to kiss his wife on the forehead. "I trust you've rested? Here's Caroline, fresh off the train and completely done in with impatience waiting for you to wake up!"

He gave a teasing tweak to the bow at the neck of her bed jacket and stepped aside, while tucking open a corner of the drape nearest Lily and motioning Caroline to step forward.

Dear Lily, straining from the pillows and smiling with her thin arms outstretched in welcome. The young woman of Caroline's recollections had aged dramatically, yet she was still beautiful. Her prominent cheekbones above sunken cheeks gave her an air of fragile nobility. Strands of white interwoven with Lily's brown hair became apparent as Caroline drew closer, yet they added an ethereal glow to her presence. It was Lily's eyes, however, that arrested her: although smudged with shadow, they were still the merry hazel eyes of Lily's youth, brimming with curiosity and mischief.

"Carrie! How wonderful! You're finally here. Do come closer, I can barely see you in the shadows." Her voice was surprisingly robust; her delight genuine. "Marco, please pull open the drapes all the way and let the sunshine in. I don't know why everyone insists that darkness is beneficial to invalids."

Caroline rushed forward and bent down into her friend's embrace as the room filled with light.

"Oh, how happy I was to receive your letter and invitation, and finally to be here! You are still my Lily, as lovely as ever."

Lily slid her hands, as light as sparrows, down Caroline's arms, pausing at her wrists. "Stop! I'm a sick woman, old before my time. But never mind. What's done is done, and it isn't going to keep us from having a grand catching-up for as long as you can stay. Marco, do bring that chair over for Carrie, please, and we'll bid you *arrivederci, caro mio*. Surely you have business to take care of?" They exchanged a look of utter devotion, without a care for anyone else seeing it.

Marco sighed. "I do indeed. I was just about to excuse myself and let you two get on with it." From beside the fireplace, he pushed over a comfortable looking easy chair into which Caroline sank without further ceremony. As Marco turned to leave, the fond, lingering look between him and Lily spoke volumes.

Once he was out the door, Lily beamed her full attention on Caroline. Life sparkled in her eyes, despite the shadows beneath them. "Now quickly, before we say anything else, I need to know you forgive me for departing all those years ago, leaving only a vague note and Sabrina's cancellation letter in my visiting diary. I understand you even paid the debts I had accumulated as a visiting girl. When I eventually wrote to the merchants requesting a final accounting with interest, they all replied that the bills had been taken care of by Mrs. John Crawford. I was mortified!"

"There's nothing to forgive. While the bills may have seemed overwhelming to you at the time, they amounted to very little in the overall scheme of things. Don't say another word about it."

Lily sank back into her pillows, eyes closed. "Thank you. I've longed to hear you say it. I've fretted about it throughout the years, yet as time went by, I became less and less certain of what I could say to justify myself. Eventually so much time had passed that I was sure I had lost your good opinion of me and there was no point in trying to redeem it."

Caroline shook her head impatiently. "Nothing of the sort. The subject is closed. Now tell me, how are you really? Do you have much pain? Are you entirely bedridden? Do you have an appetite? I must say, your Mrs. Delfini is a treasure. If she can't tempt you, nobody can."

Lily might have been taken aback by Caroline's rapid-fire directness so early in their visit, but she herself had been famous— infamous, really—for this same quality. It was as if she'd had neither the time nor the energy to dissemble. Not everyone found it becoming, but Caroline had always appreciated Lily's forthrightness. Over the years she had adopted the habit herself. Unlike many of her friends, Caroline found it useful to know exactly where things stood.

Lily clasped her hands together over the bedcovers, then looked at Caroline seriously. "Did Marco tell you what this is all about? Leukemia?"

"Yes, he explained the disease, rather graphically in fact, so I think I understand. I'm so sorry. But what does it mean on a day-to-day basis?"

"Well, first of all, let me tell you how I've had to fight to get them to tell *me* anything. You know how it is. There's always this big conspiracy of silence about illness—everyone trying to keep the truth from the patient when the outlook isn't good, fearful the patient will become upset and jeopardize her recovery. Have you ever understood the logic of that? If anyone has a right to know what's happening, it's me! I put up such a fuss, with both Marco and Dr. Jaworski, that they finally gave in and leveled with me. How ridiculous, don't you think, to keep the patient in the dark? One has to marshal one's resources, after all, to know the enemy and fight the good fight. Or if it's hopeless, to get one's life in order!"

"As you said, I'm sure they were trying to keep you from worrying." A weak reply, but it was all Caroline could think of.

Lily scoffed. "You think I didn't worry, feeling this ill with no idea why? Naturally I assumed the worst. My imagination went wild, so what were they trying to protect me from? Anyway, we got to the bottom of it. I know I'm dying, I *feel* like I'm dying, and I'm reconciled to it, most of the time anyway. But it means that I want to live every day that I have left as fully as I can. And you will help me just by being here. Oh, Caroline, I'm so thrilled to see you! Marco is so busy-busy at work, and honestly, men are not at their best in the sickroom. He frets so much about me—it renders him absolutely useless. I can make the best of every day I have left, or I can lie here in a great stew of self-pity with everyone hovering around me and wringing their hands. What earthly good would that do?"

Caroline leaned over and pushed a few strands of Lily's graying hair away from her forehead. "Bravo! I agree entirely. I'll do everything I can to lighten your days. Are you able to move about?"

"Not easily. Lettie helps me to the bathroom, and that's about it. But I'm going to ask Marco to carry me downstairs to the sunroom tomorrow. It's a lovely place now that the weather is warming up. Have you been through the house?"

Caroline shook her head. "Not yet."

"Lettie will give you the grand tour. The sunroom is bright and cheerful, especially in the morning, with a gorgeous view down to the river. The Willamette River, that is, which flows from the south and connects with the Columbia before it flows out to sea. Yes, we'll enjoy the sunroom tomorrow. I feel entirely re-energized now that you're here."

Caroline silently repeated her vow to do her best to keep Lily's spirits up. She glanced at the water carafe on the bedside table. "Who takes care of you, sees to your personal needs?"

"Lettie, bless her. In addition to being our housekeeper, she's become my personal assistant and attendant. I don't know what I'd do without her. We have a housemaid who comes in on weekdays, so Lettie just has to supervise her. Lettie's room is just down the hall, so she's nearby when I need her. She's a real blessing and a good friend. She's probably within earshot right now but giving us some privacy."

"I hope she won't resent my being here?" Caroline asked, suddenly wondering if the housekeeper might think she was trespassing on her territory.

"No, of course not. She knows how much I treasure her. Hopefully you two will become friends as well."

Caroline leaned back in her chair and relaxed. "I'm sure we shall. Now tell me about your family, Lily. Start from the beginning. Do you and Marco have children?"

A shadow crossed Lily's face, so quickly that Caroline almost missed it. "We do. Our son Mark is nineteen, still living at home—technically, anyway—and helping his father in the business. Well, at least that's been the plan. We don't see much of him these days. He's moved downstairs into the cook's room behind the kitchen. It used to be Mrs. Delfini's until she moved back home to be with her aging mother. It has its own entrance, so he comes and goes as he pleases. When he's home, he mostly eats in the kitchen, rarely joins his father in the dining room. He's a rather unhappy fellow these days. I'm...I'm worried about him."

Caroline raised an eyebrow, inviting more details, but Lily hurried on.

"Our daughter, Theresa, is not quite eighteen. She married a much older man, a widower with three young children. She's expecting her own child in about a month. We weren't too pleased about her marriage, as you can imagine, but from all reports he is good to her and the children seem to have accepted her. I beseeched her to hold off on having any children of her own, but she wouldn't hear of it. There are things she could do, of course, but she insists on following the church's teachings against family limitation. I'm not a Catholic, as you know, but it was important to Marco that the children be raised in the church. So they were. Sometimes I think it was a mistake, naming her after the Little Flower, Saint Thérèse of Lisieux."

"I'm sure that Marco, being a florist, thought the name was perfect," Caroline ventured with smile.

"Exactly. From the time she was a child, Theresa has taken her religion so seriously. At one point we thought she might become a nun. I just want her to be happy. We don't see much of her and her family these days. They live on a farm near Roseburg, in southern Oregon, a bit of a journey from here. With her confinement so near and me bedridden, I fear I may never…" Lily couldn't finish the thought. She raised tear-glittering eyes to her friend. "Do we ever stop worrying about our children, my friend?"

Caroline sighed. "It isn't allowed, I'm afraid."

Lily dashed away the tears. "And what about you? Robert the Adorable was just a toddler when I left."

Caroline's face lit up at the mention of her son. "He lives in Tennessee. I don't see him often, either, but he's doing very well. He manages his soon-to-be in-laws' horse training farm. Thoroughbreds. Last year one of his colts ran in the Kentucky Derby."

"My, that must have been exciting!"

"Yes, I wish I could have been there, but my daughter Nancy's wedding was planned for the same week. We never thought to check the calendar with him. Nancy and her husband live right down the street from me. She was born a year after you left."

Lily cocked her head sideways. "Wait. As I recall, your doctor forbade you to have another child after that miscarriage while I was still there. You told me his warning was dire—internal damage, scar tissue, that sort of thing. Don't tell me you and John disregarded…well, I guess you did."

Shamefacedly, Caroline lowered her eyes. "We had every good intention, I assure you. Yet I was so distressed over not being able to have another child. After a few months, I felt perfectly fine; everything seemed back to normal. It was hard to believe in the doctor's cautions. So when John got a little too friendly one night…"

"Well, you obviously lived to tell the tale," Lily teased. "Was the doctor wrong?"

"Oh, no, it was awful. She came five weeks early, weighed not quite four pounds. I hemorrhaged badly afterward. Fortunately, despite her size, Nancy took to nursing right away. The doctor said that was likely what saved my life, caused the after-birth contractions that slowed and eventually stopped the hemorrhaging. Meanwhile we were frantic about Nancy. We had no idea if she would survive. When I asked the doctor how to care for her, he just kind of shrugged his shoulders. To my horror, I discovered the medical establishment didn't know much about caring for premature infants. Apparently they were often just left to die—or not, if they were lucky—the thinking being that, even if they managed to survive, they'd grow up to be inferior human beings, burdens on society."

"Surely not!"

Caroline nodded. "What could I do but follow my motherly instincts? I held her, nursed her, rocked her day and night, made sure she felt warm and secure. I sang songs to her, told her over and over how much her father and I loved her. I thought if maybe she'd heard my voice in my womb, she'd find it soothing afterward. Who knows? It was a special time. Even young Robert got into the act. He often snuggled in with us to keep watch over his sister. She thrived, I'm happy to say, maybe because of all that special care. And in no way did she grow up to be an inferior human being! We've always been close in a way that might not have happened if her birth had been as routine as Robert's."

"Thank God, for both of you."

"Indeed. Nancy's been my anchor since John passed away three years ago. Heart attack. Very sudden."

Lily's hand flew to her cheek. "John, gone? Oh, I'm so sorry. I should have asked about him first!"

"We almost lost him two years earlier to the Spanish flu." Caroline's voice became grim. "My fault actually, a guilt I'll never get over."

"You, guilty? Why?" Lily drew herself higher on her pillows.

"You must have read about the Liberty Loan Drive parades in Philadelphia."

"Oh, no, don't tell me…"

"Yes, my women's group was among the organizers. This was the fourth Liberty Loan parade in the city, all of them hugely successful in selling bonds to finance the Great War. Soldiers, military bands, Boy Scouts, women's auxiliaries, floats showing off the floating biplanes made in our own Navy Yard. Afterward we had a concert, led by John Philip Souza, the March King. What we didn't know in that September of 1918 was that the Spanish flu was already among us."

Lily narrowed her eyes. "I read there were several hundred thousand spectators jammed along Broad Street, cheering for the American forces and the bond drive. The *Portland Oregonian* published the story with a photo of the crowd, but I found it hard to believe."

Caroline nodded. "All true. Add in the war bond salesmen working the spectators, along with two miles of marchers. It felt like the whole city was there. It was glorious. Spectacular! And deadly. I fell ill several days after the parade, along with thousands of other unsuspecting Philadelphians. I sent Nancy and Robert to my parents and banished John to his club. Dear Betsy—you remember our kitchen helper—she took care of me until she came down with it too. Sadly, to my eternal regret, I sent Betsy home to her family. Both she and her parents succumbed to the disease."

"Oh, that's terrible. And John?"

Caroline shook her head. "As it turned out, his club wasn't safe. Others had taken refuge there, too, and the flu spread quickly among them. The club closed down, and he came home, sick as sick can be. I did my best for him in my own weakened condition. Somehow, by the grace of God, we both survived, but his recovery took much longer than mine. I've often wondered if some lingering effect weakened his heart and caused his eventual death."

"I'm very sorry, Caroline. I was so fond of John. He always greeted me with such warmth and then discretely closeted himself in the study with his bottomless pile of manuscripts. Didn't we have such freedom in those days? No parents, no house mother, no Uncle Arnold always telling me how to behave, or rather how *not* to behave!"

"How well I remember," Caroline chuckled, happy to leave her sad memories behind.

"And then I became a visiting girl. What a crazy idea that was!"

"Why, I was rather impressed with myself for thinking of it!" Caroline sat taller in her chair and crossed her arms, with a smug smile at her own cleverness.

"I give you full credit, and for keeping it organized among our willing friends. You saved me from who knows what wretched fate. But I couldn't keep it up forever. No matter how much I looked around for a suitable young man—I was never any good at flirting, you may recall—they always seemed to prefer someone else. I had wonderful conversations with the fellows in our set, married and unmarried. Once they got used to me, they seemed to appreciate that I was up on the issues of the day and enjoyed an educated woman's point of view. One only had to read the newspapers, after all!"

"You were always an asset at the dinner table, and in many other ways."

"Or so we believed. But even though the fellows seemed to relish a spirited debate, when it came to settling down..."

"…they wanted a girl who would do as she was told and hand them their pipe and slippers as they walked in the door after work. I can't imagine you fitting into that domestic myth!"

Lily raised herself on her elbows with as much dignity as she could muster. "As it happens, I've been a good wife. Ask Marco. He'll agree wholeheartedly. But you're right—I never was the pipe and slippers type. More the, 'Let's get to the shop and rustle up some business' type. Fortunately, Marco was raised by a working mother and thought it perfectly normal.

"We've had a good life here, Carrie. Marco has been wonderful to me, and I've tried my best to return the favor. I love him madly, to this very day, and we both love Oregon. The beauty, the people, even the rain. The opportunities here have been more than we could ever have hoped for."

Caroline took a deep breath. She'd come all this way and couldn't wait any longer. "But whatever possessed you to take off so suddenly with no warning, without so much as a hint to me? When we discovered you'd left, I was frantic. I looked everywhere for you. I wrote to everyone in your visiting diary, but they were all as puzzled as I was. I inquired of all the neighbors and neighborhood shopkeepers, but no one knew a thing. You covered your tracks well, my friend. *Why?*"

Lily hesitated. "Maria, at Pretty Cat Books. Did you inquire of her?"

"Of course, she was the first one I visited. She seemed bewildered, too, said she knew nothing, just like the others." Suddenly Caroline clapped her hands in delight. "But here's some news. Remember Harry MacTavish, the Scots tobacconist around the block from Pretty Cat? You told me once that Maria loaned him books, and in return he always had an amusing tale to tell her of his life before emigrating to America. It seems their friendship blossomed. They married a couple of years after you left, and he moved into her upstairs flat. The best part is that they surprised everyone, including themselves, by producing a little girl, Marigold Maria MacTavish. She looks just like Maria but with her father's strawberry blonde hair. How do you like that?"

"What wonderful news! I couldn't be happier for them. But wait, Marigold can't be a child anymore. She's, what, seventeen or eighteen by now?"

"Yes, and you'll never guess. She's enrolling next year at Bryn Mawr and plans to go to medical school at Johns Hopkins."

Lily looked positively thrilled. "How perfect! Do I detect the guiding hand of Caroline Crawford in this turn of events?"

Caroline beamed at her friend. "Yes indeed. She and my Nancy were pals, and she spent a lot of time at our house while they were growing up. I had hoped Nancy would attend Bryn Mawr, but she had a beau and was determined to get married. There was no talking her out of it. So when I sensed a spark of interest in Marigold, the poor child didn't have a chance."

"Wonderful news indeed, the very best!" Lily paused for a moment then frowned, as if she had just remembered something. "Dare I ask about the Giannottis? Did you inquire there? Marco did send them a wire from Chicago, telling them where he was headed and that they had a new daughter-in-law."

"Yes, I asked everywhere! But Mrs. Giannotti, she wouldn't talk to me. She just scowled and turned back to arranging her flowers. I was quite put out, but I never really thought she might have known anything."

"Marco and I regret the sorrow we caused them. He wrote to them after Mark's and Theresa's births, but as far as I know he never heard back. He has been in touch with his brother, but only once or twice a year. I'm sorry to have put you to so much trouble and worry, Caroline. I truly couldn't see beyond my immediate predicament. I could blame it on my youth, my callow self-centeredness, desperate emotions clouding my judgment, but those are poor excuses and none of them good excuses for leaving you as I did."

"Enough of that. I'm here. All is forgiven, but I yearn for the full story. Please."

Lily closed her eyes. "It won't be easy, Caroline. It's much more complicated than you can possibly imagine. I desperately hope that I'll still hold your affection once I've told it. But not today. Let me simply enjoy your company this afternoon. I'm still pinching myself that you are here." She gazed contentedly at her friend, fighting eyelids that wanted to close.

Caroline reigned in her curiosity. She could see that Lily's attention was waning. They would have time to delve into weighty matters in the days ahead.

"I'm afraid I've tired you out. Why don't you get some rest, my dear, and we can visit again later."

Lily nodded almost imperceptibly. "Yes, I think you'd better get Lettie, if you wouldn't mind. Just knock on her door and ask her to come. Thank you so much for being here, Carrie. We'll get all caught up, I promise." Her voice had become no more than a whisper.

God bless Maria, Lily thought as she waited for Lettie. She had kept her promise to remain silent about Lily's reason for leaving Philadelphia all those years ago. Maria had been her only confidant during those troublesome times, a friend at a safe remove from Caroline's family and Lily's visiting circle. Maria knew *why* she'd left, but even she did not know with whom or where they went.

In the glowing aftermath of seeing her beloved friend, and the twilight of suffusing laudanum, Lily's thoughts turned to the one other person who would have made the reunion complete: her beloved sister Florence. How she wished Florence were with them now to perfect the circle of her life. She'd never stopped missing her.

CHAPTER 10

Graduation day, June 1901, finally arrived. Lily had passed her exams near the top of her class. Nothing remained but the ceremony, her final packing, and the short journey to Caroline's to take up her life as a visiting girl. She was not the least bit surprised that Uncle Arnold and Aunt Sophie had declined her invitation to attend, although Aunt Sophie sent a note of congratulations and a most welcome five dollar bill. In truth, Lily was pleased that her uncle was not there to cast a shadow on her achievement, but she wished Aunt Sophie could have shared her triumph. She was a good soul, but so hampered in her marriage to Uncle.

Florence wouldn't have missed her sister's big day for anything. Lily settled her in her own room, her underclassman roommate having already gone home. With any luck, Florence would be in this same dormitory come fall. Caroline had planned to be at graduation, too, but young Robert had come down with chicken pox and needed her at home.

The ceremony went off without a hitch, very solemn throughout until the graduates burst out of the auditorium and raced around the lawn hugging one another with unbounded glee. Lily twirled her sister around in the midst of the mayhem.

"Oh, Florence! Your life here will soon begin. College is a lot of hard work, to be sure, but the four years will zip by, I promise you. By then I'll be established, and you'll always have a home with me. Always. I promise."

Lily paused, expecting her sister to reflect her enthusiasm, even thank her, but Florence was uncharacteristically silent.

"Florence? Is anything the matter? Are you ill? Surely you're looking forward to enrolling in the fall?"

When Florence still did not reply, Lily had a dreadful thought. "Don't tell me Uncle Arnold has gotten to you! Has he? Has he beaten the dream of Bryn Mawr out of you? If he has, our mother will dig herself right out of her grave and haunt him to the ends of the earth, with me right behind her."

Florence frowned at her sister. "Shush, Lily, don't be so dramatic."

"Wait—surely he hasn't managed to use up all the money? That's embezzlement!"

"No, no, calm down. Uncle Arnold has nothing to do with it."

"Well what, then? It's obvious you're hiding something from me. Let's get out of this commotion so you can tell me." She took her sister's hand and led her away from her celebrating classmates, fending off several who beckoned her to join them in their frolicking. They reached a wooden bench under a shady tree, where Lily sat and pulled Florence down beside her.

"Out with it. Come on, tell me."

Florence took a deep breath. "I'm getting married."

"Wh...what?" Lily could barely get the word out.

"Yes, I'm getting married. Soon." She reached into the neckline of her bodice and withdrew a modest diamond ring on a thin gold chain.

"He proposed last week, and I accepted." She looked down and squeezed her eyelids shut, as if expecting a blow.

"Who? Who proposed?"

Florence opened her eyes and focused on the trees over Lily's shoulder. "I'm sure you don't know him. I met him at the youth group at church."

"Does he have a name, for heaven's sake?" Lily wanted to shake her.

"Of course. Jefferson Kirkpatrick. Jeff." Her voice softened as she said his nickname.

Lily huffed. "Okay. How old is he? What does he do?"

"He's twenty-four, and he farms with his father just west of Corning."

She grasped Florence's chin and forced her face to face.

"A farmer? You're going to be a farmer's wife?" Lily thought she would faint. "What about Bryn Mawr? What about Mother's dream for you? My dream for you? You can't do this!"

"But I'm going to, Lily." Florence hadn't raised her voice, whereas Lily's kept getting louder and louder.

"Oh, my gosh, you're not...?"

"Pregnant? No, of course not."

"Well, that's a mercy. What about Uncle Arnold? Does he know?"

Florence nodded.

"Well, surely he had something to say about it?" Maybe for once, she and Uncle would be on the same side. She wasn't sure she liked that idea.

"Oh, indeed. He had a lot to say about it," Florence replied, a small grin surfacing.

Lily thrust her fists into her hips. "For instance?"

"For instance: 'At least one of you has shown some sense. At last, a level-headed young woman who doesn't insist on stuffing her head with useless trivia.' Need I go on, Sister?"

Lily jumped up off the bench and flailed the air with her fists. A passing graduate looked at her inquiringly, but soon lost interest and walked on.

"Oh, for God's sake. Of course he would say those things, and a whole lot more besides, I'm sure. Isn't that just like him! And now he thinks he's finally gotten the better of me. He's won! Our last battle, and I wasn't even there to throw a punch. The fat old goat has won the second half of the war by default."

Florence held up her hands, palms forward. "Lily, simmer down! This isn't about you and Uncle Arnold. It's about me and Jeff. I love him, and he loves me. He's a wonderful fellow, and his parents have been wonderful to me too. They've welcomed me into their family. You and I have never had a real family since Father and Mother died, and I miss that. We plan to build a house of our own on the farm. His parent's home is a bit crowded."

"You're going to spend your days washing and cleaning and churning and cooking and weeding a vegetable garden? Florence, look around you at all these bright, educated women, the new women of the twentieth century. You can be one too! I fought Uncle Arnold for both of us. The money is there, and Uncle can't object anymore."

"I don't want to go to college, Lily. I hated all the extra studying I did with Miss Hatton. Frankly she despaired of me. She said I wasn't anything like you, with your driving ambition and independence. She told me after the first few months that she doubted I'd get into Bryn Mawr no matter how hard I studied. We agreed it was useless to go on with it."

"What? You quit your tutoring? Without telling me?"

"You were too busy fighting with Uncle when you came to Corning, so I thought it best not to mention it. I knew you'd be angry, and you are! When I told Miss Hatton that I was getting married, she hugged me and told me that was the best thing that could possibly happen."

"Traitor! How could she!" Lily slapped her thighs so hard they hurt. A strolling pair of professors turned to stare.

Florence put out a calming hand. "Lily, not everyone is like you. All the girls at school back in Corning want to get married and have a family. Please accept it and wish me well."

"And what about Mother? Don't you owe her something after all the sacrifices she made for us?"

"I've thought about that long and hard, Lily. Yes, I owe her something. I know if she were alive, she'd be disappointed, but above all she'd want me to be happy. That's what I owe her—living the life that makes me happy. I'd be miserable here at Bryn Mawr. In fact, I'd probably flunk out. I love Jeff, and I want to marry him and share his life forever. Please be happy for me, Lily."

The tears in Florence's eyes, the sincerity of her plea, cracked something in Lily's heart. She gazed at her sister, feeling entirely defeated, not just for herself but for their mother and her dreams. How could Florence have ruined Lily's graduation day this way? Lily sighed, pulled a folded handkerchief from her pocket, and handed it to her sister. She watched Florence blot her tears and found herself softening.

Florence was right, as much as it almost killed Lily to admit it. This was not about herself, nor Uncle Arnold, nor their mother. It was about Florence and her young man. Not without difficulty, Lily reined in her anger.

"You're going to have to give me a little time to adjust, Florence. And I suppose I should meet the fellow."

Florence jumped up off the bench and spun around. "I was hoping you'd say that! He's here in town, at the hotel. He came especially to meet you. We rode down on the train together this morning, and he's going home this afternoon. Don't worry, no funny business." She gave Lily a shy smile, as if to lighten the mood.

Lily just looked at her.

"I know you have a party on for later, but please, Lily, walk into town with me and meet Jeff. He's so looking forward to meeting you. Then we'll send him home and we'll go to the party, exactly as planned."

Defeated, deflated, but what could she do? Florence would be eighteen next month, of which she had considerately refrained from reminding Lily. Lily had no doubt that was the final arrow in her quiver, to be shot if Lily had been inordinately stubborn. The diamond ring, now prettily on Florence's finger, glinted in the sunlight.

As far as Lily could tell when they met in the hotel lobby, Jeff was a perfectly nice, ordinary young man. Reasonably good looking, with a high forehead predictive of early balding, but with decent manners and speech that indicated more education than one might expect of a farmer. His hands were muscular, but his fingernails were clean, another good sign. His handshake was firm. Their mutual affection was obvious. Lily couldn't deny that.

Jeff treated them to lemonade from a street vendor outside the hotel, and thanked Lily for breaking away from her graduation celebration to say hello. She nodded, the best she could do at the moment.

The girls walked Jeff to the train station a few blocks farther. On the way, Lily overheard him whisper to Florence that he didn't find her anywhere near as formidable as Florence had led him to believe. Just the same, he admitted he was grateful that he was marrying the younger, not the older, sister. Realizing he'd been overheard—or perhaps intending it—he glanced over at Lily and winked. At his cheekiness, she felt another chunk of her resistance dissolve.

Strolling back to the campus, Florence was downright giddy with relief. She'd done what she came to do, and Lily appeared to have accepted the inevitable. The wedding was set for late July, and Lily promised to be there.

"Of course you'll be there," Florence said, taking Lily's hands and spinning them around in a circle. "You'll be my maid of honor!"

That idea hadn't occurred to Lily, but again, what could she do?

Florence let go of Lily and clapped her hands. "With cousin Mavis as a bridesmaid, of course. You'd have laughed if you'd seen how miffed she was that I'm to be married before she is…and that she's only to be a bridesmaid."

Lily didn't quite see the humor, but so be it. Just before they reached the dormitory lobby beyond which the party was in full swing, Lily stopped and asked the question that had niggled at her since leaving Jeff at the station.

"What about your share of our inheritance, Florence? The money that was meant to pay for college?"

"Uncle Arnold said he'll turn it over to us the day of the wedding. We'll use it to build our house."

"But that isn't what Mother…"

"Please, Lily. We've been over that. And it's not up to you. Let's enjoy your big day."

The final turning point in Lily's feelings about Florence's wedding came when Florence asked her to help sew her wedding dress. Although she was a fine seamstress herself, having been trained by their mother right alongside Lily, Florence was sure Lily couldn't resist the opportunity to help create a wedding dress. Florence was right.

After packing up and leaving school, Lily settled in at Caroline and John's and looked forward to her first few visiting engagements. In between, she hastened to Corning with her sewing basket. The one thing she refused to do was to spend even one night under her aunt and uncle's roof. Miss Hatton had continued to supplement her income with tutoring, but never had she had a student as bright and driven as Lily. She was more than delighted to accommodate her prize pupil whenever she was in town. She happily turned over her attic and her sewing machine to their endeavors so Lily could stay entirely clear of the elder Paxtons.

The girls spent many happy hours cutting, fitting, stitching, pressing, and sewing on beads and lace. As they worked, they reminisced about their childhoods and memories of their parents. Lily, being the elder and her mother's confidant during the difficult times after their father's death, told Florence many things that Florence hadn't known or had been too young to notice.

Lily also recounted her visits to their mother in the sanitarium where she had passed her final weeks. Florence had been sheltered from the realities of their mother's illness and considered too young to go along. She now took comfort in knowing their mother had been well cared for in the mountain resort, and that Lily had been with her at the end. Lily wasn't much more than a child herself at the time, and they simply hadn't known how to talk about it.

At Florence's urging, and against Lily's better judgment, Lily made an effort to heal the breech with Uncle Arnold. As Florence said, they would both be playing leading roles in her wedding, and she didn't want to worry about sparks flying on her important day. Uncle Arnold condescended to receive Lily in his den on a warm

Saturday afternoon. The familiar smell of leather and cigars assaulted her as she walked in. She stood before him and solemnly apologized, in as few words as possible, for the trouble she had caused him and Aunt Sophie and thanked him for taking care of her and Florence after their mother died.

He accepted her sentiments without any acknowledgement of his role in their disagreements, but at least he refrained from rubbing in his delight at Florence choosing to marry instead of attending Bryn Mawr. Lily walked away feeling she'd done her best and was able to assure a grateful Florence that they would treat each other civilly at the wedding.

By the time Florence walked down the church aisle on her beaming uncle's arm, elegantly dressed in hand-beaded and appliqued satin and silk organza, carrying a bouquet of white daisies and trailing stephanotis, the girls' sisterhood was stronger than ever.

When the newlyweds' house was completed and furnished by late fall, they proudly invited Lily as their first houseguest. She continued to visit from time to time, as part of her visiting rounds, and found great pleasure in getting to know Jeff and his rambunctious family. She enjoyed the outspoken admiration of Jeff's four young sisters, who flocked around her whenever she arrived. They'd never known a female college graduate.

Despite having vetoed Bryn Mawr, Florence had landed well. Before long, she confided to Lily that she had missed her monthly period and hoped she was pregnant. Lily received the news with genuine delight and began marking the days off her calendar until she would become an aunt.

Two months later, while visiting friends in Bristol, Lily received a telegram from Uncle Arnold saying Florence was gravely ill, urging her to come to Corning as quickly as possible. She threw a few things into a valise while her host's stable boy harnessed his horse to drive her to the train station.

By the time she arrived at the hospital in the old Stearns House, it was too late. In the hallway outside the women's ward, she found Uncle Arnold frantically questioning the doctor, demanding the facts. Through the ward door, she saw Jeff sobbing quietly on his knees at Florence's bedside. Not wanting to intrude, Lily stood behind her uncle to listen to the doctor, a ginger-haired fellow in his mid-forties.

"Well, it looked like appendicitis, you see," he said, stroking his beard distractedly. "I told her husband so when he brought her in. She was feverish, a lot of abdominal pain, tender to the touch. A classic case. Her husband gave us permission to operate, which we did. We've only recently learned how to safely remove an inflamed appendix, quite the up-to-date thing, you know."

"Yes, yes, go on," Arnold demanded.

"Well, once we had her opened up, I saw that the appendix was just fine, no inflammation at all. I was perplexed, so I looked a little further. That's when I found…"

"Yes, yes, what did you find? Come on, man, out with it." Arnold raised his fist as if to strike him.

The doctor flinched, then spotted Lily. He gestured with his head to Arnold that she should leave, implying that the information he was about to impart was too graphic for such delicate ears. Following his gaze, Arnold turned around and noticed Lily for the first time. He whipped back to the doctor and said, "Oh, for God's sake, man. This woman is her sister. She's almost as educated as you are. Tell us—what did you find?"

The doctor winced and looked away from them as he reluctantly divulged the diagnosis.

"A tubular pregnancy. It's rare but not unheard of. I've only ever seen one, shortly after graduating from medical school. The…the…fetus attaches outside the… the womb, where it cannot continue to grow. Before long the whole thing erupts. It is inevitably fatal."

"You mean to say that even with a proper diagnosis at the beginning, the result would have been the same?" blustered Arnold.

The doctor nodded. "I am terribly sorry. We just don't know much about these things, I'm afraid. There was nothing to be done. My condolences to you all. Now, if you will excuse me." He made a slight bow, turned, and strode off down the hallway, his hands in the pockets of his white coat.

Lily was inconsolable. Her parents' deaths had hit her hard, but she had always had Florence. Now she was truly alone in the world. Oh, the sadness of it all, she thought, with Florence and Jeff just beginning their happy life together, and now the baby gone too. It wasn't fair.

She got through the funeral, thanks to Aunt Sophie taking it in hand. She felt her heart break at the sight of Jeff sobbing over the casket in the church. Even Uncle Arnold treated her with solicitous respect. Florence's death so soon after her wedding seemed to have knocked the wind out of the old fellow.

Caroline came to Corning for the funeral and took Lily home with her, where she gave her friend the space and loving companionship she needed in which to grieve.

CHAPTER 11

Despite her sadness over her memories of Florence, Lily slept well and felt marvelously refreshed when Marco brought her downstairs to join Caroline in the sunroom the following morning. Leticia had opened the shutters the day before for a thorough airing after a long, damp Portland winter. Scents of spring wafted in: freshly trimmed grass, drying mud puddles, and a breath of jasmine blooming below the screened windows.

Caroline stepped back after fluffing the pillows on the chaise longue toward which Marco carried Lily. Below her bed jacket, the ruffles of her white flannelette nightgown draped over Marco's arm with her sock-encased feet peeking out.

"Don't you look festive today! I always thought bed jackets had to be pale pink or baby blue or maybe ivory, colors deemed suitable for shut-ins." Caroline immediately regretted the term "shut-ins," but Lily breezed right past it.

"Not when you have friends who know you like things bright and lively. Everyone who visits me seems to think I need another flamboyant bed jacket." She patted the various flowers embroidered on the padded red sateen. "Look at these blossoms—yellow, blue, purple—oh, and here's some turquoise. One can't feel low wearing Oriental flowers. Of course my bed jackets are not all this colorful, but I've got enough to clothe an entire hospital ward if the patients were brave enough to wear them. I love every one of them!"

"I'm afraid my gift is much more sedate," said Caroline as she sat down in an easy chair facing Lily. She handed her friend a large packet wrapped in white tissue paper, tied with a yellow ribbon. "Luckily I dismissed my first inclination."

"Oh, no, not another bed jacket?" joked Lily.

"Happily not," replied Caroline with a grin.

"Oh, my, isn't this wonderful," exclaimed Lily as she eased off the wrappings. "A Pennsylvania Amish quilt. What a nice surprise, and what perfect colors. A lovely gift, quite unnecessary, of course." She beamed with pleasure as she ran her hand over the fabric.

"I knew you'd appreciate the fine stitchery, and I hoped it would bring back pleasant memories of Pennsylvania. I chose the hunter green and various shades of yellow for summer. The simple geometric design blocks framed in brown seem quite restful. I hope it gives you a bit of peace."

Lily lifted the quilt to her face and inhaled the clean cotton scent. "How thoughtful of you. I'm hopelessly in love with it. Here, help me spread it out. This will be better than any medicine. I'm sure of it!"

Lily had no idea what an incongruous picture she made in her blazing Oriental bed jacket against the demure yellow, green and brown of the quilt. But that was Lily—a fascinating mixture of contradictions.

Leticia came in with a tray of tea and blueberry scones, their fresh-from-the-oven scent drifting ahead of her. After admiring the quilt, Lettie withdrew and left them to their reminiscences. For a while the chit-chat stayed light and cheery, but when they approached the end of Lily's visiting girl days, the conversation drew to an awkward halt. Caroline took another sip of her cooling tea and looked at Lily expectantly.

Ignoring her, Lily placed her cup and saucer on a side table. She ran her fingers over the quilt again, tracing a whirl of light-to-dark yellow triangles within one of the brown bordered green squares. Last night she had promised Caroline that she would tell her why she had left Philadelphia so rashly. Now that the time had come, she could find no words to begin.

Perhaps everyone would be better served if she just stuck to the family fiction—a romantic young couple who believed everyone would disapprove of their match and chose to elope to a faraway place where they could start afresh. But she doubted Caroline would accept such a simple explanation. If it were true, surely she would have confided in her best friend before leaving. And why else had she asked Caroline to come to Oregon, but to expose the truth once and for all?

"It's a complicated story, Caroline. Let me tell you in my own way and at my own pace. It may take a few days, or more, depending on my energy. But please bear with me." And please God, she said to herself, let me tell it in the most sensitive way.

Caroline settled back to listen.

About a year after Florence's death, Lily returned to Caroline and John's home after visits with friends in nearby Cherry Hill and Chester. Her room on the second floor soon swirled with fabric, thread, pins, and ribbons. For the second time she was remaking one of her favorite dresses. She had carefully picked apart the seams, planning to alter the sleeves, bodice, and skirt in ways that would bring it into line with the new season's fashion. Skirts were slimmer in 1903 and a bit shorter; sleeves were fuller; bodices were playgrounds for tucks, lace, and fanciful embroidery.

For Lily, sewing provided a quiet, creative outlet on cloudy fall days. For the hundredth time she blessed her mother for insisting she learn to sew. When making a dress from scratch, she was intrigued by the process of following a pattern with blind faith and being rewarded for her trust. She took great satisfaction in turning a mysterious collection of flat, two-dimensional shapes into a fitted three-dimensional garment. Today's redesign called for an extra layer of creativity, which she enjoyed even more.

Her skill was a godsend, considering her Uncle Arnold's miserly doling out of her spending money over the years. The students at

Bryn Mawr were as interested in fashion as any young women their age. By necessity, however, Lily's dresses lacked fashionable fussiness. A plain design was easier and took less time to construct, while also requiring less fabric and fewer notions. With her tall, slim figure she presented a unique fashion statement on campus, always up to date, but with an elegance born of simplicity. She was widely admired for her understated wardrobe. Only her closest dormitory mates knew she was her own seamstress. Because they respected her so much, they kept it under their hats.

Once she became a visiting girl, her need for a fashionable wardrobe became acute. Her hostesses expected her to dress according to their station, to blend in flawlessly with their guests. She quickly learned, however, never to outshine the woman to whom she owed her room and board.

As fashions changed, she often found herself the recipient of her benefactors' castoffs. At first she was taken aback, unsure whether or not to be insulted. She soon realized it was just as easy for her friends to toss the outdated frocks to her as to ask a maid to take them to the nearest charity or second-hand shop. She quickly learned to accept their largesse.

The first time it happened, she and her hostess had similar figures, so she was able to wear the dress with minimal alterations, albeit waiting for an event further along in her visiting progression where it would not be recognized.

When once she was given a dress that was so hopelessly outsized as to require a total remake, she puzzled over what to do. As her afternoon was free, she decided to visit a nearby second-hand shop and see if she could sell it for a few dollars instead of remaking it. She easily set aside the ethics of such a transaction, being chronically short of cash and trusting that the donor wouldn't know or care.

While she was browsing in the shop, a dress made with a complementary fabric caught her eye. She wasn't crazy about the style, but the material was superb. She wondered if she could refashion the two dresses into a fresh new one, thereby solving the related problem of being recognized in a made-over frock.

The redesign was a resounding success. Lily had found a way to dress fashionably at a negligible cost. When a castoff dress was entirely unsuitable, she sold it for much appreciated pin money.

Life as a visiting girl was not meant to be a long term solution, Lily knew only too well, but on a day-to-day basis it kept her off the streets and out of a flea-infested boarding house—an alternative she was never far from imagining. Caroline was the key, saving Lily from the humiliation of having to ask for hospitality on her own behalf. Caroline let it be known that Lily's family had money—true, if one considered Uncle Arnold and Aunt Sophie—hinting that while she was temporarily embarrassed for funds, things would change in the not-too-distant future. Because they liked Caroline and admired Lily, their friends accepted this fiction.

Caroline, being a natural organizer, enjoyed asserting herself on Lily's behalf. She approached each potential hostess in a different way, subtly tapping into her specific personality and needs. Caroline reminded one who hated letter writing that Lily had a beautiful hand and would be helpful with social correspondence. Another would find her useful as a seamstress for her three growing daughters. Yet another, who was noted for her glittering political parties, would find Lily well-versed in matters of the day. Caroline always came up with some clever inducement that eased the way for Lily's visits. For her part, Lily always honored the promises made on her behalf, looked for ways to be even more helpful, and was always a welcome and amusing guest.

On one particular visit, her hostess's cat attacked the woman's favorite hat while the family was away for the evening, leaving a trail of shredded silk flowers and ribbons across the master bedroom carpet and down the hall. Lily gathered the remnants and took them to her room, rummaged through her odd bits of frippery, and came to breakfast the next morning having plied her needle and thread to magical effect. Her hostess was elated, and promptly gave Lily two more hats in need of refurbishment, though none so dramatically. Lily was pleased to have stumbled upon another niche, both useful and appreciated.

Nevertheless, the life of a visiting girl was fraught with discomfort and uncertainty. Some households were easier to fit into than others. Where husband and wife had a mutually respectful relationship, and the children were well disciplined and cherished, she fit in easily and enjoyed her stay. In others, the tension between the grownups could be palpable, mortifying Lily when tempers flared in her presence. Sometimes cutting and hurtful remarks flew through the air; occasionally she witnessed all-out war. She tried to pretend that she'd neither seen nor heard the ruckus, but that was not always possible.

One wife considered her a captive audience to the never-ending tale of her marital woes, which made Lily squirm. From what she observed, most of the difficulty resulted from the wife's waspish temper and unreasonable demands, yet how could she point that out to her hostess?

According to another wife, her husband's incessant demands for his marital rights were driving her mad. What could she say to that?

At another home, she sat through the husband's nightly criticism of his wife at the dinner table. No sooner had the serving maid retreated to the kitchen than he'd launch into a mean-spirited diatribe of her failings and stupidity, fueled by the several solitary whiskeys during the cocktail hour. Caught in the crossfire, Lily felt embarrassed for her friend, while wondering why she didn't speak up for herself. She couldn't wait for those interminable meals to end.

Lily avoided these unhappy situations when possible, but free lodging opportunities were finite in number. She had to accept most of what was offered.

Then there were the men who needed to be attended to with delicate sensitivity. Although it was never specified, Lily understood that one of her duties as a visiting girl was to entertain the husband and their male friends on social occasions, whether at an intimate dinner party or an outdoor summer picnic. She was expected to provide cultured and witty conversation, edged with just the merest hint of carnal innuendo, while never crossing the line into anything compromising or inviting. While she knew it was necessary, she was not a natural at this light repartee. She found it meaningless and enervating. She always excused herself at the earliest possible moment, having done her duty, and escaped to her room, where she closed the door and turned the key.

Yet there was an even greater agenda always nagging in the background. Every unattached man in their orbit was subject to scrutiny by her friends, who delighted in playing matchmaker. From time to time someone showed an interest, engaged in mild flirtation, even came back to call on her once or twice. But sooner or later their interest waned, redirected to someone more in the mold of a traditional wife, invariably to Lily's relief. She simply could not see marrying just for the sake of marrying. There had to be more to life than that.

After a year and a half of mindless peregrinations, she sensed her hostesses were tiring of her. She was tiring as well—living out of her trunk, unable to relax, and always on her best behavior. Even in the most pleasant homes, she had to be constantly on her toes—ever considerate, ever cheerful, ever helpful—and as invisible as possible with respect to the family's privacy. This emotional juggling took its toll, yet she saw no end in sight.

In addition, Lily had to count on Caroline to always have the next invitation lined up. Caroline never flagged in her efforts and certainly never complained, but she had a household to run, a toddler to manage, and soon was expecting her second child. Lily feared the day when Caroline might graciously bow out.

Increasingly, through no fault of Caroline's, gaps appeared in Lily's visiting calendar. Families traveled or moved away, new babies arrived and threw the household into chaos, aging parents moved in and required care. Florence had always welcomed her on the farm, but sadly that option no longer existed. Recently she had turned to two younger friends who were still at Bryn Mawr, where she slept on a daybed in their dorm room. At first they were thrilled that an honored graduate would avail herself of their hospitality, but after a few visits they began to find her a nuisance. As she had nothing with which to occupy herself, she distracted them from their studies. Both were intent on getting into the Woman's Medical College of

Pennsylvania and nearing their final exams. More and more, Lily ended up at Caroline's by default.

A squirrel chittered on a branch of the walnut tree to the right of the screened sunroom windows. His animated scurrying up and down the branch momentarily distracted Lily from her tale. Caroline enjoyed his antics too, then drew her friend back to her story.

"Oh, dear," said Caroline, with a hand to her cheek. "Were there really so many complications and worries involved in being a visiting girl? You certainly never spoke of it. When you returned from a visit, you always had some amusing anecdote to share. I had no idea you felt your welcomes were wearing thin. None of our friends ever hinted at such a thing to me, and of course John and I loved having you whenever you came back to us."

"I know, Caroline. I never mentioned it because I'd have seemed ungrateful, and perhaps it would have upset you. That was the last thing I wanted. I saw the handwriting on the wall, but I had no idea what to do about it. You and John were wonderful, but it couldn't go on forever."

No matter how she shifted on the chaise, Lily couldn't get comfortable. The pain was seeping back into her joints, trying its best to derail her pleasant time with Caroline.

"Do you need your medicine, dear?" Caroline asked. "Shall I fetch Leticia?"

Lily nodded her head. "Yes, please. There's lots more to tell, but I'm afraid it will have to wait." Lily tugged the quilt up to her chest, wincing at the pain. "Perhaps you'll remember one particular day when you and John were entertaining in the evening and you needed more flowers than had been delivered." Lily shot her friend a sly look. "Now that I think of it, the whole thing was actually your fault."

"My fault? Now you had really better explain!"

"I will, but later. Please ask Lettie to bring me a bit of soup too. I'll have a nap here, and you and Lettie can have lunch in the dining room. Then we'll talk again."

While Caroline sat by, Lettie spooned Lily her soup and her medicine, rearranged her pillows so she could stretch out a bit more, and tucked the quilt around her. The yellow triangle pinwheels gleamed in the midday sunlight. Lily thanked Lettie and waved them off to lunch. She closed her eyes and waited for relief.

CHAPTER 12

While Lily slept, Caroline and Leticia sat down to bowls of minestrone soup, more of that crusty Italian bread, and a lettuce and tomato salad topped with shrimp and hard-boiled eggs cut in quarters.

"You look a little confused, Mrs. Crawford. Have you never had a Shrimp Louis?"

Caroline poked at the salad with her fork, trying to decide where to start. "No, I haven't, but it looks intriguing."

"One of the many Pacific coast delights, this one originating in California, I believe. Help yourself to some dressing and enjoy." Leticia handed her a crystal sauce boat filled with something pink. "Only Mrs. Delfini knows what's in the Louis dressing; we only know it's delicious."

One taste of shrimp with Louis sauce, and Caroline was a fan.

"Lily will likely sleep for several hours," said Leticia, once the two women had finished their tea. "Before she drifted off, she suggested I show you around the house. Would you like that?"

"Only if you'll call me Caroline. Mrs. Crawford is much too formal."

"Then I insist you call me Leticia, or better yet, Lettie. Even Mark and Theresa call me Lettie. For some reason Mrs. Delfini, the youngest among us, is always called Mrs. Delfini, even though she never married. I don't know why, but there you are. Perhaps it's a

European thing. Anyway, one mustn't argue with the cook." She smiled as she said it, leading the way to the front of the house.

"This stained glass work on the two side panels and the transom was done by an artist from Germany. He came over the Oregon Trail in 1867, so the story goes, arriving in tatters but with his tools and an inventory of colored glass safely packed in sawdust in his wagon."

Caroline gazed at the beautifully executed floral design, outlined with gray lead, and the scattering of colored light across the foyer floor.

"I noticed it when I arrived. The design of entwined lilies is exquisite. Did the Giannottis build the house and commission the windows?"

"No, they bought it about eight years ago. Marco had admired it for a long time, having often delivered flowers here. One day they learned it was for sale. When Lily and Marco first stepped inside and saw the glowing lilies in the morning sunshine—that was it. Lily says they would have bought the house right then and there, no further inspection necessary. They felt immediately at home, according to Lily, and they've loved it ever since."

"I can certainly see why," Caroline remarked, as the two women carried on through the parlor and into the kitchen.

Mrs. Delfini greeted them warmly, standing at the worktable mashing a handful of greens —basil, Caroline guessed by the shape of the leaves and the aroma—with a wooden pestle in a small marble bowl.

"*Pesto*, Mrs. Crawford. To the basil I will add olive oil, garlic, ground pine nuts, and parmesan cheese. A little salt. My brother-in-law sends the pine nuts—*pinoli*—from New Mexico. The Indians gather them in the forests. You'll find *pesto alla genovese* on your plate one day soon."

"I look forward to it," said Caroline.

As they left the kitchen, Caroline glimpsed, through a partly open door, a small bedroom with an unmade bed and a messy pile of men's clothing discarded on the floor. Their son Mark's room, she surmised. Lily had mentioned that he had moved into the cook's former room when he began disengaging from family life.

Seeing the dismay on Caroline's face, Lettie spoke up. "I don't think Lily is aware of it, but Mark has not been home for more than a week. His father assumes he is with some of his more disreputable friends. He's nineteen now, graduated from high school—barely—and more or less does as he pleases. As you can imagine, Marco is at his wits' ends."

"I can imagine. How very difficult, especially with Lily in her condition. Mark must be terribly upset about her, perhaps unable to face it? Is there more to it than that?"

Lettie gave Caroline a disheartened look but said nothing. Sensing any further questions would be an intrusion, Caroline let it go. Saddened, she followed Lettie out of the kitchen.

Upstairs were three bedrooms and the bathroom across from Caroline's room, in addition to the master suite. As Lily was still downstairs napping, Leticia led Caroline into the room and showed her where a door had been cut into the adjacent bedroom where Marco now slept so as not to disturb his wife. That telltale sickroom odor lingered in Lily's absence.

"It's been so difficult, Caroline, watching her slip downward week after week. I do all I can, but it will never be enough to repay her for everything she's done for me."

"She's very lucky to have you," Caroline murmured as she followed Leticia out of the room, across the landing, and toward the room at the end of the hall. She was surprised to see that it was a suite, with a tastefully furnished sitting room, a bedroom, and a private bathroom.

"Please, Caroline, have a seat," said Leticia, gesturing to one of the two maroon armchairs that flanked the fireplace. The walls were papered with pastel flowers above the dark mahogany wainscoting; below they were painted a mossy green.

"What a pleasant room," said Caroline. "It must be cozy with the fire lit on a rainy day."

"Until now I've never had a nice place to call my own," Leticia replied. "I grew up in a big, raucous family. I count my blessings every day." As she spoke, she filled an electric kettle with water in the bathroom, set it on a sideboard, and plugged it in. She set out two cups and saucers and spooned loose tea leaves into a ceramic teapot. As soon as the kettle began to whistle, she poured boiling water into the pot. She lifted the teapot to inhale the rising steam, then wafted it by Caroline.

"Mmm, that smells wonderful," Caroline said, closing her eyes to savor the aroma.

"It's a light green tea infused with jasmine blossoms, one of my favorites," Lettie said. "I have a few of Mrs. Delfini's ginger cookies stashed away, too."

As they waited for their poured tea to cool, Caroline asked Leticia to tell her more about her family.

Leticia Grant was the eldest of nine children, born to working class parents in a downtrodden section of Portland. Her father Hank, a blacksmith, earned enough to support the family without much to spare. He liked his pint of beer on the way home most nights, so the family income never stretched far enough.

It seemed to Leticia that her mother was always pregnant or nursing a new baby. From an early age, she depended on Lettie to help her with the household chores and the younger children. School was a blessed escape, but she always had to rush home to help sort out the chaos and noise.

Lettie's memories of home were of endless washing, scrubbing, cooking, wiping dirty faces and bottoms, and marketing on Saturdays with never enough money for more than the barest essentials. Those activities were punctuated every eighteen months or so by the arrival of the midwife and the moans and groans coming from her parents' bedroom as her mother struggled to give birth. The children were terrified. They didn't understand why their mother was in such agony and feared she would die every time. Nobody explained anything to them as they huddled together, waiting, while their father hastened to the tavern at the first signs of labor.

"When her eighth child was about two months old, Mother barricaded herself in their bedroom one night with Father's rifle in hand," said Lettie. "When he rattled the door handle and banged on the door, she shouted that he was no longer welcome in their bed. Enraged with drink, he kicked down the door and dared her to shoot him. In a flood of tears, Mother hesitated, and the result was Danny, nine months later.

"This time things were different. Danny was huge, over ten pounds, and Mother was in labor for thirty-eight hours. Another woman down the street was in labor at the same time, and the midwife shuttled between them. She was a woman Mother had never used before, as her usual midwife, Josephine, was away tending to her own daughter.

"Each time the new midwife rushed in, I offered her a basin of warm water and soap to wash her soiled hands. I'd seen Josephine wash her hands frequently while tending Mother. It seemed like a sensible thing to do. This one brushed me off, saying she had no time for such foolishness.

"Oh, God, it was awful. The baby seemed stuck, and Mother kept passing out. Finally the midwife threw up her hands, cursed my father in absentia, and shouted that she didn't know what more to do. She grabbed her satchel and ran out the door. We sent one of the boys for the doctor, but by the time he tracked him down, Danny had made his appearance."

"And you witnessed all this?" asked Caroline, horrified. "You must have been what, sixteen?"

"Yes. I caught Danny myself when he finally slid out. I was terrified, praying aloud that I was doing the right things, both for the baby and our mother. The younger children were in the next room; I could hear them crying. I couldn't reassure them that all would be well, because I didn't know if it would be. We were all so frightened."

"I imagine you were," exclaimed Caroline.

"And what would I do if Mother died? We all loved her so much, but I'd be in bondage to the family forever! Everyone would depend on me. I had no idea how I'd manage." Tears welled up in Lettie's eyes as the memories swamped her.

"And...she survived?" Caroline asked cautiously.

"Thank God, yes. But not without a dreadful case of childbed fever. She was sick and feverish for ages, and in terrible pain. We found out later that the other woman who was giving birth at the same time died of it. I have no doubt the midwife passed it from her to Mother because she refused to wash her hands. The doctor said it was nonsense—what did I, a young slip of a girl, know about these things? It was a miracle that Mother survived, but she was never the same. That, and the damage Danny did on the way out, kept her in bed for weeks. I guess the only good thing that came out of it is that she never had another baby. No thanks to my father, I might add."

"Goodness," murmured Caroline.

Lettie smiled, transforming the gloom of her unhappy memories. "I love my brothers and sisters. They are all kind and generous people, and most of them have families of their own now. But I made up my mind right then and there that I would never marry, and certainly never go through what my mother did to have children. I didn't want to change another diaper or wipe another runny nose, nor tell another hungry child that we only have stale bread and lard for supper again. So you can see why I was so happy to be here with the Giannottis. Looking after Mark and Theresa was a breeze."

Caroline's eyes widened. "I see. But you've never been tempted? No handsome young man hoping to sweep you away?"

Lettie gazed out the window; her voice softened. "Yes, there was one, once. He was a fisherman, and I was crazy about him. I convinced myself that our life would be different, that I would learn how to prevent having more than two or three children, and that he would respect my wishes.

"After I promised to marry him, I began having nightmares of swarms of children clamoring for my attention, drowning me in their neediness. And I was never able to forget the bloody horror of

Danny's birth. I was terrified of having to go through it myself. Three days before the wedding, I panicked and called it off. I couldn't do it. I hurt him terribly. Four months later he drowned when his boat overturned off Astoria, where the Columbia flows into the Pacific. The fishing grounds there are rich, but the currents are treacherous and unpredictable. They never found his body."

Caroline gasped. "My heavens, I'm so sorry. I don't know what to say."

"It's all right, Caroline. I don't usually tell people these things, but my story is part of how Lily and Marco's life unfolded here in Portland. They've treated me like a member of the family." Lettie glanced at the clock on her fireplace mantle. "Speaking of Lily, I'd better go and check on her. She'll probably sleep for another hour or two, but I can't count on it. She'll want to see you as soon as she wakes up, of course."

Caroline thanked her for the tea and cookies and a pleasant visit and decided she too could do with a nap. When she awoke, she freshened up and hurried downstairs to the sunroom. The tree shadows were lengthening on the lawn; the late afternoon sun slanted through the branches, casting the room in a golden glow. Lettie was just finishing brushing and rebraiding Lily's hair.

Lily's face lit up when she saw her friend. "Dear Caroline, do come and join me. I'm still pinching myself that you're here."

"So am I, Lily! I had a nice lunch and visit with Lettie, and a nap too. I'm still not recovered from the train ride, it seems. And what's all this about Back Door Women? Marco mentioned them at lunch yesterday."

Lily winked at Lettie and asked her to bring them some iced lemonade.

"All in good time, Caroline. Let me pick up my story where I left off, on a day at your home when I was between visits and finishing a dress that we both thought was particularly clever. Remember I said earlier that everything was your fault?"

121

CHAPTER 13

The clock on the dresser read almost noon, and Caroline would be expecting Lily downstairs for lunch. Lily anchored her threaded needle in the dress fabric, planning to finish stitching the hem in the afternoon. She'd deconstructed two second-hand dresses made from lightweight merino wools. From those lucky finds, she had combined panels of pink, yellow and ivory to stunning effect, incorporating several of the decorative trims she'd removed from the bodices. She couldn't wait to show Caroline the result. She threw it over her arm and dashed downstairs.

"Why, that's marvelous," Caroline exclaimed as Lily danced into the dining room with the almost-finished dress held up against her figure. "What a splendid job you've done, blending the colors and fabrics so cleverly. You know, you could become a professional fashion designer. You could surely drum up a lot of business among our friends. They already know how clever you are. You'd have ready customers."

Lily felt her smile melt away. Was this Caroline's way of telling her it was time to pack up and move on permanently? Caroline's expression remained cheery, so Lily decided to accept the compliment and think about its possible implications later.

"Thanks, Caroline. It's something to consider, but I have to be honest. While I find it engaging to sew for myself, the thought of doing it to order and under deadline is rather daunting. Perhaps I'm just too selfish, or maybe not desperate enough. After my experience with Jeanette Miller—remember I told you how demanding she was when I offered to help with her dress last month? And how impossible it was to fit her...shall we say *sagging* figure, despite her corset...I don't think I'd have the patience."

"Well, you don't have to make a decision now. It was just a thought."

Lily set the unfinished dress on the back of a chair, and they sat down at the dining room table. While they were enjoying their tea and a light sponge cake with brandied cherry sauce for dessert, Caroline suddenly frowned.

"Lily, could you do me a favor this afternoon? I know you are trying to finish your dress, but the Duncans and the Eagletons are coming for dinner this evening, and I'm not at all happy with the flowers. I can normally count on Giannotti's to put together a decent selection and deliver them, but I forgot to order them earlier in the week. I made the mistake of sending Betsy to fetch some this morning, but that girl hasn't any sense of aesthetics. She's a satisfactory kitchen helper, but I'm afraid that's the extent of her usefulness. Could you please take a look at what we've got, and then choose whatever you think will fill in nicely in the dining room and foyer? And some for the parlor as well. It's so gloomy today; the house needs perking up."

"Of course," Lily answered. "I'll go as soon as we've finished our tea."

She wrapped up in a wool jacket, scarf, hat and gloves. The afternoon was chilly, with a breeze intent on rattling the last of the turning leaves from their branches. Lawns and sidewalks were covered with the calico of autumn, waiting to be raked into piles for burning.

The flower shop was six blocks away in an area of small wood-fronted establishments that included a bookstore, a grocery, a bakery, the second-hand shop, and a tobacconist. Lily was glad for an excuse to get out and enjoy the brisk afternoon. The errand wouldn't take long, and she'd still have time to finish the hem before dinner.

Lily often walked this route when staying with the Crawfords. The first few blocks were lined with gracious homes like Caroline and John's, set on spacious lawns. Gradually the yards and homes became smaller, until she crossed onto the block that contained the shops. Across from the shops lay a good-sized park, a favorite afternoon haunt of nannies and their charges. Graveled walkways, wooded groves, gentle rises and dips, and scattered benches—the landscape invited casual strollers, and a pond enticed children with toy sailboats.

As she neared the flower shop, Lily saw a flash of motion in the bay window of Pretty Cat Books next door. She waved to Maria Horacek, the owner, who was refreshing her window display. The arrangement usually featured a cookbook or a volume of household hints, something to do with gardening, and the latest acquisitions in women's fiction, used or new. Catering to women was good business. The well-to-do housewives of the neighborhood were reasonably well educated and, with servants to run their households and mind their children, they were often bored. One or another of the subjects in the window was bound to catch the interest of every woman who walked by. A magnificent stuffed cat made of black mink fur with gleaming jet eyes guarded the window display with unflagging vigilance. Passers-by and customers always checked to see what watchful pose Maria had settled him in for the week—peering over a stack of books, seated in a child's rocking chair, peeking out from under a satin and lace quilt. Pretty Cat was the perfect low-maintenance mascot, and a great conversation starter in the shop.

Maria kept a table and two armchairs behind the stacks where her women customers could sit and chat and enjoy afternoon tea if so inclined. Thus she overheard all the neighborhood news but only judiciously passed it on. Lily promised herself she would stop in soon and see what was currently on offer, books and otherwise.

Pushing open Giannotti Florist's door, she paused and inhaled the piney scent of fall arrangements set out on a counter that wrapped around three sides of the shop's interior walls. Autumn chrysanthemums, zinnias, sunflowers, carnations—arranged with a variety of evergreen fronds in honor of the advancing season.

A wood stove in a corner radiated just enough warmth for the customers but not enough to wilt the cut flowers. Lily stepped aside to allow a well-dressed woman with a bouquet in her arms to exit. As the woman bustled by, Lily caught a flash of rust colored chrysanthemums and yellow helianthus. She realized she'd forgotten to check on what Betsy had brought home earlier. Hopefully the florist would remember so she could choose more of the same, or perhaps something complementary—mixing and matching as she did her fabrics.

She expected to see the elderly Mrs. Giannotti behind the counter, as usual, but today a young man in his mid-twenties stood in her place, trimming the stems from a pile of white mums onto an open newspaper and arranging the blossoms one by one in a glass vase with studied carefulness. He pulled out the one he had just dropped in, trimmed off another inch, slipped it back into the vase, and stepped back to consider the result.

"*Perfecto*," he murmured to himself. Then, noticing Lily, "Good afternoon, Miss. What can I do for you today?"

He was of medium height, muscular rather than stocky, with a darker complexion than most men she knew and wavy black hair, neatly trimmed and brushed back. He wore a plaid flannel shirt with the sleeves rolled up on his tanned forearms, and a green-bibbed apron.

For a moment Lily was speechless. She'd never seen a man arranging flowers, never mind one so handsome and taking such satisfaction in it.

He braced his palms on the counter and leaned forward. "We've got mums of every color, Miss, perfect for the fall, including the brand-new bronze variety that just walked out the door. Your friends will wonder what magical land you found them in." He turned around, picked a gloriously rusty bloom from a bucket on the counter behind him, and handed it to her with a flourish. "Just tell them Giannotti's."

Accepting and admiring it gave her a moment to collect herself and get over feeling more than a little idiotic.

"It's lovely, and you're right—most unusual." She handed it back to him and cleared her throat. "I'm here on behalf of Mrs. Crawford. Her girl came by this morning, but we find we need more of the same, or perhaps something contrasting. Enough to fill out three large arrangements?"

He wiped his hands on his apron. "Of course. I wasn't here this morning. Do you know what she chose?"

Lily shook her head, embarrassed. "No, sorry. I dashed off without inquiring. How careless of me."

He rapped his knuckles on the counter. "Not at all. Let me ask my mother. I'm Marco Giannotti, by the way. I don't usually work in the shop. Greenhouses and open fields are more my territory." He grinned as he deftly wrapped the stem clippings in the newspaper and discarded them under the counter.

She watched his hands. They were not the soft, manicured hands of the men she knew—bankers, college professors, aspiring writers, physicians, architects. Though scrubbed clean, his were the seasoned hands of an outdoorsman, a man familiar with the handle of a shovel or an axe, and the reins of a team of horses.

"I'll be right back," he added as he disappeared through a curtained doorway into the back of the shop. Lily heard him call out, "Hey, Mama, what did the Crawfords order this morning?"

She didn't hear his mother's reply, but he soon returned with an assortment of zinnias and marigolds in yellows and oranges, with a variety of crisp greens. He pulled a few pieces of newspaper from a folded stack at the far end of the counter, flipped them open with one hand, and laid the flowers on them.

"This should do it, according to my mother. What about half a dozen of these bronze beauties to round things out? They'll be a terrific conversation piece, I guarantee." Without waiting for her to agree, he lifted six of the mums from the bucket behind him, added them to the mix, and secured the bundle with twine.

His eyes, so dark the pupils were almost indistinguishable from the irises, gleamed with good nature. The man was a born salesman.

"Of course. Mrs. Crawford will be delighted," Lily finally managed to say.

"It's kind of a big parcel. We can deliver them later, Miss, as soon as my wagon and driver get back."

"Oh, no, please. I'm perfectly able to carry them. It's only a few blocks."

"Wait, I have a better idea." He turned and ducked back through the curtain and reappeared with his jacket and cap. "Mama, I'm making a delivery down the street. I'll be back in a few minutes."

Mrs. Giannotti appeared in the doorway behind him, hands set on ample hips. She wore a face of unrelenting toil and gloom, the unmistakable aspect of an immigrant who has sacrificed everything for her children and now must remain alert to any threat of poor choices on their part. She was clearly not pleased to see her son poised to walk this young woman home under the pretext of carrying her flowers.

Raising a hand to his mother, he picked up the flowers before she could speak, pulled up a hinged section of the countertop, slipped through the opening, and escorted Lily outside.

The clouds had scudded off to the west and day had turned brilliant, but the chill remained. She tied her scarf a little more snugly and fished in her pocket for her gloves.

"So…you are visiting the Crawfords from out of town, Miss?" he asked as they crossed the street into the next block.

"Yes…and no, I suppose." She was flustered by his continuing to call her Miss but didn't know how to correct him without seeming overly familiar. Why hadn't she taken the opportunity earlier in the shop when he'd offered his own name?

"I don't mean to sound nosy, but it generally has to be one or the other, wouldn't you say?" He flashed her a cocky grin over the bulky packet of flowers.

She laughed. "Yes, of course. It's just…a bit difficult to explain."

"Ah. Well, then."

"I'm sorry. I don't mean to sound mysterious. I'm just…"

"Don't worry. I shouldn't be asking such personal questions. I don't even know your name."

"Well, I can at least tell you that much," she replied, relieved to finally get it out. "I'm Lily Paxton. Mrs. Crawford is my best friend. We were in college together."

He stopped and tucked his chin toward his shoulder, glancing at her sideways. She braced herself for a disparaging remark about college women. It wouldn't have been the first time a fellow had belittled her for it.

"I knew it," he said. "I knew there was something special about you. Lily—such a beautiful and intelligent flower. It's perfect for you!"

Having polished all kinds of snappy comebacks in defense of her education, Lily was flummoxed. Head down and blushing, she had no idea what to say.

He spun around and walked facing her for a few paces. "Please, accept the compliment. I meant it sincerely."

Unused to flattery, sincere or otherwise; unused to walking down the street with a man; and not at all sure what her friends would make of her strolling along with a shopkeeper's son, Lily was completely undone.

"Now I've spoiled it, haven't I?" he said, rubbing his neck with his free hand as they continued along. "Let me confess—I am not in the habit of walking a customer home, especially not such a pretty one. But it's a gorgeous autumn day, the sun is shining, the world is beautiful, and how can we not be happy to be right here, right now?"

Succumbing to his exuberance, Lily lifted her skirt and kicked a windblown heap of fallen leaves into the air. They swirled in the breeze and settled back down in a crazy quilt of browns, reds, and gold. They both laughed.

"There, you see? You just have to stop and appreciate the moment. Small pleasures, that's what life is all about. Sunshine, autumn leaves, an armful of flowers—life is good!"

"Are you always this optimistic?" she asked, casting him a sideways glance.

"Well, struggles and bad times come along without any help from me. But here we are on this magnificent afternoon. Enjoy the moment, I say. Let tomorrow, or even five minutes from now, take care of themselves. They will anyway, you know, whether we wish it or not."

Lily found his honesty and high spirits irresistible. As someone who always had to be looking and planning ahead, this was a novel concept. She'd never considered enjoying the moment, but the idea had its charm.

"Are you teasing me?" she asked, just to be sure.

"No such thing. I'm just happy to be walking down this sidewalk with Miss Lily Paxton. There. I've said it. And here we are at the Crawfords. Please, after you." He bowed slightly and motioned her to precede him up the walkway to the front door. Instinctively, and immediately regretting it, she glanced up and down the street to see if they had been observed.

Crestfallen would have been too strong to describe the look on Marco's face, but it came close.

"Ah, you don't want to be seen with Marco, the florist's son. It was just a walk down the street, Miss Lily Paxton. Nothing more." He handed her the flowers, whisked off his cap, and nodded goodbye. She was in the house with the door closed behind her before he reached the end of the walkway, where he turned to wave an unseen goodbye.

Upstairs in her room, having hastily thrust the flowers at a surprised Betsy in the kitchen, Lily wondered if her heart was beating from her run up the steps or from her encounter with Marco. Of course the latter was absurd, but the experience had been completely outside her usual interactions with men. Within her circle, the choreography was explicit. Walking alone with a man she had just met was unheard of. Not to mention that he was the florist's son.

"So that's how it all began, you and Marco," said Caroline, stretching out as well as she could while still seated in the chair facing Lily on the chaise longue. "You certainly were circumspect. I never suspected a thing."

Lily smiled softly, deepening the lines that radiated from the corners of her eyes. "I told you it was all your fault, didn't I, for sending me to the flower shop that day." Her smile faded. "From here it gets complicated, Caroline. And you are not going to like what you hear. You've come a long way, however, and I owe you the whole of it. But I'm tired now. Please bear with me. We'll continue tomorrow." Her eyelids fluttered, and her face fell into repose.

Caroline picked up the quilt, which had slipped to Lily's waist, and nestled it around her shoulders.

"In that case, let the love of a stranger who so caringly stitched this pinwheel design, give us both courage," whispered Caroline. She returned to her chair, picked up a magazine from a side table, and thumbed through it until Marco arrived after another day at the shop.

Upon his return, Marco carried Lily upstairs. Leticia brought her a light dinner, saw to her toilette and medication, and tucked her in for the night. She was content, knowing that Marco and Lettie would keep Caroline company.

When Lily awoke in the still darkness, the clock showed 3:45 a.m. She knew it would be several hours before anyone else stirred. She dreaded these long hours, hours that plagued her more and more frequently as the laudanum became less effective. In the fullness of her life with Marco and the children, she had almost banished her memory of those last months in Philadelphia. But now, with her body failing, her mind insisted on bringing up these unsettling events. How could she possibly tell Caroline the truth?

CHAPTER 14

Lily couldn't account for it, but she felt different as she dressed for dinner that evening at the Crawfords'. Life seemed to have taken a lighter turn in the few short hours since her brisk walk with Marco. Was it the dress she had just finished hemming, with its subtle pastel shades and a daringly low neckline? She had plunged the neckline strictly out of boredom. If it turned out to be too low for comfort, she'd add a pleated insert. Experimenting always piqued her interest. Besides, the frock, constructed entirely from castoffs, hadn't cost a penny.

Stepping in front of the cheval mirror beside her dresser, she tucked a stray curl into her chignon. As she turned to and fro, she ran her hands up and down her bodice, feeling their warmth through the perfectly fitted fabric. Inspecting herself from one angle, then another, she admitted she didn't have much to show off, but still, the décolletage was perfect. She smiled, rather pleased with this heightened awareness of her body.

Her only adornments were her mother's pearl and diamond earrings—each one a single pearl set in gold above a cluster of three small diamonds—and the gold chain on which she wore her mother's wedding ring. She wondered what Marco would have thought of her, so dressed up, then banished the thought as preposterous. It was highly doubtful that the Giannotti family ever thought about dressing for dinner.

Sadie and Jack Duncan and Yolanda and William Eagleton were always good company. Lily looked forward to the small gathering as she descended the stairs. Dinner was superb: a rare roast of beef with horseradish sauce, Yorkshire pudding and gravy, roasted potatoes with caramelized onions. Every so often during the meal, Marco surfaced in her thoughts, sending a thrill straight through her. His charming reaction to her name was a secret she held closely to her heart, a delight that was strictly her own and never to be shared, not even with Caroline.

Lily's dinner partner for the evening was Caroline's brother Lawrence. He had arrived for the weekend, as he often did, to join his rowing crew at the Pennsylvania Athletic Club. Being three years older than Lily and Caroline, he had generally found better things to do than to hang around with his kid sister and her friend when the girls were home on college weekends. He enjoyed teasing them, as brothers do, and often sat down with them for a game of cards. He was pleasant for the most part: a dreamy sort of fellow, tall and fair with straight blond hair that insisted on flopping down over his forehead no matter how often he brushed it aside.

Most of Caroline's school friends found Lawrence attractive. A few had eyed him hopefully, but to no avail. He had studied literature at Swarthmore College with the intention of becoming a poet. When he continued to demonstrate an appalling lack of talent in that direction, and a disinclination to pursue graduate studies toward becoming an English professor, his father stepped in and issued an ultimatum: either he join his childless uncle's insurance company in New York City, which he would ultimately inherit, or bid the family income farewell and rhapsodize to his heart's content while starving in a frigid, drafty attic.

Being fond of his creature comforts, he reluctantly chose the former, but soon discovered he was as poorly suited to the insurance profession as he was to writing poetry. As time went on, he complained that it was a waste of energy to be thinking about potential catastrophes all the time, and the financial ramifications thereof, not to mention the endless sales calls to court the business that paid his commissions. He began a slow slide into a big city life of debauchery and despair, which began to show in his drinking and unpredictable temper on his visits to his sister. Lily knew Caroline worried about him but wasn't sure what anyone could do to encourage him to take life more seriously. His father certainly hadn't had any luck in that direction.

Lily had come to find Lawrence's visits distasteful when they overlapped hers. She had never had any reason to dislike him in the past, but increasingly she found herself the object of his unwanted attention and teasing that bordered on the lewd. She sometimes caught him looking at her with an odd expression on his face, for longer than was polite. He had purposely brushed up against her in the hallway just that morning.

Instead of apologizing, he had grasped her arms and pushed her hard against the wall. Shocked, she quickly disengaged herself and hurried upstairs to her room, locking the door behind her. This was not the Lawrence with whom she and Caroline had once played genteel games of pinochle.

Earlier, she might have considered Lawrence a suitable husband. He was, after all, her best friend's brother. Upon their uncle's death, he would be gifted with a thriving business, wrapped and tied with a gold satin bow. He also stood to inherit the rest of his uncle's estate, which included a hefty investment portfolio, a brownstone in a fashionable New York City neighborhood, and a gentleman's farm on the Hudson River. On the surface he was eligible indeed.

But his attentions to Lily did not feel like those of a suitor, especially when he was tipsy. His teasing, far from brotherly, had taken on undertones of innuendo and disrespect. The more he drank, the more he leered. Toward the end of an evening, he often made sly remarks to her that no gentleman would ever make to a lady. He was careful, however, that this disrespect never surfaced when his sister or her husband was present. Lily realized that she was afraid of him.

After the Duncans and the Eagletons left that evening, Caroline and John said good night and retired to their bedroom. Tired though she was, Lily remained downstairs to straighten up while the cook's helper finished in the kitchen.

When she stepped into the library to retrieve any dirty ashtrays and empty glasses left by the men after dinner—the smell of stale tobacco nauseated Caroline, who was once again in a delicate condition—Lily stopped short. Lawrence lay half sprawled on the leather chesterfield, necktie loosened, dimly lit by a shaded lamp on a side table, holding a cigar in one hand and a glass of whiskey in the other. He raised his head at her entrance and proffered his glass in a sloppy salute.

"Well, well, the untouchable Lily. Lily white, Lily pure. It can't be much fun to live such a chaste life."

She immediately bristled, realizing he was drunk. Ignoring him, she picked up an ashtray and a half-full glass from the nearest table.

"What's the matter, Lily? Have I offended you? Hah!" He straightened around and pulled himself upright. "So dreadfully sorry. Women are so touchy. Women, huh. I should say *ladies*, ladies are so touchy. Always guarding their highly overrated virtue. What's the point? Forget about ladies; I'll tell you something about *women*, real women. A real woman knows what to *do* for a man. I suspect you have no idea, eh?"

She turned to leave. There was no point in responding.

"Hey! You looked different at dinner tonight, by cracky. Not just the new dress—oh, yes, I noticed the daring neckline. You looked...I don't know. I can't put a finger on it, but perhaps the word is intriguing. It can't be just that you took a walk out in the cold this afternoon that put that blush on your cheeks."

She swung around to face him, tightening her grasp on the glass and ashtray, sorely tempted to throw them at him. Dear God, had he seen her with Marco?

He took a deep swig of his whiskey, squinting at her over the rim of the glass.

"No, of course not. Much more than a bracing walk. You looked somehow...more alive, more attuned to the possibilities, shall we say. As if you've stepped through an important passageway in life. I wonder… has a man awakened you to carnal pleasure?"

She inhaled sharply and turned toward the door. He hauled himself to his feet, unsteady but determined.

"It shows, you know," he stated, his words slurring. "I can always tell when a woman has ripened and is ready to be plucked."

Heat flamed up her neck. She spun around again to face him. "Really, Lawrence. That's quite enough." Thankfully, he made no mention of having seen her with Marco. She didn't want Marco to be sullied by Lawrence so much as mentioning his name.

Lawrence grinned at her and brushed back his errant blond forelock. How she'd come to hate that gesture. "Aha, I knew it. Who is he? Come on, tell me."

She gasped and turned to leave again. Before she knew what was happening, he bounded across the room, grabbed her, twirled her around, and kicked the door shut behind them, thrusting her up against it. He fumbled at her skirt, but he was too drunk to be effective. The ashtray and glass slipped out of her hands as she tried to fend him off. The ashtray bounced against the glass, sending ashes, whiskey, and glass shards across the carpet. She pushed him staggering backward, jerked open the door, and ran upstairs to her room. She braced her full weight against the door, her back to it, her chest heaving as she caught her breath. Without releasing her weight against the door, she blindly slid a hand down past the doorknob to turn the key. The lock was empty.

She held her breath and listened for footsteps. Nothing. Cautiously she stepped away from the door, lifted her skirt, and scanned the floor to see where the key had fallen. The floorboards were bare. The key had been where it belonged earlier in the day, when she had locked the door against Lawrence in the morning. Quickly she searched her pockets, inspected the dresser top and drawers, the window ledge, the bedside table. It simply was not there. She knelt down to look under the bed, hoping she had inadvertently kicked it out of sight. Nothing.

Her hands flew to her neck, a vain gesture to quell her rising panic. Think! How could she protect herself without the key? Would he dare to try to come in? Caroline and John were asleep just down the hall. Surely a scream would bring them running, but did she want to do that? She stood still for a moment, hearing only her ragged breathing above the silence of the slumbering house.

The dresser—could she push it against the door? No, the noise as it scraped along the floorboards might awaken her hosts, and then she'd have some explaining to do. Would they even believe her? Believe her about what? Lawrence had done nothing more than make a clumsy, drunken pass at her. She doubted anyone would find that alarming or even credible. John might scold her for carelessly putting herself in a compromising position.

When she still heard no footsteps on the stairs or in the hallway, she began to relax. Surely Lawrence had taken another drink and fallen asleep on the library couch, or better yet, retreated to his room above the carriage house. When he awoke in the morning, he'd have forgotten all about the nasty scene, or so she hoped. She'd have to as well. After all, it was only Lawrence.

She undressed, hung her dress in the wardrobe, draped her petticoats, chemise, corset, and stockings over a chair, and slipped her nightgown over her head. She tiptoed down the hall to the bathroom, scurried back, and climbed into bed. She shivered as she stretched out between the chilly sheets. Lying on her back and pulling the covers up to her chin, she took a few calming breaths and tuned into the quiet of the night.

Why had Lawrence become so unpleasant, she wondered. Was it because he was so adrift professionally, gaining no satisfaction from a career that bored him, while yearning to live a literary life? Whatever it was, he was no longer the fellow with whom she'd joshed and played jolly card games on college weekends. Their casual friendship had taken a turn down a dark alley, and she didn't like it one bit.

A girl was taught from her earliest days to avoid situations where men might display their baser instincts. Why was this so? Why were girls and women vigorously guarded until they were safely married, rather than men taught to control themselves? It wasn't fair.

She'd best avoid him in the future, she decided, especially late at night when he'd been drinking. A girl should at least take sensible precautions. Caroline would just have to cope with the stale morning smell of tobacco in the future. As for tomorrow, she'd rise early enough to clean up the glass shards and cigarette butts and sponge the library carpet before anyone else found the mess and started asking questions. No matter how she explained it, it wouldn't reflect well on her.

A sudden grip on her jaw jolted Lily awake. Instinctively she flailed her arms and tried to shake her head, but she couldn't move. She recognized the scent of his cigars and whiskey. Lawrence!

Screams lodged in her throat but were thwarted into futile moans. With his free hand he ripped off the bedclothes. Before she could kick out, he jumped on the bed and straddled her, pinning down her legs with his weight and ignoring her ineffectual pummeling. With one hand still muffling her, he jerked up her nightgown and kneed open her legs. When she felt something hard jabbing at her most private parts, she thrashed and bucked and tried to kick him off.

The more she writhed and fought, the more excited he became and the more he pressed his advantage. With his hand still clamped on her mouth, he squeezed her nose shut with his thumb and forefinger until the world faded into nothing. She came around moments later, gasping for breath, just as he slid off her and scrambled for his trousers. He left without a word, closing the door soundlessly behind him. The metallic snick of the latch when he let go of the doorknob was his only farewell.

Sprawled atop the tangled bedclothes, Lily shivered with cold and fear. What had happened? She wasn't sure. When she turned over she felt wetness ooze out between her legs. Was it blood? Had he injured her? Had his rough treatment caused her monthly flow to begin? She reached down and touched it, rubbed it between her fingers, then brought her fingers up to her nose. It didn't smell rusty like blood, but it smelled nonetheless. A cloying scent, one she was unfamiliar with.

She slowly got up, sloshed some water from the pitcher on the washstand into the bowl and wiped herself off as well as she could. She did not want to risk encountering Lawrence—or Caroline for that matter—in the hallway to the bathroom.

She got back into bed and eased under the covers, huddling smaller and smaller, wishing she could disappear. As it had happened in the dark, she had no remembered vision of the assault, just the sounds and desperate feel of the struggle, the probing between her legs, and the smell of his sour breath before she blacked out. She had floated back to consciousness with pain in her most intimate parts, and the feeling of having been completely overwhelmed. She tried to sort it out but couldn't. She only knew something terrible had happened, something that girls were warned about and guarded against. Only this time the warnings and guarding had failed. She eventually drifted off, clutching the bedclothes around her as tightly as a shroud.

Shortly after dawn Lily awoke to the scent of frying bacon. The moment she straightened her legs and rolled over on her back, a throbbing ache radiated from the area her mother had euphemistically referred to as "down through there."

The assault flooded back: a confusion of sounds, grapplings in the dark, blunt prodding where nothing should prod, blacking out as he briefly suffocated her, then gasping for breath as he slid off, and the disgusting sticky residue. She wanted to believe it was a nightmare, but the pain in her groin rebuffed that fantasy. The damp washcloth, dumped on the edge of the basin instead of neatly hung on the stand, confirmed everything.

What did this mean? Had she lost her virginity, even though it was forced? Had it destroyed her eligibility for marriage? And—oh, God—what did it mean regarding pregnancy? Surely that wasn't possible after just one encounter. But she didn't know.

She listened for footsteps in the hallway. All was quiet except for her growling stomach. How could she possibly be hungry? But she was, ravenously. She took it as a sign that the world had awoken a better place than it had been the night before, and that she was meant to continue living in it—if she could.

On her way downstairs, she remembered the spilled ashtray and broken glass in the library. She quietly slipped along the passage toward the back of the house and pushed open the door to John's sanctuary. Not a sign of broken glass or spilled ashes or a whisky stain—everything had been cleaned up. Perhaps Caroline had assumed that Lawrence had drunkenly dropped them and asked Betsy, the kitchen maid, to take care of it. Surely it wouldn't be mentioned, for fear of discomfiting her brother.

Caroline and John were at their usual places at the breakfast table—sunshine pouring in the window, John bulwarked behind his open newspaper, and Caroline ladling stewed fruit over her oatmeal. A quick glance revealed there was only one empty place setting at the table—hers. Lawrence must have slunk off to the city on the early train. Thank God.

"Good morning, Lily," Caroline said with a bright smile as Lily sat down. "You slept well, I hope?"

Lily could only nod. Fortunately, Betsy appeared at her side with the coffee pot and leaned over to pour her a cup, blocking Caroline's view of Lily's face. With a trembling hand, she lifted her cup and took a sip, eyes lowered, as the maid backed away.

"Lily, are you all right? "Caroline looked at her more closely. John lowered a corner of his newspaper and peered at her, his attention caught by the troubled note in his wife's voice.

"Of course. I'm fine. Some nights are less restful than others, that's all."

"Well, that happens to all of us," Caroline chirped. "I was up with young Robert just before dawn. Who knows what gets into their little heads when they're all alone in the dark?"

John rattled his paper back into shape, happy to let the women deal with whatever was—or wasn't—bothering Lily.

Who knows what gets into a *man's* head when he's all alone in the dark, Lily asked herself. Well, now she knew. She was safe here for the rest of her visit, as typically Lawrence wouldn't be back for a month or more. The next time their visits overlapped he would no doubt join her, at least in public, in the pretense that nothing untoward had happened between them. But what if he tried it again?

She couldn't possibly discuss it with Caroline. Caroline loved her brother. If she believed Lily, this would cause a terrible rift in the family that had done so much for her. If Caroline didn't believe her, the girls' friendship would surely end, and Lily would be left without her only real ally in her precarious existence. Nor could she talk to John about it. She would die a thousand deaths of embarrassment, and he would probably tell her she'd imagined it.

She decided, at least for the moment, that she must take her lumps and not dwell on it. It had been an unpleasant episode, but it wasn't the end of the world. Nothing had really changed, except that she had lost her innocence. Maybe that wasn't such a bad thing. Now she knew the worst that could happen, and she had survived it. That had to count for something.

But she knew the jig was up; she could not continue to partake of Caroline and John's hospitality and hope that all would be well. Her days as a visiting girl were numbered.

Offering Caroline a brittle smile, Lily picked up her napkin, shook it out, and placed it on her lap. There on the white tablecloth, on the spot where the napkin had been so neatly folded, lay the key to her bedroom door.

CHAPTER 15

Even though Lily knew Lawrence would probably not return in the immediate future, she felt restless and uneasy in Caroline's home. During the daytime she put on her best face, trying to appear as relaxed and cheerful as possible, hoping her friend would be too distracted with her toddler and advancing pregnancy to notice her underlying agitation. She helped as usual with household tasks but found herself spending more and more time alone in her room. Taking her lumps and not dwelling on it was easier said than done.

Thank goodness for her sewing. Caroline never questioned the hours Lily shut herself away with her needles and threads, knowing it was necessary for Lily to keep her wardrobe fresh and fashionable. Although Lily found she could concentrate on the mechanics of ripping out the seams of her secondhand finds and pressing the pieces flat to get a better picture of their possibilities, the creative spark of combining and arranging them in new patterns had fled. Visions of completed garments no longer popped into her head as easily as rain made patterns on the windowpanes.

Worst of all, she no longer cared. She sat by her window for long hours, her needle stuck idly in an unfinished seam, staring into space and wondering what was to become of her. She felt ensnared, unable to leave Caroline's until the date of her next visit ten days hence. Those days stretched out interminably. And would anything be better once she moved on? She felt as if her soul had withered within her, robbing her of energy and her usual interest in the world around her.

After almost a week of this fruitless and depressing sequester, Lily took hold of herself. What am I doing, she asked herself. This unmentionable thing has happened. It can't be undone. Am I going to let it ruin my life? Lawrence was drunk. Drunk men lose their inhibitions, although that's no excuse. I have the power to rise above it and move on. Each day that goes by, I leave it further behind. The day will come when it will be but a distant shadow, no longer with any power to hurt me. I cannot and will not let it get the better of me.

She tossed aside her languishing needlework, picked up her handbag and shawl, and slipped downstairs. The house was quiet, with John at work and Caroline and Robert napping. She let herself out the front door and turned toward the shops. The afternoon was clear and crisp, with that delicious autumn chill that makes one anticipate the delight of a crackling fireplace at the end of the day. As her step lightened, she began to feel revived. A new book to read, she decided, would put a fine cap on the day. She'd drown in someone else's problems for a change.

The bell over the door jingled as she entered Pretty Cat Books. Maria Horacek, dressed in light gray that somehow looked festive on her, greeted her warmly.

"Lily Paxton, how nice! It's been a while. Welcome back! What can I entice you with today? I have the latest novels of romance, suspense, and derring-do." Quick to react to Lily's frown, she changed course. "Or perhaps something calmer? Here, have a look at this by Sarah Orne Jewett. She's one of my favorite authors. This book just came in, *The Country of the Pointed Firs*. It's a collection of short stories set in a fictional town on the coast of Maine. I just finished it myself last night."

Lily accepted the nondescript green book from Maria and turned it over in her hand. A corner of the cover was stained, so it must be second-hand, which suited her fine. The price would be low, and there was something affirming about a book that others had enjoyed before her.

"Good idea, I'll take it. Thank you, Maria." She handed Maria a few coins and watched her put them in the cash box. Pretty Cat, removed from his usual spot in the window, oversaw the transaction from atop a small stack of books on the counter.

"Lovely! Now come on back and have a cup of tea with me. It's been a deadly dull day. Only two customers before you, neither of whom could I please with anything. It must be the time of year. Everyone is as restless as the autumn leaves and can't settle down to read. Plenty of time for that come winter! I've shelved all my new books, perked up the window display, and dusted my feather duster almost bald. I could use a sit-down and some chit-chat. Join me?"

"Thank you, I'd love it," said Lily, grateful for an opportunity to fill more time before returning to the Crawfords'.

"Come along then. You know I always keep the kettle on." Maria led the way past tables topped with books and rows of filled bookshelves. Just as she'd said, the potbellied stove at the rear of the shop cast a welcoming warmth. A brass kettle steamed gently on its dull black surface. Maria waved Lily to a cushioned chair, then dumped out damp tea leaves from a ceramic teapot into a waste can, spooned in fresh ones, and filled it from the steaming kettle.

"There," said Maria as she sat down in the other chair. "We'll let it steep a bit and then we can indulge. It's my new favorite, an exotic oolong from Bengal. I discovered it recently at a new tea shop downtown. I'm quite addicted."

Lily closed her eyes and inhaled the comforting aroma, redolent of smoke and far away climes.

"I'm so pleased to see you, Lily. I'm totally dependent on friends who stop by to pass on the news of the neighborhood."

Lily was pleased to hear that Maria considered her a friend, although they would never see each other in a social setting. Maria was that rare person who listened attentively, dispensed sensible advice, and kept the details to herself. Lily had never had a reason to confide in her, but she knew that while Maria heard a great deal, she was not a gossip.

The details of Maria's own life were a bit of a mystery, which made her a delicious object of interest and speculation among her customers. She was of medium height, slender, with dark hair and deep-set dark eyes. From various bits and pieces gleaned over the years, the ladies of the neighborhood knew that she was in her late thirties and had been widowed some time ago. Her late husband, a bricklayer from Czechoslovakia, had left her a successful masonry business, which she had sold for enough to purchase this building and the one next door, occupied by Giannotti Florist. She lived in an apartment above her store, as did the Giannottis. With no rent to pay and the income from the Giannottis, she managed to live comfortably.

She was friendly with the other shopkeepers on the block and made a point of dropping in on them from time to time, even if she had no use for their products. Once she had told Lily about the tobacconist, Harry MacTavish, a particular favorite of hers with his endless supply of hilarious anecdotes about his raucous youth on the Isle of Skye and his subsequent life as a merchant mariner. Maria told him he'd be another Robert Louis Stevenson if he'd put pen to paper. She mimicked his Scottish accent perfectly when relating his reply.

"Ah, no, lassie. Writin's not for me. Leave it ta His Nibs. I canna hold a candle to the likes o' him."

From time to time, Maria loaned him a book she thought he'd enjoy. He treated them reverently and always returned them to her no worse for the wear. It was a small favor she could do, one that he appreciated way out of proportion to the effort it cost her. A fair return, Lily agreed, for the amusement he afforded her every time she stopped by.

"Lily, you always look so smart, even when you're just out for an afternoon stroll," said Maria as she poured their tea. "Whoever your dressmaker is, she is talented indeed. Wherever did you find her?"

Had she been asked this question by anyone else, Lily would have answered evasively. In the circles in which she traveled, it embarrassed her that she had to make her own clothes. Some of her hostesses knew, of course, and were generous with their castoffs, but as far as she knew they kept her secret out of kindness. When asked by other admirers, as she often was at social events, she answered with a vague reference to a dressmaker in New York City. When pressed, she'd say the woman had sewn for eastern European royalty, then fallen on hard times and emigrated to the U.S. She was now semi-retired and retained only a few select clients. Lily would whisper that she was extremely lucky to have been taken on, hinting that the dressmaker considered Lily her goodwill deed, a *mitzvah*, as the woman called it. Ending the conversation with an enigmatic smile, Lily would intimate that no power on earth would induce her to divulge this treasure's identity. The harmless fiction served them right for pressing, she always thought. Today, however, her defenses were down, and she didn't have the energy to dissemble. Nor was Maria likely to repeat what she heard.

"You might as well know, Maria. I sew them myself."

Maria set her teacup back onto its saucer and gave Lily her full attention. "Honestly? Then you are a genius! I have never seen such unique variations of colors and fabrics that come together so beautifully, and in styles that are always at the height of fashion. How do you do it?"

Lily chuckled for the first time in days. It felt good. "Your friends next door in the second-hand shop could tell a tale or two. I'm one of their best customers. I've learned to take dresses apart and refashion them. I study fashion magazines and my stylish friends' dresses. Once in a while I take the train into New York City and peruse the store windows."

At Maria's astonishment, she leaned forward and whispered, "My biggest adventure is to stand outside the Metropolitan Opera House before the matinees and observe the fashion parade. Then as I shift the reclaimed pieces of fabric around on my bed, designs just pop into my head."

145

"What an extraordinary talent! Have you ever thought of going into business? You'd be turning people away once they saw your creations."

Lily sighed. "I have thought about it, Maria. I'm afraid that if I had to sew for a living, working day and night to make dresses for others, I'd lose interest and my creativity would disappear. At the most basic level, I wouldn't even know how to begin. I have needles and thread and scissors and a measuring tape for making my own dresses, but no funds with which to set myself up professionally. I'd need a place to live and work—it would be impossible."

Maria shook her head at this young woman who knew nothing about hard times. "I've heard something about your situation, Lily. As you might imagine, people do talk. Nothing negative, I assure you. In fact, the consensus is that your life as a visiting girl must be rather exciting."

With an uncontrollable rush of feeling, Lily burst into tears. Mortified, she hid her face in her hands and fought for control, but a gusher had been turned loose by Maria's kind solicitude and there was no stopping it.

"Oh, dear, I didn't mean to set you off," said Maria. It wasn't the first time a customer had been overcome by tears in her shop. She'd heard disturbing tales of negligent or abusive husbands, unwanted pregnancies, puzzling illnesses, mistresses discovered, troubled children, and bill collectors at the door. Maria kept a supply of neatly pressed handkerchiefs in the tea cabinet near the stove for this very purpose. But none of these things could have been bothering Lily, as most involved being married. She fetched a hanky and handed it to Lily.

"What is it, Lily? What has you so upset?"

Lily took the handkerchief gratefully and blew her nose. "Oh, forgive me. I can't think what's come over me. I'm not usually a weeper." She couldn't possibly confess that she'd been attacked and violated. The shame would be unbearable.

"Well, something must have happened to upset you. You needn't tell me if you don't want to, but it often helps to let it out."

"It's just…it's just…it's just that I cannot go on as a visiting girl. It's been a year and a half, and my welcomes are thinning. My friends have been wonderful, especially Caroline, who keeps the invitations coming and puts me up more often than anyone. But I have no home, no family, no roots, no security, no income more than pin money. I'm adrift, and I don't know what to do about it." She succumbed to a second freshet of tears.

Maria held her counsel until Lily had collected herself again, then asked the obvious question.

"Marriage? Is there no one in sight to rescue you from this plight?"

Lily sniffed. "No! That's the point! I've been a social butterfly these past eighteen months, quite against my inclinations, attending every party to which I've been invited, my friends all playing matchmaker. Maria, I refuse to marry just to have a husband. A woman shouldn't have to be rescued by marriage!"

Maria patted Lily's hand. "I understand, believe me. So if marriage is not an option, at least not at the moment, and the visiting life no longer suits you, what then?"

"What then indeed!" Lily sniffed again and blotted the tears from her cheeks. "Do you really think I could make my way as a dressmaker? Could I possibly support myself?"

"If you were desperate enough, yes. Perhaps it would only be temporary. At any time you could meet the right fellow, you know."

"Not likely, if I'm stuck in a basement somewhere sewing myself blind!"

Maria clicked her tongue. "Now you are beginning to sound self-pitying. I had thought better of you."

Lily jerked back in her chair as if she'd been slapped. "Self-pitying?"

Maria smiled and patted Lily's hand. "I just wanted to get your attention. I'm way ahead of you in this game, my friend. When I was a child my family was hounded out of Odessa, in the Ukraine, because my father was heavily involved in a growing nationalist movement."

Lily sniffed and nodded, dreading what was to come and already feeling ashamed of herself.

"I was thirteen. We lost everything. My father scraped enough together by selling our household goods, at least those that were not destroyed by the soldiers, to buy us steerage passage to America. It was a ghastly voyage, everyone sick—filth and smells from the ninth circle of hell. But we arrived. My father had been a professor of mathematics in Odessa, but he spoke no English. None of us did. After we landed in New York, he managed to find work as a janitor at the College of the City of New York. He enrolled in free English classes for immigrants, and eventually he spoke well enough to resume his career as a professor.

"Meanwhile my mother and I worked in a sweatshop, making women's shirtwaists. You want to know about boredom? Losing one's creativity? Sewing under deadlines? We also took home piecework for additional pennies, working far into the night by candlelight. We lived in a tenement filled with other immigrants. Noisy, filthy, unhealthy. My younger brother died from an infected rat bite."

Lily gasped.

"Yes, it was horrible. We had a good life in Odessa. My father was a respected academic. We had a spacious apartment on a pleasant tree-lined street, fashionable clothes, amusing friends, and always plenty to eat. My mother was a wonderful cook. Her family had vacationed every summer in Vienna, where she and her mother took cooking lessons from a celebrated chef. As you can imagine, there was no fancy food on our table during those early years in New York—barely any food at all. No nice clothing, nor any further education for me. I worked, came home, ate if there was anything on the table, worked more by candlelight, and went to bed, all the while silently screaming at fate for throwing us into such a terrible life. I was an angry young woman, let me tell you. Yet in the midst of all this heartbreak, my parents never complained. They always reminded me that in America we were free. Yes, I thought to myself, free to work in a sweatshop and almost starve. But I kept quiet and did my share."

"But Maria, that's awful! How did you pull yourself out of it and end up here?" Lily gestured to the surrounding shelves of books.

Just then a series of loud bangs sounded from the floor above. Maria glanced upward and said, "Oh, pay no attention. It's just a carpenter doing some work for me." She continued her story.

"I met Janik Horacek when he came to make some repairs to our building. Please don't think our landlord cared one jot for our comfort or safety, by the way; it's just that the building was in danger of falling down. If repairs were not made, he stood to lose his income. Anyway, every day for two weeks on my way to work I passed Janik setting bricks on the building's façade. He was friendly, but respectful. The day he finished, he waited until I returned home with my basket of piecework. He asked me to walk out with him the next Sunday afternoon. He was attractive, energetic, clean, and polite. What more could a girl want? I was tired of the long hours and my aching back at the garment shop. My father had finally secured a teaching position, so my mother could retire. Without me to feed, they could manage. He asked me to marry him soon afterward, and I said yes.

"Such a wonderful husband he was. Janik honored and cherished me, as he had pledged to do in our marriage vows. His business thrived, we had a nice home, and soon a baby boy. I was so happy." Her face clouded over. "Then little Karl died of diphtheria. He was only three months old. Janik was never the same. One day at work, perhaps in a moment of distraction over Karl, he missed his step on a scaffold and fell to his death. And there I was, alone and doubly in sorrow."

"Oh, Maria! I had no idea."

Maria grasped Lily by the wrist. "I tell you this not so you should feel sorry for me. I tell you my story to show you that you can overcome anything. You can do whatever you must to survive! Did my mother and I like breaking our backs and stabbing our fingers in the sweatshop, enduring the leering eyes and wandering hands of the supervisor? No, but it kept us alive. Did my father like pushing a broom and emptying the trash at the college, the lowest person in a world where he had once been among the most exalted? No, but it was an avenue toward a greater goal. This is America, Lily! Everything is possible if you are willing to work hard, even you, who have no idea what real work is. If visiting back and forth among your friends is no longer possible, you have a talent that could support you. Think about it!"

Lily's head was reeling—shocked at Maria's revelations, not to mention her insistence that Lily's dressmaking skills could provide her a living. With so much to absorb, she picked up her handbag, stood, and gave Maria a hug.

"I'd best be getting along. Thank you, Maria, for caring. You've given me a lot to think about."

"Stop by again tomorrow," Maria said as she walked Lily to the door. "I have an idea."

Maria's mysterious smile stayed with Lily far into the night.

CHAPTER 16

Lily did not return to the bookstore the next day, nor for many days thereafter. On the night of Lily's visit with Maria, Caroline awakened in the wee hours to a rush of blood. By the time the doctor arrived, it was all over. Caroline lost her baby at just under three months. She was devastated.

In light of the severe hemorrhage, the doctor ordered bed rest for two weeks and took John aside to warn him that asserting his marital rights before Caroline was completely healed would put her in grave danger. In fact, the doctor continued, another pregnancy could prove fatal. He gave John a pointed look, which Lily caught in the mirror above the dresser as she left the room with an armload of bloody towels. They took the doctor's advice seriously. For Caroline, it meant having no further children, a realization that prolonged her emotional recovery from the miscarriage. As for John, he'd just have to make the best of an unfortunate situation.

John wanted to hire a nurse, but Lily insisted on taking care of Caroline herself. She cancelled her next several visits, grateful to be doing something more than marginally useful for a change. Although she worried that Lawrence might reappear unannounced, he did not. She trusted that he felt as mortified by his behavior as she did.

Toward the end of the second week, Caroline was able to get up for short walks around her bedroom. The exercise seemed to buoy her spirits while she grieved for the baby she would never hold in her arms. Lily's company was a great comfort to her.

Tending to Caroline and to young Robert during his nanny's hours off, gave Lily little time to think about Lawrence, or Maria's suggestion—except in the early hours of the morning. No matter what time she went to bed, she found herself wide awake several hours before sounds and scents from the kitchen signaled the beginning of the new day. She tossed and turned, with memories of the attack and anxiety over her future jostling for attention. Sweaty and exhausted, she'd finally fall asleep for another hour or so before waking up for good. On the days when that final stretch of sleep failed her, she dragged herself through her routine, wishing for nothing more than a few hours respite come nightfall.

Several weeks after her miscarriage, Caroline ran out of reading material and asked Lily to run down to the bookstore and pick up a couple of novels. When Lily set the Pretty Cat doorbell jingling, Maria was in the back of the shop shelving a crate of new books. She hurried forward to see who was there.

"Lily! How splendid to see you. I've been so afraid I hurt your feelings or perhaps insulted you with my unsolicited advice. Please tell me you forgive me."

"Nothing of the sort, Maria, there's nothing to forgive. Caroline has been ill. I've been taking care of her and helping with her little boy."

"Oh, I'm so sorry. Is she better?"

"Yes, thank you, she's well on the mend. Nothing to worry about." Miscarriages weren't mentioned in polite society. A woman grieved alone, while not understanding what had gone wrong, and fearful it might happen again.

"You've opened my eyes, Maria, to a truth I was unwilling to confront. I am that wretched being, a woman without a visible means of support, totally dependent on others. I have to do something about it."

Maria puckered her lips. "It's not a death sentence, you know!"

"I know. In the depths of some long nights I think I convinced myself it's an opportunity. And that I need to grab it. So if anything, I should be thanking you."

Maria grinned. "Go ahead."

Lily threw her arms around Maria. "Thank you, my friend!"

"You're welcome! Now, remember I told you I had an idea?"

"Yes?"

"Come with me, right now."

Maria led the way out the door and around the building to a covered staircase at the rear. Motioning Lily to follow her, she headed upstairs, paused on the second-floor landing, and unlocked a new, unpainted wooden door set next to an older one that was as weathered as the rest of the building. She stepped aside and gestured for Lily to enter. Puzzled, Lily pushed open the door and was greeted by the clean scents of freshly sawed wood and paint. She stepped into a small sitting room with a bed set into an alcove along one side, and a counter at the far end with a sink, a cabinet below, and open shelving above—a small but efficient kitchen. The furnishings were minimal—an upholstered armchair and matching hassock, a small wooden table and two cane-seated chairs, a low bookcase under a window, and the narrow bed, neatly covered with a plaid woolen blanket. It was clearly meant as a studio for a single person.

"Why, it's charming," Lily exclaimed, "but I don't understand."

Maria closed the door behind them and sat down on one of the caned chairs, gesturing for Lily to sit on the other. Pushing aside the small vase of pink carnations that she'd earlier set in the center of the table, Maria began.

"Remember when you were last here, and we heard a bump and a crash from above? And I said it was my carpenter? The bookstore has been so slow that I got to thinking about what I could do to supplement my income. It occurred to me that I didn't really need all my living space, that perhaps I could carve out an apartment to rent without missing it. The carpenter did a wonderful job. Do you see how he created the alcove for the bed? He took almost nothing from the sitting room by jutting it out several feet over the alleyway. I'm more than pleased with it."

"As you should be," agreed Lily, still a bit confused.

"Don't you see? This would be perfect for you! You can live here and sew at this table. I bet you could even find a second-hand sewing machine and learn to use it in no time. They're all the rage now, you know. That would increase your efficiency tremendously. I even know somebody who could teach you."

"Well, my goodness," gasped Lily. "I don't know what to say."

"Don't say anything yet. The rent will be modest, and with space for your work as well, you won't have to lease a workshop, at least not at first. Oh, do forgive me for being such a busybody. It's just that I can see it all so clearly, and I know you'll be such a success. Now listen. Berta and Adeline at the second-hand shop are so fond of you. They love it when you show them the fashions you've made from the garments you find there. They are truly impressed with your creativity. We all are."

"It's really just something to do on a boring afternoon," Lily demurred.

"Please, Lily, this is no time for modesty. You've made an impression! And as it turns out I'm not the only one who has extra space. By rearranging a few dress racks, the ladies have offered to create Lily's Corner, a place for you to show your one-of-a-kind creations and possibly pick up special orders as well. They will take care of sales, and you'll pay them a percentage for their trouble. What do you think?" Maria was so excited she practically bounced off her chair.

Lily was stunned. While she had been nursing Caroline, these three women had organized the rest of her life. She felt a flash of annoyance that they had done so without consulting her, then immediately felt ashamed of such an ungrateful thought. They were only trying to help. But could it really work?

Lily returned to Caroline and John's with her mind in a whirl. She'd been presented with a solution to her dilemma by a three-friend cheering section. Her stomach was a-flutter with excitement, yet the fear of branching out on her own, of having to put in long, tedious hours to please other people, of having no idea if she could earn enough money to support herself, threatened to drown any positive feelings about the idea. So many unknowns!

When she closed her eyes, she saw herself running full tilt toward a deep abyss and taking a flying leap across it—arms outstretched, skirts flapping—not sure if the opposite bank even existed, and if it did, whether her momentum would carry her safely to the other side.

Yet the ground on this side of the abyss was no longer safe. It was crumbling beneath her at an alarming rate. She simply could not continue her nomadic lifestyle. She felt more and more like an aging aunt arriving with her dilapidated carpet bag, hoping to be taken in. Nobody had said anything outright, and Caroline's requests on her behalf were only turned down when the family seemed to have a real conflict. But Lily doubted these polite refusals were entirely honest.

She truly believed that Caroline and John would have been happy for her to stay on indefinitely. Except for her fear of Lawrence, that would have been a godsend. But with the possibility of his popping in again at any time, that was no longer feasible. The mere thought of being anywhere near him sent shivers down her spine. She had to get away.

Several evenings later, when Lily returned to her room after saying goodnight to Caroline and taking a peek at young Robert, sweetly asleep in his youth bed with his thumb in his mouth, she found herself too wide awake to turn in. She tidied her room, which didn't take long, then decided to straighten her dresser drawers as well. She quickly sorted through the top drawer, rearranging her hair ribbons, handkerchiefs, her few pieces of jewelry, letter writing supplies, her visiting calendar, and such.

Opening the next drawer, she began refolding her underthings. She picked up her spare emancipation bodice, one of two she had made for herself. It was as tightly fashioned and confining as a corset, but with thick padding instead of the discomfort of whalebone or, even worse, steel stays. Daring women everywhere were ditching those old-fashioned horrors, and not a moment too soon, Lily thought. Perhaps a day would come when women would be freed of any type of confining underwear. What heaven that would be.

As she refolded the bodice and placed it back in the drawer, she noticed her monthly rags stacked neatly at the back, stained but clean, waiting for her next period. She picked one up and ran her hand across the cotton fabric. She'd been appalled when, as a young girl with budding breasts she'd encountered "the curse." What a dreadful inconvenience. Surely a God who had created butterflies and tigers and waterfalls could have come up with a better way to refresh a woman's womb after the monthly disappointment of not conceiving a child. Really, what a nuisance. Soaking the nasty rags in cold water, then scrubbing them with harsh soap and setting them out to dry in the sunshine, discretely out of sight, then folding them away for the next inevitable round.

Most of her hostesses had servants who took care of this unpleasant chore, but Lily and Florence had been taught to do it for themselves. The task was too personal and distasteful, she felt, to ask anyone to do it for her.

Lily paused for a moment, staring at the stack of rags. When had she last used them? She couldn't remember. A jolt of panic shot through her. Her cycle was reasonably regular, so she never bothered to keep accurate track of it. Her flow came when it came, and she had no reason to think about it in between. She'd been so busy caring for Caroline that she'd forgotten about it entirely.

More than a month had passed since Lawrence's assault. Had her period come on since then? She slowly shut the drawer and sat down on her bed.

When, *when* had the last time been? *Think!* She mentally traced back her activities and finally remembered feeling that warm gush when she had stood up from the dinner table at her friend Stacia's home. She had glanced down at the upholstered seat, mortified that she might have stained it. Fortunately, the flow had not seeped through her petticoat and skirt. She had hurried upstairs, cleaned herself, tied on a dry rag, soaked her blemished pantalets, put on a clean pair, and rejoined the party.

Still staring at the rags in the drawer, her stomach turned cold. Dear God, no! She opened her top drawer again and withdrew her visiting calendar. She clenched it to her chest, terrified to open it. Working up her nerve, she raised her eyes to the heavens. *Please, dear God, no. Please don't let it be.*

But there it was. She had left Stacia's seven weeks ago. Her period was three weeks overdue. She'd never been that late before. Even though she didn't keep formal track of her cycle, she was aware of its rhythm. One had to be alert and prepared in order to avoid a messy accident. The timing, give or take a few days, had never failed, nor had there been any reason for it to. Until Lawrence.

Could it be a false alarm? In romance novels, false alarms were a fallen heroine's salvation. That simply had to be it. Just to make sure, she would draw a hot bath and soak in it. She had read about that in novels, too, a sure way to bring on one's period if it was late.

Lily sat in the tub that night until the water turned cold. No sign of blood. She wondered how long it would take, or how many nights she'd have to do it. Shivering, she finally gave up and got out. Should she strap on a rag—or maybe something more capacious like a hand towel—before climbing into bed in case the flow began in the middle of the night? What, *what else*, did it say in novels? She couldn't remember.

Why, oh *why* did everything she knew about female matters come from novels? They were fiction, for heaven's sake, unreliable by definition. Had she read about the hot bath remedy in more than one book? Was it a widely known fact, or just one writer's imaginary rescue of a desperate heroine? Again she couldn't remember. Why didn't mothers pass this information on to their daughters? What was so precious about feminine ignorance?

What a horrid state of affairs, she thought, for a woman's knowledge of her own body to be a matter of secrets, speculation, and conjecture, gathered mostly, if at all, from florid fiction. If you weren't a reader you wouldn't know anything!

As she tightened a bath towel around her chest and tucked it in, she noticed her breasts seemed tender. *Oh, heaven help me.* This was something she *did* know about. Caroline had mentioned that tender breasts were—for her—one of the early signs of pregnancy. She let the towel fall and stood naked in front of the mirror. Did her breasts look slightly swollen? Gingerly she pressed them. It took no more than a gentle push to feel an unfamiliar fullness.

She fell onto her knees on the cold bathroom floor and prayed as she never had before.

Lily slept little that night. If what she suspected was true, she had fallen into the biggest disgrace known to womankind—conceiving a child out of wedlock. The circumstances hardly mattered. Whether from an honest love affair, a lapse of judgment with an inappropriate partner, or rape—the woman was left with the consequences. If it was an honest love affair, they would be married and everyone would cooperate in the fib that the baby was premature. In the latter cases, the woman would have to navigate her way through a maze of lonely, terrifying choices. And if word got out, she could be ruined for any eventual marital prospects.

She flipped over onto her back, thinking the twisting and heaving might dislodge her flow. Nothing. She tried again in the opposite direction, landing hard on her stomach. Again, nothing. What could she *do*? She refused to consider marrying Lawrence. If he had behaved toward her so brutally once, who knew how he would treat her as his wife. On more than one occasion she'd witnessed her host's husband's brutish behavior. She suspected such violence was more common than widely acknowledged, and that wives were simply expected to tolerate it.

Lawrence had never shown a violent temper during her college years. His recent drinking had obviously brought it on. She couldn't imagine living with the potential threat, always wondering when he might drink a little too much and she might provoke him again. Besides, he was a frustrated and unhappy man in his work. What joy would there be in marriage to someone so eternally discontent?

What was she thinking? Of course she couldn't marry Lawrence! Even if her previous feelings of friendship could have developed into love, he had destroyed any possibility of that.

No. She was *only* three weeks late. She would wait it out and see what happened. If she missed her period next week, she would consider her options. For now, it was useless to worry over something that might not happen. Meanwhile, in the larger picture, Maria had thrown her a lifeline, a way out of her life as a visiting girl. Let that be my focus for the next week, she counselled herself, and meanwhile I'll keep praying for the start of my wretched flow.

The week dragged by interminably. Despite Lily's resolve to put it out of her mind, not an hour went by in which she wasn't reminded of her precarious situation. She dedicated herself to Caroline and her family, churning through the days with self-imposed tasks to keep her body occupied and her mind numb. As Caroline was still taking it easy, she brought breakfast to her friend's sitting room every morning. She found she had to sit some distance away while Caroline ate her poached egg. The smell made her gag.

She read Caroline the most interesting newspaper articles; consulted with the cook and housekeeper to make sure the wheels of domesticity turned smoothly; made a nuisance of herself trying to help in the laundry; and popped in on Robert and his nanny in the nursery several times a day, much to the nanny's annoyance. She found no time to continue the dialogue with Maria.

By the end of the week, there was still no sign of her period. Mentally gritting her teeth, she carried on, obsessively checking herself for spotting as often as she could. *Nothing.* By the end of another week, she knew it was hopeless.

CHAPTER 17

The only bright note, as far as Lily was concerned, was that Lawrence stayed away. Perhaps his business claimed all his time; perhaps he was truly ashamed of himself. She didn't know and didn't care. Her own predicament consumed her. After two weeks of failed hot bath treatments, she faced herself squarely in the mirror one morning after dressing and ran her hands down the front of her skirt. Her stomach was still flat, but that meant nothing. If this thing was really happening, she'd better know for sure.

Telling Caroline she had some personal errands to take care of, she took the tram into a part of the city where she was unlikely to encounter anyone she knew. Businessmen striding by with briefcases, women with shopping bags, workmen in soiled dungarees crowded the sidewalk, all intent on their individual errands. Jostling along with them, she walked until she came upon a sign for a doctor's office. Feeling a trickle of nervous sweat inching down beneath her bodice, she gazed up at the three-story brick building. It looked respectable enough. She'd better appear respectable as well.

Spotting a five-and-dime store a few doors farther down, she entered and made her way to the back of the store, nodding at the salesgirl who smiled at her hopefully. Pretending to peruse the bolts of cloth and baskets of sewing notions on the back shelves, she removed her mother's wedding ring from the chain around her neck and slid it onto her ring finger. Then, fighting through her anxiety, she walked back out to the doctor's office.

Seated among the half dozen waiting patients were two women about her age, both noticeably pregnant, one of them holding a toddler on her lap. In a low voice, with her back to them, she asked the woman at the desk to see the doctor regarding a personal matter. The woman quirked an eyebrow, asked for her name, which she gave as Mrs. Paxton, and advised her to be seated until she was called. Greatly relieved that she had not been required to publicly state her purpose, she found an empty chair and tried to still her racing pulse. One by one the other waiting patients were called; then it was her turn.

The doctor entered the small, dimly lit consultation room holding a clipboard and pencil. Middle aged and balding, he sported a crooked tobacco-stained moustache that bounced as he spoke. Keeping his eyes on the clipboard, and not bothering to introduce himself, he asked in a bored monotone if the personal matter involved a possible pregnancy. Lily nodded, startled at his directness—and to hear the dreaded word spoken in reference to herself. Thank heavens her mother's ring shielded her from the doctor's disrespect. He cleared his throat and stroked the lower-hanging side of his moustache, then asked about the timing of her monthly flow. She stated that she had missed two periods. He licked the pencil point and made a note.

"Any other symptoms, Mrs. Paxton, such as vomiting upon awakening in the morning?" he asked.

"No, but I...I've felt queasy and repelled by certain smells. Eggs in particular."

"Hmm. Any tenderness in the mid-chest area?"

"You mean my breasts?"

He peered at her for the first time, as if she had broken a rule by calling them by their proper name. What was the matter with the man, she wondered. Surely he dealt with women every day, pregnant or not, yet he couldn't bear to hear female body parts named?

"Yes, I noticed some soreness a few weeks ago. It hasn't gone away."

He set the clipboard and pencil on a nearby window ledge. "All right, let's take a look. Up, up onto the examination table." He patted the black leather-padded table impatiently. "Recline, please."

Nervously she lowered herself on her elbows, having no idea what to expect. He gently pushed her shoulders down until she was completely prone, then smoothed her skirt over her abdomen and palpated it gingerly. Then a little more assertively just below her navel. She winced at the unexpected familiarity.

"All right, up you get." Awkwardly she did so, with no help from him. While she rearranged her skirt, he scribbled more notes on his clipboard. Finally he looked up, exhibiting an amount of enthusiasm so negligible it appeared to have snuck onto his face without his permission. His lopsided moustache twitched as he delivered his findings.

"Very well, Mrs. Paxton. I feel confident in giving you excellent news. Your baby will be born in about six months, let's say early June, give or take a week or two. Congratulations. I'm sure your husband will be pleased. Eat for two, lots of fresh vegetables and milk; rest when you can; keep your bowel habits regular; don't slip on the winter ice; avoid drafts. Return in two months and we'll check your progress."

Seated once again on a tram, surrounded by strangers, she hugged herself tightly to keep from shaking. How could this have happened? Of course she knew how it happened, she chided herself. Her entire life upended, all because that wretched Lawrence lost control of himself. The whole thing beggared belief. Yet with the various symptoms and now the doctor's confirmation, she could no longer pretend it wasn't true. *Pregnant.* Her mind flashed back to the two expectant women in the doctor's office, one with a little girl on her lap. No doubt they were both upright married women whose husbands would be delighted with the confirmation of their virility.

Absent-mindedly she twisted her mother's gold band around her finger. She had no husband and no hope of one—surely not now. This predicament was hers alone. Could she, should she, tell Caroline now that she was sure? As close as they were, and as much as she knew Caroline loved her, the old cliché was true: blood is thicker than water. Even if Caroline believed Lily that Lawrence was responsible, why would Caroline choose to sympathize with her friend over her brother?

Could she admit to the pregnancy but decline to name the father and the circumstances? Caroline would be puzzled, as she knew there was no man in Lily's life. She couldn't have Caroline assuming she'd had a liaison with one of her hostess's husbands, or, worse, a stranger somehow encountered. If she knew her friend well enough, Caroline would pester her until she broke down and confessed everything.

And if she named Lawrence, could she hold strong against Caroline and John pushing them to marry, supposing they believed her and Lawrence was willing? She couldn't imagine a life with him after what he had done to her.

Around and around her frantic thoughts went, along with the wedding ring, chasing themselves in her head until she thought she would scream. She missed her tram stop, noticing it only when the young man seated next to her stood to leave one stop later. She ran to the exit just in time to jump down to the sidewalk as the tram pulled away. In her haste she stumbled, but quickly righted herself against a lamp post. For a moment she stood there, leaning against the post, breathing deeply, and dreading her return to the Crawfords'.

Glancing around, she realized she was only a few blocks from Pretty Cat Books. Why not delay her return by dropping in on Maria? Yes, Maria was the one person she might confide in. She was older, more worldly, and not socially connected with her circle of friends. More than anyone, Maria could be counted on to be comforting and non-judgmental...or so she hoped.

While she stood dithering, two young matrons, chatting animatedly, strolled toward the bookstore from the opposite direction. They paused to point and giggle at something in the bookstore window, probably Pretty Cat, posed to delight with his black mink fur gleaming. As they entered the bookstore, Lily realized she'd lost her opportunity for a tête à tête with Maria, at least for now. Reluctantly she carried on toward home.

As she passed the bookstore and then flower shop, lost in thought, Marco pushed open the door and called to her.

"Lily! Lily of the Valley! I haven't seen you for a while. My loss," he declared as he skipped ahead a few steps, turned, doffed his cap, and bowed toward her. "I've been working in the fields, preparing them for next spring's blossoms."

In fact they had not seen each other since the day he had walked her home carrying Caroline's flowers. What an eternity ago that seemed, Lily thought. She paused, confused for a moment and not in the mood for exchanging pleasantries, no matter how kind he seemed.

Marco ignored her frown and stepped to her side.

"Have you been well?" he asked, matching his pace to hers.

This most ordinary of questions, meant merely as a conversation opener, stymied her. Am I well, she wondered? I suppose I am, pregnancy being a normal state of biological affairs. But not in my case. I am most emphatically *not* well.

She struggled to reply as noncommittally as possible, while picking up the pace. Perhaps he'd give up and return to his shop. He lengthened his stride and moved right along with her.

"Yes, I've been well," Lily finally replied, a little too forcefully in an attempt to sound convincing. "And yourself?"

Now it was his turn to frown. "Perhaps you are not so well, Lily. I can see that you are troubled."

She looked down at her marching shoes, unable to respond.

He clutched her arm, held her back while a horse and buggy passed close enough to send a whirl of dust onto them, then guided her safely across the street to the park. Seeming to have lost the impulse or ability to protest, she allowed herself to be led to a bench near a skeletal beech tree. Genuinely concerned, he asked her what was wrong. She bowed her head as her eyes teared up. How could she possibly confide in this well-meaning but inconvenient fellow who was just a notch from being a stranger? She shook her head, pulled a hankie out of her pocket, patted her eyes, and knotted it through her fingers.

"Then let's enjoy the sunshine. Close your eyes and turn your face up. There. Doesn't that feel wonderful?" He took a deep breath as if to inhale the golden glow.

Indeed it did. What a simple pleasure, to feel the late autumn sunshine on her cheeks and forehead. For a short while, Lily's troubles fell away in the unexpected enjoyment of the moment. They sat side by side on the bench until a cloud slid across the sun, throwing the park into shadow. With the shadow came a chill.

Marco stood and offered Lily his hand. Warily, she took it. For a man who worked on a farm, his touch was surprisingly tender. He pulled her to her feet and tucked her hand into his elbow, clasping it snugly against his side. This simple act seemed to Lily the most comforting gesture anyone had offered her since Florence had died. As they strolled back toward the street, she closed her eyes and tipped up her face again to savor another burst of sunshine, letting him guide her along. Then, remembering that she hardly knew him, she pulled away slightly and cut him a glance, wondering at his motive. Looking straight ahead, chin up, sporting the smile of a proud and happy man, he gently drew her back to his side. She found herself smiling too, ever so slightly. What an irrepressible fellow.

They walked the few blocks to the Crawfords' house in companionable silence. He seemed content to respect her privacy, a consideration that allowed her to relax. Their bodies touched from shoulder to hip as they strolled, but to her surprise such forbidden proximity did not frighten her. In fact, it felt reassuring. He delivered her to Caroline's doorstep, gently removed her hand from the crook of his elbow, bowed over it slightly, and murmured a soft goodbye. The immediate loss of intimacy left her feeling strangely bereft.

Lily watched Marco's retreating form until he was at the end of the walk and onto the sidewalk. As she pushed open the front door, she looked back in time to see him wave a jaunty goodbye. What an extraordinary turn of events, she mused. To be so terrified of a man she had known like a brother for more than five years, yet to be so at ease with this fellow with whom she had had only two brief encounters. And to feel such a loss as he strode away down the block, whistling of all things.

Closing the door quietly, she listened for activity in the house. If Caroline had seen them together she would have pounced with a million questions, questions to which Lily had no answer. She hoped her friend was occupied with her son in the nursery and had observed nothing. Once in her room she remembered the wedding ring. Quickly she slipped the gold band off her finger and re-threaded it onto the chain around her neck. Marco must have noticed it when he bowed over her hand to say farewell, but he had continued to respect her privacy.

CHAPTER 18

Over the next few days Lily remained quiet and withdrawn, overwhelmed by the implications of the turn her life had taken. She did her best to be sociable when required. As she was accustomed to spending great swaths of time reading and sewing in her room, Caroline failed to notice anything amiss. Lily had become so much a part of the family that her movements and moods were not much remarked upon. As Caroline continued to gain strength and resumed her normal routine, Lily had time to ponder.

During these lonely hours, various options careened through her imagination like wild horses on a mad carousel, each option less suitable than the last.

Marrying Lawrence was impossible. She must banish it from consideration and waste no time on it.

She could take a six-month tour of Europe and give the baby up for adoption there. This was the most sensible solution, a sure way of keeping her plight confidential. How melodramatic, she thought, but certainly not unheard of among young women of her class. Alas she had no money with which to finance such an indulgence and nobody she could ask for a loan. Uncle Arnold would rub his fat hands in satisfaction to see her come begging in such a predicament, then likely refuse. Aunt Sophie? As generous as she'd occasionally been, the amount needed would require Uncle's consent. Asking Caroline and John would entail confessing everything, which she must avoid for Caroline's sake. Besides, they had already done enough for her.

More practically, she could flee to another state where she was unknown, assume the persona of a recent widow, take in sewing, and live in a respectable boarding house until the baby was born. Then she could give it up for adoption, with discrete arrangements made in advance, returning to Philadelphia apparently no worse for the wear. Or she could continue the deception of widowhood, stay there, keep the baby, and raise it alone. A daunting prospect.

Or she could brazenly remain in Philadelphia, have the baby, and keep it. Oh, the scandal! Perhaps Caroline would allow her to continue living there—assuming she believed Lily's side of the story—and act as nanny to both their children. She couldn't imagine Caroline being that accepting, nor could she see herself in that stifling role, ever at Caroline's beck and call, regardless of how much she loved her.

Perhaps Caroline and John would adopt it now that they had lost their own child? Particularly if they knew it was Lawrence's child. *There I go again,* she thought, *impossible thinking.* She had to keep Lawrence out of it.

What about her nascent plans with Maria, to rent the new apartment above the bookshop and design dresses for the consignment ladies to sell? She'd been downright rude in not getting back to Maria and telling her if she was interested or not, but between her concern for Caroline and her despair over her own pregnancy, she hadn't taken the time to consider it. How could she carry on with such a plan while *enceinte*? She'd be branded and shunned as a loose woman.

Then there was the last resort: abortion. She'd heard terrifying rumors of filthy instruments, butchers masquerading as doctors, raging infections, and uncontrolled hemorrhaging, often leading to the death of the mother. And if one tried this desperate route, how did one go about it? How would she pay for it?

Every time she spiraled down to this final option, she gritted her teeth to keep from crying out in despair. Why, oh why, was female biology engineered in this way? How could something as precious as a child come about in such a thoughtless, brutal manner? How could the creation of a human life, the most precious thing we know, be subject to mere happenstance, without a lick of affection between the parties, and in her case, via outright violence?

In the same house where Caroline mourned the premature demise of a welcome child, she secretly quaked with fear of birthing one. Finally she could bear it no more. She had to confide in someone who could help her sort things out.

As Lily entered Pretty Cat Books, Maria glanced up from behind the counter where she stood tying up a parcel for a customer and gave Lily a nod. This time Lily decided she would not be put off by the presence of other customers. The end of the day was near. She would wait until the last one departed.

"Why, hello, Lily," said Georgina Mackenzie, a neighbor of Caroline's. "I've been meaning to drop by for a visit with you and Caroline. I hope she's doing well?"

Lily put on her best smile. "Oh, yes, Georgina. She's up to her ears with young Robert. You know how three-year-olds are. He never gives his mother a moment's rest."

"Surely it's time for Caroline to have another. It doesn't do to let one child claim all of his mother's attention." Word of Caroline's miscarriage had apparently stayed under wraps. If anyone had heard about it via the grapevine, it would have been Georgina.

Lily took a deep breath. "Perhaps it is, Georgina. But let's leave that up to Caroline and John, shall we?"

Maria handed Georgina the wrapped packet. "Thanks for coming by, Mrs. Mackenzie. I'm sure you'll enjoy every one of these books, and Mr. Mackenzie will be so pleased with the mystery you chose for him."

"Thank you, Maria. I'll be back for more as soon as I've read them, you can count on that." She gave Lily a guarded look. "Goodbye, Lily. It's been nice seeing you. Please tell Caroline I'll call on her soon." The bell above the door tinkled as she left. Lily released her breath, relieved to see her go.

"Lily, how nice to see you," Maria exclaimed, hurrying out from behind the counter. "I've been worried about you. Have I once again overstepped in trying to arrange your life? It wouldn't be the first time I've been scolded for being a busybody."

"Not at all, Maria." Lily glanced around the bookstore to make sure they were alone.

"Lily, what is it? Was it too much to consider, setting up shop as a dressmaker? You did tell me you want to have an independent life, and with your talent, it seemed such an ideal solution."

"No, Maria. Yes, Maria. Ah, it's more than that, much more than I knew the last time we spoke. Oh, why is life so difficult?" Lily burst into tears, instantly berating herself for yet another self-indulgent display and for being unfairly annoyed at Maria for having this effect on her.

Maria hastened to the door, turned the key in the lock, and flipped the sign in the window from "OPEN" to "CLOSED." She took Lily by the arm and led her to the private nook at the back of the shop.

"Come on now, sit down, and tell me what's so terrible. I know it's frightening to consider opening a business of your own, but I'll be here and the ladies in the consignment shop can hardly wait to set up Lily's Corner. I haven't had a chance to tell you this, but I have located a used sewing machine for you at a good price. You'll be up and thriving in no time!"

Her friend's cheerful enthusiasm made her sob all the more.

"Let it out, Lily. Cry as you must. It's safe here. No one will see you. No one needs to know." She rose, put her hand briefly on Lily's shoulder, then passed Lily a handkerchief from the folded stack in the tea cabinet. Turning to the stove, she added water to the kettle and prepared a fresh pot of tea. By the time she sat down again with two steaming cups, Lily had composed herself. She closed her eyes and inhaled the smoky oolong brew. Colorful visions of an East Indian marketplace bloomed in her mind. She took a sip and allowed her head to clear.

"Thank you, Maria. What is it about hot tea that is so comforting?"

"Mostly, I believe it's the company it's served with it. A solitary cup is nice, but sharing is nicer."

Lily smiled and nodded. Now that she had calmed down and had Maria's undivided attention, she hesitated. How to begin? What to say? She felt herself flush at the shame of it all.

Maria reached for her hand. "Come on, Lily. Something has happened. Please tell me so I can help you."

Lily took a deep breath and stared at the braided rug on the floor. She thought briefly of the doctor and his unconcerned directness. "I'm pregnant." There, it was out. Like Aladdin's genie, impossible to shove back into the lamp.

Maria's eyes widened. "Pregnant? I don't understand."

"I've been to a doctor. According to his reckoning, I am about three months along."

Maria frowned. "How is it possible? I didn't know you had a gentleman in your life."

"I don't."

"But…?"

Lily ran her hands over her hair in a gesture of despair. How could she explain without telling Maria everything? Yet how could Maria help if she did not know the full story?

"I was forced…raped." She closed her eyes and turned away, not willing to witness any judgment on Maria's face.

"*Raped?* Look at me! This is serious! What happened? Were you out walking late at night?"

Here goes, thought Lily, all my fault. She hadn't expected this from Maria..

She gulped down a mouthful of tea, then cleared her throat. "Lawrence, Caroline's brother, got drunk one night, stole the key to my room, and forced himself on me when I was half asleep. At first I had no idea what he was doing. I fought as hard as I could, but he's very strong—a champion oarsman, as it happens. Before I knew it, everything was over, and here I am, with child."

"Dear God, that puts a whole new light on things, doesn't it? What will you do?"

"I don't know. I was hoping you might help me sort through it. I can't tell Caroline. Even if she believed me, she'd surely take her brother's side. If she did stick up for me, it would affect their whole family, and I don't want to be responsible for that. Their parents were so good to me on college weekends and vacations. It's such an unspeakable predicament. Everything is stacked against me. No matter what I do, I carry the shame and the burden and Lawrence gets off scot free. It's so unfair!"

Maria sighed. "A woman's burden has always been unfair. Don't forget Adam and Eve. Humankind's descent into sin and hellfire is all Eve's fault, so says the Bible, and we're still suffering for it. Nonsense, of course, but there you are."

Lily felt her eyes tear up again.

Maria stamped her foot. "Now stop, Lily. No more tears. The obvious thing is for Lawrence to marry you. Will he do it?"

"*I* won't do it! I wouldn't consider it. I'd hate every minute of living with him, not to mention having to suffer his nightly attentions. I considered him a friend, but after this it would be hell on earth."

Maria put up her hands in protest. "All right, obviously you've made up your mind about that. A marriage lasts a long time and should at least begin pleasantly."

Lily nodded and took a calming sip of tea. "I've considered a sojourn in Europe and adoption there, but I haven't the funds. Escape to another part of the country, posing as a recent widow? I'm not sure I have the courage, either to put the baby up for adoption or to raise it alone. Brazening it out here among my friends? Unthinkable. No matter what I do, my life is ruined."

Maria put a calming hand on Lily's knee. "Perhaps it seems hopeless right now, but surely not forever. We just have to get you through the next six months. Would you consider—I can't even bring myself to say it—

Lily put down her cup and saucer on an unpacked box of books beside her chair. "I'll say it. Abortion."

Maria glanced around as if checking that nobody could overhear them, even though she had locked the door after her last customer. She leaned across the table toward Lily and lowered her voice.

"You know, my customers are very chatty while they're browsing the books. They behave as if I'm deaf, for heaven's sake. You'd be amazed at what I overhear, but I keep things to myself. Except if the information might be useful to someone. I could give you the name of a doctor…"

Lily knitted her fingers together and raised her fists to her chin. "I don't know, Maria. It sounds so frightening and desperate, not to mention dangerous."

"The person I'm thinking of, the customer I overheard, apparently emerged unscathed. She was engaged to be married but, from what I could deduce, pregnant by another man and the timing of the birth would have betrayed her. I was shocked when she came in to buy a book a week later, yattering away as if nothing had happened. Three weeks later she was married, and apparently no one's the wiser."

Lily blinked in surprise. "That sounds so cold and…harsh. I just don't know. Even if I could face it, how would I pay for it? I have almost no money, certainly not enough to pay for such a thing. And nobody I could borrow it from without divulging what it was for. And…I don't know…it may even be too late. I have no idea how timing affects safety."

Maria was quiet for a moment, her thoughts drifting off and her face suddenly saddened. Lily realized she was not thinking about finances or timing.

"Oh, Maria, I'm so sorry. You're remembering your son, aren't you? Your poor dear little boy. How insensitive of me to engage you in a discussion about…about terminating a pregnancy."

Maria's eyes glistened. "Karl would be almost finished with school by now, ready to make his way in the world. But forgive me. I have

173

no right to let my feelings intrude. You have to live with whatever you decide, not me."

Suddenly Lily wanted to be home and alone. She stood and held out her hands to Maria.

"Thank you for listening, Maria. Just talking with you has helped. I have much more thinking to do, and I'd better do it quickly. I'll run along now. You've been wonderful, truly."

Lily made it through dinner that night with John and Caroline, grateful there were no guests. She managed to respond to Caroline's light chitchat, even chuckled at a cute story she related about Robert and his new obsession with overturning rocks in the garden and squealing when bugs scurried out. Shortly afterward John excused himself with a cup of tea and a piece of cherry pie and returned to a manuscript in his study. Lily told Caroline she felt a cold coming on and thought she would turn in early. Caroline did not object, saying she'd had a tiring day. An early night suited her as well.

Lily undressed, sponged off, and tucked in, but the sandman eluded her. She got up again and donned her dressing gown and felt slippers. Up and down she paced, arms crossed over her chest.

Maria's sorrowful reaction to the topic of abortion had hit her like a bucket of icy water. What was wrong with her? All she had been focused on was *her* life being in ruins. The rape, unspeakable though it was, had resulted in the creation of a child. *A child!* A child as dear and wondrous as Robert, as darling as the sweet little girl in the doctor's office, as deserving of love as Maria's tragically lost son. Maria would have given anything to have her son alive, and here she was thinking of destroying a life just as precious.

No, she could not and would not terminate the pregnancy. The child in her womb deserved a chance at life. None of this was its fault.

But adoption? Could she really carry a child for six more months, feel it kick in her womb, go through the agonies of childbirth, then turn it over to another woman to raise? She would forever wonder if the chosen parents were good to the child, if they provided a proper education, encouraged its talents, especially if it was a girl, and most importantly, if they truly loved the child. Would a child of hers speak a foreign language instead of English? Would it be tall, short, fat, thin? Dark, fair? Pretty or handsome or plain? Intelligent or dull? Would it yearn to find her, provided it learned it was adopted, or hate her for giving it up? Or, perhaps even worse, know nothing about her at all? Oh, so many things to wonder about for the rest of her life and never to know the answers!

Shivering despite her dressing gown and slippers, she climbed into bed without disrobing. How could she live with the uncertainties of adoption? Surely an agency wouldn't give the child to anyone who would not cherish it and raise it properly, but how could she be certain? As there were with abortions, there were horror stories of adoptions—children sent out as unpaid farm laborers, or to work in dangerous factories or mines; children adopted by unscrupulous and evil parents who took advantage of them in appalling ways. How could she be sure this would not happen to her child? My God, what if no one wanted it, and it grew up neglected and unloved in an orphanage?

Sunk in despair, one of her earliest childhood memories came to her. She was four years old and afflicted with chicken pox. She was feverish and itched all over. Her mother had tied on cotton mittens to keep her from scratching. Late one evening, she awoke miserable and crying, unable to keep from scratching despite the mittens. Her mother, pregnant with Florence, tried to calm her down with cold compresses and soothing words. Nothing helped. Finally, in desperation, Mary Louise climbed into bed with her daughter, turned her on her side, and spooned in behind her. The gesture was so unexpected that Lily stopped crying. Her parents had always been affectionate, but more by word than deed. She relaxed in her mother's arms, feeling as if she were enveloped in a nest of warm goose down. Suddenly the itching no longer mattered. As she began to drift off, she felt a light push from her mother's stomach against her back, and then another one.

"Mother? What's that?"

Mary Louise hugged her tighter. "That's our new baby, stretching its legs."

"You mean the baby inside you? You can feel it move?"

"Yes, just as I could feel you before you were born." Her mother kissed the back of her head. An observant child, Lily had known there was a baby growing in her mother's stomach. Mary Louise had never hesitated to answer her questions. But still, she was astonished at this revelation. As she continued to marvel at it, the warmth and softness of her mother's body, along with the knowledge that her new brother or sister was snuggled in with them, came over her. She'd never felt so comfortable, so loved and secure. Soon she drifted off, but the memory of that feeling never left her. Even now, Lily wondered at the extent of her mother's love, that she would climb into bed and hug a child covered in scabs.

She lay on her back and laced her fingers protectively over her stomach. She pictured the child already born and in her arms. An incredible warmth suffused her, the same glow she'd felt that night with her mother and the unborn baby's kicks. She had felt it again when her mother had let her hold Florence the day she was born. And again as her mother lay dying in her arms, wrapped in the same sweet love, this time from daughter to mother. Now it came upon her again, that indescribably protective love she had experienced at those emotional milestones in her life; had yearned for all these years without knowing it. Somehow she must find a means of keeping and raising this baby. *Her* baby!

She turned sideways and snuggled deeper under the blankets. What would it be like, this child of hers and Lawrence's? Could she possibly love a child of rape, whose father she not only no longer respected but despised? Lawrence had done an unforgivable thing to her, but it would only have the power to destroy her if she let it. Surely he had not deliberately set out to harm her; sober, he would never have done such a thing. Could she rise above it to despise the act, but not the actor?

But what if the child were a boy and looked exactly like him? That would be a bitter pill to swallow. Although…she had not known Lawrence as a baby or a child, only as a young adult. Perhaps she would love the child so completely that, even if he did come to resemble the grownup Lawrence, it wouldn't matter.

CHAPTER 19

Despite her disturbing memories of Lawrence, Lily managed to doze off just before dawn. Her restless night took its toll, however. As Lettie and Caroline helped her downstairs to the sunroom after breakfast, she wondered if she had the strength to carry on recapping her tale for Caroline.

How could she tell Caroline *any* of this? She must have been out of her mind to think that making a clean breast of the past would solve anything. Now she sorely regretted writing that fateful letter urging Caroline to come to Portland. But here she was, waiting to learn why Lily had left Philadelphia without saying a word. Could she find a way to continue the story, making sense of her sudden marriage to Marco, their precipitous departure, and her silence all those years…without making any mention of Lawrence? But leaving Lawrence out of it wasn't the point, not anymore.

Settled again on the chaise longue, with the sun dancing mid-morning shadows on the lawn, Lily said a silent prayer for guidance. Lettie brought them iced lemonade and ginger wafers and reminded Lily to call if she needed anything.

Lily pulled the Amish quilt a little higher. "Did you notice, Caroline, the blue willow cachepot on my windowsill upstairs? I had one just like it in my room in Philadelphia."

"Of course. It's lovely. You left the original behind, and I've set new plants in it every spring in your honor. It still thrives on my kitchen windowsill. One of your visiting hostesses gave it to you, as I recall."

Lily hesitated as she grasped the quilt's brown border in her fists. "Not exactly. Do you remember a morning shortly before I left when you noticed that I wasn't quite myself?" The sequence of events came flooding back as she relived them for Caroline.

"You're looking a bit peaked this morning," observed Caroline, with little Robert astride her hip. "Is everything all right?"

Lily confessed that she was a bit worried about her visiting schedule. She hadn't mentioned it earlier, as she did not want to appear to be critical of Caroline's efforts on her behalf.

"I'm sorry, Caroline. You've been so wonderful about keeping me circulating, but I sense people are wearying of me."

"Surely no one has said such a thing? Certainly not to me! I can't imagine such rudeness."

Lily smiled and shook her head. "No, but I can tell my welcomes are cooling off. Even the girls at Bryn Mawr are impatient with me. I can't count on them any longer to pick up the slack. Besides, it's not much fun being there when I'm no longer a student." She stopped and put her hands up to her cheeks. "Just listen to me. I sound like an ungrateful ninny!"

"Well, you're always welcome here. You were such a help in the aftermath of my miscarriage. I truly don't know what I would have done without you. You are welcome to stay as long as you like. If it doesn't suit you to keep circulating, you can just stay here indefinitely. Let that be the last word on the subject."

Lily stood and walked to the other side of the dining table to give Caroline a hug. "You are so good to me. I don't deserve such a generous friend."

"Of course you do. We'll say no more about it. Now, I'm off to do a little shopping and meet Floria Duval for lunch. Do you want to come along?"

"No thanks. I need to sponge off a few of my dresses. When I'm finished with that, I'll fix myself a quick lunch and spend the rest of the day reading. I picked up a new book at Pretty Cat and can't wait to dive in."

"All right then. I'll just grab my coat. We'll see you at dinner, dear."

On her way upstairs, Lily stopped in the kitchen to fix herself a cup of tea. As she turned to go, through the window she saw Marco marching up the rear walkway, carrying what looked like an arrangement of greenery in a shallow pot. Puzzled, she opened the door, certain Caroline had not ordered flowers that day.

Propping the pot on his hip, Marco tipped his cap, bowed slightly, and said, "Lily of the Valley, just the person I hoped to see. The last time I walked home with you, I sensed you needed some cheering up. I've been out at the farm this past little while, so here is something to make you smile again. A pretty girl should not be unhappy."

Standing on the stoop, he held up his gift: a blue and white ceramic cachepot, planted with a seedling pine tree and a few small leafy plants, their roots nestled in moss.

"Why, I've never seen anything like it," she exclaimed as she set her cup and saucer on the countertop. "It's a miniature garden!"

"I created it especially for you, from young houseplants I've been experimenting with on the farm."

"And the bowl—it's exquisite!"

"I found it at a second-hand stall. It's genuine Chinese porcelain. See the blue willow design?" He pointed to the two Chinese figures outlined in deep cobalt against a white background, running across an arched bridge under a weeping willow tree. "See, the young couple are fleeing."

"Why? From whom?"

"Perhaps from her parents, who don't want them to marry? Maybe the fellow was unsuitable in some way. Who knows? I have crowned their tale with greenery, and they will be happy with you. Please, accept your blue willow garden." He held it out to her.

"But Marco, really, such an extravagant gift!"

"For an extravagant Lily!" He stepped closer to the open door.

She backed up a step. Accepting such a gift would break the rules of what an unmarried woman might accept from a man she barely knew, yet his expression was so endearingly earnest and devoid of any hidden agenda. She reached for it, bent over, closed her eyes, and inhaled its earthy scent. Finding the pot surprisingly heavy, she turned to put it on the counter before it slipped from her hands.

With his cap tucked under his arm and his fists in his pockets, Marco beamed at her.

"Now, it's not for the family," he cautioned. "It's for you, for your room. Put it on the windowsill so it gets some sunshine and be sure to water it moderately twice a week. I want to think of you smiling every time you see it. Will you do that for me?"

The idea of him thinking about her doing anything in her bedroom made her blush, but then she thought, why not? I have so little that actually belongs to me. Surely I can have this clever little garden in my room. It's an innocent enough gift.

"Thank you, Marco. I'll enjoy it. It's very kind of you."

"You are most welcome." He paused, twisting his cap in his hands and rocking on his heels, then looked up at her again. "May I press my luck? Will you walk out with me this afternoon, Lily? All week the neighborhood children have been raking up the leaves in the park. Have you seen the pile? They'll light a huge bonfire as soon as it's dark. Will you come and enjoy it with me?"

For a moment she was shocked, then thought, he's so handsome and so sweet. Surely it would do no harm. After all, it's the twentieth century. A woman could go walking with a fellow from down the block if she wanted to. Caroline might raise a questioning eyebrow, but she and John were invited out for the afternoon and evening, so they'd never know. Besides, she and Marco would be outside and in full view. She'd be safer than she'd been in the Crawfords' house on the night of Lawrence's attack.

She intertwined her fingers beneath her chin. "I'd be delighted, Marco."

He slapped his cap on his thigh. "Wonderful! I'll come for you just before dusk—four o'clock, let's say. Until then, be happy, Lily!"

He turned, hopped down the steps, and made haste along the walkway before she could change her mind.

Smiling, Lily watched him go. Such a good-natured fellow. She lifted the blue willow bowl, turned it this way and that to view the entire enchanting scene, then took it upstairs to her room and set it on her windowsill. When she finished sponging her dresses, she returned to the kitchen to make a sandwich and hunt for an old plate to put under the cachepot so it wouldn't mar the windowsill finish. Her tea had long since cooled, so she poured herself a fresh cup and took the tea, the sandwich, and the extra plate up to her room.

When she settled down to read by her bedroom window, she found herself captivated by the blue willow scene on the cachepot, now at eye level and perfectly lit in the afternoon sunlight. The white and blue porcelain positively glowed. Who were these two young people, and why were they fleeing over the high arched bridge? Who was that threatening figure chasing them? What had made their life at home so unbearable?

Willing herself to relax, she picked up her book and tried to read, but her thoughts kept returning to the blue willow lovers. Did the legend end happily, as the two love birds overhead might suggest? Or did it end in tragedy, lost at sea in the boat awaiting them on the other side of the bridge?

As the clock ticked slowly toward the time for their rendezvous, Lily nodded off in her reading chair, awash in the warmth of her feelings for Marco. By the time they met at the end of the Crawfords' walkway at four o'clock, well wrapped for the autumn chill, the landscape was fading. The air was sweet with the scent of late season apples that had fallen from trees along the roadway. The park swarmed with children, dogs, parents, and young couples like themselves. Many had brought lanterns, which they swung back and forth as they made their way toward the huge pile of dry leaves.

Moving toward the front of the crowd, Lily and Marco watched as several men thrust burning brands into the pile. Flames shot up, and soon the entire heap was ablaze. They backed up a few steps as the smoke assailed them. With the heat of the fiery conflagration on their faces, Marco drew Lily close to him. She glanced up, but his face betrayed nothing except fascination with the flames. She leaned in, just the slightest bit, to let him know she was happy to be with him. He turned and softly kissed her cheek. Heat that had nothing to do with the fire flashed through her. She was so startled that she later wondered if she had imagined it, but every time she thought of it, the same shocking warmth shot through her. She had never experienced anything remotely similar and had no idea what to make of it. She only knew she liked it.

Lily learned a great deal about Marco as they continued to meet every few days for an afternoon stroll. She left the house daily an hour before dusk, creating a routine that Caroline never questioned, and made sure she wasn't gone too long. She never knew when Marco's schedule would permit him to join her but was always delighted when it did.

They met around the corner, out of sight of the Crawfords' home. Lily had enough on her mind without trying to explain their friendship to Caroline. Besides, it meant nothing. It could *only* mean nothing, so there was nothing to explain.

During their walks, Lily began to comprehend what Marco meant by living in the present. She reveled in the excitement of being with him, enjoyed his irrepressible optimism, and was content with his company without making any projections into the future. They both understood that, as the immigrant florist's son, he was not a suitable caller.

As Lily spun out her story for Caroline these many years later, she recalled how Marco's live-for-the-moment attitude had colored her thoughts about the baby. When she found herself questioning her decision to keep it, a quick run-through of the options always brought her to the same conclusion. She already loved the baby; it was *hers*. Beyond that, she was unable to picture what her future with a child might look like. Intellectually she knew she needed to deal with it, but she found herself in the same stalled quandary she had faced just prior to her Bryn Mawr graduation. The future loomed ominously, yet she found herself unable to make any meaningful plans. Whenever it became too overwhelming, she reigned in her thoughts and, thinking of Marco's happy-go-lucky attitude, tried to remind herself that things would work out in some way that she just didn't know about yet. Acknowledging this memory, then leaving it behind, Lily continued her tale. As always, Caroline listened eagerly.

During their walks, Lily quickly discerned that Marco was much more educated than she might have supposed. He read the daily newspaper and subscribed to several weekly news and opinion periodicals, as well as being a steady customer of the public library. His formal education had ended at grade eight, as he was needed to help his parents in the business, but he had informed views on a wide variety of subjects, backed up by facts and figures. She found herself listening with interest as he expounded on everything from the tangles of ancient European history to local Philadelphia politics.

His English was flawless, with an occasional odd phrase he must have picked up from his parents, or an inflection that betrayed his working class background. His stories, never too long, were often hilarious, but he made sure the conversation went both ways. He wanted to learn about her, too, while respecting her boundaries. He understood that she was a woman far above him socially. He felt honored that he spent these precious hours with him and did not want to scare her away by trespassing any further into her personal affairs than she willingly let him.

When he joined her one afternoon, she saw immediately that he was out of sorts. She'd not seen this side of him before. It heartened her, as she was beginning to wonder how anyone could be so upbeat all the time. As they started along the sidewalk, Lily could barely keep up with him.

"Marco, slow down! What's wrong?" She pulled on his sleeve to stop him.

Plowing ahead, he made a fist and drove it into his other palm. "Oh, that old man. He makes me so angry."

"Your father? In what way?" She trotted a few steps ahead of him, then turned around, forcing him to halt.

He reached out and put his hands on her shoulders, a liberty he had not taken since the afternoon of the bonfire. Realizing what he had done, he dropped them immediately. "I'm sorry. Forgive me. I have no right to subject you to my angry mood."

Discomfited, they stepped along side by side again, both looking straight ahead. Then she turned to him.

"It's all right, Marco. Tell me why you are so upset."

He threw up his hands and shook his head. "Look, I go to night classes in business and agriculture. I'm learning how to farm and run the shop in scientific ways. We also learn about marketing. Do you know what marketing is?"

"I'm guessing you don't mean going shopping with a big basket for fresh meat and produce. Surely they don't give classes in that?" Lily meant it as a joke, but Marco was not in the mood.

"Certainly not. It's a different kind of marketing, a modern concept. It includes everything you might do to make your product known and increase your sales. In addition to paid advertising, it might include giving your customers something free now and again, so they like doing business with you and spread the word. Or donating your product to a charity where it will be noticed. Or making news with your product so it will be reported in the newspaper, free of charge."

"That seems fairly obvious. Why would you need to go to school to learn that?"

He turned to her, skipping sideways to maintain his pace. "Oh, Lily! I love your honesty! There's much more to it than that. I was just giving you a few simple examples. Already you cheer me up!"

Feeling a bit condescended to, Lily frowned. "Well, if that's all it takes to lift your spirits, you can't have been all that depressed."

"I can't feel depressed when I am with you. You are my tonic. You always cheer me up."

Shaking her head, she took his arm and they continued on in a more lighthearted way.

The plan was for Marco to eventually take over the flower shop, but he was much more ambitious than his father. He had newfangled ideas, and he backed them up with knowledge he acquired in his evening classes. He spent the weeks between class sessions in the country where, over the years, his father had invested in several farms and greenhouse operations—one of the things Marco had suggested with which his father had agreed. Marco learned a great deal about farming for the flower trade by pitching in with the hired hands. He was happiest with his fingers in the soil.

He had been getting more and more exasperated with his father, however, for old Mr. Giannotti refused to hear any more of Marco's ideas for modernizing the business. The man had done better than he could possibly have anticipated in America and was satisfied with the status quo. But another flower shop had recently opened in the next block, with an aggressive young owner. Their business had slowed down as the new florist sought out the opportunities that Giannotti's once had all to itself, and cultivated others that reflected his modern thinking. Marco began to believe that the only way he could get ahead was to move away and begin again on his own. He mentioned this casually to Lily one afternoon.

"Where would you go?" she asked, surprised at how much the idea distressed her.

"I don't know, but if I had a good woman to go with me, I'd leave tomorrow."

"My goodness, he said that? Out of the blue?" asked Caroline.

Lily held out her glass for Caroline to pour her more lemonade. "Yes, out of the blue."

"So you just up and took off with him? You hardly knew him!"

Lily shrugged. "It wasn't that simple, Caroline. Behind his seemingly casual attitude, Marco struck me as a serious fellow, thrifty, hardworking. He read books and newspapers, went to school to better himself. He was well informed and open-minded. But he also had a playful sense of humor. I found his company enchanting. He was so refreshingly different from the men in our set. And, of course, he was awfully good looking!" Lily fluttered her eyelashes at Caroline like a flirtatious schoolgirl. Her enchantment with her husband shone through, even after all these years.

"Yes, I can see it all turned out well, but at the time, how ever did you find the courage?"

Lily yawned behind her thin, veined hand. "Ah, therein lies the crux. Let me rest for now, Caroline. I tire so quickly. Perhaps you and Lettie could help me upstairs. I think I'm done in for the day."

But how to tell Caroline the rest of the story? Back in her bed, unable to sleep, Lily fretted. How could she tell it without destroying her family and Caroline's?

Even the maximum dose of laudanum that Dr. Jaworski allowed her was no guarantee of oblivion, but she hadn't mentioned it to anyone yet. She needed to think clearly. She lay awake in her dimly lit bedroom, trying to surmount the pain, going over and over in her mind the end of her visiting days.

CHAPTER 20

Tuesday morning's post brought a letter for Lily, addressed in Sabrina Whitman's familiar hand. Assuming it was a note confirming her visit three days hence, arranged as usual by Caroline, she tucked it into her pocket to read later. How she'd miss her walks with Marco, but it couldn't be helped. A change of scene would do her good. Perhaps she'd be able to think more clearly away from him.

At dinner that evening Caroline described a fall young Robert had taken during the day, but assured them that, aside from his injured feelings, his little knees were only bruised. John smiled indulgently, and Lily tried her best to be interested. He was an engaging child, and Lily loved him, but as each day passed her thoughts and fears regarding her own unborn child were causing her to pull away from him. He was a constant reminder of her precarious and unsettled state.

"By the way, Lawrence is coming for the weekend," Caroline said, patting her mouth with a napkin after a bite of peach cobbler. "I thought we could invite a few friends for dinner on Saturday evening. It's been a while since Lawrence has been here, more than three months, I think. I'm a little irritated with him for neglecting us. I'm sorry you won't be here, Lily. You two are wicked bridge partners."

Lily froze. She knew exactly why Lawrence hadn't visited recently. Thank God she'd be off to Sabrina's before he arrived. But how long could she keep dodging him?

"Lily, what's wrong?" Caroline asked. "You look like you've seen a ghost."

"Oh, nothing. I'm just tired. Would you mind terribly if I went upstairs after dinner? I have a lace collar to sew on a dress, and I'd like to get it done before I leave for Sabrina's."

"Of course. Get a good night's sleep. Perhaps tomorrow morning we can take Robert to the park if it's not too cold. Just before lunch, so he'll be good and tired for his afternoon nap."

"That would be lovely," said Lily, hoping her voice did not betray her. As soon as decent manners permitted, she bid them good night and retired to her room. Her plan for the evening was indeed needlework, but it had nothing to do with sewing on a lace collar. She intended to go through her dresses and decide which ones could be let out to accommodate a thickening waist. Once again she blessed her mother for teaching her to sew.

As she shut her bedroom door, she remembered the letter in her pocket. She took it out, looked at it to confirm it was indeed from Sabrina, and tossed it, unopened, into the wastebasket near the washstand. Then her sense of propriety got the better of her. One didn't just toss out a note that a friend had taken the trouble to pen, regardless of one's certainty of its contents. It might contain important information, perhaps a change in transportation arrangements from the train station to Sabrina's home.

She opened the envelope and scanned the note hastily. Then again, with a sinking feeling.

> *Dear Lily,*
>
> *I know you are counting on coming to us on Friday, and I am so sorry to disappoint you. My sister Julia has taken ill, and I must go to her in New Jersey. I'll be taking the children, as it looks like I'll be there for a while.*
>
> *I hate to disappoint you at the last minute, Lily dear, but I have no choice. Please stay in touch, and when Julia has recovered we'll be delighted to have you again.*
>
> *Affectionately, Sabrina*

Dear God, what would she do now? She crumpled the note in her hand and threw it back into the waste basket. She could not possibly stay at Caroline's with Lawrence on hand. Nor did she feel she could impose on any other friend with so little notice, especially as she'd been feeling unsure of her welcomes lately. Even the dormitory at Bryn Mawr was out—the girls had been clear about that the last time. Suddenly the trap had sprung, and she was out of options.

Unable to concentrate on sorting through her dresses, she paced the floor, from window to door and back again. After a few rounds she kicked off her shoes to prevent Caroline from hearing her and knocking on the door to inquire about her unrest. Eventually she undressed, sponged off, donned her nightgown, and climbed into bed.

She tried to still her mind by imagining herself on a pleasant walk with Marco and almost succeeded. The comforting memory of her hand tucked into his elbow. His carefree laughter, his sincere interest in her life and her feelings.

As she was finally drifting off, a new thought charged in from nowhere. She sat straight up in bed. Did a father, not wed to the mother, have rights over a child? What if Lawrence learned of the child and tried to claim it? Child welfare agencies were known to step in and remove a child from a mother they deemed unworthy or unable to care for it according to their harsh standards. They'd certainly disapprove of an unwed mother. If Caroline, God forbid, joined Lawrence in trying to take the child, they might easily prevail. Caroline could offer it a secure, traditional home; Lawrence financial security. Did an unmarried mother have *any* rights over her child if someone related and better suited contested them?

She tumbled out of bed and splashed her face with water from the pitcher on the washstand. What a dreadful thought! She could never allow that to happen. She crawled back into bed and pulled the covers tight. There she lay, huddled protectively around the babe in her womb. In the morning she awakened exhausted after a few short stretches of troubled sleep. In the early hours an idea had come to her, an idea so outrageous that she thought it might actually work. As she considered it, still tangled in her bedclothes, she gradually became aware of the sounds and scents of breakfast. A sudden surge of energy propelled her out of bed.

Nauseated by the thought of eating, she dressed, fixed her hair, donned her coat, scarf, hat and gloves, and slipped unnoticed out the back door. With determination she marched down the street toward the shops. Halfway there, her steps began to falter. Nervously she clenched her fists in her coat pockets. Could she do it? Did she have the courage? How would she live down the embarrassment if her gambit failed? And how unimaginably different would her life be if she succeeded? She daren't think about it for one second longer, or she would lose her nerve. If she had learned anything from Marco about living in the moment, this was it.

She took a deep breath and pressed forward. When she reached Giannotti Florist, she ignored the fastened shutters and the "Closed" sign in the window and pushed open the door. Mrs. Giannotti, carrying a basket of evergreen boughs, looked up from her task of filling the vases on the display counter, setting up for the day.

"Yes? We not open yet. You need something?" she asked in her heavy accent, without the slightest hint of warmth. Her severe expression told Lily exactly what she was thinking:

This girl sometimes came on behalf of one of her steadiest customers, so she dared not offend her, but she wasn't going to be pleasant either. This girl was too friendly with her son. Aside from his death, she couldn't imagine a worse tragedy than Marco taking up with a girl who was not Italian.

Lily's voice almost deserted her. "Um, actually, I wondered if...if Marco is here." God in heaven, it never occurred to her that Marco might be working at one of the farms today.

Mrs. Giannotti planted her fists on her hips. "Marco? You want him take flowers home for you again? He can do this afternoon. Right now he fix something for me."

At that moment Marco strode in through the curtained doorway behind the counter. "It's all done, Mama. The leak is stopped. No flood today." He grinned at her as he wiped his hands on his apron.

Then he noticed Lily and stopped. For a moment he was speechless, but quickly recovered.

"Ah, Miss Lily. You are early to buy flowers, but never mind. What would you like today?"

Her eyes darted to his mother, then back to him.

"Ah, yes, flowers," she murmured, as if this were the last possible reason for being there.

"Oh, uh, the yellow freesias over there and some greens." She pointed to the display vase that was furthest from Mrs. Giannotti. Silently she willed Marco to grab them, wrap them quickly, and carry them out of the shop before his mother could interfere. Anything to get away from that woman's thunderous frown.

"Yes, a dozen stalks of those," she continued. "Lovely, I can smell them from here. And yellow is so cheery on a gloomy day. What a good mix of open flowers and buds. I'm sure they'll all unfold in the warmth of the house and be perfect for Saturday's dinner party."

Now that her tongue had loosened, it chattered on mindlessly with no direction from her. She clenched her teeth in frustration. Marco must think her an idiot. Mrs. Giannotti was still staring at her, no longer hostile exactly, but looking oddly perplexed.

With a grin, Marco picked out twelve of the most luscious yellow stems, added a thirteenth for good measure, and wrapped them in newspaper with some of the nearby greens.

"Come along, Miss, I'll walk a few steps with you. I need some air. Mama, don't worry. I'll be right back, I promise."

His mother harrumphed and returned to distributing the evergreens among the vases, obviously displeased by this turn of events.

"What a nice surprise," Marco said as he offered her his arm once the door was closed behind them. With the shutters closed too, there was no need to wait until they were in the next block to keep his mother from observing this small intimacy. Suddenly Lily didn't care. The morning was crisp, the sky was clear, and she was tucked snugly against him as they walked.

Marco pulled away slightly.

"What is it, Lily?" he asked, examining her profile to get a better read of her mood. "You are not yourself today."

She was silent for a moment, then replied, "No, Marco, I'm not myself. Not at all."

"Are you ill? Someone in your family is in trouble?" She had told him of the death of her parents and sister, and of her aunt and difficult uncle, so he knew she had no living, caring relatives. But family was family, and when disaster struck old animosities should be set aside.

She stopped and turned to face him on the sidewalk, withdrawing her gloved hand from the crook of his elbow and clasping both hands together at her waist to keep them from shaking. As she glanced down to compose herself, she realized she had assumed a protective shield over her unborn child. For the first time outside the sanctuary of her bedroom, the child became real to her. What happened next would determine its future, one way or another. The staggering import of these next few minutes rendered her lightheaded. She grabbed Marco's arm for support.

He dropped the bundle of yellow freesias on the low rock wall on the inside of the sidewalk and shifted her hand off his arm so he could put it around her waist and support her better.

"Take it easy, Lily. I've got you. Let's get across the street to the park where we can sit down." Forgetting the flowers, he led her safely across and down a grassy slope to their favorite bench near the lake. As it was a school day, the only other park-goers were a couple of nannies with their charges tucked into high-wheeled buggies, crunching around the lake on the gravel path.

Feeling a little steadier, Lily let Marco guide her to the bench, where they both sat down. He put an arm around her shoulders and snuggled her against him. She melted into him, savoring the warm feeling. But there was serious business to discuss, and she was determined to tackle it. Even one more sleepless night alone in her room, endlessly exploring and rejecting possibilities, was intolerable. She had to grasp her only chance, however unlikely it might seem.

What could she say? How could she say it in a way that didn't cause him to recoil and stomp away in disgust? Did she even have the right to suggest such a thing, something that involved heartache for his family and huge challenges for them both? A leap of faith that she had no right to ask of him?

"What is it, Lily? It hurts me to see you so distressed. You must know I care for you a great deal. Please tell me what has made you so unhappy."

At the look of concern on his face, tears welled up and threatened to overwhelm her, but she fought them back fiercely. This was no time for womanly weakness. She could not allow herself to be overcome by her doubts and fears. But how could she lay her problem on such a good man? He deserved a woman of virtue, not soiled goods. "Please, Lily, out with it. I can't help you if you don't tell me what's wrong."

His anxious look almost undid her. She squeezed her eyes shut, took a shaky breath, then repeated the remark he'd tossed out on their recent walk. He had made the comment out of frustration with his father, but she grasped it as a lifeline.

"Would you really run off to a new town and start all over again if you had a good woman to go with you? I can't say I'm a good woman, but if I would do, I'll go with you."

There. It was out. She couldn't take it back. Her heart pounded, the muscles in her neck tensed, and her hands knotted in her lap as she awaited his reaction. For a moment he stared at her, as if wondering if he'd heard correctly.

"Run off with me? You'd do that?"

She nodded, steeling herself for a lighthearted admission that he'd been kidding. When he continued to stare at her, she pushed forward on the bench and stood—poised to dash away, appalled at her boldness and certain she could never face him again. He reached for her arm and gently pulled her back down.

"Really, Lily? You'd come away with me? Forever?" A lopsided grin lightened his expression and his dark eyes began to dance as he dared to believe what she was suggesting.

Lily had prepared herself for scorn, ridicule, disdain, derision—indifference at best—anything but this! She was so taken aback by his seeming pleasure in the idea that she *did* burst into tears. But they were no longer the stinging tears of despair that had plagued her night after night alone in her room. She could barely remember what tears of joy felt like, but here they were, spilling down her cheeks in the most abandoned fashion.

Marco jumped to his feet, then turned around and crouched in front of her. "Lily, my Lily of the Valley, tell me one more time—you'll really run off with me to wherever the wild winds take us?"

She nodded again and ventured a smile. Here was this good man, crouched at her feet, keen to take her away to a new life. The sheer delight in his eyes as he looked up at her, his hand on her knee, looking happier than any fellow ought to be—what more could she ask for? Then reality clamped down, unbidden, and she twisted away from him, dislodging his hand and feeling its loss. She hid her face in her palms, feeling all the joy drain away.

Confused, Marco whispered, "Lily? You're not changing your mind, are you? You really said you'd go with me."

Oh, if only it were that simple, thought Lily, struggling to clear her head. When she had thought it through last night, she knew she had to tell Marco the entire truth. She would not, could not live a lie, even if she thought he was naive enough to believe a bouncing baby born five months after their wedding could possibly be his. She'd gone this far, and Marco had surprised her. A moment ago she'd been soaring with elation, yet everything could still be lost. She brushed away her tears with the back of her hand, turned to him again, and murmured a quick prayer that she was doing the right thing.

CHAPTER 21

He sat down beside her again, puzzled but attentive. "Lily, why so serious all of a sudden?"

"Listen, Marco. Please listen." She steepled her hands at her chin and closed her eyes. She could not look at him while confessing her shame.

"I'm carrying another man's child. The child will be born in about five months. I have explored every possible option, including…including the unthinkable, but I couldn't face destroying a life that lives within me, and I can't countenance any other possibility. The truth is, I love this child, and I want to give it a good home with loving parents, as my parents did for me." She stumbled a couple of times while rushing to get it all out before she could change her mind. Then she took a deep breath and forced herself to slow down. Finally, she looked up at him.

"So you see, Marco, my proposition is not so simple. I'm not only offering to run away with you. I'm asking you to accept my child and to love it as your own. If you do not truly believe you can do that, I will walk out of your life and take another path. I'll raise the child alone and make the best of it."

Now it was Marco's turn to lose his powers of speech. An unexpected calm settled over Lily as she watched him struggle. Her tension drained away now that the dreaded truth had been spoken. The next move was up to him.

She relaxed against the back of the bench and waited, her fingers once again knitted across her stomach. She watched Marco walk slowly to the edge of the lake. He bent over to pick up a handful of pebbles and threw one with angry force over the rushes into the water. He fired off four more in quick succession, watching as each one set off ever-expanding and intersecting ripples on the lake's surface. He stood as still as the surrounding trees, bare of their leaves in the windless air. He seemed mesmerized by the complexity of the wave patterns, patterns that were as complicated as his life had suddenly become.

Lily waited, surprised at the calmness the unburdening had brought her, yet realizing that what he did next would determine her future and that of her child. When he finally turned around and began walking back toward her, his face was ashen, as serious as she had ever seen it. She leaned forward, shoulders tense again.

Marco sat down, this time at the far end of the bench, not touching even the outermost flare of her skirt on the seat.

"Who is the father, Lily? This is something I must know!" His eyes blazed, and his fists tightened in a fighting stance. Suddenly she felt afraid. What kind of fury was she about to unleash in him?

But of course he would ask that question, she realized. Any man would. Would he try to kill Lawrence? Dear God, that had never entered her mind. With Lawrence dead and Marco in prison, what good would that do anyone? And it would destroy Caroline. Dear Caroline must never know any of this!

"Marco, please! No, I don't want any harm to come to him. Or to his family. Or to you!"

"You still care about him, that you don't want him harmed? Is that it? And you think I would do such a thing? No, I just need to know, or I will wonder for the rest of my life. Please, Lily, while we are being honest, tell me. I must know everything." He relaxed his fists and pushed his hands under his thighs in a visible effort to calm himself.

For the rest of his life—did this mean there was hope? She took a sharp breath and tried to explain as succinctly and unemotionally as she could.

"You know I frequently stay with Caroline and John Crawford. Of course you do. Caroline's brother Lawrence works in New York City. He often comes to the Crawfords' for weekends, but, believe me, I had no interest in him except as a brotherly friend. He is unhappy in his work and has taken to drink. One night after a dinner party he went too far. Caroline and John had gone to bed. I stayed downstairs to tidy up. These little things are the least I can do in return for their hospitality."

She knew she was rambling, but Marco's deep brown eyes never left her own. He showed no signs of impatience, or disbelief. He could have accused her of purposely dallying late at night, believing Lawrence found her attractive. Of trying to comfort him in his unhappiness. Marco's unblinking attention gave her the courage to continue.

"The three of us were friends during my college years. Caroline and I were hopelessly young in his opinion, but when none of his buddies were around, he played cards with us, and we sometimes attended his rowing regattas. But that day everything changed. He was rude to me in the hallway after breakfast, and he tried to get his hands on me late in the evening as I was tidying up the library after a dinner party. I ran upstairs to my room, but when I tried to lock the door I discovered the key was missing. I was frightened, but as time went by the house remained quiet. I assumed he had continued to drink and fallen asleep on the library couch. I finally managed to sleep as well, trusting the danger had passed. Until I awakened to find him...well, please don't make me go any further." Tears were threatening again.

He reached across the distance that separated them and covered her hands with his.

"And you never told anyone?" he whispered. "Not even Caroline?"

"How could I? I wasn't even sure what had happened. And besides, who would they believe, me or Lawrence? Caroline would never believe her brother could do such a thing. I could hardly believe it myself! He'd usually been pleasant...until recently. He'd occasionally spoken to me disrespectfully, always when John and Caroline were out of earshot, but I never saw him lose control until that horrible night. He left the next morning before breakfast, thank goodness, and I've not seen him since. But I just learned he is coming home this weekend. I have to leave the house before he arrives. I can't possibly face him, Marco, and I have nowhere else to go. My plans for a visit to another friend's home have fallen through. In fact, I really can't carry on as a visiting girl, not in my condition. People will begin to notice."

He lowered his head and rubbed the back of his neck. "Yes, you must get away from this man. I understand. And you don't want to destroy Caroline's love for her brother. Less understandable, but I accept that. She is your friend and none of this is her fault."

"Yes, Marco! And you must never mention it either, to anyone. Promise me!"

He nodded, understanding such a promise was important to her. "But we are dancing around what really matters, Lily. If you are uncertain of what happened, how do you know you are...in a family way?" His eyes flicked down to her waistline, which revealed nothing yet, then back up to meet her gaze.

She gazed off across the lake. "I've been to a doctor."

"Ah." He closed his eyes and removed his other hand from hers. That simple gesture, the removal of the connection to a vital life force that had briefly flowed between them, a force that had given her the courage to tell the whole truth, left her feeling totally bereft. He was still sitting on the park bench with her, yet he had emotionally withdrawn all warmth and support. Baring his teeth, he ran his hands through his hair again and again. Still, he said nothing.

Certain that all was lost, Lily hitched forward on the bench and began to stand again. His hand shot out and stopped her.

"Not yet," he declared. "I haven't thought it through. You've had weeks to think about this. Give me at least a few minutes." He stood up without looking at her. "Stay here. Wait for me."

He jammed his hands into his coat pockets and jogged off along the gravel path around the lake. Lily's eyes didn't leave him for an instant. After a while he slowed to a walk, head down, with the heavy, almost shuffling tread of a man wrestling with inner demons. Her hopes plummeted as she watched his figure retreat, until it was a dark silhouette against the gray sky where the far side of the lake and the horizon merged.

As he passed the halfway point, directly across from her, Lily saw him slowly raise his head and once more run his hands through his hair. His gait gradually lengthened and lightened, as if his thoughts had cleared. His pace quickened; his coat flapped open behind him.

She hadn't moved since he'd left her. She couldn't. She was afire to know his thoughts, yet owed him this time to grapple with the challenge she had thrown him. As he rounded the lake and continued toward her, she tried to read his expression, but he was still in shadow. She felt lower than she ever had in her life. All hope fled.

Finally ending his journey, he threw himself onto the bench, his coat wide open, breathing heavily from what had become a run along the last quarter of the path. With his head tilted back, his eyes closed, he finally murmured, "Lily, my Lily of the Valley. I have loved you from the first moment I saw you walking past the shop window. I wondered, who was that young woman walking with such confidence, as if nothing in the world could ever strike her down."

She whispered, "And here I am, struck down as low as a woman can go." She felt her heart contract. What more was there to say?

He straightened up and moved closer to her, still not touching, but meeting her gaze for the first time since he'd jogged off around the lake.

"Ah, but that is not how I see it. Bad things happen, and the true test of character is how we manage these bad things. I have much time to think as I plow and plant seeds, or pull weeds in the flower beds, or drive the delivery wagon around town. In those endless hours, how else can I occupy my mind, than by considering the larger questions of life? This is what drives my father crazy. 'No think,' he says to me. 'Just do. Otherwise you pull up new flower starts with the weeds, or you drive the horse into a ditch. No think!'"

She couldn't help but smiled at the image of old Mr. Giannotti— short, stocky and balding—hopelessly exasperated with his self-educated, intellectually curious elder son.

"But you know, Lily, a walk around a lake on a cool morning is a good time to think too. So. You will go away with me? Let's do it!"

"Oh!" Lily exclaimed. A quiver of excitement ran through her, but she knew their discussion wasn't finished yet.

"Yes, but I have one more question to which I must have an answer. The most honest answer you have ever given," Marco said. Blinking, she raised a hand to stop him.

"Before you ask me that question, Marco, I have two questions for you. And these answers are also important. As much as I would like to just take off and hope for the best, I must know."

He bobbed his head and gave her the merest hint of a reassuring smile. "Go ahead. Your questions, then mine." He reached for her hands and once again she felt a surge of warmth and encouragement from him.

"Very well. This child is completely innocent. I cannot make you love it, but I do expect you to treat him or her fairly. My Uncle Arnold took Florence and me in after our mother died, but he treated us like the poor relations we were, especially me—always a burden— while showering attention on his own child. Aunt Sophie wasn't as bad, but all children deserve fairness, even if love is absent."

"Lily, look at me. I love you; therefore I will love your child. He or she will be *our* child. Not only in fairness, but in love. That I promise. As I circled the lake, I could see us together, the three of us, a happy family with perhaps a few more babies to come. I pledge to you, that I will love all our children exactly the same."

She closed her eyes and gripped his hands tightly.

"There, that wasn't so hard. Your second question, Miss?" he prompted.

"I've told you the circumstances of my fall from grace. I don't want to talk about it again, ever. Can you agree to that?"

A touch of exasperation shaded his reply. "First of all, you must get over thinking about it as a 'fall from grace' or 'being struck down,' or any other euphemistic term people use to describe these things. *Euphemistic*, don't you love that word? I learned it only last week. It allows people to acknowledge things they are taught not to name. Ridiculous." He waved an arm as if tossing the concept away.

"If this hadn't happened, Lily, I would have continued to invite you for walks, enjoyed with you such things as the bonfire, given you flowers from time to time. Eventually I would have married a plump Italian girl of my parent's choosing, all the while pining for the Bryn Mawr girl I would never have dared to court properly. Your so-called 'fall' is the biggest blessing life has handed me. A beautiful, intelligent wife and a baby, when ten minutes ago I had hope of neither. I consider myself a fortunate man." He sat up straight and thrust out his chest.

"Thank you, Marco. But you haven't answered the question. Can we leave the subject of…of…"

"Of the rape behind?" he stated with more force than he intended.

"Oh!" Lily gasped at the sheer honesty of the word on Marco's tongue.

"Yes, that's what it was. No euphemisms. Rape. And none of it was your fault. Remember that."

"All right, Marco. Can we please leave it behind?"

"Yes. I myself have no wish to speak of it further."

"And you won't allow it to erode our relationship, or your feelings for the child, by running it over and over in your mind?"

"No, if the subject comes up, I will remind myself that, regardless of how terrible it must have been for you, the result is a blessing for both of us. That I promise."

She hadn't realized she had been holding her breath. She exhaled in a rush.

"Thank you Marco." It suddenly occurred to her that she had one more question. "But where will we go?

"Not so fast. It's my turn to ask you a question. Now that I think about it, two questions. Fair is fair, agreed?"

"Oh, yes. I haven't forgotten." She tried to smile but feared these last questions might undo all the cautious bridge-building they had managed so far. Their destination really didn't matter.

He took her face in his hands and looked into her soul. "I've told you that I love you, Lily, have loved you since the day I first saw you. But can you possibly love me? I am tempted to think that I love you enough for both of us, but honestly, I do not think that works out so well. It's not so good to start married life with love on just one side. It can only result in unhappiness and resentments. What do you say, Lily? Can you love me, even just a little?"

She threw her arms around him. "Oh, yes, Marco! You are so alive compared to the other men I know. So full of fun, yet so serious when the situation calls for it. I know you'll be a fine husband and father. You are also very handsome, in case you hadn't noticed. You delight me in every way."

He pulled back from her, just enough to be face-to-face again. "Well, that is more than I had hoped to hear!"

He slid off the bench onto one knee, cap in hand.

"My last question, *cara mia*: Will you marry me?"

"Yes, Marco, oh *yes!*"

CHAPTER 22

They agreed to leave quickly, before anything unexpected could interfere. By the best of luck, the Crawfords planned to depart the next morning to visit John's family, as they often did, and would be away for a week.

In a fever of excitement, Lily spent the next two days packing her trunk, a wood-braced leather steamer that opened in the middle, with a set of drawers on one side and a rod for hangers on the other. Set on its end, the trunk served as a two-sided wardrobe, perfect for someone who took all her worldly possessions wherever she went and literally lived out of her trunk. In her traveling valise she stowed her sewing paraphernalia, a few treasured books, writing materials, a change of underwear, and a few other personal items. She still didn't know where they were going, but that was just as well. If she didn't know, she couldn't tell anyone.

She penned a brief note for Caroline. Had they been home, she doubted she'd have succeeded in keeping her excitement or activities under wraps.

> *My dearest friend,*
> *My days as a Visiting Girl are over. It was a marvelous idea, and I thank you for organizing it. The time has come for me to move on.*

As you read this, I will be on my way to a new life. I appreciate all you have done for me. You will never know how much. Forgive me for running off in the night. I cannot say good-bye; to do so would be to stay. That I cannot do either.

Please know that I am leaving of my own free will, and that I embrace this new life with open arms. When the time is right for an explanation, it will be forthcoming.

I love you, and I thank you and John for everything. Again, please forgive me.

Your Lily

Then she spied her visiting diary on top of the dresser. She thumbed through it, each dated appointment bringing back a flood of memories, most pleasant, some not. The last one, to Sabrina's on Friday, she crossed out. She retrieved Sabrina's crumpled letter from the wastebasket, smoothed it out and stashed it at the crossed-out page.

The pages that followed were mostly blank. There were only a few future visits for Caroline to cancel. She folded the note, added it to the diary, and set the book atop the dresser. She knew that nothing she could say would prevent Caroline from falling into a frenzy of confusion and concern, but she saw no other way. She would miss her best friend terribly, but she pushed aside her sadness, along with her crushing feelings of guilt, and carried on with her packing.

Toward dusk, she remembered the one person who needed a personal goodbye: Maria. She grabbed her coat and hurried down the street, only to find the bookstore closed. A glance upward at the light in the second-floor windows told her Maria was at home. She ascended the exterior stairway behind the shop and knocked on the weathered door.

"Lily! What a surprise. Come in!" A cold gust of wind hastened Lily inside and blew the door shut behind her.

"I won't stay, Maria. I've just come to tell you that I'm leaving Philadelphia with my soon-to-be child. You know my situation, and you know why I can't stay. I can't tell you where I'm going or who I'm going with. Sooner or later Caroline will come 'round asking if you know anything. I don't want you to have to lie to her any more than necessary. I'm leaving her a note, saying I'll write and explain when I'm settled. For now, that's all I can do. I've got to keep Lawrence out of it, as I've told you, for Caroline's sake. It also occurred to me that if he knew, he might attempt to take the baby away from me."

"Oh, surely not!" Maria raised her hands to her cheeks in disbelief.

Lily nodded. "Likely or not, I can't take a chance. I have no idea what my rights are and whether his would supersede mine because he's a man. I can't wait while trying to find out. So please, Maria, I beg you. When Caroline asks, please say you know nothing. It's a terrible burden to put on you, but please, *please* keep this secret for me, and for Caroline."

Maria pulled Lily in for a reassuring hug. "Of course I will, Lily. Keeping secrets is what I do. Think no more about it. I will miss you terribly, but if this is what you need to do, then Godspeed."

"Thank you, and also for all the planning you've done for me regarding a career as a fashion designer. It's ungracious to turn my back on your goodwill and friendship, but I must. Please convey my regrets to Berta and Adeline. Say no more than necessary, will you? They were very generous to offer me Lily's Corner in their shop. I apologize for letting you all down."

"There's no need to apologize, Lily. Go with our blessings. We'll all miss you." With another hug, Lily was out the door, trailing the glow of Maria's affection as she hurried along.

As she walked, Lily wondered what was going on in Marco's mind and how he would handle his own getaway. They hadn't discussed it, and she could only hope that things would go smoothly despite his overbearing mother—soon to be her mother-in-law! He had simply told her to be ready with her packed belongings at five a.m.

Late in the evening, after a last look in the empty dresser drawers and the small wardrobe in the corner of the room, she swung the two sides of the upright trunk together, fastened the brass latches, clicked the lock into place, and turned the key. Done. Now she only had to trust Marco and wait.

She stretched out on the bed, shoes on and fully clothed, certain she was in no danger of falling asleep. The next thing she knew, Marco was gently shaking her shoulder in the dark.

"Lily," he whispered. "Get up. We have to leave, right now."

"Marco! What time is it? How did you get in here?"

"The back door was unlocked. I knew this was your bedroom because I've seen the blue willow pot in the window. Come on, it's after five. I told my parents I would be driving out to the farm earlier than usual, so my mother got up and insisted on making me breakfast. Can you imagine? Luckily my suitcase was already in the wagon. I could barely eat a bite. Then she wanted to make sure I understood the sermon Father Pagliarini gave on Sunday about chastity, and how it applied to young unmarried men. Sweet Heart of Jesus, give me patience!"

Lily suppressed a grin, glad that he couldn't see her expression in the dark.

He wheeled in a dolly, onto which he loaded her trunk. He maneuvered the trunk along the carpeted hallway and down the stairs. Following behind, Lily blessed the heavens that John and Caroline were away. All that thumping would surely have awakened them.

Quickly along the downstairs hall, through the kitchen, and they were out the back door. Lily locked the door with the key that was always left under a rock beside the bottom step. Between them, they managed to shove the trunk into the wagon, followed by the dolly, while the horse stood patiently in her traces.

"Oh, that was masterful, Marco!" Lily said as they climbed up to the plank seat and Marco took up the reins.

"I had many wakeful hours thinking about how to accomplish it without disturbing the neighbors. I'll sleep on the train." He clucked to the horse. "Come on, Signorina Fiore, let's go."

"What will we do with Fiore and the wagon? Everyone who sees it will know who it belongs to."

"There are always young kids hanging around the station, ready to earn a few pennies carrying luggage and running errands. I'll pay one of the older boys to drive it back it to the shop. Fiore knows the way if she's given her head."

"Did you leave your parents a note?"

"No, I'll send them a wire from a station down the line. I didn't want to take any chances of my mother finding out too soon and sending my father or my brother to stop us."

She clutched his sleeve. "They couldn't stop us, could they?"

"No, but they could make an ugly scene. We don't need to start our new lives that way. My brother will be thrilled, because now he will inherit the business. It's not easy being the younger son in an Italian family, you know." Lily squeezed his arm in commiseration. "What about the Crawfords?" he asked. "You told me they'd be out of town."

"I left them a note, thanking them, assuring them that I was safe, and asking them not to worry about me. When I can figure out how to tell them, I'll write. But Marco, don't you think it's time you told me where we're going?"

Marco tossed his cap in the air and hollered, "Oregon!"

"Oregon?"

"Yes, *cara mia*, can you think of a better place? I've read all about the Willamette Valley, as rich as any farmland in California. A man can live free there, get his hands in the dirt, build a new flower business, and raise a family with no complications. Oregon!"

Lily didn't know what to think. She knew nothing about Oregon, except that it was a whole continent away. Yes, a whole continent away from Lawrence. She had trusted Marco this far. So be it.

It broke Lily's heart to leave the blue willow garden behind, but there was no room for it in their luggage. In fact, Lily realized, she and Marco had become the blue willow lovers, running across the half-moon bridge to a new life.

Seated together on the open wagon, the first real snowfall of the season drifted around them.

CHAPTER 23

Finally Lily's memories loosened their grip, and she dozed off. Fighting her way back to consciousness later in the afternoon, she glanced toward the chair near her bedroom window where Leticia usually sat and saw Caroline instead, head down, dozing.

In a rush, it had all come back to her—the rape, the pregnancy, and her precipitous decision to run away with Marco. How much more could she, *should* she tell Caroline? Everything had depended on Marco and his miraculous willingness to make things right for her and her child not quite twenty years ago. Now everything depended on Caroline to make things right again.

Caroline stirred, raised her head, and looked around as if unsure of where she was. Then she spotted Lily, wide awake but looking so fragile tucked under the Amish quilt, her head nestled on an embroidered pillowcase. Caroline straightened up and ran a hand over her hair.

"Oh, Lily, you're awake!"

Lily chuckled. "Looks like you had a little nap too. I'm sure you're still catching up from your train journey."

"You don't know the half of it! My daughter warned me about the many things that could befall a woman traveling alone, but even Nancy couldn't have dreamed up what I've been through."

"Tell! I want to hear everything! Enough of my stories—I've talked your head off since you arrived. I haven't even had the courtesy to ask about your journey from Philadelphia." Lily clapped her hands, animation returning to her features. She listened attentively as Caroline related her tragic misadventure with Donalee,

210

appalled by what she heard, but at the same time relieved that more telling of her own story could be put off for a while longer. She needed more time to finesse the telling.

"So that's it, Lily. The hospital said they would notify Donalee's family in Seattle and send on her remains and belongings. A police officer escorted me to the police station door, as anxious to get rid of me as I was of him. I took a taxi to Union Station, boarded the next Pullman train west, and here I am. Fortunately I encountered no further drama between Chicago and Portland, but I feel so badly about Donalee. Nobody should have to be that desperate to get out of a marriage and pregnancy, or to have to die that way."

"I hear about back street abortions all the time, Caroline. They happen way more often than anyone knows. And not always among unmarried women, as one might assume." Lily rolled her shoulders and shifted slightly on her pillows, but she wasn't strong enough to do herself much good.

Caroline rose to help her. "You hear about abortions? But why would you...?"

Lily smothered a groan with her hand. The sleeve of her bed jacket fell back and exposed several ugly bruises on her arm. Another manifestation of the leukemia, Caroline thought with a shudder.

"Forgive me, Carrie. Could you please find Lettie and ask her to come? I hate ringing that bell. It makes me feel like a hopeless invalid...which I am."

"Of course." Caroline patted her friend's hand and turned to leave, realizing she would need to pay close attention to the cues that indicated when Lily was strong enough for company and when she was at the mercy of her illness.

"Tomorrow, Caroline, I'll tell you about my life here in Portland, and later why I'm so affected by your Donalee's story. Meanwhile, Marco and Lettie will be delighted to have your company at dinner. Do ask her to come to me now, please."

That evening Caroline, Lettie, and Marco sat down to a savory roast of lamb, crusted with rosemary and served with mint sauce, mashed

211

potatoes, and nary a trace of Italian herbs. It was superb. A low floral centerpiece of lavender azaleas fluffed out with baby's breath graced the center of the table.

"We have succeeded beyond our wildest dreams," said Marco, launching into his favorite story. "If I sound like I'm bragging, please don't take it that way. We've worked hard, saved as much as we could, and embraced good fortune whenever she chose to smile on us."

Eager to learn all she could about their life in Oregon, Caroline said, "Still, it must have been difficult. None of the comforts of Philadelphia, I'm sure."

"Yes, in the beginning we could barely feed and house ourselves. I found work at a sawmill. After we'd been here for some months, I'd saved enough of my wages to start my own business. I found an abandoned wagon out in the woods, repaired it, fashioned it into a flower cart, and set up at a busy downtown street corner. If business slowed down, or someone took exception to my presence there, I just moved along. Portland was a pretty wild town back then, but the ladies were determined to tame it. Flowers on the dining table—how civilizing!"

"Where did you get your flowers?" asked Caroline.

"I walked around town, asked a lot of questions. People were friendly and helpful. After a few days, I hired a horse and rode out into the countryside to see what I could find. The Willamette Valley has some of the richest farmland on the West Coast, a big reason why so many settlers followed the Oregon Trail instead of heading south to California. Along with wheat, fruit, and hazelnuts, many of the farmers' wives had flower gardens. Several jumped at the chance to expand their plantings and supply me."

"Your delivery boy Jimmy greeted me with a bouquet of peach-colored roses at the station. They even smelled like peaches. I was delighted!"

"Ah, yes, you'll see roses all over the city during the summer. They grow like weeds here. Astonishing! In any case, it wasn't long before

I was able to open a shop downtown. It's a great location, and Giannotti Florist West is still there today."

Marco forked his last piece of roast, slathered mashed potatoes on it with his knife, European style, and popped it into his mouth. "Ah, dinner is never a disappointment here, eh, Lettie?"

Lettie raised her wine glass. "Never," she agreed.

"But let me continue. Before long we needed a house, with more space and a yard for Mark and his boundless energy. Shortly before Theresa was born, we bought a home in a quiet residential area not far from the shop."

He tossed back the last of his wine and changed the subject abruptly. "Has Lily told you about the Merry Weather Tearoom?"

"No, what's that?"

He raised his empty glass in her direction. "Not so fast! That's Lily's story to tell. I'll pop in on her for a few minutes, then I have ordering and correspondence waiting for me in my study." He rose and made a slight bow. "Ladies, if you will excuse me?"

Leticia and Caroline waved him off, then Caroline leaned forward, her forearms crossed on the table. "Lettie, what's this about a Merry Weather Tearoom?"

Lettie's eyes sparkled. "Let's not spoil Lily's fun. She'll enjoy telling you about it. She's proud of what she and her ladies have accomplished, as she should be. Meanwhile, I'll go upstairs and prepare her for bed as soon as Marco leaves her. Why don't you give us half an hour and then come along. She won't be at her best, but I know she'll want to say good night."

When Caroline joined them, Lily was freshened up, her hair neatly braided. Wearing a pale blue bed jacket with iridescent peacocks embroidered around the yoke, she reclined against the pillows, looking well cared-for and comfortable. Her smudgy eyes, however, told another tale.

"Come in, come in, my dear friend," she called to Caroline.

Lettie stepped past Caroline with an armful of damp towels and the nightgown Lily had worn during the day. "Enjoy your visit, ladies."

"Good night, Lettie, and thanks for everything," replied Lily.

To Caroline she said, "I'm sorry this is such a dull household. There are lots of books in Marco's study. Take a look around tomorrow and see if anything strikes your fancy. I remember how much you enjoy reading."

"I will, thank you. But don't worry, your household is anything but dull. And just being in Oregon is a delight. Such natural beauty! Oh, speaking of reading, I brought along a book I thought you might enjoy, *The Circular Staircase* by Mary Roberts Rinehart. She's all the rage back home in Pennsylvania. Have you heard of her?"

"No, not a word."

"She writes a ripping mystery, keeps you on the edge of your seat from start to finish. This is her first novel, made into a Broadway hit a few years ago. I thought you might like me to read it to you."

"What a lovely idea! Thank you. And what did you find to keep yourself busy this afternoon?"

"Lettie was nice enough to invite me for a cup of tea in her suite. She told me about her family, and why she is so grateful to be here with you and Marco. My, what a childhood she had."

"Yes, you'd never know it to see her today. I'm grateful to her, you can be sure of that. And you had dinner with her and Marco? Did he tell you about our early days in Portland?"

"He did, but only the basics. He hurried upstairs to visit with you, then on to business matters in his study. Just like my John."

Lily smiled fondly. "Ah, yes, John and his manuscripts. He could talk our heads off when he felt like being sociable, but in the evenings his study called. That left you free to enjoy bedtime frolics with Robert, as I did with our children. We had some happy times, Caroline, together and apart."

"We did indeed, my friend."

Lily's eyelids fluttered and Caroline could see that she wouldn't be long for the world.

"Let me get the book, Lily, and we can start reading tonight. I'll be right back." She'd ask Lily about the Merry Weather Tearoom tomorrow.

In the two minutes it took Caroline to walk to her room and pick up the book, Lily had drifted off. *The Circular Staircase* would have to wait.

CHAPTER 24

Settled by Marco in the sunroom the next morning with Caroline in the chair beside her, Lily apologized for falling asleep last night before Caroline could begin reading.

"Don't be silly! We've got lots of time. I'm much more anxious to hear about the beginning of your life here in Portland." Caroline crossed one ankle over the other, rearranged her skirt over her knees, and settled back to listen.

Feeling bright and alert after an unusually restful night, Lily couldn't wait to tell her eager listener about their early days out West. She'd fill in the gaps Marco had no doubt left in his quick sketch at dinner. And hope that Caroline didn't notice the gaps she'd left in her story of leaving Philadelphia.

Life was difficult at first for the Giannottis in Portland. They arrived with no resources beyond their youth, health, and enthusiasm. Marco had managed to squirrel away a small amount of cash from the tips he received delivering flowers back East, but the train tickets and food along the way used up much of it. They found a modest but respectable boarding house near Portland Union Station, and Marco immediately found work in a sawmill. The work was dangerous and brutal, but he was strong and willing—and he had a goal. He set aside every penny he could for his flower business.

Portland's relentless winter drizzle had already descended upon the landscape. Lily had never seen so much mud, mud, mud. On their third day there, with Marco off to work, the landlady invited Lily into her cozy parlor for tea.

Agnes Hardy recognized a fellow adventurer. She too had been a young woman of good breeding who had journeyed to the Pacific Northwest full of hopes and dreams. Over their steaming cups and a plate of shortbread cookies, she told Lily of her arrival two decades earlier with her husband, Jasper. He had worked in the logging camps up the Columbia Gorge until one day while trying to break up a logjam in the river, he slipped and was crushed to death by the shifting raft of logs. She shook her head, lost for a moment in the grim memory.

"Jasper, God bless him. He made decent money, and within a few years we were able to buy this big house. We thought we'd take in a few boarders until we needed the bedrooms for children, but the children never came along. After he died, I just kept on with the boarders, and I've managed all right. It's a lot of hard work—cooking and cleaning and settling the occasional squabble—but being so near the station, I rarely have a vacancy. And honestly, managing my boarders is a lot like managing children. They're just not as cute."

Lily laughed. "You never thought of going back home?"

"Back to St. Louis? Not on your life! Too many people minding your business, watching your manners, nosing about to make sure you show up in church every Sunday. I love the freedom here. Of course I miss Jasper, but I've made some fine friends, and I feel like I do some good in the world by opening my house to new arrivals. That's enough for me."

"Well, you've certainly made a comfortable place here. Of course, we won't be staying long. As soon as Marco gets his first week's pay, we'll need to find something more permanent." And less expensive, Lily refrained from adding. She appreciated Marco's effort to gradually acclimate her to the lifestyle of an ordinary sawyer's wife. She knew that their permanent home would be nowhere near as comfortable as Agnes Hardy's boardinghouse.

The rooms Marco found for them were on a busy street near the edge of the main business district, close to transportation and shops.

In the mornings he took a streetcar to the outskirts of the city, where he met a wagon that hauled him and his fellow workers to the mill. Lily realized it was the best he could do, so she bit back her disappointment when he first showed her their new home.

They climbed up an exterior staircase to the second floor of an old wooden building housing *Van Buskirk Mercantile, Purveyor of Foodstuffs, Dry Goods, Housewares, and Miscellany.* The staircase was roofed, but just barely, and she could see that the slightest breeze from the wrong direction would drive the rain directly at them as they went up and down. The scents of stale smoke and mildew greeted them as they opened the door on the landing and stepped inside.

The main room was furnished with a sagging sofa, two battered wooden chairs, a plank table, a dry sink set into several wide boards for a counter, and a couple of wooden fruit crates nailed to the wall for shelving. A compact cast-iron wood stove served for cooking and heating. A smaller room beyond contained a chipped white metal bedstead with rusted springs and a stained mattress, which, when they turned it over, showed blessedly fewer stains on its underside.

"It won't be for long, Lily, I promise," said Marco as he watched her struggling to take in the discouraging scene. "I'll work as hard as I can, and one day we will say to our children, 'You think you have a hard life? Let me tell you how your mother and I started out!'"

His little speech was so sincere that Lily could only throw her arms around him and laugh.

"We'll make do," she promised, "and by the time the baby is born, this will feel like a real home."

Privately, she was appalled. She couldn't imagine how she could make these dreary rooms feel like home, especially as she had no cleaning equipment with which to begin. Cobwebs crisscrossed the ceiling corners; the floor was stomped with dried mud. The zinc lining of the sink was encrusted with the remains of who knew how many of the previous tenant's meals, and the window edges sported a healthy crop of mold.

There was nothing for it but to get some cleaning equipment the next day and start scrubbing. After her father had died, her mother had looked for every possible way to economize, including letting the daily maid go and tackling the housework herself. Mary Louise Paxton had recruited her two young daughters and kept a firm hand on them until they had mastered the essentials of housekeeping.

"Someday, young ladies, you will be glad you've learned these skills, if for no other reason than to supervise your own staff properly," she told them. The girls rolled their eyes but bent to it with a will after school and on weekends, keeping themselves and their mother amused with silly banter as they worked. By the time Mary Louise was too sick to manage, the sisters were a smoothly-functioning team. The task confronting her now looked daunting, but she knew she could handle it.

Lily and Marco spent one last night of comfort at Mrs. Hardy's. After Marco trudged off to work the next day, Mrs. Hardy summoned a fellow on the street, who, for a small fee, carted Lily's trunk and Marco's bags to the Mercantile and up the outside stairs, with Lily trailing behind. It was only a six-block walk, but a world away. The skies still looked threatening after a morning shower. She walked as much as possible on the elevated wooden sidewalks, but every intersection meant crossing a morass of mud and manure, churned up by passing horses, carriages, wagons, streetcars, and an occasional automobile. By the time she climbed the stairs to her new abode, her low-heeled boots were caked to the arches.

She paid off the carter and surveyed her domain, as lonely and discouraged as she had ever felt. How—where—to begin?

Shoes first. She couldn't expect to clean with her muddy footwear messing things up as she went along. She went back downstairs to look behind the Mercantile for a stick with which to scrape off the muck. She found a pile of broken wooden shingles in the alley. Leaning against the side of the building, she scraped off as much mud as she could. Then, as presentable as she would be for the next few days, she decided it would be a good idea to meet their landlord. Perhaps he would lend her a broom, a bucket, and a mop, or advance them to her on credit. If she looked on the bright side of things, having a general merchant for a landlord and neighbor might be an unexpected stroke of luck.

She waited inside the door while the rotund shopkeeper weighed and packaged measures of dried beans, rice, coffee and a careful amount of sugar for a customer. The woman turned to leave with her purchases, nodding to Lily as she passed and leaving in her wake the intoxicating aroma of the freshly ground coffee. Lily walked up to the counter and introduced herself.

"Ah, de young missus," he said as he closed the bins beneath the counter and screwed on the sugar jar lid. "I met your husband yesterday. You are lucky he came when he did and paid the rent. Three more people asked to rent the place after he left. I should have charged him twice as much. But never mind. I am easy to get along with, as long as the rent is paid on time." His demeanor was grave, his speech deeply accented and stern. Each word sounded as if he hammered it out.

Lily blinked and took a step backward. "Well, I can assure you that we always pay our rent on time, Mr...?"

"I am Joop, Joop Van Buskirk of de Mercantile. My wife is Jannie. We say 'Yoop'; we say 'Yannie.' We come from de Nederlands, but now we are Americans." He puffed out his chest proudly.

A short, even rounder woman bustled in from the back of the store, closing the door behind her, breathless with news.

"Joop, our new tenant has just moved in. I saw de baggage going upstairs."

Not sure what to make of being called a baggage, Lily chalked it up to her landlady's unfamiliarity with English slang and decided she was referring to Lily's trunk and Marco's suitcases. Joop came to her rescue.

"You are too late, Jannie. She's already here. Meet Missus Giannotti."

"Oh, and aren't you pretty!" exclaimed Jannie Van Buskirk. "Once we get the place tidied up, it will be very comfortable for you and your husband."

Lily wasn't sure about that, but she murmured a thank you for the compliment, then decided she'd better clarify their situation in case they didn't rent to families with children. Better to know now than to have to make a move just prior to the baby's birth. "I hope my husband told you there will soon be a baby joining us?"

"Oh, he didn't say nothing about a baby," said Jannie, taking a step backwards.

Lily swallowed and replied as calmly as she could. "Yes, well, I hope that won't be a problem, Mrs. Van Buskirk. I'll make sure the baby doesn't cry or disturb you in any way. Or damage the premises." As if they could be damaged any more than they were, she mused.

Shaking his head, Mr. Van Buskirk moved away to take care of another customer. He didn't want anything to do with talk about babies. Mrs. Van Buskirk studied Lily for a moment. Then she burst out in a wide smile that popped her cheeks like rosy crabapples.

"A baby! Why didn't nobody tell me? Of course you can have a baby here. Joop and I raised six of our own, and now we have so many grandchildren I cannot even count them. But none of them are little anymore. I will be happy to have another baby here. And also happy that I do not have to wake up in the middle of the night to feed it, or wash its nappies." She chortled away at her own good humor, leaving Lily relieved and drawn in by the woman's warmth.

"Thank you, Mrs. Van Buskirk. You're very kind."

"Please, Jannie! Everybody in Portland, they call us Joop and Jannie."

"All right, Jannie. And I'm Lily. I was wondering…I don't have any cleaning supplies. Could I…" Oh good heavens, she hoped she wasn't insulting her landlady over the condition of the quarters.

"Ah, you need a broom and a bucket and what have you. That place is a mess, I know. I told him not to let it out until I clean it, but no, he don't want to lose a day of rent. That's Joop. He probably told you he could have rented it to three other people and that he should double your rent. Pay no attention. That's just his way. You come with me. I give you Joop's old stuff. I tell you, that man. He keep everything. Never throw nothing away. Many old things, broken things he cannot sell—still he keep them all. You come with me."

By way of an interior stairway she took Lily to the storeroom on the third floor, a warehouse for Joop's merchandise, mostly salable, some not.

"Ah, you see, this is how we do it in de Nederlands for many centuries. We have the shop on the street, the family quarters above, and the warehouse on the top. Just like home. Come look, see this thing."

Jannie marched over to a wide double door in the back wall that she unlatched and threw open to reveal a frightening drop to the alley below.

"You see that hook up there?" Jannie pointed up to a large hook hanging from a thick wooden beam that extended out above them from under the building's roof. "A clever Dutch way of hauling the merchandise up to the storage room. All my heavy furniture from the old country came up that way too."

Lily held tightly onto the doorframe as she obediently leaned out and looked up at the hook.

"Ah, but that is not what you are here to see," continued Jannie. "Come."

Jannie motioned Lily away so she could close and latch the delivery doors, then wove through the aisles neatly stacked with boxes and barrels of trade goods. Lily had no doubt that Joop could find anything he needed in an instant, even with his eyes closed.

"Ah, here, look at this junk pile. Where does he get this stuff, that crazy old man?"

In the corner stood a waist-high crate of jumbled, banged-up household items, a decided contrast to the meticulous order of the rest of the warehouse.

"Look at all this! Why does he keep this junk? You want to know why? Because he's a soft-hearted old fool, and every so often somebody comes along who needs a helping hand. Let's see what we can find for you."

Jannie bent over, plunged her hands into the crate, rattled around, and surfaced with a large dented bucket, a worn-down scrub-brush, and a stained string-headed mop.

"What about cooking?" Jannie asked. "You have pots, pans, dishes?"

Embarrassed, Lily shook her head, admitting she had nothing.

"Oh, these young people today," lamented Jannie, turning back to the crate. "You think these things just fall out of the sky?"

"We left in such a hurry…" Lily began.

"Never mind. I know, if you think about it too long, you don't go. Too much thinking, not so good. Here." One by one she handed Lily a collection of battered pots and pans, chipped pottery dishes and mugs, a butcher's knife with its point broken off, and two mismatched metal forks.

"Wait, one more thing." She rooted around in the bottom of the crate again and pulled out a large rusted wooden-handled spoon. "There, now you can stir the pot so the stew don't stick to the bottom." Jannie straightened up, dusted off her hands, and beamed like a lighthouse.

"I don't know what to say," said Lily, poking the spoon into the bucket with the rest of the items.

"*Dank je wel* is all you need. Now what will you cook tonight for that hardworking young husband of yours?"

Balancing the bucket on her hip, Lily shook her head. "I haven't thought that far ahead."

"*Ja, ja*, just as I thought. I bring you something later. From tomorrow, you cook for yourself."

"I can't thank you enough, Jannie. I don't know what I'd have done without you."

"Ah, please, we have to help each other, so far from home. Oh, look, let me grab that broom over there. You must sweep before you mop." Jannie took a closer look at the broom, a rather pathetic specimen. "Hmm, not enough straw left on that old thing. I get you a new one downstairs. Then you have everything!"

Jannie tossed the useless broom back into the corner, scooped up the mop, and marched Lily with her overflowing bucket down the stairs to the shop. Looking straight ahead and trying not to let her embarrassment show, Lily missed the wink the gruff old Joop gave his wife as she grabbed a new broom and two ripe apples on her way out the door.

When Marco returned from the sawmill in the early evening—cold, hungry, muddy, and bone-tired—he was welcomed by the warmth of the stove, fueled by the broken shingles Lily had found in the alley; the aroma of Mrs. Van Buskirk's stew simmering on the stove; and two shiny apples glowing on the table. The cobwebs were gone, and the wooden floor was scrubbed free of mud. Even the bed was made, thanks to sheets, a blanket and two pillows Jannie had brought along with the stew. The trunk itself stood open on its end, a wardrobe once again, making the bedroom look alluringly inviting.

"My God, Lily. You've performed a miracle! How did you do it in just one day?" he asked as he opened his arms to embrace her.

"Two miracles, Marco. Their names are Joop and Jannie. You couldn't have found us a better home."

By noon Lily had exhausted herself again with the telling of their earliest days in Portland. Lettie fed her a light chicken soup, and made her comfortable for a nap on the chaise longue.

When the two friends met again in the sunroom shortly after three o'clock, Lily appeared rested and relaxed. The bow on her flashy bed jacket was perked up and the pillows at her back newly fluffed, presumably by Lettie. The fresh-air scent of a recent shower filled the room. Just then the sun broke through the clouds. The grass flowing downhill toward the river glowed emerald in the refracted light of myriad tiny droplets.

Lily's pleasure at being downstairs, nestled under the Amish quilt with the sparkling river view outside, knew no bounds.

"Caroline, I can't think why I haven't done this every day. Well, that's not possible, is it? We close the room during the winter. It's a summer room—screened windows and no fireplace. Today's a bit chilly, but if we stay wrapped up we'll be fine. Are you comfortable in that chair?"

"Couldn't be better." Caroline tightened her shawl a bit. "My daughter Nancy has a room like this but with glassed windows—a solarium, she calls it. It's our favorite room in her house."

"When I'm finished with my tale, you must tell me more about Nancy and her family. Meanwhile, I'm still pinching myself that you're here! Did I talk your ear off again this morning? I haven't thought about those days in such a long while. Sometimes I wonder how we got through them." Lily rotated a shoulder and stretched her neck, seeking a more comfortable position.

Caroline started to rise from her chair. "Can I help you, Lily? Or call Lettie to come in?"

"No, no. A small adjustment, that's all. Did you and Lettie have a nice lunch?"

"We certainly did," said Caroline. "Your cook is a marvel. After just a few meals I've become a dedicated fan of Italian cuisine."

Lily's eyes twinkled. "It grows on one quickly, doesn't it? Around the waist as well as one's palate."

Caroline grinned, silently cheering that Lily's sense of humor was much to the fore. There was, however, no sign of Annie Delfini's talent on Lily's wraith-like figure, starkly outlined under the quilt. She dashed away the thought and prompted Lily to continue.

"Last night Lettie and Marco both mentioned the Merry Weather Tearoom but refused to tell me about it. Does it have anything to do with the mysterious Back Door Women Marco also alluded to?"

"All in good time, my friend, all in good time." Lily closed her eyes for a moment, collecting her memories.

"I shall never forget that first day above the Mercantile. Jannie and I worked so hard to make things presentable for Marco. It was a contest between Marco and me as to who was the most exhausted when he came home: Marco from his long day at the mill, or me, experiencing that overwhelming pregnancy fatigue, yet ever the good soldier with broom, mop, and pail!"

Caroline interrupted. "Lily, I have to ask. It's obvious that you were pregnant with Mark when you left Philadelphia. That's why you and Marco ran off, isn't it?

Lily nodded. "Yes."

"So that explains…"

Lily closed her eyes, hoping Caroline would take it as a sign of her embarrassment, even all these years later, and be satisfied. And that she would make the logical assumption that the child was Marco's.

"Why didn't you confide in me? I could have helped you!"

"It's complicated, Caroline. And just think…you might have talked me out of this wonderful life in Oregon. I might never have forgiven you!"

"Lily, what nonsense. But if you don't want to talk about it, fine. Please go on. So Jannie stayed to help you in addition to loading you up with supplies?"

Lily breathed a sigh of relief. She'd answered Caroline's question with a half-truth, which she seemed to accept…for now.

"It turned out Jannie and Joop had always rented the apartment to bachelors who were used to living rough. Jannie confessed that it had never occurred to her that Joop would rent it to a married couple, with a baby on the way. Jannie's a meticulous housekeeper, as I soon learned, and she was mortified that the rooms were so filthy for us."

"No wonder she was so helpful," replied Caroline.

"Yes, she felt pretty badly about the mess. She was a real chatterbox too. By the time we finished, I'd learned quite a bit about the neighborhood…not all of it complimentary. The big pot of stew she brought for our dinner was a godsend. The next day Jannie gave me a tour of the area. I met the butcher, the baker…" Lily paused, distracted by a sweet trill of bird calls from the walnut tree outside the window. None were visible, but the occasional jerk of a leafy branch further attested to the birds' presence.

"No candlestick maker?" joked Caroline.

"As it happened, that first night Jannie brought me all the candles I could possibly need." The two friends shared a giggle, and Lily knew that Caroline's curiosity—and slight annoyance—were once again tamped down. "Fortunately for us, the Van Buskirks sort of adopted us. They couldn't have been more helpful."

CHAPTER 25

Shepherded by Jannie Van Buskirk, Lily quickly made friends and picked up a few young students who needed help with their schoolwork. The neighborhood adjacent to the shops was rundown and poor, in ways that Lily had no more than glimpsed in her former life back East. But a few of the mothers recognized a rare opportunity for their children and found a way to pay her, albeit sparingly.

Once again Lily blessed her mother for teaching her to sew. Her modest earnings allowed her to purchase soft cotton fabric and lamb's wool yarn for the baby's layette. Jannie tried to teach her to knit, but Lily proved hopeless on that score. She dropped stitches and could never understand how to recover them. Her tension on the yarn varied so much that even the smallest cap or sock bulged and rippled. With a huff, Jannie took it all away and set about knitting for the baby herself. Lily kept on with the sewing, happy to translate her skills into soft little nightgowns, day dresses, neatly hemmed diapers, and such.

The day he quit the mill, Marco brought home the refashioned flower cart, a cradle he had made from lumber scraps, and a bottle of chianti with which to celebrate. The next day Lily went into labor and Mark was born with the help of a local midwife. The launch of the family business and the birth of their first child on the same day seemed an excellent omen.

Mark was a delightful child—towheaded, blue eyed, bright, and charming. He looked like neither his mother nor his father, and they both adored him. Two years later, Theresa joined the family. When Lily understood how important it was to Marco that the children be raised Catholic, she agreed. She dressed them in their finest outfits and accompanied them and their father to mass on Sundays and holy days. She enjoyed the serenity of the ceremony and the droning Latin of the prayers. But she saw no need to convert. She could not understand the importance of confession, nor the need for a priest to intercede between herself and God. She'd been taught to pray directly, and that was good enough for her. Marco saw no need to press her.

By the time Theresa started walking, Lily and Marco realized they needed to find a roomier home with a fenced yard in which the children could run off their boundless energy. They found a modest two-story house in a quiet neighborhood still an easy walk from the flower shop. Once again Lily rolled up her sleeves to make it a home.

On a promising spring day, she buttoned the children into their light sweaters. With Theresa in her buggy and Mark skipping alongside, they headed out for a walk. Crocuses and daffodils were up, and new grass was poking through the winter-dead turf.

On a whim, she decided to head for the flower shop and say hello to Marco. The children always considered this a supreme treat—they loved seeing their father looking so important behind the counter in his green apron. As she pushed the buggy along the wooden sidewalk leading to Giannotti Florist West, she spotted a "For Rent" sign in the window of the cobbler's shop next door. Curious, she shaded her eyes and peered inside. The cobbler, an older man whose wife had died recently, was boxing up his materials, apparently preparing to move on. She poked her head through the doorway and greeted him.

"Mr. Brannigan, good morning. Are you leaving us?"

"Ah, Mrs. Giannotti. Come in, come in. Look at those little ones. How they keep growing!" He reached down and tussled Mark's blond hair, which made the little boy skitter backward out of reach. Lily laughed, and Mr. Brannigan shook his head.

"'Tis a sad day, to be sure, but I've no heart for repairin' shoes now that my Hattie is gone. I'm goin' back to Wisconsin to live with my son and his family, so I am. When Hattie and I came out here, they took over our dairy farm, and I was glad to be done with it. But if there's one thing these old hands haven't forgotten, it's how to milk a cow."

He squeezed his hands open and shut in the air to demonstrate. Mark edged closer, wondering what he was up to. "At least I can be helpful and have a good meal at the end of the day. It's Hattie's cookin' I miss as much as herself."

"We'll certainly miss you," Lily said. "You've been such a good friend to Marco, helping him set up his shop and all."

"And didn't he return the favor? He found a buyer for my shoe makin' and repair equipment. The fellow is comin' by today to pick it up. I'm headin' east on the cars on Friday, with no regrets. Oregon has been good to me, but now I'm goin' home."

Lily wished him the luck of the Irish, which made him grin, and guided the children next door to Marco's. Once inside, she lifted Theresa out of her buggy and turned her loose to scamper with Mark to their father. They knew he always had soft candies hidden in one of his big apron pockets. Marco lifted them onto the counter, where they perched, happily sucking their treats.

"Marco, you didn't tell me Mr. Brannigan is going back East to live with his son."

"Well, is this such big news? He's a nice fellow, but people come and go."

"Marco, his shop is for rent!"

"That's so. What are you thinking, that I should expand, double our size? We're doing well, Lily, but not that well."

"No, not at all. Another idea just flashed into my head. I'll tell you more tonight when you get home, after the children are in bed. I need to think about it a bit."

He raised his eyebrows, but as he did with all of Lily's ideas, he gave her the benefit of the doubt. He'd withhold judgment until she explained what she had in mind. If Marco knew anything about Lily, he knew and respected her common sense.

On the way home more pieces of the idea dropped into her mind like pennies into a milk bottle. One detail after another, the ideas came together, until she was beside herself with excitement. As soon as the kitchen was tidied up, the children tucked in upstairs, and Marco settled in his favorite chair near the fireplace, Lily sat down on a corner of the hassock in front of him, careful not to nudge his feet off.

"Marco, your shop is in a perfect location. On one side the neighborhoods get nicer and nicer, with fewer shops and grander houses as the city moves up toward the hills. On the other side is the business district, so when the ladies are on their way home from shopping, it's easy to make one more stop to pick up flowers."

"Of course. You think I chose this location for no reason at all? And don't forget our delivery service, 'Delivering Happiness Every Day.' You came up with that slogan, and it works like a charm."

"Well, thank you for saying so. But think about it, Marco. When those wealthy women stop to pick up flowers, it's almost as if they are looking for a way to stretch out their shopping a little longer. I've seen them, the way they like to stand around and chat with one another, and even with you!"

His eyes twinkled. "Oh, come now, Lily. Don't tell me you're jealous!"

She frowned at him. "Of course not, silly, but think about it. They may be lonely, they may be bored, or perhaps things at home might not be so good. Maybe they just want to exchange the news of the day or have a little rest before they carry on home. For whatever reasons, it seems to me they aren't in any hurry to move along. Not everyone, mind you, but some of them, sometimes."

"All right. So what?"

"A tearoom! Right next door to Giannotti Florist West, with an open doorway in between so they don't have to go out into the weather. They'd have a place to relax, enjoy a cup of tea and perhaps a cookie or a piece of cake, meet their friends, learn what's new. Marco, it's perfect! And what luck that every table and the countertop can be decorated with beautiful flower arrangements from Giannotti's! There are saloons aplenty where men can gather, but for women—nothing except hotel restaurants, which are rather formal and expensive and farther downtown."

Up went those eyebrows again. "What makes you think you know anything about running a business, never mind a tearoom?"

She rested a hand on one hip. "And what did your parents know about running a flower business when they arrived in America? Your father was a carpenter in the old country."

"True."

"And did he run his own business there?"

"Well, no, he worked for his cousin. You know that. But at least he had the skills."

"So why didn't he use them when he came here?"

"He did, but he didn't speak the language so it was hard to get work. He finally found a guy who needed help building coffins."

"You never told me that! So how in the world did he get from coffins to flowers?"

"He noticed that no matter how poor people were, they always spent lots of money on flowers at funerals. It was a matter of family pride, of honoring the blessed dead. He didn't like the man he was working for, and he didn't like building coffins. Understandable— the customers were always unhappy—or dead. Very depressing. So he quit and began buying flowers from the sidewalk markets and reselling them to the funeral directors. He knew them all from the coffin business, and they seemed happy to do business with him, especially when he undercut the prices of their other suppliers. They learned they could trust my father to bring the flowers exactly as ordered. If the customers didn't know what they wanted, he knew what to recommend within their budget so that nobody would gossip about what skinflints they were."

"But still—not a happy business," prompted Lily.

"Right, but funerals were just the beginning. There are many other occasions for flowers, as you know. With my mother helping him, it didn't take long before they were able to open their shop, made famous lately as the celebrated meeting place of Mr. and Mrs. Marco Giannotti of Portland, Oregon."

She swatted him with a rolled-up newspaper. "Marco. Stop joking!"

"Okay, okay. They did well. Not as well as they would have if they'd used some of my ideas for improvements, mind you, but much better than they ever dreamed. They were content and secure. That is what's mattered to them."

Lily jumped up and began pacing. "Then you can understand how important this is to me, Marco. I admit I don't know much about running a business, but I didn't go to college for nothing. I studied a lot of subjects you might consider useless, like Greek and Roman history and higher mathematics, but it all added up to one thing: learning to think creatively and solve problems. That's really what business is about, don't you agree?"

Marco buried his face in his hands. "Oh woe, is me. I knew I would regret marrying a college woman."

Arms across her chest, she scoffed at him. "Don't be like that! You knew what you were getting when you married me."

"Yes—independent, full of thoughts and ideas that don't belong to a woman, outspoken…"

"…a good wife, creative homemaker, dedicated mother, entertaining conversationalist, amusing, comforting… Shall I continue?" asked Lily.

Marco grinned. "Be sure to add beautiful and so nice to wrap my arms around in the dark."

"Marco!"

"Well, it's true. These things are important to a man."

"And you've made them important to me. I do thank you for that. I'm not sure every woman enjoys that aspect of married life as much as I do. But don't try to distract me. Here's my plan: I'll start slowly and deliberately, thinking each step through as I come to it, and I'll learn as I go. We'll take a year's lease on the shop. If, at the end of that year, I've not demonstrated a reasonable level of success, I'll call it quits and have a dozen more children. But I know I can do it, Marco. I really do."

He rubbed his chin thoughtfully. "If that's what I have to do to avoid raising fourteen children…"

She gave him a light punch in the shoulder. "Be serious!"

"Serious, yes. You'll need money to start up. You need to pay the rent, purchase chairs and tables…"

"…tablecloths, napkins, teapots, cups and saucers, kettles, dessert plates, a display counter, a sign over the doorway, all kinds of things. But I'll start small, Marco. As I said, one step at a time."

Trying to suppress a grin, Marco asked, "Excuse me, but a while back you mentioned flowers on the tables and service counter? Am I supposed to just donate those to the cause?"

"Look, every morning you have to cull the open blossoms that are no longer fresh enough to sell. You just throw them away because your customers expect their flowers to last a good few days after they purchase them. What if you give the culls to me? I'll trim them and give them one more day of life before I too discard them. I'll do the same every day. It's a perfect setup, and the ladies enjoying their tea will be reminded of the beautiful flowers next door. If they haven't already, how easy it will be to slip over and pick up an assortment for their entry hall or dinner table."

"Lily, you confound me. But you haven't answered my question. What will you do for seed money? I've managed to save a little, but…"

"Thank you, Marco, but it won't be necessary. You know my Uncle Arnold was the executor of my mother's estate. I've told you about the dreadful battles I had with him over going to college. He was positively hateful, but I have to admit he was scrupulous with the bookkeeping. Every penny was accounted for, and I never had any reason to suspect he was cheating us. Florence received her share when she got married instead of going to college. Uncle gave it to her in a lump sum because she had a husband who would manage it for her. I can't tell you how many times I heard him say that a woman is incapable of handling her own finances. Backward thinking, if you ask me, that stubborn old goat."

Marco raised an eyebrow but held his peace. He'd heard this before.

"As for what was left of my share after I graduated, Uncle set it up as an investment fund that pays quarterly dividends. It provided me with spending money during my visiting girl days, modest though it was. But we left Philadelphia in such a hurry, and I…well, I didn't want him know where I was, so I never notified the bank. I know it sounds irrational, but I was afraid he'd somehow manage to yank me back under his control."

A strange look came over Marco's face. "You never thought to tell me, your husband, about this until today? When we arrived with almost no money and had to scrape by from week to week until I got established?"

Lily began to knot her hands, but then deliberately set them palm-down on her thighs, sat up straight, and looked him in the eye. "Marco, I won't apologize. No matter how willing I was, I couldn't know how things would work out for us here. A woman should always have something to fall back on." She could hear her mother's voice as clearly as if she were in the room with them.

Marco's expression remained stark, neither angry nor hurt, but not encouraging either. She knew strong feelings lived just below the surface, and he was rarely shy about expressing them.

"There must be more to it than that, Lily. Almost four years have gone by, and you haven't said a word."

"My mother was determined to make independent women of Florence and me. But it's always men who make life's rules and control the money. When my father died, our lives changed drastically. The young pharmacist Mother hired ruined us. Yet through it all, she made sure there was enough for Florence and me to go to college and have independent futures, although Florence chose otherwise. Mother never stopped reminding us of how important that was. Choices, Marco, choices Mother never had! A woman is powerless over her own life without education and choices." Lily tapped her foot on the floor. Marco knew that gesture and wisely remained silent.

"Knowing the money was there, untouched and compounding, gave me confidence and a small feeling of security after I turned my life upside down by marrying you and journeying out here. You've done marvelously for us, Marco, but think what would have happened if you'd had a crippling accident at the mill, or, God forbid, been a…a horrible husband."

She stopped suddenly with her hand to her mouth. She really hadn't meant to say that. Marco cleared his throat but didn't interrupt. She continued, but the punch had left her voice.

"A woman on her own without resources hasn't got a chance, Marco. Nor have her children."

"So you finally feel safe enough to tell me about the money, now that you plan to spend it? I could still have an accident…or die. Or demand that you turn it over to me." He raised an eyebrow imperiously. "I assume you've decided I'm not a horrible husband?"

"Oh, stop. Of course you're not a horrible husband. With a little luck—and my woman's intuition—I made an excellent choice."

"Well, thank you for that. You know you could always take over the flower shop at my premature demise."

"That's not the point, Marco. I love flowers, and I love that you're succeeding so splendidly. I see you happy and satisfied with your work as you build the business. And your customers love you. But I have no passion for the flower business. A tearoom, where women can gather informally to share ideas, exchange views, and, yes, to discuss their domestic challenges—that's what excites me. I want to give the women of our neighborhood a safe, convenient place to meet, in comfort and with no expectations put on them. Once it's established, I'll have my own income and I'll know I can take care of myself and the children should the need ever arise. Can you understand that?"

He paused before answering, his dark Italian eyes never leaving her face. Aware of a creeping sense of panic, Lily began to wonder if this would be the day their marriage began to unravel. That was the last thing she wanted.

Slowly he said, "So having left it alone these past four years, unknown to your husband and without notifying the bank of your whereabouts, sufficient dividends should have accumulated, compounded annually..."

"...that I can start the ball rolling." She drove one fist into the other open palm. "Yes!"

He leaned back in his chair and crossed an ankle over the other knee. A small smile began to lighten his face. "Or start the tea pouring, you might say?"

With his little joke, she knew she'd won. "Oh, Marco, thank you!"

He threw his hands up in the air. "Knowing you, Lily, you'll do it whether I approve or not. But, yes, you have my blessing. You mentioned creative thinking and problem solving. Let me add one more ingredient of a successful businessperson: perseverance. I have no doubt that you'll persevere from day one."

"Day one—that's tomorrow! Oh, Marco I can't wait to get started!"

CHAPTER 26

"And so I did, Caroline. The next day I made the first of many ridiculous—but happily not fatal—mistakes. I marched down to the bank to open an account so I could have my funds transferred to Portland. Well, you never saw such a fuss. The bank manager hemmed and hawed, and finally declared that I could not open an account under my own name. After all my talk about independence, my husband had to come in and sign the papers, and the account had to be in his name, with me secondary. Of course, it didn't help that I took my children to the bank with me. There I was, the perfect little housewife and mother, trying to act like a businessperson."

Caroline laughed, picturing the scene and her friend's indignation.

"And that's not all," Lily continued. "The bank manager advised me that Marco, as my husband, would have to co-sign all the papers to transfer my investment funds and future payments to Portland. That was a hard bite to swallow, too, but I couldn't let my annoyance stop me. On the other hand, we discovered that Uncle Arnold had set up the fund in my name alone, independent of himself, so there was no need to contact him."

"Were you still worried he'd somehow drag you back to New York?"

"I can't explain it, but I just didn't want him to know where I was. Anyway, we wired the Philadelphia bank that afternoon. They replied saying they would mail the necessary documents. Sure enough, within a fortnight the funds were transferred, and future payments diverted to 'my' Portland bank account. Enough had accrued for a modest beginning of the Merry Weather Tearoom."

While Lily was speaking, dark clouds had rolled in, casting the landscape in subdued shades of green and gray. Soon they were engulfed in a Portland summer downpour. Rain pounded the roof, slashed the trees and shrubs, and puddled on the lawn. A fine mist drifted into the porch through the screened windows.

"Typical June shower," Lily said, gesturing in the direction of the deluge. "Possibly the rain's last hurrah before it retreats for the summer. I love this misty feeling while we're safely inside. Are you all right, or shall we move to another room?"

"Oh, no, this is wonderful. A bit like a chilly steam bath, if there is such a thing!"

"Well said. It'll soon be over. They always are this time of year. Come July we'll have three months of solid sunshine. Pat your face and enjoy the cool radiance."

"How wonderful! My skin is drinking it in." She closed her eyes for a moment to enjoy the glow. "Now, carry on with your story. Don't leave me guessing."

"Where did I leave off? Ah, yes. New residents were streaming into the city, Caroline, new businesses popping up right and left. While I waited for the funds to transfer, I swallowed my pride and asked Marco to dip into his savings and secure the lease on the cobbler's shop. He agreed with my sense of urgency, and seemed unconcerned about being reimbursed. As soon as the lease was signed, by Marco of course, I asked him to cut a wide opening between the two shops. No door, just an open passageway, to allow customers to flow between the two shops. By the time the landlord noticed it and expressed his outrage, it was too late. He huffed away with his ears as red as lobster claws and a large bouquet for his wife. He never interfered again."

"I'm sure Marco's record as an exemplary tenant helped calm the waters," Caroline ventured with a chuckle.

"No doubt. My next errand was to a sign shop. Then I made a list of essentials, keeping to my determination to start slowly and knowing the list would increase and multiply as I went along. To the items I had mentioned to Marco, I added serving platters, curtains, trays, kettles, aprons, and on it went."

"How did you keep track of everything?" asked Caroline.

"I kept a journal, so that when I got discouraged—and there were many times when I did—I could look back and see how far I'd come. On the left-hand page I listed what I planned to do or acquire that day, and on the opposite page I listed my actual accomplishments. At the end of the day the two lists were usually quite different. I got distracted with things I hadn't anticipated, or hadn't managed what I thought I could. Sometimes the right-hand page was blank come nightfall, but overall this simple system kept me moving forward."

"I had no idea you were so entrepreneurial, Lily. They didn't teach us that at Bryn Mawr."

"Certainly not, but an educated woman can do anything. Right?"

"Right!" echoed Caroline. They both laughed.

"Well, immediately I knew I'd need help with the children. I couldn't traipse all over town with them in tow. They needed stability and routine, and I needed to be able to move quickly, not to mention taken seriously. I went downstairs to the Mercantile one morning, thinking Mrs. Van Buskirk might know of someone in the neighborhood who could look after them a few hours a day. When I told her about the tearoom, she was thrilled. She ushered me upstairs, sat me down in her parlor, poured me a cup of tea, offered me a plate of cookies, and told me all about her activities as a suffragist.

"I was stunned. That was the last thing I expected to hear. As it turned out, she had been waiting for the right opportunity to invite me to join the cause. When I demurred, at least until I had my business running, she said, 'You know, Lily, a tearoom like that, not in a big fancy hotel but accessible from the street in an ordinary part of town, might be a handy thing. Women of all sorts will feel free to stop by, meet their friends, and if a little political talk happens at the tables, what harm can it do?'

"I must have frowned, thinking I didn't want my new business hijacked by a bunch of militant suffragists, despite my belief in the cause. She saw my discomfort, bless her heart, and diplomatically changed the subject...temporarily.

"She knew just the person to care for the children while I was out and about. Lettie lived with her parents a couple of blocks away. She often shopped for her mother at the Mercantile. Lettie had just graduated from high school and wanted to go to secretarial school as soon as she could save up the fees. Her mother needed help with the younger children, so she didn't want her to do anything fulltime. Three or four hours a day was ideal for both of us.

"Lettie? That's how you met her?" asked Caroline.

"Yes, what a fortunate meeting that was. She not only helped with the children and the housekeeping, but she learned bookkeeping and typewriting and office organization over the next few years at night school. She had a natural talent for office work. As soon as Mark and Theresa were in school, Lettie took over the bookkeeping for the businesses. She's been a great help to us in so many ways. When I became ill, she moved in so she could take care of me while continuing on with the business tasks. She keeps an eye on the tearoom, now that I can't be there. Please don't tell her, but I've willed the business to her. I'd rather she not know until I'm gone. I'd be embarrassed by her gratitude."

Caroline inhaled a sharp breath, an instinctive reaction to someone heralding her own death. Lily raised a blue-veined hand to stop her.

"Now, Caroline, I know it's coming and it gives me peace to know the Merry Weather will continue on without me...and Lettie will have the independence she deserves. Theresa is well taken care of by her husband, who wouldn't dream of leaving his farm to take up a business in the city. As for Mark...well, he wouldn't be caught dead running a tearoom for women. He'll inherit the flower business someday, although he shows no inclination for it at the moment. Marco lives in hope that he'll feel differently before the time comes.

If not, so be it. Besides, it gives me great comfort to picture Lettie hearing the news."

The following morning Lily was unable to get out of bed. The excitement of Caroline's visit and their conversations over the past few days had ganged up on her, robbing her of energy. Some of the following days were better than others, and Caroline was able to see her briefly. Other days were impossible, finding her weak and pain-ridden, asking nothing more than to be left alone in her bed. Not wanting to go far and perchance miss an opportunity to sit with Lily if she felt better, Caroline took walks around the neighborhood, wrote to Nancy, read, and enjoyed afternoon tea with Lettie in her suite. Once in a while she wandered into the kitchen for a friendly chat with Mrs. Delfini.

On such an afternoon, seated on a kitchen stool, grating cheese while the cook kneaded bread dough, Caroline learned that Mrs. Delfini had come over in steerage from Sicily with her parents as a young child. Her most vivid shipboard memory was of being in her father's arms at the ship's railing, holding on in wind-whipped terror while the muslin-wrapped body of a fellow steerage passenger was cast into the churning sea. She had nightmares for years of her father letting go and her little self pitching overboard after the shrouded body.

When she was eight years old, the family joined a wagon train in St. Louis, headed for Oregon. The transcontinental train was overtaking wagon travel by then, but her father was determined to get his prized four-ox team to their new home. Far out in the prairies, he stepped on a rusty piece of discarded metal that sliced through his weathered boot. He contracted lock jaw and died an agonizing death as the wagons rolled on. She and her mother quickly learned to drive and care for the oxen. They made it over the mountains only because they had no choice. The other families in the wagon train kept an eye on them and helped them as they could, but there was little spare manpower to go around.

"What a hardy breed you pioneers were," murmured Caroline.

"Oh, yes. Once you've made the trip over the Rockies in a covered wagon, you can survive anything. Many times I wanted to crawl under a bush and die, but my mother kept us going. We sold the oxen when we got here and bought a house. Then we took in boarders to keep us going. How I hated feeding all those men and cleaning up after them. And dodging their attentions as time went by. When I was old enough to find some other kind of work, I was lucky to discover the Merry Weather. I was one of the first Back Door Women. And even luckier when the Giannottis took me on as their personal cook."

Mrs. Delfini stopped kneading the dough, looked up, and threw her floured hands up in the air. "Oh, Mrs. Crawford, stop! You've grated enough cheese to last the entire week!"

Both women threw back their heads and chortled.

Then, for Caroline, there was the sheer indulgence of afternoon naps, a habit she quickly got used to, and waking to the delicious aromas of fresh-baked bread and whatever garlic, cheese, and mysterious ingredients simmered or baked for the evening's dinner.

By the time Lily was feeling well enough to continue their visits, a week had gone by. Caroline barely recognized her friend when she entered her bedroom. Far from the animated and alert woman she'd seen just seven days before, Lily was lying on her stomach, her face turned toward Caroline. Her closed eyes were rimmed in ash, her cheeks pale and sunken, her mouth slack. Unbuoyed by her waking personality, Lily looked a frail specter of herself.

Despite the open window, or because of it, the room was stiflingly hot. Caroline unbuttoned the top of her bodice, hoping for a little relief. The sickroom smell had intensified in the heat.

Lily's eyes fluttered open and scanned the room, drifting past Caroline, finally focusing on Leticia, who had stepped aside when Caroline walked in.

"Lettie? Turn me over, please, and bring me a drink of water." Her voice was barely audible.

"Of course. Let me prop you up so it won't spill. There we go. Caroline is here to say hello."

"Caroline. Of course. How could I have missed you? You've come all this way and then I deserted

you for…how long? A week, Lettie? Now I'm developing bedsores, Caroline, so they have to turn me over at intervals. At least now I know where this new soreness is coming from. I'm so sorry. Have you found enough to keep you busy?"

"Oh, yes, please don't be concerned on that score. I'm very practiced at entertaining myself."

"Good! Where did we leave off? I still have so much to tell you. Let's see how far we get before I start to fade again."

Lily's eyes regained some of their sparkle as she elbowed herself a little higher on her pillows. Worried about those bedsores, but understanding that Lily didn't want to talk about them, Caroline pushed her chair a little closer to the bed so as not to miss a single word. Before long her friend seemed almost the Lily of old, carried along by her listener's enthusiasm.

Jannie Van Buskirk was helpful in more ways than one. After telling Lily about Leticia, she took Lily by the hand and led her into her kitchen. There on a heavy sideboard crafted of elaborately carved dark wood, sat an exquisite porcelain tea service for twelve, the rest of the set from which Jannie was preparing to serve Lily and herself tea.

"Look," said Jannie. "Here is just what you need to serve your customers. The best Dutch Amstel porcelain. It was my grandmother's, and we brought it packed in sawdust all the way from Amsterdam by ship and train. Thank goodness we didn't have to cross the Rockies in a wagon. Such a heavy barrel we would surely have had to dump along the way."

"Jannie, this porcelain is exquisite. I couldn't possibly use it to serve customers. Why, the cups and saucers would chip and break in no time. I'm not sure I'm comfortable even now drinking tea from such a valuable service."

"But look at this place." Jannie swept her hands across the modest room. "These are shopkeepers' quarters. I never entertain anyone here, except for a few close women friends who are comfortable in my kitchen. Really, what better way to announce the gentility of the tearoom than with a classic tea service!" Jannie beamed with generosity.

Lily laid a hand on her former landlady's arm. "Truly, I appreciate the offer, Jannie. But listen. I have a better idea. What if we install a shelf on the wall, at eye level like this one, and display your tea set there without actually using it. It will be the centerpiece of the décor—setting the tone, as you said—and there will be no danger of breakage. I'll sleep better if I'm not worrying about it. What do you think?"

Jannie clapped her hands. "Perfect! When you are ready, I ask Joop to install the shelf and then the whole world will be able to enjoy looking at my grandmother's Amstel service. She would be so happy!"

That was the beginning. Having secured young Leticia's capable services with the children, Lily was free to wander downtown Portland, a basket on one arm and a string bag on the other, seeking items for the shop. Knowing her budget would not cover much that was brand new, she sought out second-hand stores and sidewalk vendors, rummaging in the shops and boxes for simple treasures. She also kept an eye out for folks who were giving up on the rigors of the Pacific Northwest and heading back east. Such advertisements often appeared in the *Oregonian*, offering household goods for sale to lighten their loads. She made sure she was among the first to arrive on the day of the sale. In this way she picked up tea sets that were only missing a cup or saucer or two, sometimes the teapot itself, but were otherwise serviceable.

She also came upon numerous single cups, saucers, and dessert plates of fine bone china, which at first she passed over. Then one night it occurred to her that deliberate mismatching would be charming, much like a patchwork quilt. She retraced her steps and purchased all the single cups, saucers, plates, teapots, creamers and sugar bowls she could find, the one rule being: no chips, cracks or missing handles.

That opened the way to a variety of mismatched tables and chairs, of which there were an abundance once she began to look for them. As for tablecloths and napkins, she found some and made others with fabric from the Mercantile, which Joop added to the Giannotti account.

From a merchant across town who was expanding his business and needed more extensive furnishings, she purchased a service counter with a glass top and display front, which he obligingly carted to the shop for her. She also found several second-hand breakfronts, beautifully carved and only a little scratched, which added to the homey atmosphere. The Franklin stove in the corner would do for boiling water and keeping the place warm, and she'd worry about getting a proper cook stove when she was ready to turn the back room into a kitchen.

When approached by his wife to build a shelf for the antique tea set, Joop declared that shelves behind the counter were also needed, so he installed those as well. Within a month, Lily had the shop cleaned from top to bottom, the walls whitewashed, the floor scrubbed, the stove blackened, and flowered half-curtains hung at the windows and framing the doorway to Giannotti Florist West. A dozen tables of various sizes were set with a cheery mix of tablecloths, napkins and china in anticipation of the first customers. Teapots, cups and saucers lined the shelves behind the counter, as much for decoration as for use, looking festive in their merry disarray. To top it off, Lily had found three quilted silk wall hangings of appliqued flowers, their seams cunningly overstitched with contrasting embroidery—all different, all colorful. In a quiet moment of introspection, she wondered what tales those lively pieces of fabric art, perhaps made from once-treasured party dresses, could tell if they'd been able. She invited Jannie to see the setup on a cool fall morning.

"Ah, you have made wonders, my friend," Jannie exclaimed. "All those different cups and saucers, what a jolly idea. And isn't my grandmother's china the queen of the tearoom, perched all by itself on the wall over there!"

"Indeed it does. Joop did a stellar job with the shelving. Everything is displayed in full sight. We've created such a cheery place to relax."

"And where did you get all those charming flower bowls at the center of each table?"

"More second-hand finds, waiting to be filled with Marco's blossoms on opening day, and squat enough that our customers can see over them."

"And now, what kind of tea will you serve? And what will you serve with it?"

"Good question. I've visited the various markets in town that carry tea, and it seems to me that Joop carries as good a selection as any. In fact, he gave me an animated lecture on the long history of Dutch tea trading in the Indies. I'm sure I made his day by being such an attentive listener! I'll start with what I can buy from him in small quantities, and as the business expands I'll see if I can make a deal for larger lots at lower prices."

"Aha, you have the soul of a merchant. I wonder you aren't Dutch! Joop will enjoy bargaining with you. Just make sure you let him *think* he gets the better of you, but make sure you really get the better of him."

The two women laughed, knowing that Joop would be entertained by negotiating with a woman and never suspect that Lily would give as good as she got.

"And what about sweets?" asked Jannie. "Women must have sweets with their tea."

"Yes, that's one thing I haven't tackled yet. I'm running out of funds, and even if I could afford to buy from a bakery, I want to have treats my customers can't buy elsewhere. I want everything about the Merry Weather Tearoom to be unique, but I am a hopeless baker."

Jannie clamped her hands into her ample hips. "So what about those cookies I served you in my parlor when you told me about this venture of yours? My hazelnut crisps?"

247

Lily blinked. "They were delicious, the best cookies I've had in ages. But…"

"My own special adaptation of a popular Dutch recipe. Lots of butter and brown sugar, and instead of pecans, which we have to import all the way from California—hazelnuts—or perhaps you call them filberts—which we grow right here in Oregon. What better to serve to your lady customers?"

"But how will I get them?"

"I'll make them for you, of course! Every day, fresh from my oven. You pick them up on your way to the shop."

"You'd do that? I couldn't pay you right away."

"Forget the pay. It will come. For now, Joop is tired of having me in the store and I am tired of being there. This will give me something to do upstairs in my kitchen. I'll feel like a partner in your success!"

"That's very generous, Jannie. I don't know what to say."

"Simple, just say *ja*!"

"*Ja*, Jannie. *Ja, ja, ja*!"

One good idea led to another. The next morning Lily hopped on a streetcar headed toward the train station and the boarding house where she and Marco had stayed during their first week in Portland. Agnes Hardy welcomed her with open arms.

"Why, Lily Giannotti! It's been a while! How lovely to see you again. Come in, come in. Surely you're not looking for a place to live again?"

When Lily smiled and shook her head, Agnes motioned her into the parlor and carried on.

"I was just wondering what I was going to do today to keep myself amused. I finally hired a young woman to help with the housework and cooking. She's far too efficient, and now I find myself at loose ends by eleven o'clock. Aside from my meetings of course."

"Your meetings?" asked Lily.

"Suffrage, my dear. The vote for women. We will get it, mark my word. But the men of Oregon are not making it easy. What in heaven's name are they afraid of? That women will rule the world? Don't they know we already do? The hand that rocks the cradle, and all that. There's even a noisy contingent of women fighting against it. You're a young woman of spirit. Haven't you joined the cause?"

Lily lowered her eyes. "Well, no, although I've been asked by my former landlady. Do you know Jannie Van Buskirk at the Mercantile, by any chance?"

"Jannie? Of course! She's one of our best organizers. You said no to *her*?"

"I have two children now, Agnes."

"And Elizabeth Cady Stanton had seven! The last one born when she was forty-four, I might add."

"I'm all in favor of voting rights for women, Agnes. I'm also starting a new business. That's how I'll help."

"A new business? Isn't that exciting! A secretarial service perhaps? I do know that good secretaries are hard to find. In fact, you're just in time. We could use one in the organization."

Lily groaned. "No, no, nothing like that. I'm completely unsuited to office work. I'm opening a tearoom, the Merry Weather Tearoom—strictly for women, although that will never be said. I'm trusting that no red-blooded American man will stoop to having tea in its cozy, feminine surroundings."

"The Meriwether Tearoom? What a wonderful name! After Meriwether Lewis, our sainted explorer!" Her eyes twinkled at the intended exaggeration.

"Well, yes, but two words, Merry and Weather." Lily spelled them out. "In reference to Mr. Lewis, of course, and to the constant need to be cheerful in the face of our gray, soggy winters."

"Aren't you clever! But true Oregonians do love the rain, you know. Too much summer sunshine has us yearning for fall."

Lily nodded. "So I've learned, Agnes. What do you think—will the name resonate with the townswomen?"

"I'm sure it will. When will you open?"

"Soon, I hope. I've got almost everything in place, except for sweets to serve."

"Which is why you're here today," Agnes declared, never one to miss a beat. "Scotch shortbread. Nothing better."

"You read me too easily, Agnes. I don't want to serve bakery goods, although the Fancy Delite is a marvel. I'm glad they're there to fall back on, but I want to serve homemade cookies. Dare I hope that I might talk you into baking your delicious shortbread for me? At least until I can afford a proper kitchen and a baker on the premises?"

"You don't even have to ask. Just let me know when you plan to open, and we'll arrange delivery." She paused for a moment. "You know, I have another special cookie that my boarders love—maple walnut crescents. Let me surprise you with them. I started making them after your time, and I know of no bakery in Portland that serves anything like them."

"I accept! We'll let the customers know where they came from, and it'll be good advertising for you!"

"Marvelous! You will be closed on Sundays, I assume?"

"Certainly, Agnes. That goes without saying."

"Well, then. We'll work out payment once you are on your feet. And I'll be sure to tell all my suffragist friends about it. We're always looking for safe, unobtrusive places to discuss our strategies and tactics."

Oh, dear, thought Lily. What have I gotten myself into? She gave Agnes a hug, while crossing her fingers that the suffragists would be manageable.

That night, with the children in bed and Marco nodding off in his chair by the fire, Lily thumbed through her business diary, noting everything she had accomplished, and making tomorrow's list of what remained to be done. Something teased the fringes of her consciousness, something necessary that she had overlooked. The feeling had nagged her ever since she showed Jannie the setup a few days earlier.

She sat quietly, closed her eyes, and let the image of the tearoom float through her mind. Everything seemed fine, complete, attractive. But she couldn't shake the feeling that something was missing.

Annoyed with herself, she rose and picked up the cups, saucers, and teaspoons she and Marco had brought into the parlor with their after-dinner tea.

Teaspoons! She had not given a thought to cutlery. How could she have missed so essential an item! How amusing—even Jannie hadn't noticed. She had thought things through so carefully, so deliberately, trying so hard to be a properly organized businesswoman. Now she wondered what else she might have missed. Well, here was her opportunity to exercise that creative thinking she'd so blithely bragged about.

Giving Marco's shoulder a gentle shake, she confessed what she'd forgotten. They both grinned.

"You've ransacked the secondhand shops and carts for everything else. Why don't you try the pawnshops?" Marco suggested. "You never know what they might have. Just be careful walking the streets in that part of town."

This time he got a back-patting hug. "Thank you, Marco! What would I do without you?"

As soon as Lettie arrived the next morning to look after the children, Lily set off with her string shopping bag. Pawnshops! She'd never thought of them, but she'd seen their distinctive three-ball signs when she rode the streetcar through the seedier section of town. It would be an adventure, if nothing else.

Sure enough, there were four pawnshops within two blocks of one another. She had no idea what the protocol was when dealing with a pawnbroker, but she had nothing to lose by walking in the door and asking questions. She hit pay dirt at the Silverado Pawn Shop, the second one she tried. The shop was neatly organized, and the proprietor was young, cleanly shaven, and well dressed.

"Good morning, Miss," he greeted her. "What can I do for you?"

"I'm looking for some good quality silver-plated spoons. I thought you might…"

Before she could finish her sentence, the young man bent down, hoisted a wooden fruit flat from beneath the counter, and set it before her with a rattling clank.

"Have a look, Miss. See if these are what you're after."

The box held a jumble of tarnished and scarred spoons, forks, knives, and serving pieces.

"Well, this is quite a selection," Lily said.

"I guarantee you, Miss, with a little polish, they'll suit your table just fine and no one will know they're not sterling. Look a-here." He whipped out a smudged flannel cloth and began rubbing one of the spoons. Soon it was shiny-new, if you didn't turn it over and notice the spot on the back of the bowl where the silver plate had worn through to the base metal.

"I'll even throw in one of these magic polishing cloths for touchups. Of course you'll want a box of Red Star Cleaning Powder as well. Just got a shipment last week." From beneath his counter of many revelations, he produced a small colorful box.

"Yes, indeed," said Lily, thinking back to her visiting days. "I've polished many a table's worth of silver with Red Star. You are certainly an enterprising young man, taking care of your customers' every need."

"At your service!" He stepped back and bowed, pantomiming the doffing of a hat. "Running a pawn shop can be a sad business, Miss, dealing with desperate people, selling their valuables to buy food or pay the rent. But I treat my customers fairly, and they often come back to redeem their goods, unless of course they're selling out to finance a trip back home after failing to make good here. I hate to see that, but it keeps a roof over my family's head and food on our table."

As he looked up to greet another customer who had entered the shop, Lily carried the box to a side counter beneath a window where the light was good. She sorted through the flatware, setting aside 30 teaspoons with the least worn plating and fewest scratches and dents. The proprietor quoted her a fair price, which she paid on the way out. If the day ever came when she offered more than cookies, she'd come back for forks, knives, and serving pieces.

Lily hummed all the way home. She couldn't wait to get busy with the Red Star polish and restore her treasures to their former glory.

CHAPTER 27

Once again Caroline could see that Lily was struggling to stay awake. She shifted forward on her seat. "It sounds like the Merry Weather was all set, Lily, once you remembered the spoons. What a funny thing to forget! Let's continue tomorrow. You look done in."

Lily closed her eyes and let her head fall back against the pillows. "Sorry, I just can't keep my eyes open. No wonder, I've talked your ears off again. I feel so invigorated when I'm talking, and then— bang—exhaustion hits me like a hammer."

"We've been at it for quite a while today. We don't want another setback. Just rest now, and we'll carry on tomorrow."

"I will, thank you. But before I tell you any more about the Merry Weather, I think it's time for you to go downtown for a visit. I'll ask Marco to send Jimmy to pick you up in the delivery van tomorrow morning at ten o'clock. Lettie can go with you. What do you say?"

Caroline clapped her hands. "I can't wait! I've been dying to see it, now that I've heard so much about it, but I didn't want to take away a single second of our possible time together. However, if you think it's okay... Will Lettie mind?"

"Of course not. It's time for her to stop by again and see how things are going. Mrs. Delfini can check on me while she's gone. I'll enjoy a quiet day, and then I'll have the energy to tell you the rest of the story."

Jimmy arrived right on time the next morning. Cap in hand, he greeted Caroline and Lettie, looking as slick and shiny as the green Giannotti Florist West van itself.

"Good morning, ladies. What a glorious summer day! In you hop, and we're off to the Merry Weather." Caroline stepped up and slid along the van's bench seat, tucking in her skirt and making room for Lettie to follow.

"Thanks for coming for us, Jimmy," said Caroline. "Surely you have better things to do?"

"Nothing more important than driving two lovely ladies into town," he replied with a sideways grin.

"Jimmy, you are incorrigible," said Lettie. "How are things coming along with you and that pretty Daisy Lloyd? She's been Mr. Giannotti's bouquet maker for a while now. Quite a talented young lady."

A blush bloomed up his neck. "Aw, you know. Her father, he's not that impressed with me. Just a florist's delivery boy, sez he. But I have plans. It won't be long before I have a better position with a flashy title to match."

"Oh? A plan…for Giannotti's, or…?"

"Oh, Miss Lettie, I'd never leave Giannotti's. They're ever so good to me, but a man does need to progress."

"And does Mr. Giannotti know of your plan?"

"Of course not. It's still a secret!"

Lettie and Caroline exchanged amused glances.

"Well," Lettie continued, "you'll have to let him in on it at some point."

"Oh, don't you worry. When the time is right, I most certainly will."

Caroline sensed Jimmy was eager to share his idea. He just needed a little prodding.

"Can you tell us about it? We're good at keeping secrets, aren't we, Lettie?"

Lettie looked heavenward. "Oh, goodness, yes. You wouldn't believe the things I hear at the Merry Weather."

He frowned. "Well, you can keep all that ladies' gossip to yourself, and welcome to it."

Caroline chuckled. "So carry on, then. What's your plan all about?"

He jutted out his chin a bit, as if to bolster his confidence, and took a deep breath. "Well you see…when I'm making my deliveries to commercial establishments around town, I notice plenty of opportunities to sell more flowers, both to our current customers and other businesses along the way. Mr. Giannotti is so busy manning the store, taking orders, making sure the orders are packed correctly and sent out on time, driving out to the farms to check on growing conditions and getting his hands into the dirt from time to time. You know, all that stuff. He doesn't have a minute to look for new business, but I'm telling you, it's out there. So I'm proposing he promote me to salesman—no wait, sales manager, that's better—and turn me loose to drum up more business. He can hire someone else to make the deliveries—under my supervision, of course."

He turned to look at Caroline and Lettie, grinning at his own cleverness, awaiting their approval. In that moment of inattention, the van swerved off the road and onto the narrow grassy verge near the bottom of the hill.

"Watch out, Jimmy! You're taking us into the ditch," gasped Lettie. She and Caroline braced themselves against the dashboard, fearful of being thrown out of the doorless van.

With a yelp, Jimmy swung the vehicle back onto the street but failed to look behind him. He jumped on the brake with both feet, missed the clutch, and threw the van into a spasm of fits and sputters. Then silence.

The driver on his tail slammed on his own brakes, sending his car into a dusty fishtail, and barely avoided crashing into them. "You jerk!" the driver yelled at Jimmy as he swung past. "Watch where you're going!"

Caroline gingerly pushed back from the dashboard, as did Lettie, and looked around to see if anyone walking along the roadside had been hurt. Horns honked, urging Jimmy to get going and clear the street, but the few pedestrians strolled on with nothing more than worried glances at them.

"Whoosh," exhaled Jimmy. "That was close. Ladies, are you all right?" They assured him they were, although a bit shaken up.

"Thank goodness for that. My sincerest apologies, ladies. I guess I got carried away with my grand career plans. That'll teach me. Will you tell Mr. Giannotti? How will I ever explain it to him? He'll be furious. I've dashed my chances to become a sales manager or win Daisy's hand. This will be the end of my job, and of me and her, too." He hung his head over his fists on the steering wheel.

Caroline glanced at Lettie, who seemed incapable of speech. "Jimmy, you made a mistake. It happens. No one was hurt. You can check the van when we get to the shops. I'm sure we didn't hit any other vehicle. When you've had a chance to cool off, tell Mr. Giannotti about it calmly, hat in hand, with a sincere apology."

"I couldn't do that! He'll fire me for sure."

"Listen, Mr. Giannotti is a fair person. If you handle it manfully, you might be surprised. We won't tell, but other people witnessed the incident, in addition to the driver who almost crashed into us. He can't have missed Giannotti Florist West on the side of the van. There were other witnesses, too. Someone is bound to tell him, so you'd better get there first and tell the truth. Lettie and I will back you up, if need be. It wouldn't have happened if we hadn't been quizzing you about your plan." She shot a questioning glance at Lettie, whose color was slowly returning. She nodded in support.

"Come on Jimmy," Caroline continued. "Start the van. Let's get going before a policeman comes along."

That was all the spur Jimmy needed. He turned on the ignition and shoved the van into gear. Caroline and Lettie braced themselves against the dashboard again and held onto their hats.

Jimmy let the ladies off after a reassuring pat on the shoulder from Caroline and disappeared to park the van in the alley behind the shops. The Merry Weather Tearoom sat in the middle of a downtown block next door to its partner, Giannotti Florist West.

Twin gold and black lettering on the windows of each shop announced its business, but there the resemblance ceased. The flower shop, with its dark-green awning, matching green-painted walls, and window full of luscious flower displays, projected a neutral air. Many of its customers were women who wanted to decorate their homes, but Marco wanted men to feel welcome too. After all, they bought flowers for their wives, sweethearts, mothers and secretaries and were a healthy part of his business.

The tearoom's façade, by contrast, was feminine from top to bottom, side to side. Painted white with a dark pink frame around the half-curtained picture window and French doors, and a candy striped awning, it called out to the women of the neighborhood to drop in and have a treat.

Lettie opened one of the French doors and ushered Caroline in on a scented wave of freshly baked cinnamon buns, a babble of lively chatter, and the clink of silverware on china. A few ladies glanced up with friendly waves to Lettie. Some were fashionably dressed, wearing elaborate summer hats; others looked everyday ordinary.

"My goodness, it's not even ten-thirty and the place is filled," exclaimed Caroline.

"Yes, it's that way every day. Men can go out to the bars or their clubs. Why can't women drop in between errands while their husbands are at work and their children are in school?"

While Lettie returned the waves and greetings—a grasped hand here, a hug there—Caroline paused to take it all in. Each table sported a lush bouquet in a unique glass or china bowl, allowing easy cross-table chitchat. All the chairs were occupied by ladies tittering or listening intently, some with eyes closed, savoring a sip of tea or a bite of a confection. Most looked happy and animated; a few looked somber, perhaps with discouraging family news to share or ask for advice about. Caroline noticed but didn't linger on those unhappy souls, granting them their privacy. Several looked at her inquisitively—a new person in their comfy enclave—but soon turned back to their companions.

As Lily had mentioned, mismatched cups, saucers and small plates on assorted tablecloths created a cheery cacophony of color and design. Jannie's Dutch Amstel porcelain tea set gleamed with pride of place on its shelf between the two breakfronts.

Through the connecting door, Caroline caught a glimpse of Marco and Jimmy deep in conversation behind the counter. Marco, hands in his green apron pockets, listened intently, while Jimmy, standing tall, eye to eye with his employer, appeared to be telling his tale. A pert young woman hovered at the far end of the counter, arranging white daisies and blue agapanthus in a glass vase, trying not to appear to be listening. Marco glanced over and caught Caroline's eye. He winked at her and quickly turned back to Jimmy. She felt certain that Jimmy would get a good dressing down, but that his job was secure. And that Daisy was impressed by his forthrightness.

Lettie hurried back and took Caroline's hand. "Come on. Let's go upstairs first, and I'll show you our workroom. At this time of day it will buzz like a beehive."

They threaded their way through the noisy tearoom, past the service counter where tiered plates of assorted cookies, fancy breads, and *petites fours* were set out in an irresistible display. Several kettles steamed on a small cast iron stove behind the counter, while a hefty but impeccably dressed middle-aged woman sprinkled loose tea into half a dozen china teapots on the counter. She looked up and waved at Lettie, then turned to pick up a steaming kettle to begin filling the pots.

"That's Maybelle Mulroney," whispered Lettie as they rounded the end of the counter and stepped through a curtained doorway into the baking kitchen. "Her husband's the power behind most of the politicians in town. Fabulously wealthy, owns a fortune in forest lands and sawmills. He pulls the strings; the pols dance to his tune. But his wife is one of our treasures, God bless her."

"She does look formidable," commented Caroline.

Chuckling, Lettie steered Caroline through the kitchen, greeting one baker mixing ingredients in a large crockery bowl with a wooden spoon and another pulling a tray of just-baked cookies from an oven. They passed several rows of shelves stacked with boxes and tins of baking ingredients, then headed toward a flight of wooden stairs at the back of the room.

"Maybelle was a ferocious leader in the fight for suffrage. She never gave up, never stopped her effort to keep everyone's spirits high, day after day, no matter how hopeless things looked. Once that battle was won, she turned her full attention to the Back Door Women. She's tireless in organizing classes and ruthless in extracting money from her husband and his friends whenever they need equipment or supplies. She must be helping behind the counter today because someone failed to show up. That rarely happens, but Maybelle steps in wherever she's needed."

Caroline opened her mouth to ask again about the Back Door Women, but decided to wait and see.

Just before they reached the stairway, Lettie stopped and whispered to Caroline. "By the way, didn't that tray of cookies smell delicious?"

"Yes, it was all I could do to keep from swiping one. My mouth is still watering!"

"Me, too. I'm sure Lily told you that Agnes Hardy and Jannie Van Buskirk were her main suppliers at the beginning—shortbread and maple walnut crescents from Agnes and hazelnut crisps from Jannie—but they both retired and passed on their recipes once Lily put in the kitchen. Our bakers love experimenting, so you never know what delights will be offered from day to day. Did you smell the cinnamon buns when we walked in the door? They are our best advertisement. You can smell them all the way down the block. Nobody can resist!"

Caroline nodded vigorously.

"The bakers are all Back Door Women who learned their skills right here. See, here's the back door through which they enter from the alley. Now does it begin to make sense? We'll enjoy a snack after seeing the workshop. The tearoom may have quieted down by then, and, fingers crossed, we'll find a couple of empty seats."

As they ascended the stairs, a mechanical hum from above grew louder. About halfway up they heard a light thud, then a sudden shriek and a shuffling of footsteps. The machine noise stopped. The two hustled up to the landing to see what had happened.

The landing opened directly into a large room furnished with maybe a dozen sewing machines, all but one occupied, and wide tables for laying out fabric and patterns. Near the empty machine, a young woman hopped up and down, sucking her finger and moaning. The others had stopped pedaling and began standing to help her. Those at the cutting tables dropped their scissors and turned to join them.

"Jenny?" called an older, well-dressed woman, the first to reach her. "Oh, Jenny, what have you done? Come here, let me have a look."

Jenny popped her wet finger out of her mouth long enough to say, "I sewed my blasted finger."

"Come on," the older woman said, "stop hopping around. Let me see." The others reached them and hovered around, alarmed and anxious to help. "Give us some air, ladies. It's not an emergency, just a few stitches sewn where they don't belong. Please go back to your work. I'll take care of her."

Staring, Caroline and Lettie remained at the doorway, not wanting to add to the commotion.

"Let's go over to the window, Jenny, where I can see better. That's it." The woman took Jenny by her other arm and steered her toward the window.

Jenny shuffled along, shaking her hand in front of her to distract from the pain.

"Look, Mrs. Novak, the needle's stuck in my finger! Ow, it hurts!"

"By golly, so it is! You've broken it right off the shank. Hold still and let me get a hold of it."

Mrs. Novak tried several times to grasp the broken needle with her finger and thumbnail, but only the tiniest bit was visible and too slick with Jenny's saliva to give her purchase.

"Ow, that hurts when you try to grab it. Stop!" Jenny started hopping up and down again.

"Hold still for a moment, won't you?" Mrs. Novak tightened her one-handed grip on Jenny's finger and stabilized the girl's hand with her other. Quicker than a flash, she bent her head to Jenny's finger and plucked out the broken needle with her teeth. Jenny was too surprised to make more than a quick yelp.

"There," said the older woman, spitting out the offending sliver and wiping her mouth on her sleeve. "All taken care of. Now go over to the sink and wash your hand thoroughly. Let the cold water run over the wound for a minute. Then I'll paint it with iodine and wrap it with a bandage. It's just a puncture, only a few drops of blood. No harm done, but you'll want to leave off sewing for the day. I'll tidy up for you; you can go on home after I've patched you up." She gave Jenny a motherly pat on the rear as the girl turned, tearfully, toward the kitchen area at the far end of the room.

With a cheery round of applause for Mrs. Novak, the workers returned to their projects, not a few shaking their heads at Jenny's carelessness. One of them hurried after Jenny, in case she needed some moral support or a reminder to use soap and a clean towel.

Mrs. Novak wiped her hands on her apron, gave her mouth another swipe, then noticed Caroline and Lettie at the door. She waved and strode over to them.

"My goodness, I didn't see you standing there, Lettie. What a time to stop by for a visit!"

"Will she be okay?" asked Lettie.

"Of course. A crow crashed into the window, and everyone looked up to see what the noise was. Jenny forgot to stop pedaling and sewed right into her finger. When she jumped up, the needle broke off and there it lodged. I'm sure it hurts, but she'll be fine."

"Thank goodness. Driza Novak, this is Mrs. Caroline Crawford of Philadelphia. She and Lily were classmates at Bryn Mawr. She's come to Portland for a visit, and today seemed a good day to drop by. Although...maybe not."

"Pish-posh. Everyone's back at work, and this afternoon we have classes in nutrition and wise shopping." Driza pointed to a large slate board in a far corner, fronted by a semicircle of wooden chairs. "Let me get Jenny taken care of, then I'll join you downstairs for a cup of tea. I'll tell you all about our classes, Mrs. Crawford. I'm so proud of our girls."

Caroline glanced around the room. The women, or girls as Driza called them, were back at their machines, heads bent as they guided their pinned fabrics under the needles, feet pumping to turn the wheels that sent the shafts up and down, everything humming again. They were modestly and practically dressed, as if they had just put down their brooms at home or finished hanging the laundry. Those standing at the tables once again hunched over their pattern pieces, smoothing them out, pinning them in place, and picking up their scissors to resume cutting.

Nerves still a bit frazzled after their scare in the van and now this bit of drama, Caroline was ready for her tea and cookie—more than one, she hoped.

As Lettie had predicted, a trio of ladies was gathering their shopping bags and purses, preparing to vacate their tearoom table. Caroline glanced at the door to see if anyone was waiting to enter, thinking perhaps they'd need to defer to real customers, but the coast was clear. Lettie quickly tidied the table and stepped back for a server to give the tablecloth a quick shake-out.

"Nice to see you, Lettie, and your friend," the server said, nodding at Caroline. Again introductions were made, then Caroline and Lettie sat down to the clean table.

"What'll it be today?" asked Alexa, a thirty-ish woman dressed, as were the other servers, in a green and white gingham skirt, white shirtwaist and a white apron with a bright green sash. "We have a fresh shipment of peppermint tea, direct from a grower across the border in Washington. It's not real tea, just dried peppermint leaves, but it brews up most refreshingly and won't keep you awake at night."

Lettie deferred to Caroline, who said, "Sounds perfect!"

"Yes, Alexa, and please bring us a nice selection of cookies," said Lettie. "Driza will be joining us, so do make sure there's enough for three."

"Coming right up!" Alexa sashayed off to fill their order.

Caroline turned to Lettie. "Are the servers former suffragists?"

"No, the suffragists have pretty much stepped back unless we need someone for an emergency, like Mrs. Mulroney. Of course they are still among our best customers, reliving their war stories from their days of fighting for the vote. The servers are all Back Door Women, like the ones working upstairs. They take care of almost everything in the tearoom. I'm nominally in charge, as I'm sure Lily has told you, but the women are so efficient and organized, there's barely anything for me to do. Marco brings home the receipts every night, and I keep the books, as I do for the flower shop. I slip in here once a week to check the inventory and do the ordering, but as you can imagine, most of my time now is devoted to Lily."

Alexa returned with three cups of tea on a tray, along with a platter of cookies: chocolate crinkles, Agnes's shortbread and maple walnut crescents, and Jannie's hazelnut crisps. Caroline perked up at the bounty and reached for a crescent.

"My mother used to make these," she exclaimed. "Oh, the maple scent takes me right back to her kitchen!"

"They melt in your mouth, don't they? Have as many as you want," encouraged Lettie. "It's nice to see a woman with a healthy appetite." Caroline's thoughts flashed to Lily, whose appetite seemed to diminish more and more every day.

Driza entered the room from the curtained rear doorway and dropped into a chair across from Caroline. "Before we talk about anything else, Lettie, how is Lily?"

Lettie hesitated, as if deciding how much she should share. Caroline felt sure that whatever Lettie told her would quickly make its way around the tearoom and the workroom upstairs. It wouldn't do for Lettie to be an alarmist, knowing how beloved Lily was by everyone here. Or to violate Lily's privacy. On the other hand, gently preparing the way for the inevitable would make it less shocking when it finally happened.

"Not so good, Driza. The doctor does what he can, and we all hope and pray. But I think we need to prepare ourselves."

Driza knitted her fingers together and lowered her head. "I was afraid of that. We haven't seen her here in weeks. Marco's been looking terribly worried, but I've hesitated to ask. I'm so sorry. I'll let the others know, shall I?"

Lettie nodded. "Please, but just the barest details. And ask them not to mention it to Marco. It's difficult enough for him to deal with it without their questions and concerns. Now, why don't you tell Caroline about your classes?" To Caroline she said, "Driza is a Back Door Woman who has a great talent for organizing. She's in charge of the workroom and the classes."

Driza dipped her head, acknowledging the compliment. "With pleasure. I expect you've heard the basics from Lily. How things got started, where the women came from?"

"Not entirely," Caroline replied. "There's more to tell, I'm sure. Lily tires quickly, but we have a few good hours together most days. Once she gets going, she won't stop until she's positively worn out."

"That sounds like our Lily. We all love her and miss her." Driza picked up the pendant watch that hung around her neck on a gold chain and glanced down at it.

"Oops, I need to get back upstairs, but what it all boils down to, Mrs. Crawford, is everyone sharing what they know. At first we relied on the suffragists. They organized classes around things they knew and were willing to teach. They are excellent at training to work in fine households, manners, etiquette, as you might expect. That was valuable for women wanting to enter service, but we saw a need for more basic life skills: sewing, reading, writing, household cleanliness and organization, baby and child care, cooking and nutrition, home healthcare, managing childbirth—oh, I could go on and on. Sometimes it's just dispelling old wives tales, like putting a knife under a laboring woman's bed to cut the pain, or letting your dog lick an open wound to keep it from getting infected. Those notions are useless at best and sometimes downright harmful."

"I noticed the classes are in nutrition and wise shopping today."

"Yes, they're part and parcel of the same thing. Daughters tend to follow their mothers' examples when it comes to shopping for food. We try to open their eyes to other possibilities, broadening their baskets, you might say, while staying within their budget. Speaking of budgets, what a hit our budgeting classes have been! Of course it's hard to budget if the family income is unreliable, as it often is. Husbands whose work is erratic or whose wages are spent at the pub on their way home every night; or an emergency crops up that uses every cent saved and then some. Handling money wisely can be difficult under those circumstances, but that makes it all the more urgent. Women often have control of the family finances—at least the portion that makes it home—and they are eager to learn good spending and saving habits."

"I imagine everyone would benefit by lessons in household finance," remarked Caroline.

"Indeed, and that's just an example. Our classes are somewhat helter-skelter, depending on who's available to lead, and what's wanted at the time. Always informal, flowing with the tide. We sometimes sit around a big table so everyone can contribute. You never know who will drop in, or how many. It depends on if and when they can get away from their household chores. But it works—it's amazing how much they learn from one another with someone to guide the conversation. And the friendships made here are invaluable. It's a place to share hardships and joys, support one another, and have a good laugh at the same time. My job is to keep things upstairs somewhat organized and happening. I love being part of it."

"I can see that you do!"

Driza pushed back her chair and stood. "Which reminds me, I'd better get back to the workroom. It's my turn to lead the nutrition discussion. It's hard to think about nutrition when you're living hand to mouth, but every bit of knowledge helps. Today we're going to talk about vegetables. I've been reading up on how important vegetables are for good nutrition. We've got some great backyard gardens going. Funny thing—many of the farm girls swore they'd never put their hands in the dirt again, yet they get a kick out of coaching the city gals. And of course the coaching turned into teaching by example, so now the farm gals are among our proudest gardeners. They supply their own families, and we have a surplus sale on Fridays." She turned to their guest. "It was nice to meet you, Caroline. Please come again. Lettie, do tell Lily I was asking for her."

When Caroline and Lettie had finished their tea and rose to leave, Alexa stopped them with a white box tied with pink string. "Here are some cinnamon rolls to take home," she said, "with our love to Lily."

CHAPTER 28

By the time Caroline and Lettie returned home in the mid-afternoon, Caroline was exhausted. She hoped to see Lily a little later and share her delight in the tearoom. At the moment, however, her bed was calling. She slipped off her shoes and stretched out, intending to close her eyes for just a few minutes.

When she awoke the room was almost dark, the windows blurred by rain slicing across the glass. Startled, she rolled over and reached for the clock on her bedside table. By the radium dial, it was almost nine o'clock. Only then did she hear the light tapping on her bedroom door.

"Come in," she called, swinging her legs over the side of the bed, trying to get her bearings.

Leticia pushed open the door, carrying a laden tray. "Good evening, Sleeping Beauty. That was quite a nap!"

"My goodness, I thought I'd lie down for a few winks, and look what happened."

"Well, you must have needed it. I thought I'd better wake you up and bring you some food so you'll be able to sleep later tonight. Marco is with Lily now. She had an unsettled day. She sends her love and says she'll see you in the morning. She's most anxious to hear about our visit to the Merry Weather. I told her you'd fill her in."

Lettie set the tray on the writing desk and pulled out the chair. "I think you can eat comfortably here. There's lasagna with zucchini and garlic bread. And a glass of *vino*."

Although disappointed at not being able to see Lily, Caroline relished her solitary dinner, marveling once again at the complex flavors of an Italian dish she had never heard of. After overdoing it with sweets at the tearoom—and enjoying every bite—a savory dinner with a glass of red wine was most welcome. When she finished, she crossed the hall and indulged in a hot, lingering bath. She donned her nightgown and made herself comfortable in her reading chair. To her surprise after such a long nap, she began to nod off every few pages. Perhaps it was the wine. With her hair still damp, she gave up and slipped into bed. Stretching out luxuriously between the cool sheets, she fell asleep almost immediately. Sometime after midnight she awoke to the sounds of water dripping from the eaves and frogs croaking in the hedges. Well, at least I'm not the only one awake at this ungodly hour, she mused.

She changed positions several times, trying to get more comfortable, but her head was filled with images and snatches of conversations from the Merry Weather. What a remarkable place— all those women enjoying a ladylike tea-and-cookies respite from their daily duties. And the Back Door Women—working, learning, and sharing so industriously upstairs. She hoped young Jenny had recovered from her sewing machine needle episode.

She glanced at the clock on the bedside table. Almost 1:45 a.m. Then it was 2:20, then just after 3 o'clock. When she looked again, another quarter hour had gone by. Her long nap was the culprit; now she was paying the price.

A tumble of unbidden thoughts cycled through her mind—the tragedy of Donnalee on the train, wondering how Nancy was doing as her pregnancy progressed, small hurts she had thoughtlessly inflicted on others throughout her life and for which she had never apologized. And her concerns about Lily. She could no longer deny the haunted look in her friend's eyes when she thought she was unobserved, as if the netherworld were actively beckoning. Nor could she deny the wasting of Lily's body, thin now to the point of emaciation; her lack of appetite; her need for more and more sleep. Yet Lily's stamina for conversation defied those signs of decline.

Their time together seemed to invigorate her, until after an hour or so it became too much. Lily had apparently gotten her out here in order to unburden herself. It seemed she wasn't going to let anything, not even the progressing leukemia, stop her.

Finally Caroline could stand it no longer. She threw off the covers, donned her slippers and bathrobe, grabbed her book and reading glasses, and tiptoed down the hall, intending to wrap herself in a throw and read for a while in the screened porch. Perhaps the brisk night air would calm her mind and allow her to drift off with her feet on the hassock.

As she neared the partially open door to Lily's room, she heard a slight rustle. She hesitated, wondering if Lily had kicked off her bedclothes and was trying to pull them back up. Or perhaps her water glass was empty and she was trying to get up to refill it. She knocked lightly on the door, then pushed it open a bit more.

"Lily?" she called softly. "Are you awake? Is there something I can do for you?"

"Caroline, come in, come in. I'm having one of those dreadful nights when I can't sleep at all. So many pesky thoughts and memories chasing me around until I feel I'm going mad. Nothing helps, not even the laudanum. But here you are! Help me up a bit, please. Have you been tossing and turning too? Turn on the night lamp on the dresser. We can have a marathon middle-of-the-night chat!"

Caroline lifted her friend by her shoulders, startled by how light she was, and fluffed the pillows behind her. She untwisted the nightgown from around Lily's hips, a sure sign of a restless night, and wrapped her with a teal alpaca shawl that was draped on the back of the armchair.

"There, is that better?" she asked, as she crossed the fringed ends over Lily's chest.

"Perfect, thank you. Now, if you would quietly close the door, we'll be all set. We don't want anyone to bother us."

Smiling, Caroline did as she was asked, then pulled the armchair close enough to discern the deepening lines on Lily's face in the dim lamplight. In a blink all that disappeared, and she was back at Bryn Mawr, in that secret time of night when two giddy college girls shared their hopes and dreams and a little gossip, knowing they were safe from their sleeping housemother's sharp ears.

Lily broke the silence, her voice stronger now that their privacy was assured. "I hate these sleepless nights, but the doctor tells me it's not time yet for stronger medicine. The laudanum works well enough in the daytime, but at night I never know. The time will soon come for straight morphine, I'm told, when the pain becomes unbearable. Not something I look forward to."

Before Caroline could respond, searching for words and failing, Lily sighed, then continued. "But you don't want to hear about that. Forgive me."

Caroline caught herself yawning. Mortified, she quickly turned her head and covered her mouth with her hand, hoping Lily hadn't noticed. But Lily was too quick.

"Dear Caroline, go back to bed. You need your sleep."

"Absolutely not! That was just a little 'my-body's-getting-old' betrayal. I sabotaged myself with a long nap this afternoon, as Lettie may have told you. I've been tossing and turning for almost two hours. I'm wide awake. We can both nap all morning if we like. There's no one to stop us."

Lily giggled. "Well, if you're sure." She shifted on her pillows and fingered the satin collar of her nightgown. By now Caroline could tell when she was in pain. She'd be helping her friend through the night by distracting her, a small service she was happy to provide.

"Now, tell me all about your visit to the Merry Weather. What did you think?" Lily clasped her hands together over the shawl, a gesture of pride and anticipation.

"I was overwhelmed! It's so cozy and welcoming—that delicious aroma of fresh baked goods as one walks in, those flowered curtains and tablecloths and napkins; the various china teapots, cups, saucers and plates; flowers on every table. Mrs. Van Buskirk's Dutch porcelain tea service overseeing the room in regal splendor. It's like, well, I don't know how to say it..."

"A crazy quilt! Just like the women who frequent it. I love it when I acquire something colorful and unmatching to add to the decor, or when a new woman comes in shyly and leaves with a smile and a promise of new friends. Not to mention a bouquet to take home from Giannotti's."

"How clever you were!"

Lily chuckled. "It was a thinly conceived experiment in the beginning, based mostly on hope and imagination."

"But you marched on, just like your friends the suffragists."

"Well, you could say that. I just thought the ladies of the neighborhood might enjoy a little casual socializing and a friendly cup of tea on the way home from shopping. And if they also picked up a bouquet from Marco's, all the better. When the suffragists found it, success was assured. I couldn't have kept them away if I'd wanted to."

Lily paused, took a deep breath and pulled the shawl a little tighter. "But listen, there's more to the Merry Weather than I ever suspected. Allow me to speak of things one can't discuss in broad daylight. Like we used to do at Bryn Mawr, in our nightgowns just as we are tonight, remember?"

Caroline sighed and tucked her feet up beneath her. She'd become more and more convinced that her friend had not told her the entire story of her flight from Philadelphia, that she had cleverly skirted the real catalyst more than once. The story so far, as Lily had told it, *seemed* complete—unsuited lovers, already expecting a child, running away from Old World parental obstacles—but Caroline felt certain there was more to it. After getting her all the way out to Portland, what was keeping Lily from leveling with her?

One thought had begun niggling her: could it possibly have had anything to do with John? Caroline didn't want to believe it, but she knew John was not unblemished in his dealings with other women. If John had stepped out of line with Lily, that would certainly explain a few things. She'd waited twenty years to find out. She could wait a little longer.

Lily continued with unexpected vigor, as if she'd been wanting to have this particular discussion, whatever it was, all along.

"Let's get back to the Merry Weather, Caroline. As you know, the tearoom is only open from ten in the morning until five in the afternoon. I made a point of being there most afternoons, until recently. While there, I seated the customers and kept an eye on things, making sure everyone was properly served and taken care of.

"As time went on and it became more and more popular, I had to begin seating strangers together where there were empty seats. I held my breath the first few times, but nobody seemed to mind. In fact, friendships were struck up and the next thing I knew, these former strangers were asking to be seated together the next time they came in."

"How splendid!"

"Yes, committee women found willing volunteers for their projects. I overheard a great deal of shared housekeeping and child-raising tips. In the midst of rain and gloom and winter mud, the Merry Weather became a cheery gathering place, where women could exchange ideas, speak freely, and make friendships just as men do at their clubs. And of course the suffragists were always in and out, pressing on with their plans. I learned a great deal as I circulated the tearoom, overhearing snippets of various conversations. Sometimes I was invited to sit in and join them."

Caroline smiled. "Knowing you, I imagine you couldn't resist."

"True. You know me too well." Lily patted her hair and looked down coyly, a gesture that had always endeared her to Caroline. "What I want to tell you about happened gradually. As I became more and more attuned to the room, to the currents flowing back and forth, I caught bits of certain conversations where the ladies leaned in closer to each other, as if they didn't want to be overheard. Usually there were no more than two or three at such a table. If I approached with a single customer who needed a seat, the ladies seemed a little less sincere with their 'Please join us,' although maybe it was apparent only to me. I learned to dodge these intimate discussions and guide the newcomer in another direction."

"Were they plotting a coup d'état?" asked Caroline, injecting a little levity into the night.

Lily shook her head. "No, dear. Although I suspect an occasional household coup might have resulted."

"What were they talking about?" Caroline asked, eager for Lily to explain.

"At first I only overheard a word or two as I walked past. Then, my curiosity aroused, I found myself walking slower and circling back past the same table as often as I dared without being obvious. They were so intent on what they were sharing that they rarely noticed me."

Caroline raised her eyebrows. "Eavesdropping?"

"Indeed, and not at all ashamed of myself. There was much to be learned."

"And what *did* you learn?" Her fingers danced expectantly on her crossed forearms.

"They were discussing the marital bedroom."

Caroline stared. "You mean…"

"Yes, what goes on between husbands and wives behind closed doors. Sex." Lily hissed the word through her teeth.

"I don't understand," Caroline managed to say.

"Tell me something. What were things like between you and John in the bedroom? Before you had to turn him out?"

At Caroline's inrush of breath, Lily pushed on. "You see! Even between two old friends in the middle of the night, sex is an uncomfortable subject."

"Well, yes, it certainly is," Caroline replied, struggling to regain her composure. Did the tearoom ladies really talk about this? And, horrors, was Lily going to dive into the details? "I've never spoken about…the bedroom… with anyone. Except briefly with my doctor when it concerned my health."

"Forget the doctor. How did you *feel* about it, Caroline, sex I mean?"

"Really, Lily!"

"Listen, I'm not long for this world. As I told you in my letter, there's no time left for beating around the bush. It's important to me that we talk about this, because I have learned a great deal and I don't want it to go to the grave with me."

"But...why me?" Caroline realized she was flailing, and immediately wished she could withdraw the question.

"Because you're here, Caroline, my truest friend. Just listen for a moment. Perhaps by the time I've told you my theory about what I've learned by—hmm, yes, eavesdropping—you won't feel so uneasy. These things, so important in a marriage, are never spoken of, as we agree, yet they often dictate a woman's happiness in her marriage for the rest of her life."

"Lily, I have no idea what you are talking about."

"Exactly. So just listen.

"I did not know what to expect, in personal terms, when Marco and I ran away. On the train he was respectful. He had no choice, really, as there was no privacy in our second-class car. I was thrilled to be sitting next to him, just the two of us, holding hands and talking freely. We slept sitting up in our seats those four long nights, enjoying the closeness but dreadfully uncomfortable. After we arrived in Portland, we rested briefly at Agnes's boarding house, then she directed us to a Catholic church nearby. The priest refused to marry us without the proper publishing of the marriage banns, which would take several weeks. So we found a judge who married us on the spot. Marco was content to be legally married for the time being, and we had a proper Catholic wedding on our first anniversary.

"Back at the boarding house that first night, Marco was the soul of consideration. He knew that...certain things...had happened to me, things that terrified me about the marital act. Before he got into bed with me, he sat by my side and promised me that he would never hurt me. If he ever did anything that made me feel uncomfortable, I must promise to speak up. He wanted sex to be joyful for both of us. At the time I couldn't imagine such a thing. One of my visiting hostesses—you remember Kathleen—once said, while complaining of her husband's frequent attentions, that she followed Queen

Victoria's supposed advice to her daughter: Close your eyes and think of England. I wasn't sure how this could help me, or if it was even true, but I never forgot it—just in case."

"Heavens, I'd never heard that," Caroline interjected, at the same time realizing that things didn't quite add up. "But wait, you've already told me you were expecting Mark when you ran away. Why then would you have been frightened on your wedding night?"

Lily pursed her lips, then quickly replied. "Soon it will all make sense, but for the moment please indulge me. I was indeed frightened that night, as I huddled with the covers up to my chin. Marco pried my hands loose and held them in his own. Then he told me something amazing.

"On his delivery route there lived a beautiful and charming French widow, Nanette, who had a standing order for fresh flowers every Friday. She always greeted him politely and thanked him with a nice tip. One day, to his surprise, she invited him in for a cup of tea. Hers happened to be the last delivery that day, so he shrugged his shoulders and followed her inside."

"Oh, dear. I hope she wasn't up to no good."

"Now tell me, Caroline, what seventeen-year-old boy would turn down such an invitation from an attractive, slightly older woman of the world? She invited him in a few more times, and soon the teapot became a bottle of wine and…"

"She seduced him?" blurted Caroline.

"Indeed, in the time-honored Continental way—an older woman initiating a younger man into the mysteries of love."

Caroline's hand flew to her mouth. "My goodness!"

"Yes, she introduced him to the art of lovemaking, taught him many ways in which a man can please a woman, and how a woman can please a man. Most of all, she taught him that a woman can experience the final…shall we say…climactic event as thrillingly as a man."

Caroline, stunned and confused, could find no appropriate comment.

"You really don't know what I'm talking about, do you, Caroline?"

"No."

"Then...it wasn't like that with you and John?"

Caroline recovered her tongue, but not immediately. "John was quick and gentle, but I found the whole thing distasteful. Certainly never joyful. I couldn't wait to get it over with and cleanse myself. Once the doctor told us we had to stop for good, I was relieved. John didn't seem to mind either." No, he didn't mind, mused Caroline, but that's another story.

"And you never did it with anyone else, Caroline—I mean after John died?"

"Lily!"

"Sorry. It's just that you've missed out on one of life's great pleasures, perhaps its greatest pleasure. Marco was wonderfully patient. He slowly eased my fears, never going beyond what I could accept at the moment. As time went on I became an enthusiastic partner, much to our mutual delight. I miss those times with Marco more than I can say, and I know he misses them as well." She closed her eyes for a moment as those regrets deepened the lines near her mouth. Then she perked up again.

"So this is what I've gleaned from the conversations at the Merry Weather, Caroline: some women like it, an occasional few are crazy for it, but most consider it a duty they have to perform in exchange for being taken care of and having children. Why do you think that is?"

"Please, don't ask me. I couldn't begin to say." Caroline glanced helplessly at the clock on the mantel, which was not cooperating in bringing this discussion to a close.

"Nor I. It's just a big mystery. Someday perhaps someone will study these things, but for now it's kind of the luck of the draw, isn't it, depending greatly on the husband you get. Some are generous and considerate, and they and their wives have a healthy and enjoyable physical relationship. These may be few, or they may be many. I just don't know, but I'm grateful to have been one of the lucky ones.

"On the other end of the scale, some husbands demand their rights and take them roughly, regardless of their wives' feelings. Their wives live in dread of the night. Of course, not every woman comes to her wedding bed a virgin, but for those who do the whole tenor of their married life can be determined by how they are treated that first night in their marriage bed. How many tiptoe downstairs the next morning wondering what they have gotten themselves into? And yet, we never hear anything about it. The great charade of the joyous wedding night is often favorable only to the husband."

"Perhaps the wife's naïveté has something to do with it?" Caroline ventured, surprised that she had something to add to the conversation. "Most of us aren't prepared in the least. Certainly not by our mothers."

"I've thought about that, and I'm sure it's a factor. But consider this: You've heard the term 'frigid'? I wonder how much female frigidity is caused by selfish, clumsy—or perhaps simply ignorant—husbands."

"Good heavens, Lily. I've never given these things a thought."

"Let me tell you one more thing, perhaps the most astonishing of all. Several women confessed that their zest for sex enraged their husbands. They were told that no real lady enjoyed sex, and certainly never initiated it. They called them whores, strumpets, deranged…all kinds of dreadful things, when all she was doing was what came naturally. It's a mystifying puzzle. I have felt burdened by these observations and not known what to do with them."

"Surely you don't expect me…"

"No, no, don't worry. I don't believe anything can be done, at least not until people free themselves to speak of these things—men and women alike. But it has helped me, Caroline, to have shared my thoughts just now, even though I know I've shocked you. Which demonstrates the problem, don't you see?" She looked up and gestured toward the window. "Goodness, look! Dawn is breaking, and we're still talking."

Caroline followed her friend's gaze with eyes that had turned gritty and dry. Indeed, the sky was lightening, the trees were emerging from their shadows into daylight shades of brown and green. Something was missing. Ah, the Blue Willow cachepot was not in its usual place on the windowsill. Caroline's shoulders drooped as the full weight of exhaustion descended upon her. In the advancing light, the lines and hollows on Lily's face deepened. Pain was claiming her friend with its relentless iron fist. But Lily's spirit wasn't done yet.

"Another perfect Oregon summer day," she murmured. "I'm so glad you're here to share it with me, Caroline. We'll leave tonight's discussion for others to figure out, folk who are wiser and more open-minded. There's a bit more to tell you about the Merry Weather, and then I think I'll be able to tell you why I really brought you out here."

Caroline looked at her inquiringly. She still didn't understand why Lily had been so frightened on her wedding night when she was already pregnant.

"Yes, Carrie, I'm aware that I haven't been entirely honest, that I've dodged a few of your pertinent observations. Sins of omission, as the Church might call them. I'm still laying the groundwork, to give you a complete picture. Then perhaps you won't judge me too harshly. Let's put it to rest for now."

Caroline tried to blink away the grit under her eyelids, which only made it worse. She was indeed ready to put the conversation—and herself—to rest. She stood and tightened her bathrobe sash.

"Lily, whatever it is, I could never judge you harshly."

Lily acknowledged that with the barest smile. "Now then, Lettie will be here soon, so I'll send you away to have some breakfast and a morning nap. Doesn't that sound nice? I'm going to do the same, and we'll see each other this afternoon. Thanks so much, Caroline, for getting me through the night in an entirely unselfish manner. They can be such lonely hours."

Glancing back at Lily from the doorway, Caroline wasn't surprised that her friend's eyes were fluttering closed, her hands slumped at her sides.

279

Half an hour later Caroline lay in her own bed, snug and comfortable. She'd sponged her face with a warm washcloth, then, finding no one in the kitchen yet, she'd helped herself to a glass of milk. Then she spotted the neatly wrapped box of cinnamon buns from the Merry Weather, obviously waiting for breakfast. They wouldn't miss just one.

Upstairs again, sunshine filled her room, birds called out their greetings, and the leaves on the trees outside her window danced gaily in the breeze. Despite her fatigue, she found herself wide awake amid the raucous reminders of the awakening world. Wild thoughts and uncomfortable questions, planted by Lily, tumbled about in her head. Then, unbidden and unwelcome, came the memory of John's betrayal.

After Nancy's difficult birth, Caroline and John had never again questioned the doctor's admonition against intimacy. She had her second child, and she was content. John assured her that she mustn't feel any guilt for not being able to accommodate him. She appreciated his consideration, seeing it as a testament of his love for her. He was still outwardly affectionate, always pleasant, and never complained about it. As for herself, she hadn't missed that aspect of married life; in fact she'd been relieved to be done with it. John had assured her that her wellbeing was more important to him that anything else. She rarely thought about it as the years went by. How naïve she'd been!

A few days after John's funeral, the widowed Penelope Makepeace had arrived with a tin of cookies. Penelope and Caroline had never been close, mostly because Penelope was a gossip who exaggerated wickedly to add drama to her tattling. She was such a compelling storyteller that many had welcomed her when she had first arrived in their neighborhood—until her vicious tongue landed on one too many among them. One by one they dropped her until only a few stalwarts, whose lives were so constrained and tedious that she never found any gossip to share about them, continued to see her and thrive vicariously on her tales. She learned to insert herself into situations that didn't require invitations, such as charity fundraisers and church socials. She avidly attended funerals, where she often heard salacious murmurings about the deceased. Makepeace indeed—what an ironic name for her.

Knowing Penelope only too well, Caroline was tempted to tell Tildy to make her excuses when she saw the woman striding up her front walk, purple skirts and bonnet ribbons flying. However, on this particular day she'd have welcomed any diversion. An enervating loneliness had crept up on her since the funeral fuss had died down, and her beloved son Robert had returned to his horses in Tennessee. The steady stream of sympathetic callers, with enough cakes, pies, and covered dishes to feed half the neighborhood, had slowed to a trickle. The one person she would have liked to turn to, John, was no longer there. How odd, she thought, to yearn for John to see her through the sadness of his own death! What tricks the mind plays.

Penelope swooped into the drawing room ahead of Tildy, who had no chance to announce her. She gave the startled Caroline a near kiss, then stood back to examine her.

"Hello, my dear Caroline. How are you holding up? You do look tired, if you don't mind me saying so. When my precious Harvey passed away, I was inconsolable for months."

Feeling a little defensive, Caroline replied, "I'm doing as well as can be expected, thank you. It is a lonely time. I appreciate the cookies. Please put them on the table and make yourself comfortable. Tildy will bring us some lemonade." She could see by the woman's eager manner, by the way she perched on the edge of her chair, that she had something spicy to impart. Better get it over with, Caroline thought, hoping whatever Penelope was dying to tell her didn't reflect poorly on any of her friends.

"Well, you know I wouldn't dream of being the one to tell you this, but sooner or later someone will, and it's best to get the facts straight."

And you're going to enjoy every minute of telling me, facts or not, thought Caroline. "Penelope, I'm really not in the mood for gossip. Whatever our friends have been up to, I don't care to hear about it.

Let them live their lives, and I'll live mine. Let's just sit and enjoy the quiet, shall we?" It amused her to suggest sitting quietly to Penelope.

"No, we shall not. You must hear this from me. I've gone to a great deal of trouble to get this information, and you will want to hear it."

"My goodness, that sounds ominous."

"A good word for it, yes. Ominous. I trust you noticed the woman sitting in the back row of the church at John's service? Dressed in black, heavily veiled?" Penelope's eyebrows rose like a pair of cruising ravens.

"For goodness' sake, Penelope. Every woman in the church was dressed in black, and several of them were veiled, heavily or not. And no, I was seated at the front, as you well know. I have no idea who sat in the back."

"This woman slipped out before the service ended, didn't talk to a soul."

"Is that so?" Caroline's left foot began tapping impatiently.

"Nobody knew who she was, nor why she was at John's funeral."

"Forgive me for saying this, Penelope, but you often attend funerals of people you don't know. It seems almost a sport for you. Surely others do it as well." Caroline knew this comment would sting, but it was true. If Penelope took offense and left, all the better. Politeness never got you anywhere with people like her, and she had long since stopped caring what the other woman thought of her.

A quick intake of breath told Caroline her arrow had hit its mark. Penelope pursed her lips and seemed to reorient herself. Apparently her mission was too important to be put off by insults.

"You'd better get off your high horse, Caroline. The woman, a Mrs. Noble, lives in a house on Gerard Street once owned by the late John Crawford." She sat back and crossed her arms over her ample chest, waiting expectantly for Caroline's reaction.

"I'm aware that John owned a number of rental properties in the city. What's that got to do with anything? They belong to me now."

"Not all of them. Your husband bought the Gerard Street house in 1901, according to the public records, and two years later deeded it over to Mrs. Noble, who has lived there ever since. It was a gift; no purchase money passed between them."

Caroline felt a flush flare up her neck. "How do you know all this? And why should I care?"

"I observe, I ask questions, and I listen. I find people and their foibles most diverting. And you should care because you don't know your late husband as well as you think."

"I've heard that you also attend trials at the courthouse. Rubbing your hands together at the miseries of others." What a mean-spirited thing to say, thought Caroline, but the woman deserved it.

"Courthouse attendance is an instructive activity, Caroline. You'd be amazed at the things I learn. But don't try to distract me. Back to Mrs. Noble. Why would an attractive younger woman enjoy the pleasures and benefits of home ownership at no cost to herself?"

Caroline could take no more. She stood abruptly, almost knocking over the end table beside her chair.

"That's quite enough, Penelope. Please leave. I'm sure you'll do your best to spread this all over town, if you haven't already. I can't stop you, but I'm sure there must be a special place in hell for people like you who rejoice in the unhappiness of others."

Caroline marched to the front door trailed by a satisfied Penelope, opened it, and stepped aside. She stopped herself just in time from slamming the door on Penelope's retreating back. How she'd have loved to see the woman sprawled on her porch, skirts awry and fanny exposed.

Over the next few days Caroline found herself reevaluating her entire relationship with John. She despised Penelope for putting these thoughts into her head, but the more she considered the woman's message, the more it made sense: The lack of fuss when the doctor told them that intimate relations must cease after her miscarriage and more sternly after Nancy's birth. The nonchalance with which John moved into a separate bedroom. His lack of complaints about the situation as time went by. His outward cheerfulness and continued affection, but, after Nancy, never hinting at anything more.

From her point of view, nothing had changed except that she had their bed to herself. No more of that messy nuisance, which she had tolerated because it meant so much to John and, of course, was the avenue to children. Most of all, she no longer had to fear death by childbirth. John had made an attempt to teach her how to satisfy him in other ways, but she found them distasteful in the extreme. He quickly demurred and never mentioned them again.

She had heard the expression, "men have needs," but apparently she had not understood how strong those needs were. Now it seemed he'd taken a mistress who took care of those needs in return for a home, probably an allowance, and a certain amount of affection.

Caroline was completely flummoxed. Hurt, too, she had to admit. Even though John was no longer welcome in her bed, she had always considered him her best friend. She didn't doubt the feeling was mutual. They had a rich social life, two beloved children, and a pleasant home. She'd had no indication that things might be otherwise. But of course—all those evening meetings with authors and poker nights at his club—he must have been at Mrs. Noble's. She couldn't put it to rest. After four days of fretting about it, she phoned their attorney, a longtime family friend. She plunged right in before losing her nerve.

"Bradley Olmsted, I have a question for you. Did John have a mistress by the name of Mrs. Noble, and has she owned the Gerard Street house all these years? Deeded to her by my late husband in return for love and affection?"

She heard a quick intake of breath across the wire, then a raspy clearing of the attorney's throat. "Whoa. That's more than one question, Caroline."

"Stop it, Bradley. I want a straight answer, more than one if that's what it takes. Immediately."

"Now, now, Caroline, these aren't things discussed in the presence of women."

"What a ridiculous thing to say. Don't try to squirm out of it. I want to know exactly who this Mrs. Noble is, and what her relationship was with my husband."

A long silence ensued, punctuated by the rustling of papers on his end. Caroline could be just as stubborn as the next person when it suited her. John had taught her long ago that when negotiating or trying to pry information out of someone, there comes a time when the next person to speak loses. It amused her to think that she was using his own tactic to worm information about his secret life out of their attorney. This tiny tendril of absurdity loosened up a tightness in her chest. Her sense of humor was still alive. Perhaps she would get through this.

"Caroline, are you there?"

"Yes, Bradley, I'm still here. Please proceed. I'm sure you have better things to do than sit there with the receiver to your ear, rearranging papers that have nothing to do with why I'm calling." She could almost see him switch to drumming his fingers on his desktop.

"Ah, yes, well. It seems you've pretty much sized up the situation correctly. John purchased the property in 1901 and gave it to Mrs. Noble several years later."

Caroline gasped, then exhaled slowly in an effort to calm herself. The punch had left her voice. "Thank you, Bradley."

"You didn't give me much choice, Caroline. Was there anything else?"

"No." She took a deep breath. "We have an appointment next week to decide what to do about the publishing business."

"We do indeed, Caroline. I'll see you then."

"Yes, Bradley. Goodbye."

Once she'd settled down, Caroline found herself puzzled by her lack of anger at John for his deception. After all, her health had caused the break of their marital contract, and she'd been too squeamish to satisfy him in other ways. Perhaps he *was* entitled to find satisfaction elsewhere. It wasn't his fault any more than it was hers. He'd handled it discretely, to be sure, never subjecting her to embarrassment or anguish. Nor had it appeared to impact their comfortable finances. The arrangement seemed simple when she looked at it logically. He was a good man, and she'd loved him dearly. Still...

CHAPTER 29

Several hours later Caroline awoke gradually to that delicious coming-to-consciousness that is neither here nor there. She stretched out luxuriously, enjoying the soft slide of the sheets on her legs and arms. All thoughts of John had fled. Abruptly the mood broke as Lily's midnight revelations came flooding in. She felt like a door into a forbidden corner of her mind had been smashed open, leaving her gasping at the unwanted sights within.

She remembered something that had happened when she was perhaps four years old, something she hadn't thought about for decades. She had awoken in the dark hours of the night, frightened by a nightmare perhaps. Dragging her blanket, she had padded down the hall to her parents' bedroom, looking for comfort. Half asleep, she pushed open their door and stopped. Some great lumpy thing was moving up and down under the bedcovers, making strange moaning sounds in her father's voice. Nightmare forgotten, she shot back to her room and scooted under her bed, where she huddled with her blanket for the rest of the night. She never mentioned it to a soul, and never went to her parents' bedroom again after dark.

Hearing footsteps in the hall, Caroline sat up, dangled her feet over the side of the bed, and took a minute or two to collect herself. Then she quickly dressed, tidied her hair, and stepped into her shoes.

When she reached Lily's door, Lettie was just leaving. "Caroline, your timing is perfect. Lily's awake and feeling renewed. She'll be delighted to see you. It's almost noon. I'll bring some lunch for you both in a little while. Meanwhile I've left a fresh pot of coffee on the dresser. Will you help yourself?"

Overhearing, Lily called out, "Caroline, come in! Pull up that chair. Now that you've been to the Merry Weather, I can't wait to tell you how I got it staffed and running."

Had their conversation of last night really happened, Caroline wondered, or had she dreamt the whole thing? If not, was Lily just going to carry on, oblivious to how she'd shaken her friend's naïve understanding of married intimacy? Should she bring it up if Lily didn't?

Then she noticed again the absence of the Blue Willow cachepot. It had been on Lily's windowsill ever since she, Caroline, had arrived. It hadn't been there late in the night, and it wasn't there now.

She looked at her friend, trying to interpret her expression. "Good morning, Lily. I hope you rested well."

"I did. You too, I trust?" Lily's smile was cheery and bright, overcoming the bruised gauntness of her features. "Morning naps after a sleepless night can be quite restoring."

Caroline nodded, waiting for Lily to mention the reason for her sleepless night. But she didn't. She seemed to have said her say about marital sex and was done with it—relieved to have passed on her observations to someone else. For what reason, Caroline could not imagine, except to unburden herself of one more thing before she died. But the real unburdening, the reason Lily had brought her to Portland—that still lay around the corner.

Lily was dying, Caroline had no doubt about that. Although her lively storytelling belied the seriousness of her condition, her day-by-day decline was apparent. It now occurred to Caroline that perhaps Lily was doing more than recounting her life's journey for Caroline, more than simply bridging the twenty year gap in their friendship. Was she also reviewing her life for her own sake, looking at it honestly in her remaining days, perhaps to see how others might judge her, or how she might judge herself? If, by being there to listen and care, Caroline was providing a last, loving service to her friend, she felt honored to do so. Eventually Lily would get to whatever was truly bothering her.

Gesturing toward the window, Caroline asked, "Where's your Blue Willow garden, Lily? It's not there."

"Oh, every summer Marco takes it to the shop for a little invigoration. He carried it downstairs after dinner last night so he wouldn't forget it this morning. Sit, sit, I've more to tell."

So she hadn't dreamt it. Last night and today were the only times she'd seen the cachepot gone from the windowsill. Caroline's discomfort eased a bit. She sat down to listen.

"You've met some of the Back Door Women, Caroline. I love telling the beginning of their story. So here it is: Prior to opening, Marco and Jannie helped me set up the tables and chairs at the Merry Weather, hang the curtains, that sort of thing, but I quickly realized that I couldn't run the place by myself. So I did the easiest thing possible, or so I thought. I hand lettered a cardboard sign and propped it in the window.

OPENING SOON
HELP WANTED, WOMEN ONLY
APPLY TOMORROW AT 9:00 A.M.

"You never saw such a gaggle of women, young and old, waiting excitedly at the door when I arrived the next morning. Marco said some were already there when he arrived at five o'clock to receive the flower deliveries. I was terrified!"

"Terrified? Why?"

"All those women looking for work, and I could only hire a few. How in the world could I sort them out and determine which ones would be best, or needed employment the most? I didn't even know how many I required or what qualifications I should look for. The worst part was knowing I'd have to disappoint most of them. Suddenly I wasn't sure I was hardhearted enough to be a businesswoman."

"So what did you do?" asked Caroline.

"I hastened past the crowd and snuck in via the back of the flower shop, took a few deep breaths, and asked Marco to send for Jannie with a cry for help. She came right away, thank goodness. She'd hired and fired many workers at the Mercantile and knew just what to do. I realized I'd have to toughen up quickly.

"We asked the women to come in and sit down. We'd set out 28 chairs. Once they were seated, only one remained empty. I explained the situation to them, then Jannie and I interviewed them one by one. She took half, and I took half. We wrote down their names and our impressions of each one, then told them to return the next morning. After we compared notes, we made a list of the six most promising. In the morning I posted their names in the window, with instructions to return the following afternoon. I added a note thanking the others for coming. Peeking from behind a curtain, I watched the women come by to see who had been selected. I shall never forget the disappointment on the faces of those who were not on the list. I vowed to make it up to them somehow. But thank God for Jannie. Five of the six turned out to be terrific workers who were with us for many years. In fact, several of them are still with us."

"And what did you do for the others?" asked Caroline.

Lily clapped her hands. "They became my first Back Door Women. More on that in a minute. The tearoom has succeeded in ways I couldn't possibly have imagined. Jannie and Agnes no sooner spread the word than I was inundated with suffragists. At first I was shocked. The news of their counterparts on the East Coast being beaten by police, jailed, and force-fed was appalling—just for exercising their First Amendment rights of free speech, peaceful assembly, and to petition the government! There was much marching here, too, let me tell you. Portland was a hotbed of women campaigning for the vote. Oregon granted it statewide in 1912, but there was still much to be done on the national level."

"Yes, we couldn't stop with the states," exclaimed Caroline. "I actually marched in the D.C. suffrage parade down Pennsylvania Avenue the day before President Wilson's inauguration in 1913. He was dead set against the whole idea, and, mercy, was he furious!

Spectators attacked us while the police just watched. They finally sent in the cavalry—the cavalry!—to calm things down. You must have read about it?"

"Yes, what a scene! You weren't injured, were you?"

"Luckily not, but I would have considered it a badge of honor. Four years later I joined the Silent Sentinels who picketed the White House day in and day out in the months leading up to Wilson's second inauguration. I left just before some of the major arrests, because I promised John I'd only be away for a week. Some of my best friends were arrested and thrown in the Occoquan Workhouse in Virginia. You must have read about their hunger strike and forced feeding. That's a form of torture, you know, a rubber tube jammed through your nostril and down your throat with swill sloshing into your stomach. It's painful and degrading, not to mention the injuries the prisoners suffered while resisting."

"Oh, yes, front page news in the *Oregonian*. Simply appalling."

"Right. Then there was the Night of Terror, when the superintendent got fed up and ordered the guards to brutalize the women. They were beaten, choked, kicked, slammed up against the walls. Many sustained serious injuries. Finally, enough was enough. They were released, but not without generating a whole lot more sympathy for the movement. I've felt guilty ever since that I wasn't there to face that music with them."

"Good Heavens, Caroline, you marched on the front lines! I'm not sure I'd ever have thought it of you."

"I don't need to tell you what a woman can do when she gets her dander up! What about you?"

"I marched in the city as often as I could," Lily said. "But my biggest contribution was providing a safe place for the neighborhood suffragists to meet. Many an unlikely woman was converted to the cause over tea and cookies at the Merry Weather. You didn't have to be rich or well-dressed or educated. Women of all sorts came and met, regardless of social or financial status. I also opened the room to them in the evenings to host their speakers. Louise Bryant and Sara Bard Field often dropped by. One night we had the honor of hosting Abigail Scott Duniway. She was a tireless leader of the cause here in Oregon. We set up every chair we could scrounge, including a dozen or more in Marco's shop where they could see and hear through the opening. Still, it was standing room only, with more women peering through the window to get a glimpse of her."

"How wonderful!" Caroline clapped her hands.

"Yes, and we almost had Susan B. Anthony, but after Duniway we realized we needed a much larger venue. Thank goodness, or our old wooden building might have collapsed out from under us!"

"I heard Miss Anthony speak in Philadelphia," remarked Caroline, "along with Mrs. Stanton. What a privilege, and what a tragedy that neither of them lived to see their goal finally achieved."

"It was indeed. So tell me more about the campaign back home in Pennsylvania."

"Oh, my goodness! Surely you heard? In 1915 we cast a replica of the Liberty Bell and named it the Justice Bell. We toured it through every county in the state, demanding justice for women at every stop. Five thousand miles on the back of a pickup truck! We chained the clapper to its side, vowing never to let it ring until universal suffrage was the law of the land. When the Nineteenth Amendment was ratified three years ago, we took the Justice Bell to Independence Square, unchained the clapper, and rang it forty-eight times, one for every state in the union. My, did it peal! What a thrill after all those years of struggle!"

"How wonderful. Just think, Caroline, a hundred years from now most female citizens will have been born with the franchise. Will they appreciate what we went through, how hard we fought to give them the vote? Will they exercise it with passion?"

"We can only hope, Lily. And if they ever have to, let's hope they fight to keep it."

Lettie arrived with their lunch on a tray. "Do you think you can manage a sandwich today, Lily? The bread is thinly sliced, and the egg salad filling is soft. I've cut it into small pieces for you, no crusts. There's milk to dip it in, if you like."

"Thanks, Lettie. Caroline will help me. We were just talking about the fight for suffrage. You danced in the street with the rest of us the day the Nineteenth Amendment was ratified."

"Oh, my gosh, yes, that's a day I'll never forget! We whooped and hollered until we were hoarse. And you can be sure that I will never neglect the privilege."

Caroline and Lily beamed at her. Lettie turned to leave with a lightness of step she rarely exhibited in these days of Lily's declining health. Lily shifted a bit on her pillows and asked Caroline to put the lunch tray on her lap. She carried on with her tale between dunked bites of her sandwich.

"When the fight for the ballot was over, I wondered if I'd lose my Merry Weather customers. But the most amazing thing happened, Carrie. I'd never been able to rid myself of the image of all those hopeful women I'd had to disappoint the day I hired my first employees. I continued to see them, and others like them, on the streets, in the shops. Downtrodden, bowed with maternal responsibilities, yet with inklings of pride, perhaps in meeting their difficult lives' demands and still managing to carry on. Occasionally I'd find one peering in the front window, no doubt wishing she had the means and manners to sit down inside for a genteel cup of tea.

"One day I had a brilliant idea. Before I could talk myself out of it, I put a handwritten sign in the window that said,

IF YOU HAVE NEVER HAD
LADIES AFTERNOON TEA IN A TEAROOM,
YOU ARE INVITED ON SUNDAY AT 2 PM.
ALL WELCOME
COMPLIMENTS OF THE MANAGEMENT

"Marco thought I was out of my mind. Good, I told him, sometimes the best ideas come from moments of insanity. I roped Agnes and Jannie into helping me again, as well as some of the suffragists. When I opened the doors that afternoon you wouldn't believe the number of women who were waiting outside, all scrubbed up and in their Sunday best. Some of them were hesitant, not truly believing they were welcome; some of them were downright frightened, judging by the looks in their eyes. But mostly they were excited. We welcomed them and brought out the extra chairs we kept in the back room for lecture nights. We managed to seat everyone—just. The tea kettles steamed nonstop. Luckily I had erred on the side of abundance in ordering cookies from the bakery that morning—against my principles, as they weren't homemade, but for these guests bakery goods were a luxury.

"I stood before them, waited for them to quiet down, thanked them for coming, and invited them to relax and make new friends if there were strangers at their table. My only thought was to provide them with a pleasant, once-in-a-lifetime experience. I had cautioned my suffragist servers to treat them like ladies, regardless of their appearances. Despite a few doubtful looks, I knew I could count on them.

"As I stood there making my brief remarks, I expected to see a roomful of discouragement and despair, yet what I saw instead was excitement, hope, and resilience of spirit, the resilience that allows a mother from the poorest tenement to do her best for her children, and never give a thought for her own wants and desires. I realized that most of them, if given a chance, could rise above society's expectations, and their own expectations for themselves. All they needed was a chance.

"I don't know what got into me, but I began to ask questions. What do you need to get ahead in the world? What would make a difference in your life? How can you help your children to succeed?" The suffragists, who were standing quietly at the back of the room in their starched aprons, shot me some questioning looks, but Agnes and Jannie nodded their encouragement.

"Only a couple women responded at first, rather timidly, and then the dam broke. Such a din you never heard! When I finally got them to calm down, I asked them, one at a time, to describe the one thing that would help them the most. Another torrent, but this time I heard them. 'Steady work. Better pay. Reasonable hours. Domestic training for running their own households. Learning to read and write better. Learning to serve in a fancy home. Cooking lessons. Running water. Indoor plumbing. Help with children. Fewer children." That last one—fewer children—brought the outpouring to a halt. That such a thing should have been spoken aloud! I knew of Margaret Sanger's birth control campaign, and the legal difficulties she faced, but I doubt many of them did. You should have seen the startled looks on the faces of the suffragists, many of whom by the way, managed to limit their families quite nicely.

"I nodded at Agnes, and she winked back at me. We had our mission. And that's where the term 'Back Door Women' came from. After that they came in via the back door and up the stairs for their classes and workshops, while the ladies of the neighborhood sipped their tea in front, thereby paying for the whole operation."

"Wasn't the term a bit condescending?" asked Caroline.

"Well, it just kind of evolved. I don't even remember who came up with it. But if you ask around, you'll find many successful home managers and domestic employees, not to mention a few who have started their own businesses or found office employment, who were once Lily's Back Door Women—and proud of it."

"Come to mention it, Mrs. Delfini had a few proud words to say about that."

"Yes, she was one of the first, and I'm so lucky now to have her in my kitchen. So, as soon as the women left—tumbling over one another in expressing their gratitude—Agnes, Jannie and I sat down and made a list of everything we could remember."

"You always were a great one for making lists."

"I had to be, to keep my visiting life organized!"

Caroline grinned. "Of course you did. But go on. What happened next?"

"We couldn't help with everything, but there were many ways in which we could. Like learning to read and write better, better penmanship for those who already knew how to write—that was Agnes's idea—training for domestic service, childcare, cooking and sewing lessons, and fewer children. I wasn't exactly sure what we could do about that last item, but with Margaret Sanger so active back East, I knew eventually we'd find out. Women who are continually giving birth can't get ahead, not to mention potentially ruining their health or dying in the effort. The one thing I'm not sure we're ever going to be able to change is husbands asserting their marital rights, pregnancy be damned. So it has to come down to methods a woman can employ for their own protection.

"Another thing that came up during that discussion was unsafe abortions. We knew that wealthy women, like our suffragists, could usually find a qualified doctor to help them, but poor women often resorted to desperate means. We weren't sure what we could do about that either, but we thought that by providing correct family limitation information, clandestinely of course so we wouldn't be arrested like Mrs. Sanger, and keeping our thinking caps on, we might be able to make a difference. We're still trying. So you can see why the story of your Donalee touched me."

Caroline nodded sadly as the vision of the frivolous young woman, hemorrhaging in the Pullman sleeper berth, flashed through her memory.

"We couldn't do anything about indoor plumbing," Lily continued, "or steady work, better pay, reasonable hours, but we believed that if we tackled the possible items, the things on the 'impossible' list would someday become possible. The upstairs space above our shops was rented out by the landlord as warehousing for another merchant. Marco decided it was time to buy the building. We turned that upstairs space into a workroom, which you saw, and set out to teach our Back Door Women the skills they needed to better their lives."

"And who better to teach them than the suffragists!" exclaimed Caroline, grasping the overall picture.

"Right. Between them they had many skills, and it turned out they loved teaching and feeling they were making a difference once again."

"Wasn't there a settlement house in Portland, like the Lutheran Settlement House in Philadelphia or Jane Addams's Hull House in

Chicago, where immigrant women and others could come together for guidance and learning?" Caroline asked.

"Yes, the People's Institute Settlement Work was founded in 1905 but soon turned its attention from social work to health care for the underprivileged. The Neighborhood House was founded the same year, but it's a good distance from us. We wanted to provide what we could, informally, in our own neighborhood. The income from the tearoom was surprisingly steady, enough to provide what we needed for supplies upstairs and so on."

"Bravo!" echoed Caroline.

"Before we knew it, we had neighborhood women coming in for all kinds of things, sometimes in groups, sometimes one-to-one. Take something as simple as penmanship. It didn't take much instruction, and they could practice to their heart's content at home. All they needed was a pen, a bottle of ink, and a lined booklet, which in many cases were beyond the family budget. So we supplied them. Having a beautiful hand did wonders for the way they felt about themselves. I saw it happen again and again."

"You have beautiful handwriting, Lily. I always admired that about you."

Lily chuckled. "Remember Ramona Boyden? She was one of my last visiting hostesses. She'd just had her first child at a rather advanced age and received a million and one gifts for the little tyke. She asked me to write all the thank-you letters, flattering me for my nice lettering. By the time I finished, I swore I'd never write anything again except shopping lists and one obligatory note to each hostess after a visit. Period."

"I don't blame you," quipped Caroline.

"Right. So the suffragists donated a couple of old sewing machines, and we picked up a few more at second-hand shops. You'd be amazed at what the women produced once they mastered the machines. And my lessons in refashioning were a huge hit. They learned how to take apart old dresses, eliminate the worn parts, and reconstruct them just as I did to keep my visiting wardrobe up to date. Sure, patching was easier and quicker if a dress wasn't entirely worn out, but everyone loves a new-looking dress. I've often wondered if our friends ever knew how much time I spent in my bedroom, desperately stitching to keep myself in style!"

"You were so clever at it, Lily. Even I didn't know the extent of your labors. I usually thought you were reading or napping."

Lily smiled wryly. "Not all the time. I even made patching into a fine art and passed that on to the Back Door Women as well, so they never had to be ashamed of when patching was all they could manage."

Without planning it, and surprising even herself, Caroline abruptly changed the subject. She was interested in what Lily was telling her, but her patience had finally worn out.

"Speaking of those days, Lily, won't you tell me *really* why you left so suddenly? I sense it was more than your visiting schedule wearing thin and coincidentally meeting Marco. I swear if I have to spend one more day without knowing, I shall go berserk. I promise, whatever you have to say, I won't blame or judge. It's been a long time, and I've come all this way." She reached out and took Lily's hand, at rest on the Amish quilt. "Please."

Lily sighed from the depths of her being. For a long moment Caroline feared she'd gone too far. But she'd been in Portland for several weeks, waiting patiently for Lily to get to the heart of the matter. A few times Lily had led her right up to the brink, then handily swerved into more recollections of her early life in Portland.

She already knew that Lily had been pregnant with Mark when she and Marco left Philadelphia. And that Mark was born five months after they arrived. So what else was she hiding?

When Caroline considered how much she had worried about Lily over the years—and frankly, how thoughtlessly Lily had run off in the night all those many years ago, leaving bills unpaid and no explanation—she felt she had a right to push for an answer. After all, that wasn't how one usually repaid friendship and hospitality. Caroline wasn't proud of these thoughts but saw no reason not to think them.

She waited.

Lily had shut her eyes, her expression completely blank. Had she fallen asleep?

Finally Lily looked up and spoke wearily. "Yes, it's time. But Caroline, regardless of saying you won't blame or judge, you have no idea what kind of Pandora's box this will open. Lives will change. If not for the better, I will have unleashed a whirlwind."

Before Caroline could murmur anything reassuring, the door to Lily's bedroom burst open. A tall, fair young man rushed in, bristling with rage.

CHAPTER 30

"Mother, you must tell Father to quit harping on me!" Seeing Caroline, the young man skidded to a stop. "Oh, I'm sorry. I didn't know you had company. But please, Mother…"

Caroline, struck dumb by the young man's appearance, jumped up from her chair and sidled behind it, holding onto the chair's back for support.

"L-L-Lawrence?" she stammered. "*Lawrence?* It can't be!"

Letting go of the chair, she rushed toward him, then halted and hesitantly reached out to touch the solid weave of his jacket sleeve. *How could this be?*

The young man, equally stunned, backed away.

"Mother, who…who is this?" he stammered. "And who is Lawrence?"

Lily grasped the quilt and pulled it halfway over her face, leaving only her distressed eyes showing.

Caroline turned toward her. "Yes, Lily, what *is* this about? He's the image of my brother Lawrence!"

At that moment Leticia rushed in. "What's going on?" she asked. "Lily, are you all right? Mark, you shouldn't be upsetting your mother!"

"*Mark?*" Caroline gasped. "This is your son Mark?"

Lily squeezed her eyes shut. "Lettie, please call Marco and ask him to come home right away."

Leticia, as confused as the others, backed out of the room and hurried downstairs to the telephone.

"Mark, come here, son. Sit down on the bed beside me." Lily patted the quilt, looking as serious as Caroline had ever seen her. "This is my friend Caroline Crawford of Philadelphia. We were at Bryn Mawr together. You've heard me speak of her. You haven't been home much recently. Perhaps you forgot she was coming for a visit?"

Mark nodded briefly at Caroline, and then turned back to his mother. At first Caroline thought he might refuse her request to sit down, but the apprehensive look on his mother's face softened him momentarily. Caroline collapsed back onto her chair, more puzzled than ever.

"Dear God, where to start," moaned Lily.

"Why don't you start with why I am the only one with blue eyes and blonde hair in this family," said Mark, in a barely civil tone. "I've never belonged. I wonder if you picked me up off the street, the child of one of your sainted Back Door Women!"

His hostility stunned Lily into silence.

Finally she spoke again, her hands kneading the quilt. "This is what's been eating at you all this time, Mark, isn't it? And your father and I too blind to see?"

Mark stood and began pacing, his blonde hair flying each time he whipped around in the confines of the bedroom.

"You have to admit, Mother, it is strange. I don't fit in with Father's Italian friends and their children. Theresa looks like them, but not me. The Italian kids at school teased me relentlessly, saying I look like a Mick or a Bohunk. In their minds, one is as bad the other."

Lily seemed beside herself with agitation, but she inhaled deeply and forged ahead. This young man who looked so much like Lawrence—was he Lily's real reason for bringing her here? But it couldn't be! For the moment she held her tongue.

"This is going to be hurtful and embarrassing, son, but there's no way around it. You see, I... I found myself pregnant soon after college, and Marco was kind enough to marry me. He's been a good husband to me, and I love him so much. And he's been a loving father to you." She paused, as if daring him to contradict her. And knowing instantly that this glib explanation would never suffice for either Mark or Caroline.

Mark sneered. "You 'found yourself' pregnant? You don't just 'find' yourself pregnant, Mother."

She looked down at her shaking hands. "No. One doesn't just find one's self pregnant."

For Caroline the facts continued to click into place. She had to speak.

"*Lawrence*? Is my *brother* responsible? Is that why you left without saying a word?"

Lily closed her eyes and nodded. "Yes. I couldn't face him, and I was terrified it might happen again. Nor did I want you to know. I had to get away."

"But you two were no more than casual friends! You never spent any time alone together...as far as I knew."

"It wasn't like that, Caroline."

"But..."

For a long moment nobody spoke. Mark stopped pacing and flicked his glance between Caroline and his mother, taking in their expressions and waiting for...what?

"You don't mean...?" Caroline felt her cheeks flush. She couldn't finish the thought.

Lily nodded, eyes brimming.

"He...he violated you?" Caroline blurted.

"Yes." A whisper so soft it was barely audible. Caroline leaned closer.

"When?"

"I stayed downstairs one night after a dinner party to tidy up. You and John had gone to bed. Lawrence was in the study, quite drunk. He made some rude remarks as I picked up a dirty glass and ashtray, but I ignored him. When I got upstairs to my room, I went to lock the door but the key was missing. I searched my pockets, the floor,

302

everywhere in my room but couldn't find it, nor could I think where else it might be. He didn't follow me upstairs. The house remained quiet, and I eventually fell asleep. I awoke to find him on top of me. I tried to fight him off, but he was too strong. Before I knew it, it was over and I wasn't even sure what had happened. Six weeks later I knew I was…in trouble."

"You were raped?" gasped Mark. "That makes me…"

"The beloved son of your father and me." Lily said it firmly and clearly, looking straight at him. "Marco adored you from the moment you were born, and he has never wavered in that love. You know that, Mark."

Mark snorted with disgust. "How can either of you love me, knowing where I came from? A child of *rape*? That's disgusting." As he paused to absorb it, a flush crept up his neck. Caroline wondered if he was reassessing his opinion of his mother, a woman who allowed such a thing to happen. If so, she prayed that he would keep such a misguided thought to himself.

With a surge of strength, Lily elbowed herself up on the pillows.

"I spent many a sleepless night, Mark, when I discovered I was carrying you. Should I run away to Europe, or to another town in America, and give the baby up for adoption? I even wondered, Caroline, if you and John might raise the child. You'd just miscarried, so I thought you might be willing, but that would have meant admitting Lawrence's role and causing a great rift in your family, or so I imagined. Or should I find a doctor who was willing to…" She looked away, unable say it in front of her son. Then she gathered her strength again and looked back at him.

"Or did I have the courage to admit my circumstance and raise you alone? The only thing I knew for certain, son, is that I loved you from the moment I reconciled myself to your existence. I determined to do my best for you—you who were innocent of any fault."

"But Father—Marco—he knew?" Skepticism replaced the anger in his voice. "And accepted me as his own?"

"Yes, you know he did. I was completely honest with him before I agreed to marry him. And he never wavered, not once. Did he, son?" She raised her chin, challenging him to contradict her.

Mark bit his lip and remained silent. Absentmindedly he brushed his fallen lock of blond hair off his forehead, a gesture so familiar that it brought tears to Caroline's eyes.

"Lily, I still don't understand why you didn't tell me. I could have helped you!"

"You did so much for me, Caroline. All those months as a visiting girl—you kept my calendar full, making sure I was welcome in our friends' homes. And you and John continued to keep me when my schedule started to tatter. How could I tell you that your beloved brother had assaulted me? If you'd believed me, it might have meant the end of your relationship with him and a great rift in your family. Considering how much I'd loved my sister Florence, I couldn't bear that possibility. And if you didn't believe me, well, what then? You'd have cast me out as a troublemaker. Marco came to the rescue, miraculously. Even though we'd only known each other casually, it seemed the best solution for all."

"Lily, I would never..."

Mark interrupted, arms crossed on his chest. "Except for me, growing up like the ugly duckling, feeling totally out of step with the rest of the family and all our dark-eyed Italian friends. At least now I know why." With that, he dashed for the door, promptly colliding with his father.

"Whoa," said Marco, grasping his son by the shoulders. "What's the rush?" He held on while looking around Mark's shoulder. "Lily, are you all right?"

"Let me go," shouted Mark, twisting out of Marco's grasp. A shocked silence ensued in the bedroom as the young man bounded down the stairs and slammed out the front door.

Despite the million and one questions Caroline wanted to ask, she could see that Lily was spent. This then, was the reason for her summons to Portland, and it had taken all that Lily had to finally get it out. She leaned over and kissed her friend on the cheek, murmured that she should try to get some rest. She nodded at Marco, trusting he would stay and soothe Lily, and retired to her own room. The day was warm, but she felt chilled to the bone. She nestled into the easy chair beside the window and took refuge under the afghan.

In her wildest imaginings, she could never have conjured Lily's real reason for leaving Philadelphia. But it must be true—Mark was the living image of Lawrence—tall, fair and slender, with straight blonde hair and vivid blue eyes. Not to mention that frequent, useless effort to tame his blonde forelock and, yes, now that she thought about it, their father's distinctive patrician nose.

Why else would Lily have left so suddenly, leaving no trace? Of course she wanted to get far away from Lawrence, and far enough away to give herself and her child a fresh start. But to do it in complete secrecy, not mentioning a word to her best friend? What unbelievable loyalty, to have made such a sacrifice to protect her, Caroline's, love for her brother, who certainly didn't deserve it.

Picking at a loose blue thread in the afghan, Caroline found herself wondering how she would have reacted if Lily had told her everything at the time. She had no idea. Would she have believed her? Or would she have jumped to her brother's defense? From what Caroline knew of rape, the finger of guilt almost always pointed at the woman: looking at a man in a "come hither way;" dressing provocatively; being in the wrong place at the wrong time against all motherly warnings. Witness Mark's flush a few minutes ago as he appeared to consider his mother's role in the whole thing. It was so unfair. She *hoped* she would have stuck up for Lily and demanded that John kick Lawrence out of their house and forbid him to return. She *hoped* she would have helped Lily find the best way to handle her pregnancy. She *hoped* her friendship for Lily would have been as strong as Lily's had been for her. She *hoped*, but she would never know. What a muddle.

And no wonder Mark felt so out of step with his family. Perhaps a fellow with a different disposition might not have given it a second thought, or learned to fight back against the schoolyard teasing. From the few flashes she'd experienced of Mark, he appeared to be a sensitive soul, much like—yes, the better part of Lawrence. He had never been mean. When the girls were home from college, Lawrence had always been pleasant, companionable, cheerful. An occasional dark side had indeed showed itself, though, as he got older.

While reluctantly making his way in the insurance business in New York City, Lawrence had visited Caroline and John every few months to drum up clients in their area. Caroline had seen how the business was wearing him down, how much he truly hated it while he continued to trudge on. He began drinking to excess and sinking deep into gloom following the binges.

But rape—how could he have done such a thing, and to Lily, who had been such a cherished guest in their home? *Rape*—the worst thing a man could do to a woman short of murder. In fact, maybe rape was the greater crime, for the woman had to live with the trauma for the rest of her life; with murder it was over and done with. Caroline could scarcely believe it, yet she had no reason to doubt Lily.

She shifted in her chair and gazed at the trees outside the window, gently shimmering in a light afternoon breeze. An unexpected peace soon settled upon her as she realized she had a God-given chance to repay Lily's long-ago sacrifice on her behalf.

Dinner that evening was subdued, with just Marco and Caroline at the table. Leticia stayed upstairs with Lily. As Mark had never yet joined them for dinner, his absence went unremarked, but Caroline silently sent him a blessing with the hope that he was safe and able to begin assimilating his newfound history.

Once Mrs. Delfini had finished serving the sour cream and walnut pie with chamomile tea and closed the dining room door, Marco cleared his throat and cautiously opened the conversation on the unspoken subject that was hanging over them.

"I'm sure this all comes as a tremendous shock to you, Caroline. I truly apologize. You came here with the best of intentions, simply to renew your friendship and cheer Lily up with reminiscences of your earlier days. Now you're thrown into a full-blown family crisis.

I'm as shocked as you are. I had no idea of Lily's true purpose in inviting you. After you left the room this afternoon, she confessed her wish to connect you with Mark, a last-ditch effort to get to the bottom of what she suspected was bothering him, his growing feeling of alienation within the family." Marco took a bite of his pie, wiped his mouth with his napkin, set down his fork and pushed the plate away.

"He'd been such an agreeable fellow until a few years ago. Then his personality flipped almost overnight. We were terribly distressed but had no idea what to do. He refused to discuss it with either of us. Granted, it's natural for a young man to push away from his parents. I certainly did. It's part of growing up. But this was more than just a boy's awkward transition into manhood and independence. After considering every other possibility and based on a few things he'd said, Lily apparently concluded that he felt he didn't belong with us. The confusion, she felt, was driving him into melancholy. Does that make any sense to you?"

Caroline stirred her tea to cool it. Like Marco, she had no appetite for the pie.

"I guess it makes as much sense as anything," she said. "What a blow to find out about his parentage so abruptly and unexpectedly. I hope it doesn't send him deeper into the abyss."

"Lily's worried about that too. She told me she vacillated until the very moment she sent you the letter, then agonized that she had done the wrong thing. She didn't mention any of this to me, by the way. Once you arrived, she still wasn't sure she'd done the right thing. First she had to find a way to tell you about Lawrence's involvement, having no idea how that would go. Then, hoping for the best, to confront Mark with it. It occurs to me that perhaps she thought Mark would take one look at you and somehow divine the truth."

"Rather naïve," Caroline said with a hint of a smile. "We didn't look at all alike, save for our coloring…or what was our coloring. As you can see, my hair is no longer its former youthful shade."

Marco bowed his head. "True, but as Lily told me, she didn't have much to go on and time was running out. She hoped desperately that if Mark knew the truth, he'd understand why he was so different from the rest of the family, eventually accept it, and get back to rights. She had only a mother's intuition, and the desperate wish to die knowing her firstborn would be able to carry on."

Caroline poured herself another cup of tea, silently offering the same to Marco. He shook his head. She set the teapot back on its trivet.

"I wonder, Marco…do you think Lily only got as far as hoping the explanation of his parentage would explain why he looked so unlike you and the rest of the Italian community, thus offering him an opportunity to make peace with it? Could she have failed to take into account the knowledge that he is the product of…forced attention? Not to mention that if he subscribes to the common notion that women bring this kind of thing upon themselves…"

"…it could shatter his feelings—his respect—for his mother, so soon before her death and be left with no chance to reconcile." Marco finished the devastating thought for her. "I hadn't thought of that. What destructive power secrets have."

"And here I am, in Lily's opinion, the key to the whole thing," Caroline mused. "Never imagining the truth would burst upon all of us in such an explosive manner."

"Indeed. Your reaction to Mark's appearance—as Lily described it to me—thinking for an instant that he was Lawrence, shocked her as much as it shocked you."

"I wonder, as Mark was growing up, did his resemblance to my brother never bother her? Wasn't Mark a constant reminder of Lawrence and the harm he did her?"

"I asked Lily about that. She said she hadn't known Lawrence as a child, so in his early years there was no reason to compare him to Lawrence. He was just Mark, completely himself. As he grew into adulthood, and the resemblance became obvious, she said she thought about it occasionally. But, as she said, he was just our Mark."

Marco hesitated before continuing. "This may change things between you and your brother, but I hope not. It's the one thing Lily wanted to avoid, the reason she left Philadelphia without telling you in the first place."

Caroline looked at him sharply. "No, Marco. It won't change anything between Lawrence and me. Lawrence is dead, you see, so there's nothing to be done about it."

"Dead? Oh, Caroline, I'm so sorry. I had no idea. Forgive me."

She shook her head. "There's nothing to forgive. Perhaps it's for the best. I'm not sure how I would have handled it otherwise."

"But surely he didn't deserve to die!"

Caroline waved her hand in the negative. "No, of course not. That's not what I meant. He had become such an unhappy fellow. He wanted to be a poet, you see, but our father forced him into a career in life insurance with our bachelor Uncle Corrigan. Lawrence would eventually inherit the business and our Uncle's extensive estate. But he hated selling insurance, couldn't cope with the demands of the job—always hustling for business and suffering heaps of rejection for every sale. He began sliding downhill—drinking a lot, associating with unsavory types, exhibiting rather bombastic behavior while visiting us, but never to the point of being dangerous. Such a thought never occurred to us."

"May I ask how your brother died?"

She brightened slightly. "As a matter of fact, it was a bit of a miracle...until it ended badly."

"A miracle? That's an odd way of putting it," replied Marco.

"As I said, Lawrence wanted to be a poet. Or any sort of writer, as it turned out, but he couldn't see a way through. My husband John encouraged him, as he would any aspiring writer, but he warned him he'd better stick with insurance to pay the bills. Everything changed with the Great War. His imagination caught fire, and he decided to become a war correspondent. He had no journalism background, but he knew one of the editors at the *Philadelphia Enquirer*, the father of a college chum. The fellow told him he could not send him over in any official capacity, as he had no experience or credentials. But if he could get himself there and come up with some good material, he'd take a look at it and see if he could use it on a freelance basis."

Marco lifted an eyebrow.

"By then Lawrence had stuck with insurance for almost ten years and had saved a fair amount of money. He managed to get to Europe in one of those zig-zagging convoys of war matériel that we sent to the Allies before the U.S. entered the war. He never said a word to us before he left, fearing no doubt our father would try to stop him. He cabled home from France, and by then it was too late."

"Daring of him," conceded Marco. "Shows a lot of gumption."

"Yes, enticed by the war, all thoughts of poetry flew out the window. Off he went, for the adventure of a lifetime. As it turned out, Lawrence was extremely gifted at writing tales of civilian life in war-torn France, of ordinary families coping with the terrors and deprivations of combat in their fields and forests. He'd studied French in college and quickly become fluent. He was likeable, unobtrusive, and I guess people trusted him enough to share their stories with him. When his dispatches began to appear in the *Enquirer,* we were thrilled. Soon they were syndicated throughout the country.

"And then, shortly before the war ended, the stories stopped. We later learned that he had been following the Allied forces in France during the Hundred Days Offensive. He ran into a group of stranded German snipers who shot him on sight. They shot him on sight. When his body was found, there was a sheaf of handwritten drafts in his rucksack. Those last dispatches were published posthumously."

"Wait a minute. Are you talking about Lawrence Lindholm, the famous war correspondent? *He's* your brother?"

"Yes."

"I'll be damned. I followed his stories in the *Oregonian* with great interest. Everybody did. I really felt for those villagers and farmers whose homes and crops were destroyed by the fighting. The country people he wrote about seemed so real, their suffering so immediate. He had a tremendous gift for bringing the civilians' hardships alive to his readers half a world away. Thanks to his articles, I was eager to register for the draft when the U.S. entered the war."

"Thank you for saying so," murmured Caroline. "I was heartbroken when I learned of his death. My only consolation was that he had died doing what he loved. Now of course, I wonder if he was also running away from what happened with Lily."

"We'll never know," replied Marco. "Lily said he knew nothing about the pregnancy."

"No, I'm sure she never saw him again."

"And you? Has it changed your feelings for your brother?"

She replied thoughtfully. "I don't know. That will take some time." She did not want to discuss her feelings for her brother with Marco or anyone else just yet. She reached for another topic. "But tell me…I didn't know you were in the war."

"I wasn't actually. When the draft came along in June of '17, I was over the age of thirty so it didn't apply to me. However, when they extended the maximum age to forty-five in September of '18…"

"Weren't you in an exempt category, with a dependent wife and children?" Caroline asked.

"Lily had her own thriving business, so she wasn't technically dependent. So that exemption may not have applied if I had chosen to invoke it. Which I didn't. Patriotism had caught up to me—thanks in part, as I've said, to your brother's reporting—and I was willing to serve. I registered with the Selective Service and waited to be called. The Armistice was signed two months later, so the call never came."

"Good thing! You'd have been sent for training at the peak of the Spanish Flu epidemic. Soldiers died right and left without leaving the camps. You made a lucky escape."

"With a bit of guilt attached. So many soldiers died before they reached the battlefields. Lily was pleased, of course. No wife wants to see her husband go off to war. What about your husband? Did he see action?"

"As with you, the war ended before he got his marching orders."

Marco reached for a decanter of port wine on the sideboard and two glasses. He gave Caroline a questioning look, which she returned with a nod. He poured them both a glass, then held his up to the chandelier and studied the glowing ruby liquid.

"Mark my words, Caroline, the Great War didn't finish anything. Germany's staggering under the reparation demands and unbearable humiliation. She's biding her time. She'll come back at us again, you wait and see." He took a sip of wine. "Sometimes I think Mark just needs a good war to straighten him out. Then I pray to God it never happens. It's not a cure I wish on anyone. But back to Lawrence Lindholm. I do remember reading about his death. It was nationwide news. We'd come to feel we knew him, that we'd lost a friend."

"Lily must have seen his stories too. Did she never mention she knew him, that he was the man who fathered Mark?"

He thought for a moment. "No, never. When she told me about her…condition, back in Philadelphia, I asked her to tell me everything, including the identity of the man responsible. If I was going to live with it—and be a father to the child—I had to be able to put it to rest and not let unanswered questions plague me for the rest of my life. Lily understood. She too did not want to always be waiting for the next shoe to drop, never knowing when I might bring up the subject again. It had happened, it was over, and we had a life to live. After we talked about it that one time and she told me that the man was your brother Lawrence, we agreed we would never mention it again. And we never have."

"The name Lindholm meant nothing to you?"

Marco slowly shook his head. "I knew you by your married name, Caroline Crawford. Lily never mentioned your brother's last name, not then, and certainly not afterward. There were occasions when we discussed his articles—everybody did. She never let on, not even for a second." He huffed. "Amazing."

For a moment they sat in silence. Caroline too marveled at Lily's ability to so completely protect Mark from the past—until now. Then an idea occurred to her.

"I kept a scrapbook of my brother's published articles," she said. "I was so proud of him. I thought Lawrence would enjoy seeing the collection upon his return and sharing them with his future wife and children. I don't know if it would help, but if you think it's a good idea, I'll wire my daughter and ask her to send it. Perhaps knowing that Lawrence was an honorable—well, mostly—and talented fellow might be comforting to Mark. He'd get a vivid picture of the transformative years of Lawrence's life, if he's interested."

Marco's face brightened for the first time that evening. "Perhaps it would. I'm totally at sea as to how to handle this," he admitted. "But I don't believe it would hurt. Thank you for offering."

"I have a stake in this, too, Marco. I'm actually Mark's aunt, aren't I? Lawrence never married, nor had any other children. That makes Mark the only nephew I'll ever have." She hurried to add, "Not that I'd want to cause him any more confusion, but…well, you know what I mean."

"Of course. He'll have more of a family than he ever imagined."

"Let's hope he sees it that way."

CHAPTER 31

Lily's emotional exertions following the revelation of Mark's true parentage caused her a serious setback. The doctor came in the next morning and decreed that she needed complete rest with no visitors except Lettie and Marco. She slept most of the time, with Lettie hovering nearby, attending to her needs.

Caroline, struggling to make sense of it herself, wished she could have helped with Lily. With Mark, at least, there was a way. She wired Nancy, asking her to send the scrapbook, saying she'd explain everything when she got home.

The next day, still restless and worried about Mark and Lily, she broke away for an afternoon at the Merry Weather Tearoom. She was greeted warmly by Lily's friends, all of whom inquired after Lily and asked Caroline to give her their love. Those few hours of cheery camaraderie sent Caroline home in a calmer frame of mind. Mark was nowhere to be found.

On the third morning, the house was quiet again, with Leticia upstairs tending to Lily and Mrs. Delfini off to market. Caroline was reading in her chair on the screened porch when she heard a door open and click shut. Curious, and feeling the need for a stretch, she got up and followed the sound. She found Mark in the kitchen, poking through the pantry for something to eat. He turned around at the sound of her footsteps. His hand, holding an apple, stopped halfway to his mouth. His disheveled clothes and hair, muddy shoes, and bloodshot eyes told their own story. One look at him brought back all the anxiety she had earlier felt on his behalf.

"Hello, Mark," Caroline said.

He nodded. "Mrs. Crawford."

She fumbled for her skirt pockets, unsure of what to say. "This is all very awkward, isn't it? I feel as upset as I'm sure you are."

"No offense, but I don't think you can possibly know how upset I feel." He took a defiant bite of the apple and turned as if to leave.

"Mark, wait. We've both got something at stake here. Your...connection...with my brother, I mean." She took a couple of steps toward him, then stopped, fearing he would flee. When he halted and turned back toward her, she gathered her courage, softened her voice, and continued.

"Let's have a cup of tea, Mark. It sounds ridiculous, but this is what English people famously do whenever their lives are falling apart, or when they just want to have a word with someone. Your mother has built a thriving business on the theory. Perhaps we could try it?" She ventured an encouraging smile at him.

He frowned at her, crunched another bite of apple, but didn't move.

"Please. I know some things about my brother that may interest you. Won't you hear me out?"

Still looking distrustful, Mark moved slowly to the work table in the center of the kitchen and pulled out a stool from beneath it. He sat down, wrapped his feet through the rungs, and rested his forearms on the table.

Caroline found cups and saucers in the cupboard, set them on the table, then prepared a pot of tea. Taking her time, she hoped that this simple task, which he had doubtless watched his mother do for as long as he could remember, would soothe him enough to overcome his wariness.

Puttering with the tea also gave her a few moments to figure out how to continue a conversation that she hoped would be the first tentative step toward building a relationship with the young man. Perhaps, if she treaded carefully, she might be able to help him as

Lily had envisioned. She began in the most innocuous way she could think of.

"You know, Mark, Mrs. Delfini made some delicious aniseed cookies yesterday. I bet if you looked in the pantry again, you might find a few."

He hesitated, then wordlessly slid off the stool and did as she suggested. He brought the cookie jar to the table, opened it, and sat down again. "You're right," he muttered around a mouthful of crumbs. "I love these cookies."

Soon the tea was steeped, and she poured them both a cup. Mark bent over his and inhaled deeply, eyes closed. "For as long as I live, English Breakfast Tea will always be the scent of my mother. I don't think she ever wears perfume. She always smells of tea." He had whispered so softly that Caroline had to lean in to hear him.

"You love her very much, don't you?" Caroline asked.

Tears gleamed in his eyes as he looked at her. "I've been pretty awful to her lately, haven't I? And I don't even know what's wrong with her. Nobody tells me anything." He stopped, unable to continue.

"Perhaps you haven't been around much for anyone to tell you anything. No offense," she added wryly.

That brought forth a twitch at the side of his mouth.

"None taken." He stared down into his cup, as if the answers might lie there. "I'm not proud of myself. But I haven't known what to do. They're all so quiet, always tiptoeing around, everything hush-hush. I just seemed to be in the way. So I decided if I stayed away and didn't know what's wrong with her, nothing bad would happen." He looked up at Caroline. "Crazy, huh?"

Caroline took a sip of her tea, then replaced her cup on its saucer. "We do all kinds of crazy things to protect ourselves from hurt, Mark. Would you like me to tell you what your father has told me about your mother's illness?"

He narrowed his eyes, as if he hadn't expected that getting information was as easy as asking for it.

"Yes, please! Why does everything have to be top secret?"

Trusting she was doing the right thing, Caroline outlined what Marco had told her about Lily's leukemia. He sat quietly, staring blankly across the room, trying to absorb the information, apple, tea and cookies forgotten.

Finally he asked, "Isn't there anything the doctor can do?"

Caroline shook her head. "I don't believe so. Dr. Jaworski has corresponded with doctors in the East, but apparently, even there, not much is known about leukemia. At this point, they can just keep her as comfortable as possible, as I understand it. Laudanum eases the pain and sometimes helps her sleep. I expect she'll need something stronger toward the end. Leticia has become very skilled at caring for her, which is a blessing."

He nodded thoughtfully. Caroline waited, astounded yet again by Mark's uncanny resemblance to Lawrence. Shouldn't she now despise her brother for the pain he'd caused her best friend? But it was so long ago, and Lawrence was dead. Whatever eternal justice he'd earned would have been meted out by now on the other side of the divide.

Mark looked up and focused on the crockery on a shelf above the sink. He blinked a few times, and a single tear crept from the corner of an eye. He dashed it away so quickly that Caroline almost missed it. In his ignorance about his mother's illness, he had no doubt imagined the worst, but to have it confirmed seemed to have stunned him.

"It's all right to cry, Mark. Sadness is an honest emotion and not the least bit unmanly. It's a terrible thing to lose one's mother."

Mark lowered his forehead onto his intertwined fists on the table. His shoulders shuddered with sobs. Caroline rose and stood behind him with a light hand on his back, as any aunt might.

"On top of all this, you've discovered why you are so different from everyone else in your family. So many shocks."

Mark raised his head and twisted around on his chair to look up at Caroline, as if wondering how far he could trust her. She lifted her hand and stepped back. He swiped the tears from his cheeks with his shirt sleeve and responded angrily.

"All my life people have teased me about looking like a Mick or a Bohunk in a family of Wops. For a long time I didn't understand. By the time it made some sense to me, Mother was sick and I didn't want to add to my parents' problems. I even wondered if I was adopted, but I was afraid to ask. It would have hurt them terribly, and frankly I didn't want it to be true."

Caroline's heart went out to the troubled young man. "I understand. There was no one you could talk to, no place to go for answers. That's enough to sink the most seaworthy ship. But listen, speaking of ships, our family name, Lindholm, is Swedish. Would it be so bad to have descended from Vikings? They were ferocious in battle and daring on the seas." Then her bright idea fizzled. Vikings were also known for raping and pillaging. "Although perhaps they were not *always* admirable," she quickly added, attempting to make light of it.

Mark cut her a glance, but kept his thoughts to himself. Caroline returned to her stool.

"Mark, I love your mother too. I'm devastated by her illness. And I've quickly become fond of your father…Marco. He's a wonderful man." She determined right then never to refer to Lawrence as his father. Marco was his father in every way that mattered; nineteen years of loving and caring outweighed one dastardly act.

"It seems your mother brought me here to somehow help you find your way through the puzzle of your parentage. She had only her motherly intuition and her overwhelming love for you to guide her. Will you let me help?" She had no idea how. She'd just have to follow her own inner guidance, flowing with Mark's responses as things unfolded.

He looked at her long and hard, his fair eyelashes still glistening with tears. She recognized the struggle in him, wondering how he could confide in this woman he barely knew, and how he could possibly admit that he needed help in sorting out his feelings.

When he slipped one foot from the stool struts onto the floor as if he were about to stand up and leave again, she said, "Mark, when your mother and I were in college, we did a great deal of talking on walks through the campus and her family's neighborhood. Come on, let's take a stroll. You can show me your favorite landmarks along the way."

After a pause, as if deciding whether or not to go along with her invitation, he rose and took their cups to the sink. She covered the cookie jar and turned toward the pantry. As she passed him, Mark lifted the lid and grabbed a few more cookies, then opened the kitchen door and held it for her. She put the cookie jar away, grabbed her straw hat from the hat rack, and followed him out. At least his appetite and his manners hasn't deserted him, Caroline thought. She took that as a hopeful sign.

They walked past Mrs. Delfini's herb garden, where a pair of pale yellow butterflies flirted among the leaves. Once on the road, the hilly neighborhood of tall trees and stately homes sparkled around them after an early morning shower.

"This is isn't easy, Mark, is it? For either of us."

He stuffed his hands into his pockets and nodded. "You could say that."

"You'll forgive me for interfering, won't you? I am, after all, your aunt."

He stopped and looked at her, as if startled by the idea. "I...never thought about it that way. I suppose you are."

"Let's make the best of it, shall we, Mark? For me, it's nothing short of miraculous that I've found my brother's son. I thought I was seeing a ghost when you walked into Lily's bedroom! You're the image of him at your age."

He frowned again, not at all thrilled by the comparison. She quickly moved the conversation on.

"Let me tell you about my brother. He wasn't all bad, you know. Why don't we begin with that, and see where it takes us?"

Mark popped the last cookie into his mouth and kept walking. "I'm listening." But there was one thing Caroline felt she had to get out of the way

"Before I begin, let me say I'm absolutely appalled by what Lawrence did to your mother."

"Do you believe her?" he asked sharply.

Caroline was taken aback by that question. But then, when the bedrock of his life had been so shaken, why would he trust anyone about anything?

"Yes I do, Mark. It all fits together. My brother abruptly stopped visiting us for several months with no explanation. When she heard he was coming for a weekend, your mother left without saying goodbye, in great haste and secrecy. Now I know she was expecting you at the time. During our early talks here, she let me assume Marco was responsible. A sin of omission, she later called it, stalling until she felt ready to tell me the truth. As I've said, she didn't invite me here just to strike up an old friendship and make amends for leaving Philadelphia. That was a ruse. I believe she thought that if she brought us together, you might begin to understand and some of the gloom would lift. So, let's get back to Lawrence."

She told him about their pleasant childhood; their easy companionship with one another, and eventually with Lily; his love of rowing; and his desire to be a poet. The recitation required nothing of Mark than to listen.

"Our father was dead set against a writing career," she said. "As I'm sure you know, poets tend to be paupers unless they have a private income, which Father refused to consider. Father was a practical man, and he wasn't about to see his only son waste his life in useless scribbling, as he termed it. Lawrence was more or less forced to join our uncle's insurance business, with the promise of inheriting everything upon Uncle Corrigan's demise. He'd have been a wealthy man eventually, but apparently that meant nothing to him. He worked diligently at the insurance business, I'll give him that, but he became more and more depressed, his lifestyle not one to be admired."

Caroline glanced at Mark to see if he was absorbing her words. His neutral expression revealed nothing. Polite, humoring his mother's friend, but only marginally attentive. Caroline pushed on.

"Then the Great War came along. By pulling a few strings, he became a freelance war correspondent for the biggest newspaper in

Philadelphia." At this, Mark turned to look at her, his attention now piqued.

"So he became a writer after all," he said.

"Yes. As it turned out, he had a knack for colorful background stories of how the war affected the beleaguered people in the French countryside. He reported stories of heart-wrenching survival against all odds. His dispatches were read throughout this country, and eventually the world. He made quite a name for himself." She watched him to see what impression this was making. His gaze no longer concentrated on the sidewalk, but focused off into the distance, perhaps imagining his progenitor slogging through the war-torn French countryside with a camera hanging from his neck and a notebook in his rucksack.

"So he wasn't a ne'er-do-well after all," Mark spat. "Just a bloody rapist."

Caroline let that go by. There was nothing she could say to contradict it or make it less than it was. She continued, trusting she could help him see the Lawrence she'd known and loved.

"Lawrence was unsuited for the business world, plain and simple. When he found his true calling, he thrived, despite the horrific circumstances."

"I suppose that's understandable," Mark mumbled. "Where is he now?"

Caroline took a few steps before replying, fearing this would be yet another shock.

"I'm sorry to say the story doesn't end happily, Mark. He was killed just before the war ended. Shot in cold blood by German snipers. We learned about it months later. His last dispatches were published after his death."

They were crossing a bridge over a deep, shrub-filled ravine that widened as it ran down to the river. Their footsteps echoed on the weathered wooden planks. Mark stopped and grabbed onto the railing, hunched over and gasping for breath. Caroline stepped to his side and put an arm around him.

"Mark? I'm sorry. Forgive me for being so graphic."

"Jesus. I just learn that I have a father I never knew about, and then I discover he's dead."

"I'm so sorry. That was brutal. But…"

"Mrs. Crawford, please leave me alone."

Caroline peered down into the ravine and shuddered.

"Not here, Mark! Please come back with me."

He turned to face her, his voice harsh. "If I'd wanted to do away with myself, I'd have done so by now. Please, Mrs. Crawford, leave me alone. I'll see you back at the house later. I promise."

With a heavy heart, she had no choice but to comply. She turned and began walking back to the house. One backward glance revealed he was still hunched over the railing, staring at the gulch below. Understanding that he needed space and time to absorb this unsettling news, she walked on, sending him a silent blessing. She spent the afternoon fretting for his wellbeing, trying to settle down and read, but with little success. When she heard Mrs. Delfini greet him in the kitchen several hours later, she breathed a sigh of relief.

Late that afternoon, Lily was finally recovered enough for Caroline to visit her. She swallowed several times before she was able to speak. Seated at Lily's side, Caroline reached for the water glass and helped her friend take a sip. Even so, her voice was raspy in a way Caroline hadn't noticed before. Her first question was about Mark.

"Where is he, Caroline? He must be terribly upset. Marco says he left the house after learning about Lawrence. Has he returned?"

"You're not to worry. He's home. I heard him in the kitchen a little while ago. He and I took a nice long walk this morning, and I told him about Lawrence: our happy childhood, his college days, his career. You knew, didn't you, that my brother Lawrence was Lawrence Lindholm, the international war correspondent?"

Lily played nervously with the ribbons of her bed jacket. "Yes, I almost fainted the first time Marco called one of his stories in the *Oregonian* to my attention. To my horror he read the whole thing out loud. He commented on what a sensitive fellow the writer must have been to have captured the devastated feelings of a farm wife whose husband and two sons had been killed on the battlefield, leaving her with three younger children. I must have gone as white as a ghost, but he was so fascinated by the story that he paid no attention. Of course it could have been a different Lawrence Lindholm, but after Marco left the next morning I found the article. There he was, photographed leaning against an old rock-walled farmhouse with the family. That erased any doubt. With a little practice and a few deep breaths, I learned to take it in stride when Marco commented on yet another Lindholm story. We had promised never to speak of him again. I'm sure Marco had no idea."

"Yes, he and I talked about it. He hadn't known my brother's last name and had no reason to make the connection." Caroline hesitated for a moment. "You know, too, that Lawrence is dead."

"Yes, we read about it just after the war ended. I was sorry for you, Caroline. I know you loved him."

"And you left my home to protect that love. I'm overwhelmed that you did something so selfless on my behalf."

"I've never regretted it, Caroline. It's over and done with. Lawrence was not a bad person. I know that."

"He hated always being on the hustle, trying to sell an insurance policy whether a person needed it or not. Some people enjoy the sales game; Lawrence decidedly did not. I thought it would help Mark to know that he was a talented and internationally respected writer."

"It's all such a jumble, Caroline. I apologize for getting you here under false pretenses. I truly wanted to see you, to reminisce about our school days and my crazy life as a visiting girl. To ask your forgiveness for ducking out without an explanation. As the years went by, I became more and more embarrassed about it. I don't think I'd have had the courage to write to you recently if I hadn't been so worried about Mark. Can you forgive me for dragging you into this mess?"

"There's nothing to forgive, you silly goose. Now that I'm over the shock of meeting Mark, I'm thrilled to find out I have a nephew. I just feel terrible about the circumstances. Those weeks when you bravely carried on with your visiting schedule, so worried about what to do—you must have been frantic. I do wish you'd been able to confide in me."

"It was a long time ago, Caroline." Lily closed her eyes, then looked up at her friend mischievously. "Besides, how many times did I declare that I would never marry just to get married?"

"That was practically your anthem," Caroline teased back.

"And then I did exactly that, although I was enchanted with Marco from the beginning. I've had a wonderful life with him. We'd never have married otherwise. I'm very grateful, even to Lawrence. Now if only I can help Mark make peace with it."

CHAPTER 32

That evening at dinner, Caroline told Marco about her walk with Mark. "The poor boy is awash in confusion, Marco. So much to sort out, so many things to assimilate."

"At least we know, or think we know, what brought on the melancholy," said Marco as he helped himself to a slice of meatloaf. "But how to help him out of it?"

Caroline tore off a piece of Mrs. Delfini's warm crusty bread and slowly buttered it before continuing.

"Consider for a moment, Marco, what you just said. The rape of his mother was a terrible thing, and now he understands why he felt so out of step with your Italian family and friends. From here it's a matter of how he deals with it, and only he can work that out. He knows we're here to support him."

"I hope to God you're right." With a swipe through his mashed potatoes, Marco popped a bite of meatloaf into his mouth.

"And then there's Lily," Caroline said softly.

He set his knife and fork on his plate and looked at her, deep sadness in his eyes. "Lily."

"Yes, Marco. Soon you'll lose your wife and Mark will lose his mother. As difficult as it will be for you, you'll need to reach out and comfort him. He can't deal with it by himself, not on top of everything else."

Marco scoffed. "Surely he knows I love him?"

"Intellectually, perhaps. But emotionally, I don't know. I gather you two haven't been particularly close lately."

"That's certainly true. He has been rather difficult."

Caroline ignored the annoyance in his voice. She reached across the table and put a hand on his sleeve.

"Marco, it will be up to you to make the first move, to reassure him that you are and always have been his father. By the way, he mentioned that he's been told very little about Lily's illness, and that has surely added to his feelings of alienation. I hope I didn't step out of line, but when he asked me about it this afternoon, it seemed a good time to tell him what you shared with me."

Marco glanced away. "Well, I guess I didn't want to upset him. One never knows how much to tell a child."

"He isn't a child anymore, Marco. He knows his mother is seriously ill, and I'm sure the worry is as upsetting as the reality. Who knows what his imagination may be serving up, and then learning about Lawrence on top of it. Nobody would be able to handle that, especially not such a vulnerable young man."

"What do you suggest?".

"Have a talk with him, right away. Apologize for keeping him in the dark about Lily. Invite him to ask any questions he might have. And don't be afraid to let your own emotions show. Let him see that it's okay for him to feel sadness and grief. And fear! A young man his age has no idea what to do with such feelings." She peaked her eyebrows. "Perhaps you don't either."

His voice quavered. "I have to be strong for everyone. I *can't* let my feelings show."

"Try it. You may find it helps to restore the bond between you."

Marco glanced at her doubtfully.

"And tell Mark how Lily told you that day at the lake that she was expecting a baby. Tell him how you were prepared to love him from that very moment, and that you proposed to her on the spot. How the two of you traveled out here a few days later like the Blue Willow lovers. It's a touching and romantic story, you know. Have you or Lily ever shared it with him?"

He shook his head. "I certainly haven't, and I doubt Lily has either. I guess we feared it would bring on questions—questions we didn't know how to answer."

"Then talk to him, try to be completely open, no matter what he asks."

Marco frowned. Caroline lifted her chin and tipped her head, silently challenging him.

"All right," he finally agreed. "I'll try, provided he'll sit still and listen."

Caroline broke into a smile. "Good. Start with the apology. That always softens people up."

Getting ready for bed later, Caroline wondered if she had overstepped with her advice to Marco. What gave her the right to give counsel on a matter of such sensitivity? She'd spoken from her heart, but good intentions often went awry. Well, she could only hope that her advice was worthy, and that he would act on it.

Marco was late getting home the next night. Reading in her bedroom after dinner with Lettie, Caroline heard him come in and immediately climb the stairs to see Lily. She waited for almost an hour until he went downstairs again, then followed him to his den. Seated at his desk, he looked up as Caroline knocked softly on the open door. His eyes were undershot with dark circles, his expression grim. Alarmed, she clenched her fists and prepared herself for devastating news about Lily.

"Caroline, come in. If it's not one thing it's another. My best grower of leafy winter greens told me today that he won't be able to supply me this year. After closing the shop, I drove out to the farm to see what the problem was. Leaf-boring larvae, he told me. The whole field is infested. He'll have to uproot and burn everything, then plow it all under and leave it fallow for a year. I'll have to find another supplier. But never mind, you're just in time to distract me. Will you join me in a glass of wine?"

She nodded, wanting to feel relieved that worry about Lily was not forefront on his mind, but still anxious for her friend. She sat on a chair facing his desk as he topped his glass and poured one for her.

"Lily—is she all right?" Caroline inquired.

He grimaced. "As much as can be expected. She's resting comfortably for the moment. Lettie is with her."

"Thank goodness." Caroline tipped up her glass, took a sip, and breathed over it in her mouth before swallowing. "Mmm, a bit raw, but decent."

Marco grinned. "You get used to it." She began to relax.

"Tell me, Marco, how is it you always seem to have a good supply of wine on hand? Isn't Prohibition enforced out here?"

"Yes, but certainly not in the way it was intended. Do you know Oregon's history with Prohibition?"

"Not at all."

"Lily could tell you a lot about it. From the vivid stories of her Back Door Women, she's learned only too well how alcohol can undermine domestic harmony. She and her suffragist friends pushed all the harder for the vote, because they knew that they would then be able to vote for measures restricting the sale of alcohol. Oregon women got the vote in 1912, and sure enough, Oregon passed statewide Prohibition in 1914, effective two years later.

"Over time, our chief of police and the mayor of Portland worked things out between them. The police control the confiscation and clandestine storage of liquor, and the Mayor and his cronies control the distribution. If you are well connected and can afford the outrageous prices, you can get whatever you want. And of course fortunes are being made all along the way."

"And those less fortunate are made scapegoats, I imagine, arrested and jailed for petty violations."

"That's the way the world works, isn't it?" Marco mused. "The 'haves' and the 'have-nots'."

Caroline could only nod, accepting that they were both among the fortunate 'haves.'

Marco went on. "Of course there are dramatic raids on speakeasies and such, with public displays of bottle breaking and booze running in the streets, but that was just for show. By 1920, when the federal Prohibition law kicked in, the city of Portland was way ahead in the bootlegging game, including a vigorous contraband trade across the border with British Columbia."

"But you don't drink hard liquor, at least not that I've noticed."

He made a fist. "*Sono Italiano*—I'm Italian! Why would I drink booze when I can have *vino?*"

"But wine is just as illegal as liquor."

"Aha! Several of my flower suppliers grow grapes and make their own vino. They put a few bottles in with the flowers and invoice it as 'vine flowers.' Haven't you noticed that the bottles aren't labeled? And, as you said, it can be a bit raw."

Caroline glanced at the bottle on his desk. Sure enough, no label. When served at the table, the wine had always been in a crystal decanter.

Marco chuckled. "In an emergency there's always sacramental wine. Too sweet for my taste, but many of our parishioners have come to appreciate it. From time to time I trade the good Father a bottle of this farmer's red, for which he is most grateful, for one of his sacramentals. I give it to Mrs. Delfini to use in cooking. Perhaps you've noticed the sweetness of her tomato sauce?"

"So that's her secret. I might have known."

"As long as the wine hasn't been consecrated, she's delighted to have it. But back to Prohibition—I don't imagine the situation is all that different everywhere else in the country. Bootleggers, speakeasies, mobsters everywhere. The law has spawned all kinds of unintended consequences. Frankly I think we've set in motion a hurricane from which we may never recover."

"You may be right. Only time will tell. But enough of that, Marco. Have you had a chance to speak with Mark?"

Marco shook his head. "I haven't been able to catch him at home, and he hasn't shown up at the shop. I just don't know what to do. Lily gets agitated every time we talk about him. I think she fears...she fears dying before they can reconcile." He blinked rapidly, beating back tears.

"I believe that's exactly what she fears," whispered Caroline.

"She's getting weaker and weaker, Caroline, and her pain has intensified. Several days ago Dr. Jaworski taught Lettie how to inject her with morphine. Laudanum is no longer effective."

Caroline's hand flew to her cheek. "She never said!"

"No, she wouldn't. She'll soldier on until the end."

A new idea came to Caroline. "What if we invite Mark to participate in Lily's care, keeping her company for a while each day, or maybe just sitting with her while she sleeps. It would do Lily a world of good to have Mark beside her. Just knowing he's there might start their healing process."

Marco looked at Caroline doubtfully. "It could also upset her. He hasn't been very pleasant to either of us lately."

"Marco, all it would take is a few humble words from Mark. One sincere sentence. This whole exercise of getting me out here was an attempt to help your son regain his footing and restore the loving relationship that once existed between them. We can't let Lily leave him the way things are."

Marco nodded.

"There's something else to consider, Marco. If we focus on helping Lily and Mark reconcile, it will also go a long way toward you two men being there for each other when Lily is gone."

Marco winced and looked down at his hands, clasped together on his desk.

"You owe him that, Marco. He deserves an opportunity to be close to his mother in her waning days, to clear up the unhappiness that's between them. But he won't do it on his own. Think how horrible it would be for her to die with him still feeling so mixed up. Once she's gone, the opportunity is gone."

He shook his head. "I can't imagine that he'd do it. He's had no experience in a sickroom. Men don't do that sort of thing."

"Come on, Marco. You spend time with Lily every day, and so can Mark. I bet all you have to do is give him a little encouragement. He might even be pleased to be asked."

Marco drained his wine glass and wiped his lips with the back of his hand.

"I don't suppose you'd have that conversation with him?" he asked, rather shamefacedly.

"No, Marco. You need to mend your own fences with him. While you're at it, why don't you ask him to join us for dinner from now on. It's getting rather grim, just the two of us muddling along while Lettie is upstairs with Lily." Mark must be tired of apples and cookies from the pantry, she thought to herself.

Caroline fell asleep easily that night, but an hour later found herself wide awake, her restless mind spinning through her concerns and worries about Lily and her family. She tossed and turned, but found no reprieve. Finally she got up, donned her robe and slippers, and went downstairs for a glass of warm milk. Heading toward the kitchen, she approached the partially open door to Marco's office. Voices rose and fell from within. Realizing that Marco had finally caught up with his son, she paused to listen.

"So you see, Mark. That blue willow cachepot on your mother's windowsill tells the whole story. From the day she told me, sitting by the lake, that she was expecting you, I have wanted you and loved you. I can't express it any more clearly than that."

Mark's reply was barely a whisper. "Thank you, Dad. That helps."

"I'm glad you think so, son. Before you go, I have one great favor to ask of you. It's about your mother."

"Yes?" Caroline heard a chill in Mark's voice.

"There's no use denying it—her days are coming to an end." Marco's voice caught as he spoke. Caroline could only imagine the pain reflected on both their faces. "It would do her a great deal of good if you would spend time with her, daily if you please. Sit with her, listen to her, give her the chance to say what she wants to say to you before she goes."

Without waiting for Mark's reply, Caroline stepped quickly past the office door, trusting that the two men were too deeply engaged in their conversation to notice.

CHAPTER 33

Lily awoke two mornings later to find Mark sitting on a chair beside her bed. Wondering if she were hallucinating, she struggled to raise herself on an elbow to get a better look.

"Mark? Is that really you?" Her whisper was so soft, she wondered if he'd heard her.

"That's not a very friendly greeting, Mother. How are you feeling?"

"Pleasantly surprised. Could you please hand me that glass of water, son?"

He helped her raise her head and held the glass to her lips while she sipped.

"Thank you," she said as he eased her back on the pillows. "What's happened?" she finally asked.

"You mean why am I here?" He looked down at his hands and frowned. "Mrs. Crawford finally told me about the…the leukemia. Father later apologized for keeping me in the dark. He said he wanted to protect me, but of course that was the last thing he achieved."

Lily grinned at him. Her lips were chapped, her gums had receded painfully, but her spirit was still strong. "Marco and Dr. Jaworski tried that strategy with me, too, but I forced it out of them."

"No one could ever say no to you, Mother. Anyway, Father asked me if I would spend some time with you. At first I was a bit…"

332

"...wary?" she finished for him, knowing this would be hard for him to admit.

"Yeah, you could say that. But, considering..." His eyes teared up, much to his consternation. He looked away and blinked hard.

She reached out and took his hand. "Mark, can you possibly forgive me for also keeping you in the dark about...about who you are?"

"Honestly?" he asked, struggling to keep the anger out of his voice. "I can't imagine anyone telling her son he's the child of rape. I had this big, dark hole in my life, but I couldn't fathom its cause. It writhed around in my gut like a snake. Still, you could have kept it to yourself, you and Father, and let me go on in despair. It took nerve to ask Mrs. Crawford to come out here and help you set the record straight. It could easily have backfired, you know—with me taking it the wrong way and leaving things worse than they were before she arrived."

"Yes, I knew I was taking a terrible chance. But Mark, I was willing to do anything to help you find your way again. Anything. Luckily Caroline has been a brick about it."

"She's been amazing. Sort of taken me under her wing like..."

"...like an aunt! She's very fond of you, Mark, and wants so much to be a real aunt to you."

Lily expected Mark to respond to that idea with at least some enthusiasm. Instead he scowled and looked away.

"Why is that troubling, son?"

"For me to know I was fathered by such a...such a beast? How do I accept that? How do I know I'm not just like him? I've heard people talk about tainted blood, that you can't escape your family background. Remember when Dan Confessore's father hanged himself? I heard people say it was only to be expected, because his own father had done the same thing."

"Mark, I don't believe that for a minute. Even if it were so, Lawrence wasn't a bad person. Yes, he did a terrible thing, but it wasn't the hallmark of his personality. I think we are all capable of dark deeds under certain circumstances. You'd be shocked by some of the stories I hear at the Merry Weather. You can truly hate the sin but still love—or at least not hate—the sinner."

Mark pushed aside his bangs, such an endearing gesture, Lily thought. Yes, that was Lawrence's gesture too, but only occasionally had she been mindful of it. She had rarely thought of Mark as Lawrence's son. He was simply Mark.

"We ached for you, son. We had no idea what was going on in your mind, in your heart. We just knew you'd lost your way. Marco, worried as he was, had his work to distract him, but as I got sicker I had nothing to do but to lie here and stew on it. Finally I reached the point where, if I didn't act, I knew I would go to my grave full of regrets, and leave you even more adrift."

Mark shifted in his seat, looked away from his mother, and gathered his legs beneath him as if to rise and leave the room. "Mother, please don't talk about…"

Lily raised a thin, blue veined hand. "…about going to my grave? Mark, look at me. Look at my arms. Shriveled matchsticks! I'm a mere shadow of myself, barely able to sit up against the pillows. I *am* going to my grave, much as I'd rather stay here and enjoy the life we've worked so hard for. I've faced the finality of it, and so must you."

Mark covered his eyes with his hand, as if he were willing to continue listening but couldn't bear looking at her. Lily understood.

"Mark, do you know how much your father loves you?"

He shrugged. "I know how much you love me." He hesitated. "And, yes, I suppose Father too."

Tears sprang to Lily's eyes. "Do you mean that, Mark? Do you truly know, truly *feel* that Marco is your father, in every way? That he loved you from the first moment he held you in his arms, minutes after you were born?"

"I'm trying hard to believe it, Mother. Right now, that's the best I can do."

From then on, Mark spent time with Lily in the mornings or the early evenings, depending on how she felt. He dined with Marco and

Caroline most nights. He was reasonably pleasant company, although there were obviously things that troubled him. Some nights he had his dinner on a tray with Lily. He still occasionally went out in the evening with his friends, but the nights of reveling until dawn and arriving home wasted, or staying away for days on end were over. He even began to take an interest in the flower business, a gesture he silently offered to keep the peace during his mother's waning days. His father seemed grateful, and that was what mattered.

CHAPTER 34

The scrapbook of Lawrence's articles arrived. Caroline couldn't hide a surge of pride when she handed it to Mark, yet he sensed that she was still grappling with her feelings about the brother she had loved.

Mark took the scrapbook to his room and spent the next few days pouring over it. Stories of elderly farmers hiding lost soldiers in their barns and attics; young mothers trading sexual favors for food for their children; people burying valuables in the woods and scarce foodstuffs under floorboards; old men murdering marauding soldiers and burying their bodies among the trees in order to save what remained of their families; husbands, brothers, and sons who never came back, fates unknown. The big battles were waged from the trenches with guns, gas, bayonets, and horse-drawn artillery, but small battles were fought at home—day to day, hand to mouth, in quiet desperation.

That the man who had violated his mother could have written so sensitively and caringly about complete strangers in a faraway land broke something loose in Mark's heart. He began to believe what his mother had said about people being neither all good nor all bad. And that one could hate the sin but not the sinner.

He brought the scrapbook to dinner one night and handed it back to Caroline, thanking her for sharing it with him. "These are remarkable articles, Mrs. Cr…Aunt Caroline. I'm impressed."

Smiling in surprise at his familiarity, she handed the scrapbook back to him. "This is for you, Mark. Keep it as a connection to the family you never knew you had."

He hesitated, then nodded. "Thank you. I'll treasure it."

"That's nice of you, Caroline," echoed Marco. Struck by the tension in his father's voice, Mark wondered what it cost him to say that. Did he resent this tangible reminder of his son's paternal ancestry? Mark had often heard men saying how important it was to have a son of their own blood to carry on the family name. Italian men in particular. Mark Giannotti had the name, but not the Giannotti blood.

While Mrs. Delfini cleared away their main course and returned with dessert, Mark placed a hand on the scrapbook, cleared his throat, and said, "Dad, I've had a lot of time these past few days to think about my future. I've come to some conclusions."

Marco picked up his dessert fork and began to turn it by the handle between his forefinger and thumb, a sure sign of annoyance with which Mark was only too familiar.

"Have you, now, son?"

Mark plunged on, hoping he wouldn't set off a tirade, but willing to chance it. "You know my best marks in school were in English and history."

"Yes?"

"I loved the history books we read and the writing assignments, especially the stories about the settling of the West."

"So you want to be a cowboy?" Marco peered at his son from beneath his eyebrows.

Mark sharpened his own gaze, checking to see if Marco was serious. "No, Father, nothing like that. I'd like to be a writer."

"A writer, eh? Beats chasing cows across the prairie. Pretty precarious way to make a living, though," Marco declared.

Sarcasm was the last thing Mark expected from his father. He'd thought that things had straightened out between them over the past few days. He hoped his father was simply unprepared for his assertion of independence. He didn't want to consider that Marco was annoyed to learn that Lawrence's literary bent had trickled down to his son. He took a deep breath.

"Perhaps, Dad, but I'd like to give writing a try." Mark waited a beat, then glanced away.

"And what do you plan to write about, pray tell? You have no training, no background, and no dramatic arena from which to tell tales, as Lindholm did. I won't wish another war upon us, just so you can earn a living." Again the sarcasm—where was this coming from?

"I don't know yet, Dad. I'll continue to work for you until I figure it out." Mark looked at his father again, this time holding his gaze. "Provided you still want me."

Somewhat mollified, Marco responded gruffly, "Of course I do, son. We're busier than ever, since that rapscallion Jimmy wiggled his way into becoming our sales manager. And that farm I purchased up the Gorge takes way more work than I anticipated. I could split myself in three and still not handle it all."

"Fair enough," said Mark, greatly relieved that his father was calming down. Perhaps he was thinking of the lengths to which he had gone to get out from under his own father's thumb and was aware of history beginning to repeat itself. Perhaps they were both making accommodations to keep the peace because of Lily. Whatever it was, he was grateful.

Marco stroked his chin for a few moments. "I'll tell you what, son. Give me two years and put your earnings away to help pay your tuition at the University of Oregon. I hear they have a well-respected journalism program there. If you are determined to do this, then learn what you can, get your degree, and you'll have a much better chance to make something of yourself. I'll pay the shortfall, provided you keep your grades up. You'll have my blessing, and I'm sure your mother will agree."

Mark was stunned. He hadn't given college a thought. High school had been such a bore, except for his senior English teacher who brilliantly dramatized the novels they read, and his American history teacher who had made the Revolution, the Civil War, and the taming of the West come alive by his animated storytelling. But college? Although both teachers had urged him to enroll, assuring him he was college material, he'd dismissed it outright. Four more years of studying? Not for him.

"If I may interrupt," said Caroline. They looked at her as if they had forgotten she was there. "As you know, my husband owned a publishing company, which I sold shortly after his death. Last year the new owner approached me with the idea of consolidating Lawrence's wartime dispatches into a book. Books about the Great War are popular right now, and Lawrence's viewpoint was unique. Not to mention that his name is a household word throughout the country. The publisher has every expectation that it will be a big success."

"And what has that got to do with us?" Marco asked.

"He died intestate, and with no wife or children…that he knew of. Our parents had passed on, so as his only sibling, I was declared his heir. The book is being edited right now. Nothing would please me more than to sign over the copyright to you, Mark. It's rightfully yours, and the royalties are bound to be considerable."

Marco looked at his son, gauging his reaction. Mark fumbled for a response.

"I don't know what to say, Aunt Caroline. Father, does this make sense?"

Marco huffed. "It makes about as much sense as anything does right now, son. But it could open up your future, give you the wherewithal to pursue your writing."

"Would I still have to put in two years at Giannotti's?"

"You rascal! From what I know about the publishing business, which I admit isn't much, it will be a while before any royalties roll in. Am I right, Caroline?"

She nodded her head.

"So let's compromise. Give me just a year in which to adjust to the increased business and the new farm, and I'll send you off to the university with no strings attached."

Mark's head was reeling when he said good night to his father and Caroline. An inheritance? He couldn't yet grasp what that might mean. And college, when he had barely scraped through high school? But he'd be studying subjects he liked, living away from home, and he'd have the time and opportunity to explore the possibilities. Perhaps journalism; perhaps he'd write novels or historical biographies. Maybe even teach history or literature or writing. Thanks to the scrapbook, he took silent pride in his sire's talent and trusted some of it had been transmitted to him. Yes, it made perfect sense. He'd enroll at University of Oregon next year and begin the rest of his life.

He fell asleep with the scrapbook beside his pillow, one hand splayed on the cover.

Several evenings later, Mark stood at the kitchen door, gazing out at Mrs. Delfini's herb garden, still visible in the lingering summer twilight. He recalled the happy hours he had spent with her each spring, helping her turn the soil, build up neat rows of dirt, and plant the various seeds for her Italian seasonings. She hadn't had to ask him twice, as he'd loved being outdoors and getting his hands in the soil, just like his father. It had become their annual ritual…until this past spring. He had not been in the mood and now felt a little ashamed of himself.

She was just finishing tidying up the kitchen after dinner. He turned to face her. "Mrs. D, I'm sorry I wasn't around to help you with the garden this year. It looks like you did pretty well without me, though."

She stopped wiping the counter near the sink, rag in hand, and turned around. "You had troubles of your own to think about. I missed you, but I got the job done." She smiled as she said it.

"I've always been proud to be part of it," he said. "I mean, watching the plants grow and then enjoying how delicious they made the food you cooked for us."

"It was a pleasure for me, too. You were very helpful, and I enjoyed your company. But time marches along, and you have much more important things to do. That's as it should be." She said it with a firm nod of her head. It felt like a blessing, an encouragement to move on.

Later, when he was in his bedroom and the house was quiet, he sat on his bed and tried to empty his mind of the demons that had tortured his thoughts and dreams for so long. He expected they would always be there, lurking in the background, occasionally roaring to the forefront when he least anticipated them. When they did, he hoped he'd be able to face them squarely and banish them until the next time. For now he would try to move forward with new interests to explore, new places to discover, new people to meet.

He tucked into bed with, "*Astoria: Or, Enterprise Beyond the Rocky Mountains*" by Washington Irving. John Jacob Astor had commissioned the book as the official history of his company's 1810–1812 expedition to Oregon. What an astounding story—this German immigrant fur trader who founded the town of Astoria at the mouth of the Columbia River, then turned New York City real estate magnate. What a life that man had lived, although, Mark had to admit, not an entirely admirable one.

What had it been like for the teenage son of a butcher to leave his small German town and land in America right after the Revolutionary War, finding opportunities aplenty for a young man with brains and daring? Butchering had led him to dealing in hides, which led to a fur trading empire that spanned the country. With his profits invested in Manhattan real estate, Astor became one of the richest men in America. The era of daring deeds was over perhaps, but there was a great deal of history to research and write about. And wasn't Astor another example of a person not all good nor all bad?

This is what he wanted to do, he thought to himself, to get under the skin of these heroic yet flawed people, find out what motivated them, what led them to such adventurous lives—to take such risks, to rebound and return to the fray after bankruptcies, swindles, and failures. Yes, he wanted to be a writer, and it no longer seemed impossible. He drifted off, content to feel at home for the first time in a long while.

Unusually for him, Mark awoke well before dawn. The house was quiet except for the ticking of the kitchen clock just outside his door. For a reason he couldn't explain, he felt compelled to throw off the covers and put on his dressing gown. He made his way through the kitchen and dining room to the stairs, splashed by multicolored moonlight shining through the stained glass door panels. Up he went, reassured by the familiar creak of the planks. He turned toward his mother's room and found the door partway open. He stopped and listened. All was quiet, all seemed well, but still he pushed open the door and stepped in. Lily lay sleeping, propped up on pillows to help her breathing, barely visible in the shaded light of the small lamp on the dresser. He stood gazing at her for several moments, swamped with memories of how wonderful she had been with him and Theresa: playful, funny, yet guiding them gently in positive directions, diverting them from danger, picking them up and hugging them when they were hurt or upset.

Seeing that she was sleeping peacefully, he turned to go back downstairs, but something uncanny stopped him. He turned again, and, without knowing why, made himself comfortable in the upholstered chair at Lily's bedside. Somehow it seemed important that he stay and keep watch. She had aged dramatically over the last few weeks, but in repose and soft lamplight, it barely showed.

All at once Lily strained forward, opened her eyes, coughed, and then gasped, "Take care of Marco, son. He needs you."

Startled, Mark shifted to the edge of the bed, where he tenderly gathered his mother in his arms. Perhaps her breathing would ease if he held her upright. She was so shockingly fragile; there was almost nothing left of her. She gasped two more times, exhaled softly, then slumped in his arms, a marionette whose strings had been cut.

"Mother? Mother?" he whispered hoarsely. "Are you all right?"

Looking around frantically for help but finding none, he eased her gently back onto the pillows. She had no more substance than an armful of twigs. He put his ear against her chest but heard nothing. He sat back and gazed at her, tears pooling in his eyes, stroking her soft, pale cheek and graying hair. He knew it was over.

Mark remained on the bed and brushed back the stray wisps that had escaped from her braid. Her skin was as soft as the breast feathers of the eider ducks he'd kept in a backyard pen as a child. Her face had relaxed, all signs of pain erased. She was once again the beautiful mother of his youth.

He knew he should alert the household, let his father know at once what had happened, but he also knew that this would be his last chance to be alone with her. Soon the many people who loved her would crowd in, and the ceremonies for the dead would begin. He had a profound sense that this was his mother's last gift to him: the privilege of holding her in his arms while her soul took flight; sharing with him the peace of her passing.

Tears cascaded down his cheeks as he whispered, *Oh, Mother, I've only begun to appreciate everything you gave me and everything you gave up for me. You left behind all that you knew and took a chance with a man who was almost a stranger—just to give me a home and a father. How could you have loved me, knowing how I came to be? Yet you did. You were the best mother anyone could ask for. And I never felt any difference in how you treated me and Theresa. We were always equal in your loving eyes.*

And you were the one who saw I was foundering. You took a terrible chance by inviting Aunt Caroline out here to try and clear things up. How did you know that was the right thing to do? Aunt Caroline spoke of intuition. I looked it up—understanding something without conscious reasoning. Was that it? Bringing her here was the most loving thing you could have done.

He sat quietly for a few more minutes, holding her hand as it began to cool. Soon he knew it was time.

He pulled up the Amish quilt, leaving her serene face exposed, and kissed her on both cheeks. Then he opened the door to his father's room, went in, and laid a gentle hand on his sleeping father's shoulder.

"Dad. Mother's gone."

CHAPTER 35

Friends from the neighborhood and beyond attended Lily's funeral service: former suffragists, neighboring shopkeepers, the tightknit Italian community, and Back Door Women of every circumstance and occupation. Automobiles and carriages and black-clad walkers streamed into the churchyard. Marco and Mark had filled the church with joyous bouquets in celebration of Lily's life and their love for her.

So this is how it ends, mused Caroline, having coffee with Marco in the sunporch the day after the service. Gentle rain fell, splattering the leaves of the walnut tree and soaking into the ever-accepting soil. The chaise longue was empty, sending a silent cry throughout the room that Lily would never recline there again. Once more, she knew the meaning of a broken heart. The physical ache was so acute, she felt as if her heart had been ripped from her chest.

Lily's bright light had gone out, but not before she had accomplished what her letter to Caroline had intended. The two friends had shared Lily's final days, and Mark had been given the knowledge and support to begin setting his life in order.

Marco, sitting across from her, looked grim and exhausted. Sorrow had carved deep creases on either side of his mouth. His hair was mussed, and he needed a shave.

"I'll help Lettie with Lily's things," Caroline offered softly. "And, if you like, I'll write responses to the condolence letters you've been receiving. I can't tell you how often Lily wrote notes of all sorts for her visiting hostesses."

Marco gave Caroline a tired nod. "I guess if it were left up to me, they would never get written, eh? Social niceties involving pen and paper have never been my strong suit."

She patted his arm. "I'm happy to do it for you. You and Mark get back to your customers. Keeping busy is the best thing you can do right now. I'm sure it's what Lily would want. And don't worry, I'll head home as soon as those tasks are done."

Marco looked startled. "Oh, no, you mustn't leave us. You've become part of our family." The sincerity in his voice was touching. She'd become so fond of Lily's family.

"Well, I won't leave immediately, but soon. I have a life in Philadelphia, you know, and I feel it calling. My daughter Nancy's baby is due in four months—my first grandchild."

"Ah, yes, grandchildren," said Marco. "I received a telegram from Theresa's husband this morning. She gave birth yesterday to healthy little girl. Mother and daughter doing well."

"Congratulations! Lily would have been so happy to know Theresa is safely delivered and that a new child has joined the family."

"Yes." Marco smiled through his sadness. "Guess what they named her—Lily Angelique. For Lily, of course, and Angelique for her other grandmother.

"Why, that's lovely! Lily Angelique. Our Lily would have been honored and delighted."

"I haven't told Theresa about Lily's death," continued Marco. "I didn't want to upset her just prior to the baby's arrival. Now I'm thinking I'll take Mark for a visit with his sister and give her the news in person. It's the least I can do. And I want to meet my new granddaughter."

"Of course you do. I'm glad you're taking Mark. You'll both be a great comfort to Theresa. It will also be an opportunity for Mark to tell his sister what he's learned about his own identity—if he wants to. And for you and Mark to spend time together. He needs you so much."

Marco looked directly at Caroline, elbows on his knees. "I've been harsh with Mark, I realize, expected too much of him as he struggled with his doubts and fears."

"But you had no idea, Marco. Only Lily suspected what was going on, why he felt so alienated from the family."

He shook his head. "She took a dreadful chance in bringing you here. Thank God you came, and that she was right."

"Sometimes a mother's hunch is a deeper truth than anything that proceeds from reason. And when one is dying, all caution falls away, as Lily reminded me more than once. She knew this was the last thing she could do for Mark. And since you introduced the subject of Mark, he seems excited about planning for college."

"Yes, I admit I'm surprised. Perhaps he just wasn't ready until now. It's the best thing for him, I'm sure of it."

Lettie entered the sun porch holding a coffee pot. "Refills, anyone?" she asked. She too looked done in with grief for her friend and mentor, even as she made an effort to sound cheerful.

Marco held out his cup. "Fill 'er up, please. Caroline?"

"Yes, please."

As Lettie poured out the steaming brew, Marco said, "Sit down and join us, Lettie, please. I was just telling Caroline that I'm planning a trip with Mark to visit Theresa and meet my new granddaughter. Why don't you come with us? Theresa loves you, and I know you feel the same about her. Although she'd been expecting it, word of her mother's death will have hit her hard. Among the three of us, we can console her and give her a full picture of Lily's last days. I think she'd appreciate that."

Surprised, Lettie set the coffee pot on a table near Marco and Caroline. Marco pulled up a chair for her, which gave her a moment to consider this unexpected invitation.

Once seated, she asked, "Go to Roseburg? To see Theresa?"

"Yes. I'll keep the flower shop closed for another week, and you can decide what to do about the Merry Weather. And Mrs. Delfini deserves a paid vacation. How about it?"

"Wait, I can decide about the Merry Weather?"

"Yes. Actually, it's time you knew. Lily has given it to you in her will. The lawyers have drawn up the paperwork, and we'll make it official as soon as we return."

For a moment Lettie looked dumbfounded. "She...she's given it to me? The Merry Weather?"

"Indeed," said Marco. "And she liked to picture your surprise when you found out. She wouldn't have been disappointed."

Marco and Caroline both grinned. "You've worked as hard as Lily to make it a success," Marco added. "You deserve it."

"My goodness! That will take some getting used to," Lettie murmured.

"You can do that in Roseburg. What do you say?"

Her face shone with pleasure. "Oh, I'd love to see Theresa and her family."

"Excellent! We'll leave on Friday. I'll wire Theresa today. She'll have a lot to cope with—a new baby on top of the sadness of her mother's death, but I know she'll be pleased to have us there."

Three days later, Marco and Mark drove Caroline to Union Station, with fond farewells and many thanks. Later that afternoon the two men and Lettie boarded a train south to Roseburg, with heavy hearts but looking forward to a change of scene and precious healing time with Theresa and her family.

As her train chugged east up the Columbia Gorge, Caroline watched the stunning panorama flow by: the sparkling river racing past her; the orchards, wheat fields, pasture lands; then wild forests stretching up, down, and all around. Above the trees, naked peaks crowned with snow, even in mid-summer. She had five leisurely days to digest her time in Oregon. Yet she knew it would take the rest of her life to truly sort it out. And what a tale she had to tell Nancy!

AFTERWORD

This is the story I wanted to tell, inspired by the early life of movie star Katharine Hepburn's mother, Katharine Martha Houghton Hepburn, as recounted in the book, *Katharine Hepburn*, by Barbara Leaming. A friend sent me the paperback more than a decade ago, and I was mesmerized by the elder Katharine's struggle to attend and graduate from Bryn Mawr College, class of 1899. The term "visiting girl," and all that it implies, comes from this book. Perhaps today Lily might have been known as a sort of high-class guest room surfer. I owe a great deal to Ms. Leaming. Acknowledging the inspiration, this story is my own.

That said, I wondered what might have happened to the characters after Caroline returned to Philadelphia, and Marco, Mark, and Lettie returned to Portland from their visit with Theresa and her family. Here's what I think:

Marco refused to hear a word about Lettie moving out of his house. She had been with them for many years, and he couldn't imagine his household without her. During the months following their trip to Roseburg, a subtle change took place in their relationship—a surprise to both of them when they finally realized it. A year and a half after Lily's death, they married in a quiet ceremony at the Catholic church. With her husband and children, Theresa journeyed north for the occasion, pleased that her father had found happiness with someone she also loved.

Mark put in his promised year with his father at Giannotti Florist West, which gave him time to grieve for his mother, steady his relationship with his father, and think more about his future. Shortly before his father's marriage to Lettie, of which he heartily approved, he enrolled at University of Oregon in Eugene.

On that lush, forested campus, nobody cared that he was blonde and blue-eyed with an Italian last name. He joined a fraternity, where he was just one of the guys. He majored in journalism but took every creative writing course he could. He also dipped into a variety of other subjects that interested him and formed a platform for further exploration in his literary future: science, history, anthropology, geography, economics, astronomy, ethics, and so on. At the beginning of every term when he stood in line to register for his classes, he felt as if he was choosing from an endless buffet of knowledge just waiting for him to savor. He also became an accomplished oarsman for the Oregon Ducks.

After graduation, Mark took a job at the *Portland Oregonian* as a beat reporter. It was the best thing he could have done. He won high praise—and death threats—for his exposé of the bootlegging business run by Portland's chief of police and the city mayor. Many of his newspaper stories later worked their way into his best-selling novels.

Mark stayed in touch with his Aunt Caroline. At first their correspondence was mostly one-sided, but as his confidence as a writer grew, he enjoyed their lively backs and forths.

He married a daring young lady reporter who did not know how to take "no comment" for an answer. On their honeymoon they took an extended trip back East, including a week in Philadelphia with Caroline. While there, Caroline told him that her and Lawrence's childless Uncle Corrigan had died shortly before Lawrence, leaving Lawrence everything in spite of his change of career—the insurance business, several valuable properties, and his extensive investment portfolio. Upon Lawrence's death it all went to Caroline. She sold the business and added the proceeds to Uncle Corrigan's stock portfolio. Seeing for herself that Mark had settled into responsible adulthood, she turned everything over to him as Lawrence's rightful heir. He and his family lived comfortably thereafter while he reveled in the up and down world of a professional novelist.

Caroline settled back into her life in Philadelphia, missing Lily and her family, but happy to return in plenty of time to welcome her first grandchild. Her garden bloomed pristine, thanks to her faithful gardener, and Tildy bustled about cheerfully in her kitchen again. It took a few days to share her Pacific Northwest adventure with Nancy, who marveled at every twist and turn. Even though her sadness over Lily's death still hurt, Caroline enjoyed the sharing. Lily came alive again every time she spoke of her.

She also took the tale to Maria Horacek MacTavish at Pretty Cat Books. Maria was astounded to hear, all these years later, of Lily's life out West, and saddened to hear of her death. Maria never let on that she had held in confidence a piece of the puzzle when Caroline had asked her long ago if she knew anything about Lily's disappearance.

Finally, Caroline pondered over what to make of Lily's musings about marital sex in their strange middle-of-the-night conversation, and what to do with the information. She simply couldn't bring herself to discuss it with Nancy, or anyone else, for that matter. So she bought a brand new notebook and wrote down everything she could remember, and added her own ruminations on the subject. Then she wrapped the notebook in a square of muslin fabric, tied it with string, and stashed it in the bottom of a trunk in her attic. Perhaps some woman in a future generation, braver than she, would find it useful...or at least interesting.

Acknowledgements

I began writing The Visiting Girl in 2013. Seven years into it (with many long interruptions), the Covid-19 pandemic hit and there I was, like many others, isolated and bored. What to do, but finish the book.

Barbara Salice, a friend from our young mother days in Hawai'i, could not possibly have known that the box of second-hand books she sent me almost ten years ago held the treasured *Katharine Hepburn* by Barbara Leaming, which inspired me to create Lily and Caroline's story.

I was struck by the struggle of the elder Kate (movie star Katharine's mother), who, as an orphaned teenager in the 1890s, hired an attorney to force her guardian uncle to honor her mother's instructions in her will to enroll her daughters at Bryn Mawr College. Kate's mother left a legacy for this very purpose, but their uncle did not believe in higher education for women. Kate won the desperate fight, then had to buckle down to conquer the college's overwhelming entrance requirements.

As the titular visiting girl, Kate eventually married the up and coming Dr. Thomas Hepburn and the rest is history. *Mahalo* to both Barbaras!

The fictional Lily's life, of course, took an entirely different turn.

Many thanks to my "first readers" Diane Chance, Carol Chroneos, Madelyn Denbeau, Jill Engledow, Kenn Grimes, Anne Irons, Jana Hollenbeck, Connie Kent, Nancy Maxwell, gaël Doyle Oroyan, Lynn Pappas, Ann Sutton, and Judy Van Zile. I was overwhelmed by the diligence with which each of these readers tackled the manuscript.

gaël Oroyan (she prefers the lower case "g") set me on my writing path in the early 1970s when I lived in Kaneohe, Oahu, and she was a writing instructor at Windward Community College. Kenn Grimes kept me at it in recent years, as I tried to keep up with his relentless output. He's still way ahead.

A shout out to Critique Circle, an international writer's critique website based in Iceland. By submitting my chapters for feedback, one at a time, and critiquing others' work in return, I learned more than I can begin to describe from writers whom I will never be able to thank in person. Critique Circle is free—you earn credits by critiquing other writers' submissions, which you can then "spend" to have your own work critiqued. At last look, Critique Circle had 3,500 members from all over the world, although most work is submitted in English.

Special thanks to my talented daughter-in-law Heather Walls for the beautiful cover design.

**If you enjoyed The Visiting Girl,
I hope you'll put a review on Amazon.com!**

About the Author

Madge Walls lived most of her life in Hawai'i, the setting for her two previous contemporary novels, *Paying the Price* and *Buyers Are Liars*. With *The Vising Girl,* she challenged herself to write a story set on the Mainland in an earlier time period. She graduated from the University of Oregon and currently lives in southern Oregon, closer to her three sons and their families.

Please visit her website: **www.madgewalls.com**

Book Clubs

Madge Walls has attended many book club discussions of her novels—in person and via Zoom, Skype, and WhatsApp. She'd be delighted to participate in yours. Email majwalls@comcast.net to arrange a date.

Book Club Questions

1. Shortly before graduation from Bryn Mawr College, Lily is forced to confront the uncertainty of her future. She has no immediate family, she's short on funds, there is no potential husband in sight, and she has not been brought up to work. The first three are understandable, but the fourth? Why does she not simply bite the bullet and get to work as many a young woman in her situation would? Does this make you think less of her?

2. Caroline's idea of setting Lily up as a visiting girl seemed like a stroke of genius at the time. Yet there was a growing thrum of discomfort on Lily's part, of which Caroline and their friends were unaware. How did this contribute to Lily's bold decision to throw her fate into Marco's hands?

3. What do we learn about Marco by way of his thoughtful but quick decision to accept Lily's pregnancy and raise the child as his own?

4. The theme of intuition runs throughout this story. How is intuition important to the plot?

5. The matter of marital sex sneaks in as the story unfolds, until Lily and Caroline's frank (at least on Lilly's part) discussion in the

middle of the night. Does Lily's theory ring true, that what happens on a woman's wedding night can affect her attitude, positively or negatively, toward marital intimacy ongoing? Even today are you comfortable discussing this? If not, how far have we actually come regarding sexual freedom for women?

6. When Caroline learned of John's "betrayal," she was shocked. Was it really a betrayal for a husband to take a mistress under such circumstances, at a time when there was no reliable birth control and abortion was illegal? When the doctor advised Caroline and John that another pregnancy would likely kill her, why did she take John's easy acceptance of this as a sign of his love for her?

7. People sometimes make life-altering decisions based on how they believe another person will react, when in fact the other person might react in a totally unexpected way. People also sometimes make silent decisions in order to protect others. Both of these factors influenced Lily's decision to run away with Marco. Discuss.

8. Although Lily planned to write Caroline with an apology and explanation for her abrupt departure, as time went by she began to feel that nothing she could say would be sufficient to undo the harm. Have you ever felt this way, perhaps in the end being too embarrassed by the amount of time gone by to write or pick up the phone and clear the air?

9. Keeping secrets can be very destructive. Yet the ultimate unveiling of a secret can be the first step on the path to healing. How does the revelation of Mark's parentage affect those involved?

10. How do you think Mark felt to learn he was a child of rape?

Selected Bibliography

Barry, John M. *The Great Influenza.* Viking Press, 2004

Davis, Kenneth C. "Philadelphia Threw a WWI Parade That Gave Thousands of Onlookers the Flu." www.smithsonianmag.com, September 21, 2018

Dodds, Linda and Carolyn Buan. *Portland Then and Now.* Thunder Bay Press, 2001

Dundas, Zack. "The Scandalous History of Booze in Portland." *Portland Monthly*, December, 2015

Garrett, Laurie. *The Coming Plague.* Farrar, Straus and Giroux, 1994

Horowitz, Helen Lefkowitz. *The Power and Passion of M. Carey Thomas.* University of Illinois Press, 1999

Knight, Louise W. *Citizen: Jane Addams and the Struggle for Democracy.* University of Chicago Press, 2005

Lansing, Jewel. *Portland: People, Politics, and Power 1851-2001.* Oregon State University Press, 2003

Leaming, Barbara. *Katharine Hepburn.* Avon Books, 1996

Morrison, Dorothy Nafus. *Ladies Were Not Expected: Abigail Scott Duniway and Women's Rights.* Atheneum, 1977

Mukherjee, Siddhartha, *The Emperor of All Maladies.* Scribner, 2010

Raffel, Dawn. *The Strange Case of Dr. Couney.* Blue Rider Press, 2018

Stein, Elissa, and Susan Kim. *Flow: The Cultural Story of Menstruation.* St. Martin's Press, 2009

Stookey, Jeff. "1920s Prohibition in Portland, Oregon." www.jeffstookey.com, 2018

Tye, Larry. *Rising From the Rails: Pullman Porters and the Making of the Black Middle Class.* Henry Holt and Company, 2004

Welsh, Joe, Bill Howes, and Kevin J. Holland. *The Cars of the Pullman.* Voyageur Press, 2010

-------- "Care of Premature Infants." *Penn Nursing.* www.nursing.upenn.edu

-------- *The Justice Bell Story.* Justice Bell Foundation. www.justicebell.org

The Visiting Girl

The Visiting Girl

Made in the USA
Columbia, SC
26 January 2022

54382800R00217